THRONE OF NIGHTMARES

ALSO BY KERRI MANISCALCO

KINGDOM OF THE WICKED

Kingdom of the Wicked

Kingdom of the Cursed

Kingdom of the Feared

PRINCE OF SIN

Throne of the Fallen

Throne of Secrets

THRONE OF NIGHTMARES

KERRI MANISCALCO

First published in the United States by Little, Brown and Company in 2026
First published in Great Britain in 2026 by Hodderscape
An imprint of Hodder & Stoughton Limited
An Hachette UK company

The authorised representative in the EEA is Hachette Ireland, 8 Castlecourt Centre, Dublin 15, D15 XTP3, Ireland (email: info@hbgi.ie)

1

Copyright © Kerri Maniscalco 2026

The right of Kerri Maniscalco to be identified as the Author of the Work has been asserted by her in accordance with the Copyright, Designs and Patents Act 1988.

Print book interior design by Taylor Navis
Map by Virginia Allyn
Interior art: Phoenix illustration © ArtCreationsDesignPhoto/Shutterstock.com;
Botanical illustration © Lisla/Shutterstock.com

All rights reserved. No part of this publication may be reproduced, stored in a retrieval system, or transmitted, in any form or by any means without the prior written permission of the publisher, nor be otherwise circulated in any form of binding or cover other than that in which it is published and without a similar condition being imposed on the subsequent purchaser.

All characters in this publication are fictitious and any resemblance to real persons, living or dead, is purely coincidental.

A CIP catalogue record for this title is available from the British Library

Hardback ISBN 978 1 399 71574 4
Trade Paperback ISBN 978 1 399 71575 1
ebook ISBN 978 1 399 71576 8

Typeset in Sabon LT Std

Printed and bound in Great Britain by Clays Ltd, Elcograf S.p.A.

Hodder & Stoughton policy is to use papers that are natural, renewable and recyclable products and made from wood grown in sustainable forests. The logging and manufacturing processes are expected to conform to the environmental regulations of the country of origin.

Hodder & Stoughton Limited
Carmelite House
50 Victoria Embankment
London EC4Y 0DZ

www.hodderscape.co.uk

For the bookworm who dreams of falling into the pages of their favorite fantasy world, this one is for you.

Villains in stories proclaim all the glory,
Until they meet a foe more wicked than sweet
and suddenly find their hearts stumbling a beat.

POEMS FOR THE WICKED, VOLUME THREE

In a snow-covered realm called the Seven Circles, seven morally questionable princes rule over their Houses of Sin.

Wrath, Envy, Gluttony, Sloth, Lust, Greed, and Pride.

Some princes prefer to play devilish games, while others delight in all manner of sin, seeking pleasure to feed their power.

Outside the Underworld they're called the Wicked and are spoken of in hushed tones, making them especially intriguing to those with curious minds.

Even on the magical Shifting Isles—a peculiar island off the coast of the Underworld where different eras and dimensions overlap unbeknownst to its inhabitants—where this tale begins, rumors of them often run as wild as the debauched royals throughout the small villages.

Some stories claim a single kiss from a prince could convince even the most hardened cynic to sell their soul, hoping for another taste of oblivion.

Others liken them to the tricksy Fae, unable to lie directly but so clever in their wordplay and bargains they manage to twist the truth to their whims anyway.

Then there are darker stories that speak of their violence, their cunning in battle. Most worry about the Prince of Wrath, but the wisest recognize it's the quiet, watchful ones who pose the greatest threat.

Regardless of which brother is deemed most ruthless, none wish to meet the sinful immortals on the killing field, especially when they draw their strange, glowing daggers, which seem to desire blood as much as the creatures wielding them.

Whether feared or secretly craved, all agree that if one of

the Wicked crosses your path, you're either very lucky, or very cursed.

This is the story of the enigmatic Prince of Sloth. A prince who knows the mind is the deadliest weapon anyone possesses, and hones knowledge into the sharpest of blades.

Most believe Sloth's sin makes him lazy, uncaring—that couldn't be further from the truth. While his circle and court are dedicated to academics, and that pursuit of knowledge is the main way he fuels his power, Sloth can be more merciless than the Prince of Wrath when provoked for one important fact he's aware of.

Books hold the power to break worlds and remake them and Prince Sloth has studied them with singular focus.

But for all his intelligence and cunning, he isn't at all prepared for Lore Brimstone, the small-town librarian who secretly dreams that one day her mundane life will become as adventurous and romantic as her favorite books.

As the wisest of mortals have said, be careful what you wish for: it just might come true…

PROLOGUE
Prince Sloth

MOUNT LYRA, BELLINGTON. SHIFTING ISLES.

"You're sure this is the temple, Your Highness?"

Xavier's low voice only held a small note of doubt, but the fear rolling off him in waves was impossible for my heightened senses to miss.

His concern had nothing to do with the artifact we'd come for and everything to do with retrieving it, though it would be wiser to fear the book more than the deadly fall we now faced.

"Yes."

My assurance didn't calm his nerves; if anything, they flickered more erratically.

I had no doubt we were where we needed to be.

So far, the chamber located inside the labyrinth of tunnels built into the snowcapped mountain fit the description exactly.

Towering walls made of a smoky, opaque black stone, with silver mica set deep within, glittered like a thousand tiny stars had frozen inside, the whorls forming undiscovered constellations.

I surveyed the cavern's edge in the spill of moonlight trickling down from a hole carved into the mountain's peak, calculating the best path for our descent.

There weren't any good options to choose from—just bad or worse.

The climb down from our tunnel was mostly a sheer drop that I gauged to be around four hundred feet before it ended with large, brutal stakes driven into the ground at slight angles.

One slip would be the last mistake anyone ever made.

Skeletons of those who'd attempted to steal from the goddess before were impaled on many of those crude torture rods, the flesh not fully rotted on some.

For others, their bones had been picked clean by whatever monsters called this treacherous place home and acted as pale warnings emerging from the shadows.

Temple Knights—a small sect of religious warriors who served one of the most infamous old gods and who lived only in this dimension—crafted locations like this to hide any remaining holy treasure, places rigged with nasty surprises that gave their favorite goddess the blood tithes she craved.

While some might enter the temple, none would leave without paying a price.

Judging from the corpses littering the ground, that had been true.

Until tonight.

I *would* be leaving with the book, even if I had to fight the gods themselves.

Temple Knights had mastered the art of ensuring their goddess's secrets remained hidden from those intent on stealing power they weren't owed. They'd share just enough information to lure people *to* the temples, but once one was inside, there was little chance of escape.

No god had been more vicious with their games than the Goddess of Night.

She liked to watch the ones she toyed with suffer, finding joy in their pain.

Ancient myths described her as a deity who originally held power over dreams but soon discovered her taste for nightmares outweighed any mercy she once possessed.

In the twisted world of the gods, fortune favored the depraved.

Nyantha had been a dark, glittering jewel during the height of her reign, and many mortals sought to please her by celebrating everything associated with the magic of night: the stars, the moon, dreams, and darkness. All brought a sense of comfort and wonder. Until the darkness grew teeth and nipped at the faithful.

The mountaintop had even been partially carved off an eon before to serve as a window for the moon to watch this underground chamber, offering a prime view of all who entered uninvited.

The temple's imposing entrance was also meant to strike fear into the bravest of men, to remind them they were mere specks in the eyes of the gods.

It was fortunate that I wasn't mortal.

And even more fortunate that the old gods and goddesses had not held any true power over this world in ages.

Most had disappeared to other realms long before my brothers and I ever set foot in the Underworld.

Others we'd helped to send on their way.

Unlike the few goddesses who were born of this realm and still remained, the old gods were something else.

Most were forgotten, their names existing only in the oldest of books—several of which were secured in my private collection, far from curious minds.

Once mortals began to fear the night, they stopped offering gifts to the deity who tormented them, and what little power she'd retained faded even more.

Though remnants remained in places like this.

I exhaled slowly, my breath floating through the frigid air in an ominous warning of its own.

My brothers and I were considered lethal to most, the midnight monsters feared by man, but even we Princes of Sin knew when to tread carefully.

Xavier shifted from foot to foot beside me. His nerves were understandable but distracting as I silently plotted and he grew more tense.

In several archival ledgers, I'd read that not only was the chamber at the bottom warded against magic users to prevent us from easily entering the sacred space below, but it was also haunted by the souls of those who'd come hunting for its treasure before.

In the unnatural stillness of the subterranean chamber, with only the empty eyes of the dead watching us, I didn't doubt those tales.

Something slumbered here.

Something of immense and terrible power.

I felt the odd magic begin to pulse deep within my chest like a slow second heartbeat.

Whatever lurked below had cracked an eye, waiting.

I wasn't devout, unless sinning was considered a religion, but prayed it was the Liber Noctem.

The dark book had evaded me for centuries, but I'd persisted, tracking every story, every careless note or poem or fable written, trying to find its location after the old gods had spirited it away and refused to grant me access to it.

The Liber Noctem was also more commonly called the Book of Nightmares, with good reason; it could be used to create just as easily as to destroy.

But that wasn't the worst it could do.

"I'll go down first." I glanced at Xavier. His face paled, rivaling the color of the bones below. "If you want to wait here, I'll retrieve the book and be back soon."

"No. I'm coming."

His jaw set in a hard line.

As the master librarian for my House of Sin, he was just as eager as I was to see the mythical Book of Nightmares in person.

Unlike me, he wasn't immortal.

I nodded once, dropping the subject.

We'd already discussed the dangers before setting out on this recovery expedition. There was no need to rehash the risks.

I turned back to the ledge, the strange power below sending out more pulse waves, a slow tempo forming in the beat, tempting me like a siren's song.

I wondered if Xavier sensed it too, if it was tormenting him the same way or worse.

There was only one way to put an end to it.

"Watch where I step and follow my movements exactly."

Without another word, I hoisted the leather satchel I'd brought onto my shoulder and began my descent.

I dropped to the ground, pushing myself back until my legs dangled over the edge of nothing. Xavier drew in a sharp breath as my boots slid over smooth stone, searching for the slightest foothold while I methodically moved one hand at a time, locating tiny crevices to grip.

There were barely any, and my fingertips quickly began to cramp from holding my full weight, the agony only serving to harden my resolve.

No matter if I broke every bone in my body, I wouldn't leave this temple without the Liber Noctem.

As if to test my silent vow, one of my knuckles snapped loudly, dislocating.

I gritted my teeth and kept moving. Slowly. Excruciatingly. My flesh ripping on sharpened spots, the slippery blood adding an extra layer of strain.

I wasn't foolish enough to think the journey would be easy, so I didn't waste time cursing the difficulty. Anything worth having required hard work and sacrifice or else it wouldn't be that valuable.

Cuts would heal; bones would mend.

But failure would mean destruction for every realm.

I tuned out everything, the fear emitting from Xavier, the strange pull of dark power—all that mattered was the next handhold or foothold.

Each movement brought me closer to victory.

Sweat dotted my brow, dripping into my eyes, the salt of it burning.

I didn't dare brush it away.

Finally, with the ground in sight, I pushed off the cliff, gracefully landing between two stakes. My boots slapped hard-packed earth, dust flying up to greet me, dirtying my leathers.

Blood continued to seep from my fingers, and I watched, oddly transfixed, as a single drop splattered onto a skull.

My healing powers normally stitched together any wound in seconds, which meant the rumors of the temple being warded against invading magic were true.

Relief speared through me. I was glad I hadn't tried to test it out.

The subtle pounding of magic grew more intense now that I was closer

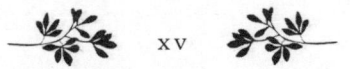

to its source, making me wonder if the book sensed my power or if it simply hoped for another sacrifice.

While Xavier began his descent, I pivoted in place, my gaze raking over the cavern in a slow, methodical sweep. It wasn't what I expected.

There were no runes. No altar. No book.

Only the bones of those who'd tried and failed to steal the Liber Noctem and the increasingly strong foreign power thrumming through me.

It felt wrong, like a chord plucked violently in a favorite song, making a once comforting sound suddenly foreboding.

I shoved the invasive pulse from my thoughts, forcing myself to focus on what we needed to do next. The faster we retrieved the book, the faster we could return to my House of Sin and secure it in the archives.

I needed to ensure the book never found its way back to its master.

The runes were supposedly the next step to unveiling the book's location.

I scanned the chamber a second time, taking in every inch.

The walls were the same glittering black stone, but there wasn't a carving or blemish to be found in the smooth surface.

There were no doors or openings, no way out aside from the tunnel we'd climbed down from. As far as temples went, it was spartan.

Anyone casually stumbling upon it would never think it was associated with the Goddess of Night. However, if they'd come looking for the goddess of death, then they might believe they'd found her.

The more recent corpses stunk this close. There were an alarming number of fresh bodies. If I were superstitious, I'd think the Goddess of Night had been preparing for this moment and needed sacrifices. Or maybe her Temple Knights were to blame.

I'd sometimes wondered if they'd ever attempt to free their goddess.

I shifted between the stakes, bloodied fingertips brushing their barklike surface, searching for any markings. There were none.

I glanced up just as Xavier jumped. He landed with a muffled curse, arms windmilling at his sides as he flew backward onto the dirt.

He'd narrowly missed impaling himself.

I offered him a hand, which he slapped away, glaring, his mood darkening

by the second. I flashed my teeth, the grin more feral than friendly as I jerked my chin at the chamber walls.

"Help me search for runes."

Xavier gave me a strange look as he got to his feet.

"You don't remember?" he asked, skepticism plain in his voice.

I silently envisioned eviscerating him until calmness descended again.

"Clearly not."

"They won't be visible yet." He nodded to the hole in the top of the mountain. "Not until the moon sits directly above us."

I followed his gaze and slowly released a breath. The moon had almost fully risen; it wouldn't be much longer.

I left Xavier and moved throughout the chamber, trying to work off the strange feeling settling over me. The brutality of my thoughts was curious.

I wasn't used to feeling so... on edge. Tense. Those emotions were better suited to my more volatile brothers, Wrath especially.

I had nothing to gain by fueling the rage building within. My magic was replenished by knowledge, by stoking the unquenchable thirst to learn all I could. It's why my circle in the Underworld was thought to be standoffish and lazy. We were a court of readers first.

The power of the dark book combined with the lack of my magic had to be to blame, though Xavier's temper was closer to the surface too.

Something was very wrong with this chamber.

Unease trickled in again.

I could no longer tell if it was coming from Xavier or me.

Moments later a cloud passed over the moon, briefly shrouding us in darkness before silvery light shrugged it off and bathed the temple in its glow.

As if the Goddess of Night was truly looking down upon us, the chamber walls began to sparkle.

The mica that had seemed to just be sprinkled in natural formations revealed a different truth: in the wash of moonlight, they were runes.

All around us, ancient words emerged.

I spun in place, translating them as quickly as I could.

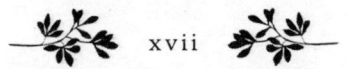

"There." I pointed to the west-facing wall, locating the beginning of the passage. *"Beware of waking the gods; their dreams are often our nightmares. Carpe noctem."*

"Seize the night?" Xavier's voice echoed loudly. "What in the frozen hells does that mean?"

I cursed. "It's Nyantha's motto for her mercenary wraiths."

"Her... wraiths. Yes, yes, of course."

My gaze sharpened on him. His research should have turned up that information; almost every historical text mentioned them in passing.

Nocturnas were her shadow warriors, legendary in their own right.

And they were currently locked away in Somnia, the dream realm where Nyantha had been banished. I glanced back at the runes; there was something familiar about the message that made me think of an old druid spell. I swung back to face my master librarian.

"Xavier..."

Suddenly, dozens of shadows peeled away from the temple's walls.

One by one they dropped into the skeletons and decaying corpses, the force of their merging rattling the bones.

As swiftly as the shadows had fallen, they rose in their new forms.

Eyeless skulls swiveled in our direction, the sockets now glowing with a strange crimson light.

My skin prickled from the ravenous hunger I saw there. The need.

Shadow wraiths wanted what they no longer possessed. A body. A soul.

Not truly vampires or zombies, they fed on their victims' fear, not their flesh.

That didn't mean they couldn't cause physical harm, though, especially while inhabiting a host body.

It should have been impossible for them to be here.

Xavier whimpered beside me and the Nocturnas' attention turned to him, his fear stirring them into a frenzy as they all took a step toward us in unison.

I unsheathed my House dagger from its scabbard, the blade glowing in anticipation. I palmed the cool hilt, which had been molded after the tree of knowledge, my House crest, and adjusted my grip to its familiar weight.

The same dark power that stoked my rage made me crave blood.

A killing calm descended.

I locked onto my targets, already envisioning their destruction.

The Liber Noctem would *not* be taken from me.

"Do you still have the blade in your boot?" I kept my attention on the advancing shadow wraiths, forcing myself to wait before striking. "Xavier. *Focus*. Where's your blade?"

"I...I'm not sure."

One Nocturna seemed to be hungrier and bolder than the others.

It stalked forward disjointedly in its reanimated corpse body, the flesh gray and half rotted hanging loosely from its limbs.

The stench was foul enough to make my eyes water as it closed the distance.

A small tremor went through the floor. Followed by a deep, reverberating rumble.

I jumped back, watching as the skull I'd bled onto sank into the earth.

Xavier dropped to his knees and began to pray. I'd never seen him do that before.

I would have shot him a questioning look, but I was transfixed by the altar of bones slowly emerging from the gaping hole beneath the cavern floor.

It resembled a macabre pedestal that must have been hidden for centuries.

Something in its center stirred.

Skeletal fingers unfurled, the joints cracking as they stretched wide. The hands clawed at the darkness now pouring from the center of the altar, creeping higher, straining as if they'd been praying for this exact moment.

I stood rooted to the spot, ignoring the Nocturnas creeping closer.

Slowly, impossibly, the hands sank back into the shadows and began to lift an object into the dim light. My heart thrummed madly. Fear erupted from whatever was hidden in the shadows as if it were the very essence of the emotion.

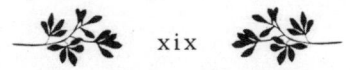

The skeletal hands rose higher, clearing the shadows, and I stared at a book, cradled reverently in the dead's embrace.

My heart ceased to beat for a second as I drank it in.

Its cover was black with one striking image—a gold phoenix rising in a blaze of vengeance. Sparks flickered across its feathers, sending prisms of light across the altar it rested upon.

The whole altar seemed to shiver...in fear. Or anticipation. A prickle of unease went through me. It was no ordinary book.

The Book of Nightmares was truly here.

After all these years, all this hunting...it was so close I could smell its ancient pages. The most alluring of perfumes.

Xavier's emotions flared wildly, his panic striking out.

He'd seen what I had. The Liber Noctem was finally within our grasp.

I lunged for it. My blood had released it from its hiding place, and that somehow made me feel bonded to it in a way I couldn't explain.

I snapped the bones as whatever magic fueling them continued to keep them locked in a death grip around the Liber Noctem.

The moment my bare hands made contact with the book, a wave of dark power rushed through me, forceful enough to make my knees buckle.

It was temptation, taunting, fear, promises of unending power, vengeance. It was chaos and destruction, and it took *everything* in me to hand it over to Xavier and not race out of here with it.

It was *mine*.

As if acknowledging the peculiar connection, gold light flashed out from the book and a searing heat flared across the skin on my torso and arms, the delicate lines creating a design I couldn't afford to remove my leathers to look at now.

Within mere seconds the pain stopped, making me wonder if I'd truly felt it at all.

There was no time to ponder what had just happened; the shadow wraiths swayed with agitation. They'd paused while the book emerged but wouldn't be still much longer.

"I'll draw them away," I said. "You take the book out of here."

I shoved the book into Xavier's arms even though it was the last thing I wanted to do. Then I sprinted into the advancing undead soldiers, letting instinct and muscle memory direct my every blow.

The first of the fresher corpses staggered toward me, its jaw slack and milky eyes weeping pus.

I brought my blade down, cleaving through its exposed clavicle, and its arm flopped uselessly to its side, held by nothing but a rotten strip of sinew now.

I swung again, severing its head in a powerful blow. It hit the ground and splattered open, the gods-awful stench temporarily overwhelming my senses.

Another Nocturna snapped at my shoulder, and I spun, ramming my elbow into what remained of its face. Rotting teeth shattered with the impact.

I hacked and slashed, clearing a half circle around me as decaying body parts flew in all directions.

Putrid blood and other gore slicked my palms, and I skidded in foul viscera as I tried to keep my footing steady despite the increasingly slippery ground.

A third Nocturna, missing half its skull, came at me with a broken sword.

I parried with my dagger, ignoring the whine of metal against metal before driving my blade up through its ruined head.

I fought without pause, unleashing the full force of my fighting abilities, and even without my magic to aid me, I was violence made flesh.

Wrath might be the general of war, but each Prince of Sin was lethal.

I had thousands of texts on war and anatomy and had studied the most effective ways to disarm and destroy.

My wings snapped out from where I'd kept them, shielding me from blows and swiping out the legs of several Nocturnas.

The feathers were the color of my eyes and made a striking contrast against the dark stone walls.

I hit the dirt hard, the impact rattling my bones as I kicked out in a powerful arc, shattering both of the wraith's kneecaps with a sickening crunch.

Once it went down, I sprang back to my feet, already taking on the next shadow wraith.

I drove my fists into its decaying flesh, punching clean through its stolen body, then pivoted and struck the next, leaving a trail of destruction in my wake.

On and on they swarmed around me, desperate to reclaim their beloved Liber Noctem.

Each time I managed to fend one off, another emerged, ready to take its place. Their strikes came fast and fierce, but I was not one to surrender.

My focus was set entirely on the dance of death.

Step, strike, retreat. Head severed, arm cracked, leg shattered. One by one the Nocturnas fell, the bodies of their hosts ruined.

I snapped the neck of the next wraith, a clean, efficient kill.

The lifeless form slipped from my grasp, thudding softly against the temple's ground. I moved toward my next target, completely in sync with the brutal rhythm of battle.

I pivoted as jaws snapped near my jugular, laughing darkly at the failed attempt to incapacitate me. Even on the Shifting Isles and away from my court and my ability to replenish my magic, it would take more than a torn throat to take me down.

Claws dragged over the leathers covering my chest and I yanked the Nocturna toward me, driving my dagger up and through its ribs.

If it had a heart, it would have been speared.

I dropped the body and went to the next.

My wings flared out, sending more shadow wraiths sprawling.

I didn't think about the passage of time, or about the book or about failure.

I was a being forged with a singular purpose: to kill, and nothing more.

It felt freeing—to slow my endless thoughts, to act on instinct and not solely on intellect. Though I never quite let go of my studies, my sin wouldn't ever fully release me. Nor would I want it to.

Each movement was meticulously plotted. A calculated step forward, a lethal strike, a swipe of my wings, followed by a strategic retreat.

I executed each hit by the book.

Soon, I'd leveled them all and the stillness of death jolted me from my trance.

Xavier's fear spiked impossibly higher in the aftermath.

I understood. Out of all my brothers, I was the academic. Not many in my court had seen me with any weapon in hand other than a book. I'd even train in secret with only my brothers; no one would be able to withstand a true fight aside from them anyway. If I was training for battle, I wanted it to serve a purpose aside from the fun my siblings considered it to be.

I didn't turn to look at Xavier yet, wanting to be certain the desire to maim had fully faded from my expression.

There was no need to frighten him any more than I had.

I tucked my wings away; the pale blue feathers had been splattered with blood and gore.

I wiped my blade on my leathers and swept my attention around the chamber, ensuring the wraiths hadn't risen again.

All was quiet for the moment.

Finally, I faced my master librarian. The time for coddling was over.

We needed to act. I wouldn't rest until the book was magically bound in my library, where Nyantha would never get near it again.

Some monsters needed to remain caged for eternity.

Xavier had the book in his grasp, a single tear streaking down his cheek.

"We need to hurry. They'll reanimate soon." I collected my satchel from where I'd dropped it. "Hand me the book so we can climb out of here."

Xavier clutched it to his chest and took a step back.

Dark suspicion rose in me again.

The book's allure had been hard for me to resist; for Xavier it would be even harder.

I calculated the space between us, the possible moves he might make, mentally running through the most efficient counterstrikes.

Xavier might be my master librarian, my most trusted member of court, but I wouldn't hesitate to take him out if he posed a threat.

"I'm sorry," he said simply, his regret overcoming his fear for a moment.

Before I could fling the hilt of my dagger at him to knock him out, he shoved his hand into his pocket and removed a single glittering rock.

Recognition fell on me like a boulder, stilling my movements.

He'd brought a portal stone. Whatever his plan, it wasn't a result of the book's allure tempting him. He'd come prepared for this outcome.

I stared, barely breathing, while my mind spun with ways to defuse the situation.

Cold, efficient, analytical—the three aspects I valued above all and that usually served me well were giving way to dread.

Xavier's hand tightened on it, his knuckles turning white.

To use a portal stone was simple: you needed to think of a location while holding it.

If you had no specific location in mind, the portal stone automatically transported you to Somnia, the land of dreams, where it was rumored to be mined from. And with magical wards in place to secure its borders, I couldn't simply transport myself to Somnia without one.

An individual stone could be used several times before the magic that fueled it faded, but if he destroyed the stone, there would be no coming back.

Not many people ever chose to venture to Somnia—the realm had a bad habit of trapping them there in their nightmares until they withered to nothing.

"Wait..." I held my hands up like I was soothing a cornered animal. "Let's discuss—"

"Carpe noctem!"

Without another word, Xavier crushed the stone in his fist and was instantly ripped from this realm, taking the Liber Noctem with him.

I dove forward, knowing it was too late.

The book and my companion were gone.

I stared at the glittering aftermath of the portal's magic, my heart thudding wildly. Betrayal was as cold and unforgiving as a blade to the gut.

An icy rage burned through me that had nothing to do with dark magic now. This darkness belonged only to me.

My master librarian had stolen the Book of Nightmares.

He'd taken the only portal stone I'd had from my House of Sin.

He'd found some way to get around my ability to detect lies. He'd *planned* this heist. Meticulously. For the hells knew how long.

If my magic wasn't bound in this chamber, it would have frozen every surface with my displeasure. Bone turned to dust in my hands.

I glanced down. I had no recollection of picking up the skull.

My thoughts turned over the events of the night. Nyantha's wraiths. The manipulative power seeping from the chamber, infecting us.

Both clever distractions.

Xavier knew I'd fight, granting him time to secure the book and get far enough away that I couldn't simply grab him. And I suspected, based on his withholding of pertinent information, and his shouted decree, that he must have always served the Goddess of Night and had used my court to locate the Book of Nightmares.

Which meant there was only one place Xavier was likely going with it now. Somnia. The very location we'd needed to keep it from.

I shivered at the thought.

If Nyantha got her hands back on the Liber Noctem, I had little doubt she'd destroy my House of Sin for the pivotal role I'd played in her downfall.

I cursed the day the old gods had come knocking at my door, looking for help. Neither myself nor my brothers had ever seen them since. They sent messengers occasionally—ones whose memories were always wiped clean aside from their missives. The secretive pricks.

I stormed through the chamber, thoughts racing as I plotted and began to climb. I would use a spell to find the nearest portal stone and follow Xavier into the bowels of that hellish realm.

Then I'd become every nightmare the myths claimed my kind to be.

And more.

House Sloth was docile until provoked.

Then we waged war with cold, brutal efficiency.

My House was one without mercy, and I aimed to remind those foolish enough to cross me just how vicious I could be.

PART I

Once Upon a Time . . .

ONE
Lore

I FUMBLED IN the dark, ungloved hands frantically roving across walls papered in tattered silk, cursing at the thick layer of dust marking my every move.

I might as well light a torch and wave it around for the Collector.

Perhaps he'd think me mad and look for less troubling prey.

I tucked that away as my last option, still hoping to escape this neglected manor the good old-fashioned way first: by jumping out a window and running for the woods. That always seemed to work in my favorite books.

Though maybe it was time to stop pretending I was in a mystery novel.

Stories had gotten me into this nightmare. It was a tall tale that drew me here in the dead of night, searching for my own adventure.

Foxglove Manor was supposedly haunted by the killer's victims, and when the hunter moon rose, ushering in the harvest season, curious souls could spy the dead seeking revenge.

What the folktales failed to mention was the very real, very bloodthirsty murderer who still stalked these abandoned grounds, hoping mystery-loving fools ventured here alone.

How else might the infamous Collector harvest more souls to add to his collection?

Rain thrashed against the lone window at the end of the narrow corridor, sounding as frantic as my heartbeat.

I'd come upstairs because of the promise of freedom the window had offered, unaware that it perched too high to reach, its single eye impassively watching my attempt to cheat death.

I pushed against the solid wall, refusing to admit I'd found a dead end.

A single sconce without a candlestick seemed to mock me.

Or maybe it was trying to get my attention. Blessed, dusty thing.

I gave the misunderstood yet valiant candleless sconce a little tug, and chunks of plaster crashed to the hardwood in a loud, unmistakable invitation for the Collector to come kill me.

Why wasn't there ever a secret lever when you needed one?

Maybe the old manor house was the true villain.

I drew in a deep breath, trying to ignore the walls of fate closing in.

Main characters *always* got out of trouble at the last possible second. There was an art to dramatic effect. One they perfected.

If only I could channel my inner heroine under duress.

At this rate, I'd be lucky to even be considered a side character. At twenty-four, I was about to die in some brutal, ritualistic death, and I'd only *just* entered this cursed manor house.

Thunder boomed menacingly, rattling the windowpane.

I couldn't tell if the storm was trying to scare the life out of me before the killer arrived, or if it was just as upset about my soon-to-be violent ending.

I shook my head. I'd now reached the anthropomorphizing stage of denial.

A floorboard creaked on the stairs, followed by another.

Like any rational adult facing certain demise, I squeezed my eyes shut, debating my next move.

I could either pretend my fierce yet fluffy animal familiar had finally come to my rescue or admit that the dagger-wielding lunatic had caught up with me and I was as far from a main character with a magical sidekick as one could be.

Logic was so boring. No wonder I was doomed.

Lightning flashed, illuminating the hulking shadow of my stalker before plunging me back into darkness. He was here, he was inches away…

A rough hand clamped onto my shoulder, shaking me.

"Lore!"

I screamed, jolting upright...blinking as reality came crashing back and the book in my lap fell unceremoniously to the floor.

It took another long second to piece together what had happened.

I was still in the library where I worked.

Little half-eaten pastries, empty mugs of tea, and uncorked bottles of sparkling wine were scattered across low tables.

The monthly book club I hosted had met earlier tonight to discuss the first release in the Collector series, a thrilling murder mystery that featured a fearless heroine tracking a killer who'd attacked her twin in the opening installment.

It was all terribly brutal and thus thoroughly engaging.

My best friends, Blake and Agatha, offered to help me clean, but I'd sent them off so they could dive into the sequel.

I'd stayed behind to read one more chapter before locking up, and, well...one chapter quickly turned into ten.

I blamed the author for whatever addictive substance she'd woven into the story. It was like a delicious potato chip—eating one was simply out of the question.

I glared up at my brother.

"Gods' blood, Fable. Don't you ever knock? I was just getting to the good part."

He gave me a bemused look. "It's a public library. And we're late."

"Late for..."

"The traveling—"

"The traveling caravan!" I glanced at the clock and cringed. We still had some time to wander around, but we needed to hurry. "I completely forgot."

"I figured. Blake stopped by and said I probably needed to drag you out of here." He plucked my novel from the floor and shook his head at the title. "You started rereading *Harvest Moon* already?"

I snatched the book from his grubby paws and dusted it off.

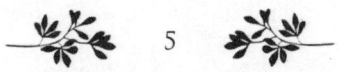

"After our discussion tonight, I wanted to scan a few passages. I must have dozed off for a minute."

A knowing smirk curved his lips. "You mean you and your cohorts were obsessing over the villain again."

"Obsessing is a bit overstated." I wrinkled my nose. "He's just..."

"Dark, brooding, misunderstood?"

"Layered, you snob. He lives by his own moral code, killing the worst of society."

My brother's grin widened.

"You're rationalizing violent, sociopathic behavior because his cheekbones are described as: 'as sharp as the blade he wielded.'"

He wasn't wrong, but, as the youngest sibling, I would never admit it on principle.

I placed the book back on its shelf and started quickly gathering up the discarded plates while Fable went for the empty mugs.

"Say what you will, but vigilante justice makes for exciting stories when it's done well."

"Because committing murder is *such* an admirable quality in a mate."

I waved off his very logical response.

"No one wants to read about normal, well-adjusted people. They want the misunderstood villain with the sassy pet dragon. Tell me you're not more intrigued by the man who will torch the world for his true love rather than sacrifice himself for the greater good. The first creates glorious tension; the second makes you bawl until you're a snotty, distraught wreck, lying catatonically on your bed, staring at the ceiling while wondering when you became such a masochist. No one wants to watch their true love die a horrible, slow death, even if it's honorable."

My brother barked a laugh. "I would worry about you, but a sassy dragon is hard to beat."

"You, sir, are a man of infinite wisdom, no matter what your fellow professors say."

It was a dirty lie that had both of us grinning at each other.

My brother was wickedly intelligent, especially when it came to dissecting novels, and I adored teasing him.

He'd been away teaching at the most prestigious university on the island for the last few months, and I'd missed him and our lively debates.

It felt good to have him back, even temporarily.

Blake and Agatha never shied away from dissecting every book we read, but teasing my brother was one of my favorite pastimes.

Fable's main area of study was the emotional impact of stories on mortals.

Like everyone in our family, he was just as *obsessed* with fiction.

Wholesome, good-natured. My brother looked the part of a storybook hero.

Dark hair, dark eyes. And enough easy banter to carry him through an entire narrative on his own. He had eligible men and women fawning over him, not that he ever seemed to notice. His first true love was reading.

I matched him in coloring but missed out on the leading-lady gene.

Unlike my brother, I had no horde of adoring suitors lining up.

Even with a name like Lore Brimstone, which practically *begged* for a dark, romantic adventure, I was doomed to never be a main character in real life for one insurmountable reason—I had no tragic backstory.

No dead or terrible parents.

No murdered sibling or dark family secrets.

No snarky animal familiar to speak with, mind to mind.

And—much to my constant dismay—no fated mate trying to strike a questionable bargain with me.

Just a bookish family who spent our evenings passionately discussing our favorite reads of the week over dinner.

Worst of all? We all loved one another. Fiercely.

With so much stacked against me, I accepted my lot in life as a secondary character destined for cat ownership, and that was that.

I liked cats and books, and honestly that wasn't the worst fate.

Well, that wasn't *entirely* true; I wanted to fall wildly, madly, wholeheartedly in love like the characters in my books.

Surprisingly, I wasn't someone who fell in love easily, though. I only courted a few suitors, and while they were perfectly lovely, there was always *something* missing. I didn't want to marry any man; I wanted the right one for me. Someone who loved me and my quirks, not despite them. The same way I wanted to adore who he authentically was at his core.

I grabbed my cloak from the peg on the wall and fastened it around my shoulders, preparing for the cool evening air.

Before I turned off the lights, I swept my attention around the little library, ensuring all was well for the morning shift.

The books were returned to the shelves, the chairs had been rearranged back into the seating section, and I'd put out the fire.

Satisfied everything was in place, I followed my brother out and locked up.

The library was nestled on top of a hill, surrounded by towering evergreen trees that stood so close together it was only accessible by foot.

We set off down the dirt path that led into the village center, and I inhaled the cold, salty breeze blowing in from the ocean.

Bellington was a small port town that was famous for…well, not much. But it was a quaint place that seemed to be taken directly from the pages of a novel.

My father shared old oral histories that claimed our island was magical, that travelers could come here from other realms, and that our time period was unique to us. If those stories were true, then Bellington could be replaced by other cities and places and all new inhabitants and none of us would be any the wiser.

Dimensions sitting on top of each other was a lot to take in, but my father loved unearthing more folklore about our home, and I'd always sit at our table, entirely rapt.

Other legends claimed this island could manifest any setting—from a Regency-era world complete with a king and queen, to a primitive world where mythical creatures roamed the shores and skies.

I'd certainly spent a lot of time looking for the impossible, especially since there were several stories from a few generations back where villagers were said to have manipulated the elements, but nothing was ever too notable.

Thus far, our little town was as normal as anything.

I had the opportunity to study in a larger city up north like Fable but loved the library too much to leave, even if I craved adventure.

My book club was filled with people who were as into the latest releases as I was.

Blake and I were both antihero-obsessed and didn't care who knew it. And Agatha and I could talk for hours about our favorite romance tropes. The three of us spent an unhealthy amount of time theorizing about sequels and plot points, and sometimes we'd just spend all day reading in our separate corners, together but completely absorbed in our own worlds.

I worried that moving to a larger city would somehow feel less personal, though I knew Fable had found the opposite to be true.

Maybe I was just scared to take that first step into the unknown.

Across the way a crescent-shaped cove offered a stunning view of Mount Lyra, a forbidding summit superstitious locals rarely traveled to for fear of angering the old elemental gods.

A temple had been carved into the mountain, and while some out-of-town adventurers hiked there, I had no desire to venture into the space.

Not because of the old gods, but because of the rumors of dead bodies. The hike into the mountain was treacherous.

I glimpsed its snow-covered peak rising through the trees and clutched my cloak tighter, swearing it felt colder somehow, like the very land itself was seething over something.

Internally, I shook myself. The mountain wasn't raging. I was probably crashing from too much sugar consumption tonight.

I silently vowed to not mix that many chocolate-covered raspberry jellies with wine again.

Everything in moderation, nothing to excess.

The sage advice from Father flitted through my head. For the most part I followed it, except where books were concerned.

I was a gluttonous little fiend when it came to devouring novels. Father supported that addiction, though, mostly because as a folklorist he suffered from it too.

In fact, our parents named us Lore and Fable because of their shared affection for those kinds of tall tales—loving fiction was my destiny.

If someone cracked me open, they'd find ink in my veins and stories in my soul.

Reading was transportive; the moment someone picked up a book they stepped into the characters' journey, following them through battles and heartache and cheering when good eventually defeated evil and they found their hard-won happily-ever-afters.

Watching favorite characters overcome obstacles and never give up inspired *real* hope that transcended fiction.

If they soldiered on, even in the darkest of times, then so could we.

Through books readers lived a million lives and felt a million emotions. I adored them all, but romantic adventures were my favorites.

The tension, the impossibly high stakes, the yearning. The moment the characters stopped fighting their fate and gave in to their hearts.

I sighed dreamily at every declaration of love and kicked my feet like a giddy schoolchild.

I was a hopeless romantic, emphasis on *hopeless*.

I followed my brother's careful steps and concentrated on not tripping over any roots as we descended the trail and the village proper slowly came into view.

Every time I rounded the corner and took in that first glimpse of the tiny wharf town below, I couldn't help but smile.

Small rows of stone buildings with charming thatched roofs were stuffed together, forming a village square filled with family businesses.

There was a baker, a butcher, a cobbler, a dressmaker, and even a forge at the far end of the main road. When I was younger, I used to daydream about marrying the blacksmith's son like the heroine in my favorite romance novel.

"What do you want to check out first: the tarot reader or candied apples?" Fable asked as we approached the edge of town and the caravans' wagons came into view.

A hive of activity had sprung up in the hours I'd been at work; it looked like the entire village was out partaking in all the fantasy and fun the newcomers had brought.

My gaze skipped from one covered wagon to the next.

Acrobats in a rainbow of colors twirled around from ribbons they'd strung up between buildings, fire-eaters breathed flames from on top of whiskey barrels, where villagers stood riveted by the show and the scents of caramel corn and apples filled the air with the sweetest aroma.

I wanted to experience *everything*, storing all the magic and fun away to revisit in my memories during the long, cold winter that was fast approaching.

My attention skimmed down the long train of covered wagons that had rolled in, pausing on one that stood out from the rest.

It was older, shoddier, and from what I could see of the many glass jars lining the shelves inside it, looked to be selling items for spells.

The story lover in me went on high alert, and before I'd made the conscious decision, I was heading directly for it.

"Lore?" Fable called after me. "Where are you going?"

"Be right back!" I glanced over my shoulder. "I'll meet you at the card reader!"

My brother mumbled something about things never changing and headed for the line. A strange thread of excitement tugged me deeper into the festivities.

I couldn't help but wonder if something wonderful was about to happen.

TWO
Lore

I MADE MY way through the crowd, smiling at familiar faces as I edged around families and couples strolling through the square. The closer I got to the wagon, the more my skin prickled with an odd sense of foreboding.

When I finally arrived, there was no one tending to it.

"Hello?"

I peered up at the jars—this close I could clearly make out dried flowers that seemed to be tea and not occult items like eye of newt and preserved dragonfly wings.

I sighed. My imagination had gotten the best of me again.

There were no secret witches or grimoires or spell candles for finding my one true love. No enchanted pendants or rings. I could probably find an herbal mixture to relieve bloating the next time Father made his infamous beans, though.

I turned around, searching for Fable as the crowd surged toward the acrobats.

Fireworks lit up the sky, the sudden crackle and pop making me inhale sharply as I watched the embers rain down, then fade.

I thought of the mountain, that strange feeling of angry gods, and internally slapped myself.

I'd read one too many fantasy books.

The gods were fables meant to keep us in line, the mountain was like any other natural landscape, and I was wasting time being lost to daydreams instead of living in the moment.

I'd taken a step away when a warbled voice spoke behind me.

"Gift for the gifted?"

"Blood and bones!" I spun around, my hand pressed to my heart.

It thrashed like a fish caught on a line.

A tiny woman with silver hair and eyes took my measure. Her face was lined and weathered, matching the sound of her voice.

I placed her roughly between ninety and nine thousand.

An ancient aura settled around her, furthering my suspicion that my mind was working overtime tonight.

She wore a black hooded cloak and looked like she'd been plucked from the pages of a fairy tale. Except she was the wicked poisoned-apple-wielding character sent to make the heroine's journey an epic disaster.

It was a good thing I'd resisted getting candied apples first.

Every internal instinct I had warned me to run. I tamped them down, not wanting to give in to my sugar-fueled imagination again tonight.

Maybe she was my fairy godmother in disguise.

It took another second to get over my surprise and process what she'd said.

"I'm not magically gifted, but thank you for the offer."

Magic wasn't unheard of here, but according to my father's research and my own curiosity, it had been a long time since someone had wielded anything supernatural.

Feeling terrible, I motioned to the jar with dried petals.

"I would love to buy some tea from you, though."

Her eyes narrowed as she followed my gaze, her head shaking slightly.

"You don't want tea, girl. What you want is adventure." She looked me over again, and I had the oddest feeling she could read my soul. "Are you ready to shed the mundane and live your dreams?"

"Who wouldn't be?"

"Few want to work for it. And even fewer are brave enough to face their fears first. You think you are?"

If she wanted me to play along, I was game. "Brave enough to face my fears? Definitely, especially if that means I get to live happily ever after."

"Good. You agree to see this quest through to its end?" she asked.

That escalated rather quickly—from facing my fears to agreeing to a random, mysterious quest—but since this was clearly hypothetical, I nodded. "I agree."

A distant rumble of thunder shook the ground. I glanced around; there wasn't a cloud in the sky. The old woman harrumphed.

"Take this. You'll be needing this to get you on your way."

With reflexes far faster than should have been possible, her hand shot out and icy fingers closed around my wrist. From her other hand, she dropped something smooth and cold into my palm, then closed my fingers around it.

I almost convinced myself it hummed against my skin.

"Hurry along, now." She let me go and hobbled back. "He'll be coming any moment. And forces of change rarely make things easy."

My brows rose. That didn't sound ominous at all.

"I'm sorry, but I think you have me confused with—"

"I know precisely who you are, Lore Brimstone. Now, focus on your quest and *go*."

I subtly pinched myself to see if I was dreaming, then rubbed at the sore spot on my arm. I was definitely awake and now I'd have a bruise.

The woman looked like she wanted to smack me over the head, but her attention abruptly shifted behind me, her eyes widening.

"Who are you?" I asked.

She motioned to a silver pin I hadn't noticed on her cloak.

If she expected me to recognize the sigil, she would be sorely disappointed. It looked like a sun wedged between two crescent moons that faced outward on either side. A sword speared down the center of the sun.

Something about it felt a little menacing.

"A friend."

Before I could comment on it, her gaze grew distant before snapping back into focus.

"He's here. And he's ready to begin."

Her voice fell to a whisper so low I almost missed what she'd said.

If it wasn't for the fine hair rising along my neck, I would have thought I'd imagined it.

"Begin? I thought the quest was hypothetical. I don't really want to—"

Heat rolled along my spine, like someone had locked me in their sights and was taking their time drinking me in.

Which was absolutely out of the question.

I slowly twisted in place, following that strange sensation if only to prove myself wrong.

My gaze scanned the crowd—acrobats, families, sugary treats, fire-breathers, the same as before. On second thought, that wasn't quite right.

People were milling about with frothy mugs of ale now. I made a mental note to snag two before I met Fable at the card reader.

There wasn't anything...

All at once I knew exactly who the old woman meant.

He strode into view, his gait long and confident, looking like the kind of man from generations past. Battle hardened, cold, his emotions locked away behind an impenetrable wall.

A dark cloak billowed out behind him, showing glimpses of the equally dark fighting leathers he wore beneath it.

His hood was drawn low over his face, covering all but his full mouth.

For a moment, all I could do was stare, my attention riveted to the mysterious man.

He had the square jawline given to all leading villains, and irrationally, I wanted to run my fingers over the pale stubble I could just make out.

His shoulders were broad, his hips narrow, and without being too bulky overall, he looked muscular enough to toss a few hundred pounds without breaking a sweat.

I couldn't even see his features, but there was *something* about him that made me stop and take notice—as if some long-forgotten instincts kicked on and alerted my brain to a primal need he could fulfill.

He was dangerous but would likely defend those he loved without mercy.

I gave him an appreciative look.

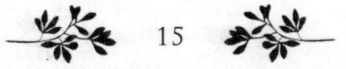

I'd put his talents to use and send him out to collect overdue library books.

I glanced up, wondering if I'd somehow fallen out of the stupid tree and hit every branch on the way down.

The man probably murdered without remorse and had a stash of bones he guarded like an ornery dragon with its treasure.

Only a fool would consider getting on his bad side.

Or even his good side.

He was trouble and not in the fun fictional kind of way. He was the kind of man who had an objective and didn't stop until he'd reached it. And if someone got in his way, I had little doubt he'd crush them without hesitation.

My heart decided it was a wonderful time to beat twice its speed when he parted the crowd and continued walking as if he owned the road.

Men and women alike paused to watch him pass; even with his face hidden, he exuded raw masculinity mixed with power and animal grace.

He moved with purpose, with singular focus. An apex predator locked onto his prey.

I pitied the unfortunate soul who'd caused his ire.

I was so caught up in that strange intersection of both admiring and fearing him that it took much too long to realize he was coming straight for *me*.

I staggered back from the force of his attention and shot an accusatory look at the old woman. "Did you steal this pretty rock from that nice lethal-looking gentleman?"

She smiled wickedly. "No. But if I were you, I'd run along now, girl. He'll take pleasure in the chase."

"Or the kill."

Her grin widened. "Same difference."

"In what universe?"

She didn't bother to respond.

So much for a fairy godmother; I'd gotten one straight from the bowels of hell.

And she'd sent a devil after me.

The stone in my palm pulsed, the heat unmistakable.

I glanced down—it was *glowing*.

Except it wasn't emitting a bright shining light; it was dark and dangerous, with hints of red, like an ember slowly dying in a fire.

Or sparking to life.

Ribbons of shadows suddenly streamed out from it, winding up my arm.

They were oddly warm as they crisscrossed under my long sleeves.

For some inexplicable reason, I'd always imagined shadows being cold. They slithered higher as if amused by my thoughts.

My mind crashed to a halt at that.

Shadows couldn't understand emotions; that was absurd.

Oh, gods. I must be in shock.

Having read so much, I thought I'd be more prepared to act swiftly if I ever encountered something paranormal. That was sadly untrue when faced with something so beyond any frame of reference.

My brain tried desperately to reason away the unreasonable.

Instead of throwing the stone or screaming or passing out, I watched, unblinking, as I tried to make sense of it all.

There was no way this was real. Rocks didn't spew out shadows, and old women didn't send people on quests to achieve their dreams.

And yet I didn't think I was having a psychotic break...which was probably what everyone who'd experienced one thought too.

The shadows wound themselves tighter, almost like they were feeding off my growing alarm and becoming agitated themselves. The more I tried to calm my nerves, the more my pulse raced and the shadows writhed.

"Holy gods—"

In the next breath, what could only be described as a glittering portal yawned open, engulfing my arm entirely.

Now I couldn't throw the damn stone if I wanted to; half of my body was just *gone*. Darkness swirled like an angry storm growing, enveloping more of me.

It all happened so quickly; I had no time to scream.

Someone grabbed my other arm, and the heat from where he'd latched on indicated exactly who'd caught up to me.

I wasn't sure if I was grateful for his presence or not.

From somewhere far away my brother shouted my name, and before I could yell back, the stranger and I were suddenly ripped away from Bellington on a warm midnight breeze.

We fell, through time, space, and the gods knew where else, finally landing in a painful heap, with me flat on my back, on hard-packed earth.

Next to me, my homicidal companion didn't make a sound.

Maybe his neck snapped in the crash.

I lay there, eyes squeezed shut, waiting for the world to stop spinning. This absolutely *couldn't* be happening.

Yet the physical pain hinted otherwise.

Maybe it was just a very vivid dream. I tried to think of the last thing that was normal before I'd met the fairy godmother from hell.

Fireworks had gone off. I exhaled slowly.

I could have gotten smacked in the head with an errant flare.

Rocks and pebbles dug into me as I shifted a little to see if I could move. Nothing seemed to be broken, but it felt like I'd been torn into a million pieces, then crudely stitched together again.

I studiously ignored the fact that the village streets were hard-packed dirt in most places, or cobblestone, and they didn't have any pebbles like the ones I was sprawled on. Reality was closing in hard and fast and I really needed a minute to come to terms with things.

I debated whether I should just stay there until I woke up.

There was no way any of this was really happening. Any minute now Fable would shake me out of this bad dream, and we'd laugh about it.

Two large hands settled around my waist, then unceremoniously hoisted me to my feet. My eyes snapped open.

He let me go so swiftly I almost thought I'd burned him.

He turned around, surveying our surroundings, and I caught the most unexpected smile on his face. Like this was all completely *normal*. And he was pleased.

Wonderful. I had a sociopath for a companion.

I drew in a sharp breath that had nothing to do with pain as I skimmed over the mercenary assassin who was now glaring at me and took in our new surroundings.

I couldn't seem to wrap my mind around what I was looking at.

I stared, unblinking, and tried to come up with any excuse that didn't hint at magic. There was no way we'd fallen through a portal to a new world. And yet...here we stood, very clearly in a different, unfamiliar place.

This was not Bellington. That much I was certain of.

There was no hint of the ocean, no Mount Lyra, no crowded street.

We'd fallen onto a mountaintop in the middle of a vast range of mountains, with no signs of civilization for as far as I could see.

I focused on maintaining even breaths, or else I might begin to hyperventilate, and I did *not* want the stranger to know how scared I was.

Something cautioned me to treat him the way I would any threat.

He hadn't been terrified or even surprised by magic. He'd been after the stone I held, which meant he knew what it was and how it worked. Maybe he'd been after his own quest and now he'd kill me and be on his way.

Perfect. We were trapped together...wherever we were.

The sun had already sunk below the horizon, taking its last rays with it as night crept in. Shadows reached long fingers across the rocky terrain, shrouding the narrow pass where we'd landed in darkness.

I forced myself to compartmentalize.

Magic was real.

I glanced down at the rock in my palm, feeling a strange sense of bittersweetness. I'd always daydreamed about going on an adventure, but this was a little too much to handle. Maybe if Blake and Agatha were here, or my brother, it might feel more tempting. But I was alone with a man I didn't know, who hadn't spoken a single word, and I was overwhelmed.

The old woman had said I needed to experience my worst fears before I could live out my dreams. And that had lost its appeal the second we landed here.

Maybe the old folktales my father told about Bellington were true—maybe this was some other dimension and all I had to do was use the stone to go back home.

Unfortunately, the stone no longer glowed or felt warm. I squeezed my eyes shut and tried to summon the shadows... to no avail. A sound that raised the fine hair along my arms brought my attention back to the here and now.

A darker, much larger shadow peeled away from the others, and I had a sinking suspicion that things were about to get worse.

We needed to get off the mountain.

And that would be treacherous without any light.

That was the least of our troubles.

I swallowed thickly as I formulated a plan.

"Are you injured?" the devil from the village square demanded.

His low voice had me shivering for all the wrong reasons. He sounded like a dark fantasy come to life.

I shook my head, uncertain if that was true but not wanting to admit to anything he could potentially use against me if he was as dangerous as he appeared.

He seemed to read the slight hesitation on my face anyway.

His hood had fallen back during our descent to hell, granting me my first real look at him.

Pale hair, a shade of blond so light it was almost white, hung messily across his forehead. It was longer in the front, shorn close on the sides, and I had the strangest impression the dishevelment wasn't something he normally condoned.

Eyes the color of blue winter skies and just as cold stared back at me.

My focus slid along his perfectly carved features—his cut cheekbones, that square jaw with a fine layer of ash-colored stubble, the full lips twisted into a frown.

There was something rigidly analytical about him, like he saw the world strictly in logical terms and cared little for emotion.

We couldn't be more different if we tried, even in coloring.

I was dark and comforting like the night and he was the light of a harsh dawn rising with a vengeance.

He looked like an angel, the kind who'd fallen and preferred it that way, while my greatest sin was staying up too late reading.

I swallowed hard as he assessed me in that cool, quiet manner.

It felt like he was trying to determine if I was a friend or foe, and I wasn't sure what he'd do when he settled on an answer.

And selfish reasons aside, I needed him to direct his homicidal tendencies elsewhere.

"If you're done staring at me," I said, impressed I sounded so calm and collected, despite one of my biggest fears making an appearance, "you might want to look behind you. We seem to have a welcome party."

THREE
Prince Sloth

I TOOK IN OUR surroundings, then flicked my attention toward the purple haze at the edge of the horizon. The mountain range was real, but not quite natural. It was too sharp, too menacing, too dark and saturated. There was a peculiar quality about it all, one that was similar to the strangeness of dreams.

I had a strong feeling I knew where we'd landed.

Somnia. The land where nightmares roamed and could be twisted and used to torture anyone foolish enough to cross over its wards. Long before the old gods banished Nyantha here, the realm used to be known for its dreamlike beauty. Now it was a reminder of what could happen to our realm if the Goddess of Night escaped.

I released a slow breath and fought another smile. The woman had brought us exactly where I needed to go to track Xavier and the book.

I kept half my attention locked onto the enigmatic woman standing before me as I allowed our stalkers to move in for the kill.

I wasn't afraid, but given the nightmares creeping closer, the realm must be feeding off one of her surface-level fears.

I scanned her and quickly logged details; heart-shaped face, pert nose, long mocha-brown hair with strands of caramel, similar eye color, pale skin with a hint of warmth.

If my brother Lust were here, he'd make some loathsome quip about peaches and cream.

I wasn't my brother.

I looked deeper, searching for hints of treachery and deceit.

Quiet chittering raised the fine hair along my neck, the sound growing closer.

I still had a few moments.

The spell I'd used to find the nearest portal stone had brought me to the village across the cove from Mount Lyra, and I was more than a little put out that someone else had beaten me to the stone. Now I'd need to keep her safe until I could send her back and then use it to travel here again.

I didn't need one more complication as I hunted the Liber Noctem.

And there was something about this woman that set me on edge.

I scanned her for any information on who she was and what her motivation for leaving the Shifting Isles might be.

Assassin, poisoner, seductress.

Or possibly someone hunting the dark book.

She could easily fit into any of those categories.

Her eyes were fringed in thick lashes, her lips plump, and her scowl was an impressive weapon aimed directly at me.

Given my height of just over six feet, I placed her around five and a half feet, maybe an inch or so more.

Her long-sleeved dress was simple, a dark peach that complemented her skin tone but was made of cotton and had no frills, much like her dark cloak.

Not highborn, then.

Her lack of fighting leathers or weapons indicated she was no warrior either.

Unless that was a clever deception she used to lure her prey, letting them believe she posed no true harm until it was too late.

I wasn't convinced she spent nights coldly slicing her enemies' throats, though. But I wouldn't be surprised if she was after the Liber Noctem. Rumors of the magic it contained had spread across realms.

Power was a seduction to most.

Pebbles skidded over the edge of the cliff; the hunting party was growing.

My pulse raced in anticipation.

It wouldn't be long now.

My attention swept down; no calluses or burns on the woman's hands. Which confirmed she didn't spend her days training or doing manual labor.

Not a baker, laundress, blacksmith, or farmer.

Boots that appeared to be well-worn peeked out from her hemline, allowing her to run swiftly if she had to.

If she wasn't hunting the Book of Nightmares, I had no idea why she'd want or need a portal stone.

From my brief observation in the village, she didn't seem to be in duress or escaping from someone.

She was an equation in need of solving. I didn't deal well with variables.

Nobility or not, I'd imagined several logical paths the woman *should* have taken when confronted with traveling through realms: hysterics, denial, potential fainting spells.

Reactions most mortals would have to being yanked through a portal by shadows and spit out into what I suspected was the world crafted from nightmares.

The way she'd issued the warning, using that dry tone with a touch of humor, wasn't expected at all.

Especially if the creatures closing in on us were what I imagined them to be.

She had no idea I was a Prince of Sin; she'd think I was mortal too. Therefore, she should be exhibiting signs of terror that these might be our last moments.

Unless she wasn't entirely human.

I dismissed the notion of her being *other* until I found proof otherwise. If she knew of the Book of Nightmares, then that explained why she wasn't surprised to end up in this realm.

Maybe she *had* chosen to come here.

I'd think she was fearless if I didn't detect a slight hint of the emotion coming from her, but my abilities couldn't differentiate between her being scared of me, of losing the dark book, or of our impending attackers.

I narrowed my gaze on her. She was keeping secrets.

Which made her infinitely more dangerous than the beasts surrounding us.

She arched a brow, her expression clearly indicating she thought I might be slow. "Do you speak the common tongue?"

I bristled.

"I'm fluent in many languages."

"Wonderful. Right now, I only care about you speaking with a sword or a knife or whatever killing method a sociopath of your caliber normally prefers."

A sociopath of my caliber. I restrained from resting my hand on the hilt of my dagger. "What, exactly, are you suggesting?"

Her assessment wasn't far off, but she'd struck a nerve.

I wouldn't hesitate to slay anything that stood in my way, even the pretty, doe-eyed deceiver staring me down, but I was surprised she'd pieced that together after only briefly looking me over.

She promptly ignored me, and I suspected it wasn't because of the beasts that were almost within striking range.

This woman refused to answer a stupid question.

My jaw strained from how hard I was clamping it shut. That was twice in as many minutes that she'd questioned my intelligence.

My sin's hackles were getting raised.

Today wasn't doing any favors for my patience.

"They're right behind you." Her focus slid from them to me. "And they look hungry."

The smile that curved my lips was meant to instill fear.

She simply raised her brows, irking my sin more with her silent assessment. She clearly found me lacking in more areas.

No one was that calm when faced with a Prince of Sin; even not knowing what I was, most mortals sensed the *otherness*.

Which meant I really needed to figure out who she was before I found myself with a dagger to the back.

"I know."

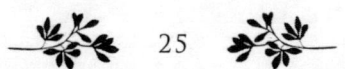

Surprise flashed in her face as I shot forward and lifted her up, spinning around and depositing her behind me.

My blade was already in my fist when I pivoted back to confront them, its familiar weight a comfort as I drank in my opponents, pleased despite our dire predicament.

Based on the nearly silent chittering of their mandibles and the occasional hiss, I'd hoped to find these creatures—a pack of Lycosidae: supernatural spiders that stood almost as tall as horses and were just as wide.

Their bulbous hair-covered bodies had eight long, sturdy legs coming from them, indicating they were built to run and pounce like the wolves they were named after.

And they looked primed to do just that.

They swayed back and forth, their many legs planted in place for now.

A few of them crouched and began bouncing a little, moving at different intervals in a disjointed dance.

I didn't suffer from arachnophobia but fought the urge to shudder.

"That's horrifying. Why are they moving like that?"

I kept my attention trained on the spiders. "To frighten us."

"Mission accomplished."

"Fear breeds carelessness. They're hoping we make a mistake because we're not focused. And right now, you're feeding into that."

She muttered something under her breath that I ignored.

I analyzed their massive size and the distance between us. A few steps and they'd have us pinned against the mountainside with nowhere to go.

Lycosidae were a native species of spiders found only in Somnia that had been plucked from mortals' nightmares and now lived and breathed and were as real as anything.

From the skittering sounds they'd made climbing up the cliff, I'd judged there to be around half a dozen.

I'd been close—there were eight I could see.

Unless more were clinging to the side of the mountain.

Masters at ambushing their prey, they chose specific locations to attack that put their opponents at a disadvantage—like cornering us on the side of this rocky mountain.

The more impaired our senses, the better.

The natural terrain would be difficult to navigate without the added complication of fending off any attacks. As if to drive home the fact that we were in danger, a gust of wind slammed into us, howling its own warning.

Of course the woman would bring us *here*. By a nest of predators.

My grip on the dagger tightened, the handle rough against my calloused palm.

I would not retreat or surrender. I would finish this, figure out a way to send the woman back home, then set out after the Liber Noctem alone.

"No matter what happens," I said, "stay behind me. And do not get bitten."

"Perfect. I'd already planned on using you as a human shield."

I focused on the rocky soil beneath my boots, grounding myself and ignoring the woman's ill-timed snark.

I'd trained in all conditions; the uneven footing would be inconvenient but not impossible to contend with. My main concern was keeping them from slipping past me to attack the woman.

Unlike her, I hadn't been joking.

One bite or stab would be the end for her.

She had the portal stone, which meant she had my full protection for the time being.

The spiders grew bolder, skittering forward another few feet, then crouching. They'd expertly formed a semicircle around us, their onyx eyes glittering in the twilight.

They were testing the boundaries, gauging my reaction to their nearness. They wanted to see if I was afraid or if they'd need to change tactics.

Soon they'd discover they'd gone hunting for a lamb only to find they'd cornered a lion.

I widened my stance, both to ensure they focused on me and to prepare myself.

Patience won battles and wars more often than brute force. The best strategies were plotted carefully, not incited by emotion.

There were no Princes of Sin more patient than me.

The spiders' bouncing intensified, the erratic rhythm turning more frenzied. They were growing restless; most of their prey probably panicked by now.

The damp heat of their breath swept over me, the sulfurous scent like rotten eggs. They'd fed recently.

A savage part of me hoped Xavier had found his end.

A quiet gag sounded behind me, the noise so unexpected I shook my head in disbelief.

Perhaps the woman was trying to distract me enough for the spiders to attack—then she'd haul herself down the mountain while they were otherwise occupied and race after the book.

"What?" she asked, voice irritated.

"Pungent breath is what you're upset about right now?"

"Everyone has their limits."

"Yours are simply strange."

"Says the maniac choosing to have a *conversation* instead of focusing on the giant, creepy spiders surrounding us."

"A *strategic* conversation."

"Well, as long as it's all part of your diabolical plot to keep us alive, carry on."

My senses prickled. It was the only warning I received.

"Stay back!"

I moved on instinct as one Lycosidae sprang forward.

I might not be able to die as an immortal, but they could bring me back to their web and inject venom into me, feeding in an endless cycle until I went mad.

I shifted to the side, narrowly avoiding another crushing blow as it pounced for me again, mindful of keeping it far from the woman.

Using my full strength, I kicked its midsection, launching it back several feet. It collided with its pack, then reared up, raising its front legs like a spooked horse.

Based on its size and viciousness, I wagered it was the alpha.

Before it brought those lethal legs down, I lunged forward, shearing the front two limbs off at the upper joint, then raced to the side to do the same to two more legs, my blade easily tearing through its tendons and skin.

It wasn't enough to end this.

I dove under it and swung upward, carving into its abdomen, then jumped back as gelatinous fluid seeped out.

Dark blood sprayed out from the severed limbs, splattering across my leathers.

It all happened within seconds.

For one drawn-out breath, silence descended.

Then the maimed Lycosidae screeched as it stumbled to the ground, the unholy sound seeming to possess a hundred voices rolled into one.

Death would not be swift for it.

I watched, emotionless, as it thrashed, spilling blood faster with each frantic movement.

The brutality of my attack was meant to warn the others off, to spare them their lives. But these were creatures born of nightmares; they welcomed violence, craved it.

They took it as a challenge, not a deterrent.

Nature didn't believe in mercy; there was only predator or prey.

The pack screamed their rage, their hackles raised as they screeched a mournful promise of vengeance. Their chittering grew so loud it rattled in my skull.

I swore.

There were too many of them for us to slip past and use the distraction to our advantage.

I considered carrying the woman but didn't want to chance slipping or being rammed by a spider and losing my footing.

One mistake or misstep and we'd fall over the mountain's edge.

I spared a quick glance back; the woman's eyes were wide and fixed on the gore. All humor had drained from her and shock seemed to be settling in.

That wasn't good.

Movement caught my attention as the alpha finally stilled.

"Run when I tell you to."

The woman didn't seem to be in the present anymore; she was completely lost to fear.

"Peaches. You need to focus."

Her gaze snapped to mine, a new fire burning within it.

"Did you just call me *peaches*?"

"Keep your wits about you. If you die, it's not my problem."

She swore roundly, calling me several colorful names, which I ignored.

I twisted around as the remaining seven beasts leapt at me, attacking as a unit.

I retreated to that cold, dark place fit for killing.

I became as dangerous as a storm, unleashing myself upon the nightmare spiders as I drove them back toward the cliff's edge.

I ended them swiftly, landing mortal wounds that would ensure they didn't suffer.

Stab, strike, retreat.

It didn't matter if they were Nocturnas or mortals or underworld beasts—my blade was indiscriminate, my dance of death unmatched.

One went down quickly. Then another.

A sharp metallic tang lingered in the air, a repulsive mixture of blood and gore. I ignored it as I stabbed and slashed.

The creatures shrieked in frustration as another of their rank went down. There was no mercy in this death song, only kill or be killed.

I had no time to waste on distractions; every moment I spent here was a moment the Book of Nightmares got farther away.

My cloak flew out behind me as I struck at the approaching creatures. They were just as ravenous to destroy me.

I clenched my jaw and gripped my blade tightly, wielding it like an extension of my body.

The steel glinted under the moonlight as I swung it in wide arcs above my head, bringing it down repeatedly with all my might.

The giant spiders kept lunging at me, their glittering eyes filled with savage bloodlust as their hairy legs scuttled across the ground.

Their mandibles clicked menacingly as they attempted to overpower me.

In my periphery I tracked the woman as she huddled against the mountain.

Another war cry drew my attention back. The beta struck out, narrowly missing my heart.

I hurtled out of reach, then doubled back, teeth bared.

I plunged my dagger into an attacker, the warmth of its blood coating my skin. It went down, leaving only three more spiders to deal with.

Instead of taking turns, the rest of the pack jumped as a killing unit.

In and out, one after the other, striking, biting, retreating, masters of their own death march. They were learning my moves, anticipating them.

They were much more cunning than the Nocturnas had been.

I shut all thoughts down save for one: ending this battle.

Spiders attacked with a renewed frenzy, their clawed legs tearing through my leather armor, slicing into my skin with frightening ease.

Venom seared through my veins, but thankfully the gashes weren't debilitating.

I clenched my jaw, channeling all my determination into each strike, my dagger whirling overhead before I smashed it down onto my enemies.

Blood drenched the grass beneath me, transforming the ground into a slick battlefield that threatened my balance with every step.

My muscles strained with each swing and parry, but the spiders were feral now, the battle raging in a chaotic dance of blood and steel versus claws and teeth.

I rammed the hilt of my dagger into the center of one spider, flinging myself back as a hundred smaller spiders erupted from within.

Their bodies were the size of small dogs.

I froze for a moment at the sight before spinning on my heel.

We needed to retreat. *Now.*

FOUR
Prince Sloth

I WRENCHED MYSELF INTO action.

My attention swept across the mountain, searching for an escape.

Fighting nearly a dozen fully grown spiders had been difficult, but with the new numbers circling us, running was the best option, even if we fell down the mountain.

Annoyance flickered through me. I cursed this realm and its first obstacle.

I'd known the nightmares roaming the land wouldn't be easy to deal with, but this was worse. Especially with the woman's presence I hadn't factored in.

I couldn't fend off that many spiders and guarantee she would survive without a bite. But I could wrap my body around hers if we went over the cliff.

Not ideal, but the plan would suffice.

A bloodcurdling scream sent ice through my veins.

I pivoted in time to see one of the smaller spiders leaping at her.

It was a blur of legs and fangs, too fast and too close for her to escape. With how swiftly it was moving, the impact would knock her off the side of the mountain.

I flung my blade at it, the slick thwack indicating it found its target.

A beat later the spider collapsed in a twitching heap at her feet, its venomous legs mere inches from delivering a fatal blow.

My heart thudded aggressively—that had been too close.

One more second and I would have been too late.

If she'd gone over the edge of the cliff, I would have lost the portal stone and my way out of this realm.

Her frightened eyes met mine before she screamed again.

"Behind you!"

Pain slammed into my side, sharp and flaming.

I looked down, confused by what I saw.

A spider's leg speared me like a sword.

Seconds later, it wrenched it out, its victory screech splitting the night.

Had I been human, it would have been a killing blow.

My breath hissed through my teeth as warmth flowed out of me, my blood gushing out in a torrent down my side.

I stumbled forward, knees crashing to the ground, and pressed a hand to my wound. It did little to staunch the flow; my fingers were slick within moments.

The world grew dark at the edges, fuzzy.

It wouldn't be long before the potent venom completely dragged me under, immortal or not.

I gritted my teeth, furious with Xavier for his betrayal again.

What little chance I'd had of picking up his trail was lost now.

"My dagger."

The woman dropped to her knees before me, her hands fisting in my leathers.

"You can't fight like this, are you mad?"

Blood seeped through my fingers. "Take...it. And run."

I wasn't being altruistic or selfless.

When I recovered, I'd be able to track her with it.

She moved out of view and I released a breath.

That took less convincing than I'd thought it would.

At least she had a decent sense of self-preservation and a subtle ruthlessness I could respect.

My attention shifted.

The mountain loomed like a great beast, its jagged edges clawing at the sky. I squinted, almost convinced the mountain had *actually* rumbled.

My pulse slowed. The mountain definitely trembled beneath us. Through the haze descending, I was struck with a realization: it was no regular mountain—we'd landed on a volcano.

And it was about to erupt.

Gods-damned nightmares. *Of course* they'd find a way to literally twist the ground beneath our feet.

I'd hoped my companion had made it far enough away with the portal stone, when she appeared again.

I narrowed my gaze. Surely, *surely* I was hallucinating and she hadn't fetched my dagger and rushed back to my side.

I gritted my teeth. "Did you sustain a head injury?"

"No." She searched my face. "Why?"

I drew in my remaining strength. "I swear I told you to run."

The woman gave me a scathing look, then muttered something I couldn't understand, her frustration outweighing her terror.

Perhaps she'd been joking earlier because she was absolutely mad instead of fearless. At the end of her tirade, it sounded like she'd called me an ungrateful, coldhearted prick.

She was only partly correct in that assumption.

My eyes shut but I wrenched them open.

A shadow rose behind her.

She swore, then jumped on top of me, shielding my body with hers, furthering my suspicion that she was insane.

I was badly injured but would survive; she wouldn't. And there was nothing I could do to save her from her misplaced heroics.

If she died, it would be her own damned fault.

And I'd be forced to find a way to drag her soul back from Death's domain to make her help me search for the portal stone. With the wards in place, I couldn't simply use my own magic to transport out of here.

I would *not* be pleased with the delay.

Though I supposed if a spider ate her, I'd just have to hunt the swarm down and gut them all until I found the stone.

None of that would be necessary if she just listened and ran.

Ribbons of shadows shot out and wound around us, seeming oddly sentient. She held me tighter, and the press of her body against mine felt like fire as her curves branded my chest.

The ribbons bound her to me in a move that felt more possessive than protective.

My focus drifted across her face. Embers ignited in her eyes, tiny specks glowing like golden flames.

I struggled to recall details of the venom, wondering if vivid hallucinations were part of the symptoms or not.

It seemed highly likely they were.

One moment we were on the mountaintop, and the next it simply… fell away. Like it had folded in on itself and someone had turned the page of a pop-up book.

Darkness held us tightly in its fist as the ground gave way to nothingness. We floated in a void, weightless but tethered together until gravity came crashing back with a vengeance.

The shadows loosened their grip and faded away as quickly as they'd appeared. Hard earth slammed into us.

Fresh blood poured out from where I'd been impaled, the agony all-encompassing as I drew in a shallow breath and tried to orient myself.

A warm hand slapped my face.

"Wake up, Sociopath. You can't die on me now."

I blinked as our surroundings slowly came into view. We'd traveled to a new location. Soft, damp grass cushioned my head.

I rolled to the side, another explosion of pain stealing my breath.

My vision turned black at the edges, but I refused to submit to the darkness just yet. I forced my eyes to stay open, expecting to see the spiders preparing for the kill, or the mountaintop raining down lava.

All was quiet. No pack of Lycosidae, no other enemies closing in.

We were sprawled in a meadow of tall, sweet grass and wildflowers.

Alone.

About a hundred yards away a stone cabin sat near the edge of a dark wood. No smoke wafted out from the chimney, but that didn't mean it was abandoned.

Cool drops fell across my face; I glanced up.

Rain. I couldn't recall if I'd seen a storm rolling in on the mountain. I didn't think so.

Thunder sounded in the distance, the force of it shaking the ground.

My eyes fluttered shut.

The venom felt like fire in my veins as it traveled deeper into my system. I couldn't fight it much longer. Or maybe I'd already succumbed to it and was lost in a delusion while it worked its way back out of my system.

That was the only logical explanation for how we ended up here.

Unless she'd somehow used the portal stone, and I hadn't seen it.

"Someone, help!" the woman cried out, startling me.

No. Was what I would have said if words didn't fail me. She had no way of knowing there was no help to be found in Somnia.

Not even I could be trusted.

This world was built on dreams, on fantasy. And the goddess who ruled it cleverly twisted them to her whims without anyone being the wiser.

My head rolled to the side, the sound of approaching footsteps barely rousing me.

"By the gods. Who *are* you? What happened to him?" a different feminine voice responded in the common tongue.

I tried to shove myself into a sitting position, but my limbs didn't cooperate.

"Well, that's kind of an interesting story..."

They exchanged more words, but I couldn't hold on to the rapid conversation.

Despite my best efforts, I fell into a dreamless sleep and didn't get up.

I woke with a start in an uncomfortable bed, the straw from the mattress jabbing into my wound.

The pain hadn't roused me from sleep; some gnawing sense of unease had.

It felt like the room had drawn its breath, waiting to see what happened next.

I gingerly sat up and the thin sheet covering me fell away.

I glanced down at my bare chest, frowning.

Gauze was wrapped tightly around my torso, but that wasn't what caught my attention. I tugged the bandage off and stared.

A large intricate design covered my entire chest and both arms, the careful lines dipping below my trousers. A tattoo.

Unlike the House Sloth tree of knowledge crest I had inked onto my back, I had no recollection of getting this one.

It was hard to tell from this direction, but it looked like each arm had a wing tattooed onto it and the bird's body was inked onto my chest.

The lifelike gold feathers looked lit from within, the ink shimmering against my skin.

My brother Envy would appreciate the artistry of the image.

I only felt that sense of unease growing further. It was the same phoenix design that had been on the cover of the Liber Noctem.

The phantom burning slowly came back to me.

With everything that had happened, I'd almost forgotten about the odd sensation I'd felt back in the temple.

I wasn't sure what the tattoo meant, but it couldn't be anything good if the Book of Nightmares was involved. I focused on breathing steadily to keep my icy wall of calm in place. On not letting my annoyance give way to rage.

Something *marked* me. Without my knowledge or consent.

I hated the violation even if my curiosity about it was piqued.

"A phoenix is an interesting choice. Why'd you get it?"

My attention snapped up.

I hadn't noticed the woman sitting in the small chair off to the side of the bed. With annoyance, I realized I couldn't keep referring to her as *the woman* in my head.

"What's your name?"

She gave me a bemused look.

"Peaches. Don't you remember? I thought we bonded."

I coolly stared at her.

Her mood was cheerful despite the chaos we'd survived.

I couldn't decide if I was slightly impressed or worried about her mental state again.

I settled on annoyance. I never trusted an optimist.

And I certainly didn't trust this woman.

After a minute of strained silence, she leveled me with the same cold look I was giving her.

I didn't acknowledge it at all, which made her mood darken.

I swore shadows flickered in her eyes before she blinked them away.

My hallucinations weren't quite under control yet.

I focused on breathing in and out steadily.

My healing abilities had been working hard to restore me, and it wouldn't be much longer before I was completely healed.

I'd give myself two more minutes, then get the portal stone from her and head out to start tracking Xavier and the Liber Noctem.

"How long was I out for?"

"An hour or so." She dragged her gaze from my tattoo to my face. "If you're worried about your virtue, I only took your tunic off to clean your wound. I also disinfected it with some alcohol I found in the cabinet. You thrashed pretty good, so I assume it helped."

I arched a brow at the radiant smile that crossed her face when she mentioned thrashing but said nothing.

She was like the sun, having a bright disposition, but still capable of a violent burn. Lust would already be in love. But that wouldn't be surprising; he had no common sense.

That strange feeling of discomfort reared its head again. I didn't think it had anything to do with her, but after Xavier's betrayal, I wasn't sure.

My senses were alerting me to some unseen danger.

I scanned the small single-room cabin.

One cot, two chairs, a table, and an overly large fireplace. Along the far wall sat a wooden cabinet filled with jars.

Herbs, dried meat, beans. A small stack of plates and utensils.

A chamber pot, washbasin, and screen were stashed in the opposite corner. An impressive collection of axes hung near the door.

Rain softly pattered against the tin roof; the storm we'd arrived in hadn't blown over yet.

I finally recalled that there had been another woman at some point.

"Where are we?"

"Some nice woman named Jessa Maya's cabin. She's out gathering supplies for a poultice. Not that you asked. Or seem to need one. Your wound is healing remarkably fast. Almost like you're not human."

Her dark gaze bore into mine, unflinching and sharp.

There were no shadows this time, and her expression was easy enough to read because I suspected she *wanted* me to know how she felt.

She didn't trust me and knew I had secrets of my own.

If she thought I would confirm her suspicions and give her any information she could use against me, she would be disappointed.

I only needed to figure out if she was also searching for the Liber Noctem, then come up with a way to convince her to hand over the portal stone and return to her kingdom.

She sighed when I offered no information.

"My name is Lore."

I surveyed her. "Lore's an unusual name."

She shrugged and got up, grabbing a chipped mug from the side table and offering it to me. "Jessa Maya said to give you this when you woke up."

It smelled like an old carcass.

I wouldn't have been surprised if it was poisoned.

Lore's lips twitched like she knew what I was thinking, and it gave her a dark sort of glee to inflict the sludge on me.

I held the steaming contents but refrained from sipping it. I'd need to be dragged and dumped at the gates of the Great Beyond before I ingested it. Even then true death might be preferable.

"Are you going to tell me your name or keep me in suspense?"

I gave her a slow, wicked smile in response.

Princes of Sin guarded our true names with savagery. They granted someone power to summon us, among other inconveniences and potential threats. I saw no reason to share that information with her now. Or ever.

Instead of glowering or making demands of me, a spark of challenge flared in her eyes.

Gods only knew what she was plotting.

"Why did you bring us here?" I asked.

She arched an impertinent brow but said nothing. Frustrating woman.

We sat in silence, analyzing each other.

As the thick fog of venom slowly dissipated, more memories came back.

Shadows streaming out from Lore, the odd folding in of the world around us, the embers I swore I'd seen in her eyes. Ending up in a seemingly different part of this realm within moments.

"You used the portal stone again?" I asked, watching her closely.

"Portal stone?" She gave me a blank look. "Oh! You mean this?"

Lore stuck her hand into her skirt pocket and pulled the stone out, holding it up for me to inspect.

I hadn't gotten a good look at it before and swallowed thickly.

A smooth onyx teardrop lay flat in her palm.

Chills raced along my spine.

I'd never seen it in person, only illustrations and sketches, but I'd recognize it anywhere.

I'd been searching for it for as long as I'd been hunting the book.

That wasn't a portal stone. It was a phoenix tear. And it had once come from the cover of the Liber Noctem.

Myths suggested the first, and most powerful, phoenix had lost her mate and flew across the realm of the old gods, leaving a trail of tears.

All but one exploded upon contact with the terrain. But the Goddess of Night herself had caught the final tear in her palm and cradled it close, grieving along with her friend.

By all accounts, the original phoenix was never seen again, and when it left the realm of the old gods, the few remaining of its kind disappeared too.

Some claimed the old gods had captured the original phoenix to further their wicked plots, and others swore the ancient birds traveled to a new dimension, one where all manner of mythical creatures ruled the land.

I hadn't found such a place, but the universe was vast and complex and not even I dared to believe I knew all the secrets she held.

Legend claimed that the Goddess of Night mourned the loss of her favorite companion so much, she'd turned her back on dreams, focusing only on nightmares from that day forward.

Without any shift in my expression, I let my magic flow out, subtly testing the woman sitting beside the bed.

If she knew the full potential of the phoenix tear she held, all my strategies needed to be reworked. And if—gods forbid—she was a creature who could *access* that potential, we were already in far deeper than even I could have accounted for.

I didn't sense any magic in Lore, but my tension didn't ease. It was possible she was shielding her power from me.

It certainly made me more suspicious about who she really was. It also forced me to consider the possibility that she'd plotted with Xavier.

There were no such things as coincidences. And the fact that the Liber Noctem and the phoenix tear were both found in the same small village on the Shifting Isles where she was set me further on edge.

This had the makings of a plot that had been in play for a long time.

Xavier was smart. He knew all the legends as well as I did.

Which meant he also knew the missing link that could damn us all.

He had the book, the phoenix tear was in play, and if he was attempting what I believed he was, then all he'd need was a dreamweaver.

I worked to keep my reaction from my face.

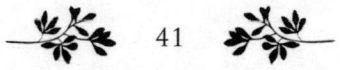

Little had been written about dreamweavers, but I'd collected just enough to understand they were world-builders beyond compare, descendants of the old gods. And if Lore *was* a dreamweaver in possession of the phoenix tear, then I needed to get them both out of Somnia as soon as possible.

My heart thudded against my chest.

That growing sense of unease was back and was getting more insistent than it had been before.

My magic had definitely sensed the threat.

The very one that leaned closer, her brows pinching together as she studied me with the same intensity I'd been aiming at her.

"Is everything okay?" she asked.

I scanned her features. I didn't detect any false notes in her tone or expression, but that didn't mean anything.

"What exactly do you do in Bellington?"

She frowned. "I don't see how that's relevant."

I didn't think she'd answer, but it had been worth a try.

I jerked my chin at the phoenix tear, my cool mask of indifference sliding into place.

"Give me the stone; I'll bring us back to Bellington."

Something unreadable flashed in her face, her hand tightening on the stone. It happened swiftly, but I'd been watching for her reaction.

Lore didn't *want* to give up the phoenix tear.

Even if handing it over meant she'd safely go back home to her family and world.

It wasn't the reaction most would have when given an easy option.

Either she knew what it was or she was suspicious of my motives.

Neither of those options was good.

Xavier's treachery might be far more damning than I'd originally thought. If he'd managed to not only smuggle the book into this realm, but get a dreamweaver here as well, that meant one thing.

He wanted to enact the Trials of Unbinding.

Avoiding them was *one* of the reasons I'd hoped to lock the Liber Noctem away in my collection.

I studied Lore like I would any potential adversary. She could be far more dangerous than I'd originally thought.

"If you want to transport us yourself, then by all means." I held my hand out, palm up. "Let's get back to your realm."

FIVE
Lore

THE HANDSOME — AND exceptionally talented — spider assassin had gone preternaturally still when he first saw the rock the fairy godmother from hell had given me.

I didn't need to possess any extraordinary powers of deduction like my favorite detectives to realize whatever I held wasn't the portal stone he'd mentioned.

He'd tried hard to convince me to hand him the stone without being obvious about it, but there was no way I'd give him the one thing I knew could bring me back home to my family.

Dreaming of embarking on a fantasy adventure was thrilling from the safety of my room, but I was quickly discovering that living it was a bit of a nightmare.

I never had to worry about *actually* being impaled by giant spiders in Bellington. I'd give anything to be back there now, with the exception of handing over the one object I knew could bring me home.

There was no guarantee that the sociopath would take me with him.

I gripped the stone in my palm, trying to summon the same warmth I'd felt from it back in my village while the quiet assassin watched in that unnervingly intense way.

Nothing happened.

I peered back at him, hoping for any hint of how I was doing, but he might as well have been carved from marble.

His expression was completely closed off and void of any warmth.

I'd read enough fiction to know the villain always turned up the charm right before he double-crossed the heroine.

Thus far, I wasn't in any danger of swooning.

This man was as friendly and approachable as the mythical ice dragons I'd grown up reading about.

He *did* have all the physical trappings of an exquisite antihero, though, right down to his beautiful, ruthless features.

I needed to be on guard while we were stuck in this predicament.

The last thing I needed was for my fiction-loving brain to kick on and start imagining him as the leading love interest.

He kept that frosty gaze locked on mine as I struggled to wake the not-likely-a-portal-stone up. It wasn't the easiest thing to ignore.

I kept trying to focus on the matter at hand and not think about his little slip and all the terrible things it could mean.

He'd called Bellington *my* realm, not his.

Gods only knew who he was or where he came from. If I let myself start freaking out over that, I'd end up in the fetal position and I didn't want to be that vulnerable in front of him or Jessa Maya when she returned.

It had been more disquieting than comforting to see another woman. Which was odd, but something had been off about her, something I couldn't quite put my finger on. It was a nagging sense of déjà vu that made no sense.

That feeling of foreboding persisted even now.

A prickle of unease traveled down my spine the longer the silence stretched between us and the stone remained as magical as a lump of coal.

"How does the portal stone work?" I finally asked. "It's not coming to life like the first time I held it."

Something flashed in his face, much too quickly for me to read.

"Concentrate on your home and picture yourself being there. The magic will do the rest."

I closed my fingers around the stone and waited for the telltale sensation I'd felt before. The warmth, the shadows streaming out...

I imagined my small village, then shifted my attention to my library. I spent so much time there, it was easy to envision the space.

Every time I unlocked the door and stepped inside the small, squat building, I felt the same sense of wonder that I had as a girl when my parents took us there. I could see the slant of warm afternoon light that illuminated the worn shelves, mismatched wooden chairs gathered around a coffee table and fireplace like old friends, and the hush that wrapped around me like a favorite quilt.

I wasn't thrilled about potentially dragging this ice king there with me, but sacrifices needed to be made.

A few minutes ticked by. I squinted.

We were still in the cabin.

"Is it possible it got broken on the trip?" I asked, flipping the damned thing over, searching for any cracks or hairline fractures.

The assassin shocked me by leaning in and wrapping his hand over mine, his warm, calloused fingers brushing against the stone in my grasp.

"Empty your mind. I'll transport us back."

I raised a brow at his clipped tone.

He ignored me and closed his eyes, no doubt attempting to get the magic rock to work.

I wanted him to succeed, so I refrained from silently cursing him for his surly attitude.

A minute passed. Then another. The rock didn't get the message that he was impatient and possibly a serial killer.

It remained stubbornly inactive. I could almost believe it was tormenting him on purpose. An odd kinship sparked in my chest at that. I doubted many people ever challenged him.

His jaw ticked.

He wrenched his eyes open and glared at the stone.

I gave him a few seconds to come to terms with his annoyance and did my best to not stare at the ridiculously toned chest he had.

When he'd leaned over to hold the stone, he'd inadvertently brought that wall of muscle mere inches from my face, and it was difficult to ignore.

With definition like that, he would *definitely* be a villain in my romantic fantasy adventure stories. It was practically a criminal offense to look like a god and have the attitude of a sinner.

I made another mental note to not get on his bad side. He could probably snap my neck and bury my corpse without breaking a sweat.

"Lore?" He snapped his fingers in front of my face. "Did you hear anything I just said?"

If I had a dagger, I might have stabbed him with it.

Instead, I grabbed his tunic and tossed it at him.

Even injured, his reflexes were unlike anything I'd ever seen; he snatched it from the air before it hit him in his beautiful chiseled face.

He arched a brow but dutifully shrugged his gore-splattered shirt back on.

I released a breath. Thank the gods *that* was taken care of.

"You were saying?" I asked brightly.

A frown tugged at the corners of his mouth as he considered the stone again before responding. "Does any of this feel...strange?"

I waited for him to crack a smile for obvious reasons.

He didn't.

He held my gaze, waiting.

"If by 'this' you mean falling through a portal, being attacked by Jurassic spiders, then ending up in a cabin in the woods with a nameless, mortally wounded assassin who miraculously healed in under an hour seem odd?"

I tapped a finger against my lips, feigning contemplation. He could not be serious now. *Of course* this was strange.

In fact, we'd crossed so far beyond strange, I was wondering if we'd created a new state of mind altogether.

Now that I wasn't focused on staying away from the death spiders and he was awake and we were not magically back in my village, the shock was wearing off. I was seconds away from diving into the deepest end of the insanity pool and floating around there until reality came back.

"No, it's just another normal evening in my world. Why, are *you* feeling like it's a bit strange?"

His attention fell to my mouth and lingered.

If we were in a book, this would absolutely be the time he'd quip about my smart mouth.

For a moment, he looked like he was about to do just that.

Instead of playing out that secret fantasy I didn't know I had, he brought that icy glare back up, respectfully staring into my eyes.

I released the breath that had suddenly lodged in my throat; the tension had been glorious there for a second.

"When you used the stone on the mountaintop, what were you imagining?" he asked.

I lifted a shoulder. "My parents' house."

"Does this look like your family's home?"

I shook my head. "When nothing happened, I started to think of where I'd feel safe. The next thing I knew, I was picturing a cabin in the woods, far from giant spiders."

He stared at me for an extended beat.

"Do you recognize this particular cabin?"

"Is that really important right now?"

He simply arched a brow, waiting. Gods, he was infuriating.

If he wanted to play out his own fever dream, I'd humor him.

While his general attitude left much to be desired, he *did* take a spider leg to the gut for me. If that wasn't deserving of a quick ride on the delusional train, I wasn't sure what was. Plus, I was a little concerned about my brief conversation with Jessa Maya earlier.

I looked at the room with a critical eye.

Honestly, there had been a few peculiar things I'd stuffed into my mental "to deal with later" file. It was obviously time to open it.

"Everything here is very close to a book I've read."

Jessa Maya's name, her moon-pale skin and crimson hair, even the forest and meadow of sweet grass were identical.

In the story, legend claimed her hair was the color of her victims' blood. She wasn't exactly human; she was a redcap. A murderous goblin.

One of the more creative aspects of the novel was how instead of dipping her cap in blood, she dipped her locks in, and her hair grew darker the more she killed. Though she did also *drink* the blood, so there was some confusion about how the magic actually worked.

The woman I'd met here had medium auburn locks, which, if we were insane and were going by the author's world-building, would be a little concerning.

I finally brought my attention back to his. "That's strange, right?"

He didn't look surprised by the revelation; if anything a grim sort of resolve set into his features.

"What happens in the book?" he pressed.

I glanced out the lone window, nibbling my lower lip.

"Well..." It struck me that this would be an awkward plot summary, no matter how I tried selling it. Best to give as little information as possible. "Jessa Maya has a bit of a murdering addiction."

"And?"

I grimaced. "She's a cannibal. Well, technically, she's a goblin. She looks human, though, which is why I think she gets confused for a cannibal."

His brows shot up.

"It's all very allegorical, though," I added quickly. "She only attacks those who've been warned against touching her belongings. Really, it can be read as a study of why society finds women who stand up for themselves unappealing and villainizes them."

I'd read the book right after a particularly bad breakup and felt a kinship for Jessa Maya. I'd been the one who ended the courtship, but I was villainized for breaking his heart. In reality, he hadn't really wanted me, and he'd let it slip that he was in love with someone else who'd given her heart to another. Apparently, I'd been the safe, second option. It was perfectly acceptable for him to settle, but I knew it was a recipe for disaster down the line.

I'd saved us both from a loveless union, yet I was the villain.

I felt my blood pressure rising and took a deep breath to center myself. Honestly, the way female characters were held to a higher, impossible standard in fiction was one of my biggest gripes.

A woman was branded as unlikable and irredeemable if she behaved the same way a man did. It was unjust how we demanded perfection from some characters while praising the flaws of others as growth.

That unfortunately wasn't restricted to the pages of novels, either.

That notion often bled into reality.

So, yes, Jessa Maya *might* kill and eat her victims, but that was beside the point. The moral of the story was to respect others or suffer the consequences because you never knew when you were messing with a rage-fueled cannibal who was *extremely* particular about her belongings.

I knew I was careening over the edge, but focusing on something familiar was keeping me grounded for the moment.

The assassin seemed to choose his next words carefully. "Did the woman you spoke with earlier say anything similar to you?"

I thought of her parting words.

"She said, 'Touch anything, and I'll gut you like a pig.' Then she mimed a very convincing stabbing motion, laughed, and flounced off into the woods."

He stared at me for a solid moment, seeming lost for words.

I had a feeling it was more my description of her frolicking into the forest rather than the subject that had thrown him.

"Dark humor is an acquired taste," I pointed out, "so I didn't hold it against her."

The woman lived alone in a world where giant spiders impaled people, and I doubted she had visitors over for tea very often.

Far be it from me to judge what she found funny.

"How, exactly, did this cannibal goblin story make you feel safe?"

I bristled at his tone. "It's not like the book started off with the cannibalism. It was very pleasant up until it wasn't."

I left out the part about my dissolved courtship and how I'd felt an odd kinship toward the villainess in the story.

He pinched the bridge of his nose and took a deep breath.

"How long ago did she leave?"

"Maybe an hour?"

I lifted a shoulder. I hadn't thought to check the nonexistent clock.

I'd been preoccupied by addressing his wound like any normal adult dealing with a post-monster-attack crisis. The least he could do was thank me for playing nursemaid and remaining calm and clearheaded enough to focus on his trauma.

Up until this unfortunate event, I didn't even know I *could* help someone back from the brink of death. His manners clearly needed work.

"She helped me carry you in and went to collect the herbs a few minutes later."

He glanced around the room, a new alertness in his gaze. The apex predator returned.

"Did you use anything without permission?"

I opened my mouth to say no, then stopped, an eerie sense of déjà vu coming over me. "I used some alcohol on your wound."

"That's something that happened in the story?" he guessed.

My attention returned to the cabinet of supplies, my pulse beginning to tick faster.

In the book the main character had been left alone for days and finally took a sip of what she thought was water. She planned on refilling the bottle as soon as the winter storm had passed.

It had been a trap—Jessa Maya spiked the drink and attacked when the toxin had kicked in. She'd taken her ax and hacked her into a hundred little pieces.

"Lore. Did this happen in your book?"

I shook myself out of my growing unease. "Yes. But not exactly; there are a few similarities is all. It's not the same plotline."

His brows knit together. "What do you mean?"

"For starters, it's not winter. The setting was an integral part of the book. And Jessa Maya stayed in the cabin for the first few days. Then she left during the worst of the blizzard. When she came back, that's when the axing began."

Instead of questioning my taste in fiction, he flung the sheet off his legs and got to his feet like the devil himself had torched his ass.

"Grab supplies and hurry."

I watched, uncharacteristically subdued, as he retrieved his dagger from the nightstand and moved faster than any mortal could, flinging open the cabinet, inspecting jars.

He was a blur of motion, pausing only when he noticed I was still rooted to the spot where he'd left me.

I wondered if he was really *that* fast or if my adrenaline had finally crashed and shock had settled in, making me sluggish. Though healing from being impaled in an hour kind of indicated he wasn't human.

It was one more thing to tuck away until I could deal with it later.

There were only so many impossible things I could reasonably handle before dinner.

"Why aren't you packing? Are you sick? Did she make you eat or drink anything?" he demanded.

"No, I'm perfectly fine."

He narrowed his gaze, not believing the obvious lie but not calling me on it.

"Then grab anything you can in case we need to sleep in the woods for a few days. We need to leave before she returns."

I couldn't believe I was about to be the voice of reason, but here we were.

"It's only a story. And you should really rest."

Miraculous healing aside, he'd been impaled an hour or so ago.

He looked like he was silently debating something.

The fact that he seemed more worried now than when I summarized my cannibal murder book said a lot.

He hadn't missed a beat then.

Footsteps scraped across the stairs of the front porch.

He swore, moving again in that supernaturally fast way.

Within seconds, he snatched a blanket, a waterskin, and several other jars and stuffed them into a leather satchel.

He grabbed my hand and drew me out from around the small bed.

"This isn't similar to the book; it *is* the story."

I stared at him. "I think you need to lie down again. You're obviously feverish."

"I am not ill. And right now"—he paused like the next thing that came out of his mouth would cause physical pain—"right now there is a goblin cannibal about to walk through that door and I'd rather not have to fight her with my magic while I'm recovering. I suggest we discuss this *after* we escape."

I was at a complete loss for words.

For starters, he'd just admitted to having magic. And even after a day of impossibilities, my skepticism went on high alert.

Or maybe it was my sense of survival. I had no way of knowing if he was luring me outside to kill me with his aforementioned powers.

"Why don't you just kill her?"

I couldn't believe those words left my mouth, but here we were.

His brows shot up. Wonderful, I'd shocked a sociopath.

"Goblins are immortal," he said like this was completely normal. "I'd rather save my energy for what's to come."

I doubted the night could get any more terrifying than that.

A key twisted in the lock, the doorknob slowly turning.

I could slap myself for not thinking the night could get any worse. Whenever main characters did that, the plot always took offense.

My senses prickled in warning, growing so tense my hands began trembling.

The main character in the book had also been locked in the cabin.

How many coincidences needed to occur before they were no longer coincidences?

That was a philosophical question for another day.

Right now my gut said to run, and I never ignored that wise little wretch. Any reader knew that was the kiss of death.

My attention jerked up to the assassin; he gave me a patient look.

He might be out of his mind, he might have ulterior motives, but the churning sense of dread told me to trust his brand of crazy and move.

Now.

I shot across the small room, and the assassin with questionable sanity shoved the window up, using enough force to crack the stone frame, forgoing silence in favor of speed.

We'd *definitely* need to discuss what he ate to fuel that kind of immense power later.

I grabbed on to the ledge and hoisted myself up as the front door crashed open.

An ax flew past my head, embedding itself in the wall.

I froze. *Holy gods.*

Stone splintered from the force. Jessa Maya had one hell of a throwing arm.

A second ax whizzed by, skimming my ear.

"Move, Lore!"

His warning wasn't necessary—I was already falling through the window and running as fast as I could. I slipped over the rain-soaked grass, the storm pelting down on me with a vengeance, but didn't stop.

I charged through puddle after puddle, my boots getting soaked through.

My toes prickled uncomfortably from the icy water, but I'd worry about that later. My stockings were sopping wet and kept making a squelching noise that no amount of thunder could hide.

I never would have thought damp socks might be my undoing.

Hopefully the storm would drown out sounds of wet footwear.

The assassin easily caught up and grabbed my arm, hauling me alongside him at breakneck speed.

My feet practically floated over the ground as he lifted me higher.

A beat later, I heard the pounding of... paws?

I glanced over my shoulder and *really* wished I hadn't.

Jessa Maya was riding a wolf. And not just any wolf, but something truly out of a nightmare. It was easily the size of an elephant, and its fangs looked sharp enough to rip my limbs off in one bite. That definitely hadn't been in the original story.

The sociopath swore and yelled at me to move my ass faster.

Together we raced across the meadow and aimed for the woods, the furious Jessa Maya chasing close behind us with a bloodcurdling cry I'd never unhear.

Thunder shook the earth, the force of it powerful enough to make me stumble.

A moment later, a whip of lightning struck near us, igniting a dead sapling in a blaze of white flames.

I let go of the assassin and careened around the scorched earth before grabbing on to him again.

My cloak, now completely saturated with rainwater, added weight to my frame that was getting harder to ignore.

I wished I'd spent more time climbing the trails up the mountains in Bellington with Fable. Or hefting around heavier books.

If I survived the raging cannibal and her death wolf, I made a mental note to add strength training to my weekly schedule.

Running for one's life wasn't as thrilling as fiction made it seem.

I had a stitch in my side that could possibly be an early sign of a heart attack and was wheezing already.

The wolf was gaining on us, and if we didn't make it to the woods soon to slow it down, we would die. Flashes of my parents and Fable spurred me on. I would *not* meet my end here.

We ran so hard my lungs squeezed painfully in my chest, and I thought I'd die if I took another breath.

While we'd been inside, the temperature had plummeted several degrees, the cold air stinging with each sharp inhalation.

Even being injured, the homicidal sociopath showed no such strain.

He moved with lethal grace while I huffed along at his side.

We finally reached the forest's edge moments before the wolf and his screeching rider.

The assassin charged forward with the force of a battering ram, slicing through the dense, tangled greenery to create a jagged path for me to follow.

I hurled myself into the eerie woods after him, my adrenaline surging through my veins as the wolf howled in frustration and began snarling and tearing at the undergrowth, trying to rip an opening large enough for it to squeeze through.

The dense trees would only keep it at bay for so long.

I hoped the sociopath knew what he was doing, or we were doomed.

Giant spiders, shadow portals, nightmare wolf riding, immortal goblin cannibals… What was behind door number three?

I was about to find out.

SIX
Lore

It was so dark I could barely see his light hair in front of me.

Branches and vines lashed at my arms and face like whips, brambles snagging fiercely in my hair and skirt. I couldn't afford to slow down, not even for a moment to wipe the rain blurring my vision.

My pulse pounded violently, a frantic drumbeat of impending doom.

Any second could be my last.

Jessa Maya's death wolf was closing the distance, and the sound of her pet from hell crashing through the forest behind us was sending my heartbeat into full panic.

I did not want to end up as her dinner.

I had all sorts of horrific images fluttering through my head—being basted on a spit with an apple stuffed in my mouth was just one scenario haunting me.

I kept my attention on the here and now.

At the base of a wide tree, the assassin abruptly stopped and swung around.

Like the supreme predator I was, I crashed into him at full speed and bounced off his chest, landing ungracefully in a bush.

I swiped a lock of wet hair from my face, wondering what I'd done in a previous life to warrant this kind of karmic retribution.

To add insult to injury, I'd probably get a black eye from smashing into that wall of hard muscle.

He hauled me up, his face an expressionless mask as he plucked a leaf from my hair. I got the feeling that if we weren't being chased, Lord Serious might have actually cracked a smile.

"Get on my back."

He didn't have to tell me twice.

I jumped up and clung to him like a barnacle, my arms and legs locked around him in a death grip.

For a breathless second I felt the solid heat of his body under mine, strong, steady, and completely unshaken despite the circumstances. I held him a little tighter, sinking into the safety he offered.

His hands shifted just enough to anchor me against him, a fleeting, almost tender gesture that left me wondering if I'd imagined it as he took off again, moving so fast my hair whipped behind me in a gust of wind he created.

The night held no dominion over him.

He leapt over fallen logs, dodged low-hanging branches, and wove in and around saplings, moving like it was daylight and the sun was streaming down, not like it was full dark and more treacherous from the raging storm.

I had no idea *what* he was but was thankful for whatever made him move like a freight train.

Eventually, the sound of pursuit faded, and our pace slowed.

Instead of stopping completely, he circled a thick copse of trees.

I couldn't see his face from my position, but judging from the way his head cocked to the side, he was analyzing the ground for any tracks we'd left.

"Hold on tightly."

It was the only warning I got before he started climbing the largest evergreen I'd ever seen. It looked like it had eaten half the forest.

Gravity was clearly another law he enjoyed breaking.

He moved up the tree with ease, swinging from one branch to the next, then confidently letting go, undisturbed by being airborne with me still locked around his neck.

I closed my eyes, pretending like I was one of the acrobats who'd been at my village tonight, flying through the air without any fear of falling.

Gods. Had I walked into town with Fable only a few hours ago? It felt like a lifetime.

The assassin finally stopped climbing, then shimmied me off his back.

I dropped to my feet, the weight of my waterlogged cloak causing me to teeter to one side.

My boots slipped over the rounded surface of the branch, but before I went careening to my death, my unwitting hero spun around and wrapped an arm around me as he pressed my back securely against the tree.

"Move down slowly," he commanded, "and use the trunk as a support."

He didn't offer soft words of comfort like "I'll make sure you don't fall, Lore." Or "Don't worry, I've got you." But his cool, steady gaze remained locked on mine as he offered his hand.

He wouldn't let me die by tree tonight. Hopefully not by goblin cannibal or any other monsters either.

I gripped his hands tightly as I slid down, mindful of the bulky material pooling at my side.

My butt hit the branch, and I reluctantly let go of him.

I'd never been clumsy before and knew it was a sign of a bigger issue I'd need to address soon.

Once I was sure I wasn't about to slip again, I tucked my chin against my chest and closed my eyes as full body shivers wracked through me.

The thick greenery helped shelter us from the worst of the storm, but I was still soaked through and freezing.

The air already felt colder than it had a few seconds ago, and if the temperature dipped any lower, the rain would turn to sleet or snow.

My teeth started to chatter, and I cursed them for making any sound that could draw attention to our perch. I doubted Jessa Maya and her demon wolf were the only beasts hunting in these woods.

In the distance the shrill screams of the cannibal pierced the night.

My grumpy savior pushed to his feet, standing completely still, his attention set on the forest below.

I had a thousand questions but kept them stuffed inside me.

We weren't safe yet.

Several tense but quiet moments later, he turned to me again, squatting until our gazes were level.

I couldn't stop myself from scanning him.

His damp hair somehow looked effortlessly stylish as an errant lock fell across his forehead. He didn't seem impacted by the elements or his earlier run-in with the spiders at all.

If I hadn't been with him, I would think he'd simply walked out in the storm or had just taken a refreshing bath.

His focus drifted from the top of my wet head down my convulsing body, then back up.

I guaranteed he wasn't thinking *effortless* or *stylish*.

Rats everywhere would rejoice—my name would now be synonymous with drowned appearances.

"Do you still have the stone?" he asked, drawing me from my rodent musings.

I nodded, trembling so hard I didn't trust I wouldn't accidentally bite my tongue off if I tried speaking.

I needed to get out of these wet clothes and get warm, or else the murderess stalking us would be the least of my concerns.

He assessed me in that unnervingly intense way.

His expression hadn't shifted, but I still saw the moment he'd come to the same conclusion I had.

He glanced down at the forest floor.

"I'll scout the area for shelter." He looked me over again, frowning a little this time. "Do you have enough strength left to not fall?"

I swallowed hard, knowing I had to be honest.

As much as I wished to be as indestructible as my favorite characters, the truth was my body felt like lead and the combination of exhaustion,

cold, wet, and complete shock of traveling via shadow then running for our lives, not once but *twice* in short succession, had finally caught up.

I slowly shook my head.

No judgment showed on his face, only an inward shift where I could practically see the gears turning as he flipped through some mental list of options before settling on one.

A moment later, he pulled off the leather satchel, which I'd forgotten all about, wedged it between us, then undid his cloak.

He ripped a strip off at the hemline, then rummaged in the bag, removing the blanket he'd stolen, and started tying the ends together.

Once it was to his liking, he looped it around the monster-sized tree trunk and knotted it at my waist.

He tugged hard, almost knocking me clear off the damn branch, then sat back on his heels to inspect his dastardly work.

A smile twitched at the corners of his mouth as I wriggled.

Of course a sociopath would find amusement in tying someone up to a tree.

He tucked his cloak around me and arranged the hood so I could use it as a scarf to breathe into. It helped a little, but I was still shivering so hard my muscles hurt from the tension. The temperature had plummeted again.

"Don't move."

I arched a brow. He knew full well that would be impossible since he'd also bound my arms. Who knew Lord Stoic could be funny?

"H-hilarious."

"I have *many* admirable qualities."

He looked me over again, slowly this time, his gaze lingering far too long on my mouth.

No hero looked at a damsel in distress with that much heat.

When he dragged his attention back to mine, he stopped fighting his amusement and openly grinned at my annoyance, the smile lighting his whole face.

He really was a pretty bastard.

"I'll be back soon, Peaches."

I narrowed my eyes, and he *winked*.

Before I could curse him for his poorly timed flirtation, *he stepped off the branch*.

He didn't climb down, didn't jump to the next branch; he literally stepped aside as if the ground wasn't a hundred feet below us and simply dropped.

I was so shocked, I stared for a long moment, unblinking, at the space he'd just occupied, straining to hear any sounds of him going splat, but there was only the soft patter of rain falling.

At least he hadn't killed himself and left me trussed up in this tree.

My irritation replaced my moment of stunned silence.

Irksome man. Or whatever hard-to-kill male being he *actually* was.

While I sat there, quietly fuming and huddled into his cloak, I slowly realized what he'd done. I was no longer focused on the cold or my draining energy; I was alert and thinking of an equally vexing pet name for him.

Revenge really was an excellent motivator.

Mr. Coldly Analytical had seen how tired I'd gotten and had purposely tried to get a rise from me.

I knew it wasn't kindness that motivated him.

It was entirely self-serving—I suspected he had his own reasons for keeping me safe.

Which made me even more wary. He must be afraid that I'd die before he could get what he wanted.

And if a stone-cold assassin was worried about my survival, that meant I was in much worse condition than I'd thought.

I sat there, struggling to keep myself upright, focusing on what I could control. Which, to be fair, wasn't much. I could barely wiggle my toes.

My breath misted in front of me in what I hoped wasn't a ghostly premonition of my fate.

I didn't want to die in this strange realm, far from my family.

Now that I was alone with my thoughts, I could admit I was afraid. Adventures in books were safe, and this was anything but.

The reality I faced was grave—I was stranded in a nightmarish world with a man who clearly wasn't mortal and was probably more ruthless than the goblin cannibal and spiders combined.

The fact that he hadn't left me meant he needed me.

And whether I liked it or not, I needed him to survive.

An ache that had nothing to do with the temperature built inside me—my family must be beside themselves by now.

I wished I could be there, comforting them.

I would give anything to be sitting around our crammed dining room table, talking about books and eating a meal we all made together—Mom's freshly baked rosemary and roasted garlic flatbread, my favorite garden salad with dried cranberries, goat cheese, and toasted walnuts, Dad's infamous herbed white beans, and Fable's best chocolate dessert—while laughing over wine.

There would be no laughter in our household tonight, and I hated that I was the cause, intentionally or not.

I swore I felt their pain through the realms, and I vowed to return to them, no matter how impossible that seemed now.

From the time I was little I'd always been one of those wildly optimistic people who broke down *impossible* into *I'm possible*.

Hope felt like a single candle that burned in my center, and I nourished that light even on the dimmest days.

All it took was one tiny spark to banish the darkness of despair.

I applied that to most areas of my life, though I hated to admit how hard I struggled to maintain that optimism when it came to love.

Part of me feared there was something unlovable about me, something wrong that others sensed.

It wasn't true, I knew that rationally, but logic didn't rule the heart.

Mother encouraged me and Fable to find the silver lining in any situation because hope was one of the most powerful weapons a person had, second only to knowledge. She'd put her rolling pin down and playfully smear flour on our noses, telling us we always had all the power we needed inside us, just like the heroes in our storybooks.

I ignored the icy claws of the rain digging into my bones and the ache in my heart, and focused on the positives.

I'd escaped death via nightmare creatures not once but twice today.

I wasn't alone. Well, technically, I was at the moment, but I had someone I knew would come back to me, even for selfish reasons.

I had the weird portal stone the old woman had given me, but I couldn't get it to work again. Yet.

But I bet the assassin knew other methods for us to try, and I'd find a way to get the information out of him so we could get back to Bellington. *Soon.*

A soft, eerie howl emerged from somewhere below, its haunting note lingering in the crisp night air, immediately followed by another, slightly more distant but equally unsettling cry.

These sounded different from the death wolf Jessa Maya had ridden.

A shiver ran down my spine like an icy finger, and I instinctively burrowed deeper into the murderer's cloak.

The oppressive darkness of the forest seemed to close in around me.

Before long, the night was filled with the chilling, echoing calls of wolves, their mournful cries weaving through the trees and surrounding me.

I wondered if Jessa Maya's death wolf had summoned its pack. Then I wished I wasn't bound to the tree without a weapon.

I silently begged the ruthless assassin to hurry back.

If he protected us from what I imagined were wolves from the death wolf's pack, he could call me Peaches as much as he liked.

I had a growing suspicion the creatures howling weren't the ones we had to worry about the most; there were probably many scarier things creeping silently through the undergrowth.

The temperature dropped again, drastically this time. I blinked ice crystals from my lashes and tried not to panic.

A twig snapped near the base of my tree.

I closed my eyes, praying I'd simply imagined it.

Another branch cracked, this one much, much too close to ignore.

I took a deep, steadying breath.

It was time to channel my inner main character and face my fears.

With luck, maybe this was already the dark-night-of-my-soul portion of the journey.

I opened my eyes and realized immediately this wasn't the turning point for me yet; my troubles were just getting started.

And they were getting bigger and badder by the moment.

My pulse raced as I stared into two glowing yellow orbs that gazed back.

The wolves had arrived.

SEVEN
Prince Sloth

Lore screamed so loud the woods fell silent.

I froze on the branch below hers, not wanting to elicit another strong reaction from her as I assessed her from a seemingly safe distance.

I'd been gone for just over an hour, leading the goblin and her wolf away, then scouting the area for a secure location to start a fire and rest. The temperature had steadily continued to drop, and Lore's condition had only gotten worse.

Hypothermia could set in under normal circumstances in two hours when the air temperature was just at freezing. But Lore was soaked through and therefore that time frame dropped drastically. In freezing water, it could occur in as little as fifteen minutes.

Her pupils were blown out, her lips tinged a bruised shade of blue, and her skin had turned so pale it was a miracle she was still conscious.

She looked like a ghostly winter sprite that had come to haunt me for previous sins.

I shifted a little, gauging her response.

She trembled violently at the sight of me, her gaze wide and unblinking.

Terror permeated the space between us, the sharp, prickling sensation setting me on edge from its force.

It was worse than expected.

I swore under my breath.

The temperature plummeted again, unnaturally fast, the wind even more biting and brutal than it had been just seconds ago.

I felt the invisible walls closing in on us and forced myself to not growl in frustration.

I would prefer to fight a hundred spiders or shadow wraiths instead of two foes I had no advantage over: time and the elements.

I breathed in slowly, then exhaled, forcing myself to remember who I was. I would not be rattled. I would not fear.

I had one task to focus on, and at its core, it was simple: I had to bring Lore to safety as swiftly as possible.

It was like a game of chess, except these stakes were not win or lose; they were win or die.

A cold calm descended upon me.

These were terms I could work with.

"I'm going to untie you, Peaches."

She gave no indication she understood what I'd said, but the fear coming off her escalated.

I slowly moved along the branch below her, putting myself within range.

I reached for her, mindful of not making any sudden movements, but she screamed and thrashed as I leaned closer. This time the sound came out much weaker and each inhalation ended with a wheeze.

I lunged around the tree trunk, sliced the makeshift rope off, snagged the blanket before it fell, then stuffed it into my belt, all within seconds.

Lore scrambled forward, then lost her balance, but I was waiting to catch her before she fell from the branch.

She slumped into my arms, head lolling against my chest, and didn't stir.

I heard the weak beat of her heart, but its rhythm was off.

"Shit."

I tucked her against my body, taking care to keep her head and neck protected, sighted the ground, and jumped.

I landed with a soft thud on the carpet of pine needles, pausing to listen for any sounds of imminent danger. Lore hadn't moved.

Rain suddenly shifted to snow, the flakes falling fast and hard, quickly sticking to the forest floor and to our clothing.

I swore under my breath, cursing Somnia for this new gift.

It was another set of complications we didn't need.

Even with the canopy of trees providing a bit of shelter, snow still blanketed the ground.

I gritted my teeth and started running as swiftly as I could without jostling her too much.

My heightened senses picked up several beasts roaming the forest far to the west, the sounds of their soft snarls resounding against the dampened silence of snow.

Knowing Somnia, they could be any nightmare creatures given form.

I hurtled through the forest in a blur.

My senses were in overdrive, flickering between anything that might cross our path and the winding trail I'd scouted earlier.

I flew by markers I'd subtly left before. We were close.

I pressed Lore against me, running faster as the sounds of rushing river water greeted me and the crevice I'd discovered in the base of a small mountain came into view.

I ducked behind the dense, needled branches of an evergreen that obscured the entrance, its dark green foliage offering a natural camouflage.

I charged into the narrow cave, my footsteps echoing against the cold stone walls.

I didn't slow my pace until the short, confining tunnel expanded into a larger chamber, where the ceiling soared above.

I gently set Lore down and bolted back outside, gathering stones that had broken away and tumbled off the mountain over time.

As soon as I had enough rocks, I scanned both sides of the river, seeking out any tracks in the snow. Other than mine, there were none.

I exhaled, thankful something had gone right.

So long as nothing had followed us, it *should* be the perfect location to spend a few hours holed up.

The rapid flowing water would help cover up any sounds we made, and the tree branches were wide and low enough to block the cave's entrance from view.

I snatched a branch and swept away my own tracks, then rushed back inside to make a fire pit with the rocks.

Utilizing my supernatural speed, it took only seconds to complete.

I dumped the twigs I'd collected earlier into the center, then used a bit of magic to send sparks into the kindling.

Within moments a roaring fire blazed, warming our cave.

Lore's lips had already turned a deeper shade of blue; if I didn't get her out of those wet clothes now, the warmest fire in the realm wouldn't matter.

I hesitated for only a second. Given the choice between modesty and death, I imagined she would happily rip the clothes off herself.

I swiftly removed the cloak I'd given her, then divested her of her own cloak and clothing, taking pains to not resort to shredding her garments off or cutting them with my dagger.

Her arms were limp as I carefully yanked her dress up and off and tossed it aside.

I ignored the quickening beat of my heart at her lack of response and focused on the task at hand. I unlaced her boots and tugged them off, setting them by the fire to dry.

Next, I rolled her stockings down, cringing at the sight of her frozen toes.

Without sparing another second, I worked her undergarments off and added them to the small circle of clothing around the fire.

Once all her cold, wet clothing was gone and was drying by the open flames, I stripped mine off. Since we had nothing to change into, body heat was the safest way to warm her up.

I placed my clothes and the blanket I'd stolen by the fire to dry next to hers, then settled down behind Lore, pulling her flush against my body.

I winced. Her skin felt like ice.

I smoothed the wet hair off her face, then skimmed the pulse point in her neck. It fluttered softly, weak but still present.

I resisted the urge to roll us closer to the fire, knowing how important it was to warm her up slowly or I'd potentially cause more damage.

I lay there, listening for any change in her breathing, my own muscles tense as I mentally flipped through all the information I'd learned about hypothermia over the centuries.

Medical texts I'd studied indicated it was imperative to keep the center of the body warm and worry about the extremities later.

Until it dried, I had no blanket to use, so I placed my hands over her torso, envisioning warmth flowing into her from me.

I silently counted the seconds, focusing entirely on the icy body in front of mine.

After enough time had passed, I arranged Lore's feet so the soles rested on my legs, hoping the added warmth would help save her toes.

The first sixty minutes crawled by.

I strained to hear any shift in her pulse or breathing. Her temperature had barely improved, but near the end of the hour I swore there was an increase in it.

I wasn't prone to acts of delusion, so that meant even the slightest improvement was promising.

The following hour had me questioning myself.

How well *was* I versed in healing?

It was the second time tonight I'd been unsure, and I loathed it.

I forced myself to think of my House. I had an entire wing of my library dedicated to mortal science and medicine, and it was as extensive as the rest of my collection on the healing arts.

Like all the members of my court, I'd spent years devoting myself to learning all I could.

From what I recalled, she wasn't making as much progress as she should be by now.

Lore's pulse was still weak, her body barely warmer than a corpse's.

I gritted my teeth, warring with myself over what to do. I could attempt to use the phoenix tear again, or even my own magic. But the cost of leaving Somnia might be losing the Book of Nightmares.

I gave it a few more minutes.

I cursed her and Xavier and the realm itself for this situation.

I should be spelling the book shut for eternity and locking it away in my House of Sin's collection, not playing royal healer.

I emptied my mind of those thoughts and focused on Lore.

My body burned higher naturally, so it should be speeding the process of her recovery, not hindering it. I suspected her condition was related to this cursed realm.

Finally, after internally debating, I closed my eyes and imagined my magic transporting us to my House of Sin.

I couldn't let her die. For several reasons.

My magic crackled as soon as it felt the call, the telltale smoke whipping around us to carry us away... then disappeared.

Frustration welled inside me as I pushed more magic into the transportation spell I used. It was more difficult to use this kind of magic in Somnia, but it should still be *possible*. From my understanding, the wards allowed people to leave if they had a portal stone. Except for the Goddess of Night. Her magic was blocked entirely and rendered useless here.

I channeled all my power into the next attempt.

Smoke curled through the cave, winding around us.

And it blew away in some phantom breeze.

"Fuck."

This wasn't good. I had a feeling the wards weren't the only thing keeping me here.

I exhaled slowly, forcing myself back to that cold, calm center. I would deal with the fallout of this revelation later.

Right now, Lore needed help.

I inched us closer to the fire and tentatively ran my fingers through her long hair, gently detangling the strands to help them dry faster. The chocolate strands mixed with caramel were annoyingly soft and pretty.

I shifted her locks every few minutes, allowing each section to have equal time by the flames.

It was a slow, tedious process, but eventually it dried.

At least it was one less avenue for her to lose heat through.

With that task complete, I focused my attention on the next area. All the while, I kept forcing my mind to not wander back to the fact that I *couldn't* get out of this realm.

The idea of being trapped didn't sit well. It put me at the mercy of others. And even if I weren't a Prince of Sin, that would be a problem.

Lore's hands and feet were still blocks of ice, but her center had warmed a bit more.

I nestled closer, keeping one palm flattened across her torso for her organs, and started rubbing warmth into her hands with my other.

Holding her in place, I slowly rotated us to the other side, wanting to ease any discomfort from lying in one spot for too long while also giving her other side equal time near the fire.

I switched hands and continued my ministrations on her extremities, working to restore warmth to her fingers before moving to her palms and wrists.

I would do this all night if I must.

If the worst had come to pass, which I strongly suspected was the case, then the fate of my court and the realms depended on Lore now.

Which meant she had my protection, whether either of us liked it or not.

Two hours later, her hands and feet were cold but significantly warmer than they had been, her hair was completely dry, and her skin had a pleasant flush beginning.

It was too soon to celebrate; anything could change from one moment to the next, but I was cautiously optimistic.

I released her long enough to see if the clothes and blanket were dry yet.

There were still damp areas on her dress and undergarments, and my pants were no better, so I shifted them around and did the same with our boots.

Hopefully it wouldn't be too much longer before we could redress; the more layers I could get back on her, the better.

I added another log to the fire, stoking it as I did so.

It had warmed our chamber well, but snow was still falling hard outside, and our supplies were limited.

I would need to make another run for wood and try to find some dry brush before daybreak.

When the time came for me to venture out again, I'd have preferred for Lore to be more stable before I left. I didn't want her healing to backtrack when she was finally making headway.

I checked the blanket, relieved it had fully dried.

I tugged it over us and pulled Lore against me again.

Her skin was still too cold for my liking, but it was significantly better than when we first arrived.

I wrapped my arms around her and tucked her head beneath my chin, feeling the warmth spread.

I wasn't prone to letting my thoughts wander like some of my brothers, preferring to utilize my time more efficiently, and it was a trait that served me well now.

I spent nearly an hour counting the beats of her heart, comparing the strength of it every few moments. As the next hour dragged on, her breathing improved.

In place of the short, raspy gasps, she now inhaled and exhaled steadily, the sound more akin to a deep, restorative sleep.

The worst of her symptoms were over.

She wasn't healed yet, but if she made it this far, she'd more than likely survive the night.

I kept my attention focused on her for the next half hour, noting more positive shifts.

Assured she was indeed out of critical condition, I split my focus between monitoring her and plotting our next moves.

I could no longer cast off the truth of our situation.

Lore was more than likely a dreamweaver. A fact I still needed to test, but I prepared myself for the unfavorable outcome of it being true.

We were trapped in Somnia.

And that meant Xavier had succeeded in setting the Trials of Unbinding into motion. Otherwise, my magic would have worked to transport us out.

I should have known better than to think any simple binding spell was enough, especially when given to the old gods, who were masters at creating loopholes.

Every lock had a key.

And every villain had a chance for redemption. After the old gods had taken the druid spell I'd given them, they secretly created their punishment for Nyantha. It wasn't until much later that I first heard rumors of the Trials, and by then it was too late to counteract them.

The Trials of Unbinding were a way for Nyantha to gain back all she'd lost. I cursed myself for not ensuring the original spell couldn't be manipulated.

A dreamweaver would act as her champion, for lack of a better term, going through the Trials for her.

The easiest way to prevent Nyantha from winning would be to remove Lore from the game by any means necessary. But there was a catch: anyone outside the Trials who attempted to harm her would suffer her same fate; even an immortal could find True Death.

Technically, I wasn't part of the tests and couldn't risk my court.

Now that I knew the Unbinding was activated, and Lore was probably a dreamweaver, I'd need to use extreme caution from here on out.

And to do that, I needed information from my personal archives.

I checked Lore one more time, and the sounds of her even breaths were enough to convince me she'd be all right while I... utilized the full potential of my magic.

I closed my eyes, centered my thoughts, and called upon the secret power of my sin. No one knew, not even my brothers, that I could connect with the ancient tree of knowledge in House Sloth. While we respected each other, each prince kept certain truths to ourselves. Especially where our circles were concerned.

Within the walls of my mind, I now stood in the heart of my enchanted library, leaning against the base of the ancient tree.

I took a moment to appreciate the beauty of the space, knowing it might be a long time before I could see it again in person.

Then I called for the Library to awaken.

EIGHT
Prince Sloth

LIBRARY, I HAVE need of your services.

I waited for it to deign to respond and enjoyed the momentary peace. This chamber was my favorite section of the Library—the tree soared up, the branches reaching across the vast expanse of the room.

A handful of books hung from some of the branches like ornaments; those were the tomes the Library was currently reading.

The leaves on the branches were all different colors—some deep greens, plums, blues, golds, and silver.

I'd had a glass dome installed to allow the light to trickle in, but the stained glass had been coated with a special film to keep the light from harming the books.

Form meant nothing if the function wasn't ideal.

I glanced up at the towering shelves, filled with my most prized books on magic, myths and legends of the old gods, and the histories of the many realms in this universe.

While I waited for my ornery Library, I inhaled deeply, wishing I could actually smell the worn leather of the texts located in this section.

I was no more solid than an apparition—when I projected this way it was closer to what mortals thought of as remote viewing or astral travel.

My body was solidly in Somnia, but I didn't need to be physically present to utilize the knowledge found in my House of Sin.

Since my entire library was enchanted, I could mentally call upon it to do my bidding. The tree's magic rivaled my own, and most of the time it behaved itself. But like all sentient beings, it had its petulant moments.

I felt when the Library finally took notice of my presence and waited for me to address it again.

Bring me all the texts I have on the Trials of Unbinding.

A beat passed without any movement or acknowledgment. I held my tongue. The Library was in a pissy mood.

I braced myself for the sass.

This century would be nice, Library.

I felt its indignant huff and knew better than to comment now.

Perhaps I would be more motivated by a simple show of manners and respect. Something akin to "Please, most perspicacious of Libraries. Grant me a favor of grand proportions with your unmatched perception. Pull forth the spellbinding knowledge only someone as magnanimous and erudite as yourself can achieve. O master of fate, wizard of wisdom, pull back the curtain of my inadequacy and let me swim across your sea of enlightenment."

"Swim across your sea of enlightenment" was a rather inflated self-description, which indicated I was in for a lecture, but I kept my frustration locked deep inside where it couldn't sense it.

Forgive my insolence, O self-important one. Xavier stole the Liber Noctem, managed to get a dreamweaver into Somnia, and I am currently trapped here. If the Goddess of Night's power is restored, I believe that would be disastrous for all. Snap out of your mood. I need those texts.

The Library sniffed.

Xavier was a sniveling slug.

You disliked him because you wanted the title of master librarian.

And now it seems there is a job opening. How fortuitous for me.

It would pull the wrong texts, or flat-out ignore his solicitations, just to make him work harder in his role. Xavier would storm into my private study, furious to be thwarted over the simplest requests.

I need information now. There's not much time.

What is time? It is but an infinity loop where the past, present, and future all collide. This moment has already been, has yet to occur, and is happening now.

I mentally growled. *Save the philosophical musings for when I'm home and the realms and our own court aren't in danger. I need those Unbinding texts.*

You're just upset you misjudged the slug.

You do realize if House Sloth falls, you will also cease to exist, correct? And you don't like anyone. He showed no deception, or I would have sensed the lie.

I tolerate you well enough. Even when your attitude leaves much to be desired. But I suppose I can look beyond your shortcomings to save the realm this once. I am but your most loyal of servants.

Loyal, yes, humble, no.

I heard that.

Without further argument, the Library pulled three texts and placed them on a long table set up in the corner of the room.

I stood over them, scanning the pages it flipped to.

The first text outlined the druid binding spell.

I'd provided it to the old gods when I came up with a plan of action for them to take, and they'd insisted they would enact it on their own. Without the Book of Nightmares to study, I had no idea what conditions they'd woven in, though. I only knew with certainty the outcome was the creation of the Trials.

Punishment from the old gods could be anything.

The Library sensed my need for more information and set another book down in front of me, flipping until it paused on a more detailed theory of the Trials.

> **Legends suggest that once the Trials of Unbinding are enacted, Somnia will lock itself down from anyone who attempts to leave.**
>
> **No magic, no object, no sacrifice, will lift the spell that**

erects the wards. However, it is important to note, the wards won't stop travelers from coming into the realm via portal stone only.

That confirmed why I couldn't use my magic to get out of the realm. Just as I'd suspected. I tamped my frustration down; it was a useless emotion right now.

The Library flipped to the next page.

Most scholars who've extensively studied the old gods and their punishments believe the Unbinding will consist of five rounds, or chapters.

In this instance, the tests are thought to be tailored to the individual dreamweaver based on the tales they spin, but there are strong indications each round will in part be designed to test the dreamweaver's strength and spirit in a way befitting the god they champion for.

If keeping in line with the old gods' favored punishments, each test will attempt to strip the participant down to their baser fears, not only to test them physically and emotionally, but also to test the very fabric of their soul.

Folklorists argue over whether the dreamweaver is in total control of the story they tell, or if Somnia itself plays a larger role in determining which scenes come to life since the land toys with dreams and nightmares.

Others believe it is the Liber Noctem itself that reshapes the tests.

I straightened from where I'd been leaning over the book, letting the information soak in. It was odd that I hadn't recalled these details on my own, but with the amount of knowledge stored in my head, it wasn't too surprising some information was hazy.

The Library thumbed through several chapters and paused.

> *Myths collected from former Temple Knights claim that the Liber Noctem and Somnia itself will do all they can to ensure the dreamweaver doesn't succeed in winning the Trials of Unbinding.*
>
> *Not much is known why. Most think it's because the Liber Noctem wants to protect its stolen magic.*

This wasn't giving me anything to work with. Just conjecture and theories. Neither of which were concrete areas for me to analyze.

The Library suddenly pulled another book from one of the highest shelves and set it down, flipping through pages until it landed on what it had been searching for.

I glanced at the title before it opened the book.

PHILOSOPHY OF SACRIFICES THROUGHOUT THE AGES

> A case study of points and counterpoints in the quest to determine if good versus evil exists beyond theory in mortal trappings.

> Is a monster born or created? Some posit that if such a vile thing can be made, then it should be granted the power to be unmade.
>
> Who decides fate, redemption, or the concept of being deserving? The gods? Some other higher source?
>
> Surely it is not up to us but rather the individual being tested.
>
> What is evil without the chance to be good? In turn that begs the question of how good can be measured if it's not tested for evil and emerges triumphant. Can either exist without their inverse to challenge them?
>
> It's a philosophical question asked throughout the realms.

But to deny evil's potential undoing would be to deny that dreams and nightmares cannot begin as one only to end as the other.

Who are we when we're stripped to our core? When our fears are laid out for not simply others to see, but for ourselves to see as well?

It felt like there was a connection I was hovering near.

Somehow it tied into the Trials and the dark book and the Goddess of Night, but *how* remained a mystery.

Library, pull the most recent legends surrounding the Goddess of Night. I want to know—

The book slammed shut.

In the next instant I was suddenly wrenched out of my library.

I blinked at the cave, disoriented by the unexpected shift, my senses on high alert. I'd never been torn from my projection before. I slammed the wall on my emotions down so I could think clearly.

It took another moment for me to be grounded in the physical. Lore still slept soundly; there were no indications we'd been discovered.

All seemed well.

Still, I listened and waited. Something had yanked me back here. Several moments passed and nothing crept out from the shadows, no nightmare creature attacked. I must have simply run out of time.

I considered the information I'd learned.

The Library was sentient, but it also was attuned to my subconscious. I wasn't sure if I wanted to know more about legends surrounding sacrifices, or if the Library thought it would be beneficial.

The part concerning dreams and nightmares was certainly intriguing. But I was still troubled by the actual Trials themselves.

If the dark book could take control over them...

I exhaled slowly, not wanting to consider how bad things might get. The book *was* Nyantha's essence, for all intents and purposes.

All the dark, twisted things she was had been transferred to it.

I wasn't sure of everything a dreamweaver was capable of, but as soon as Lore woke up, I'd start teaching her how to create a mental shield. It would be a way for her to keep the book out of her mind and maybe prevent or mitigate any damage it could do by manipulating her.

Lore stirred as if troubled in her sleep.

I held on to the dwindling hope that I was wrong, that she was just some mortal who was hunting the book I was after. And that she wasn't another victim of Xavier's treachery.

I called upon my magic again and tried to transport us out of this realm. It answered my summons only to dissipate again.

We were well and truly trapped.

I closed my eyes, trying to piece together the best course of action.

From the howling wind beating against the cave, I guessed the storm had turned into a blizzard.

In Somnia the weather followed no normal patterns.

Snow could fall in the summer as easily as the fall and winter, dumping several feet before disappearing as suddenly.

Getting Lore healthy wouldn't mean much if we had to go back out into the storm. Until she woke up and we could test her abilities, there wasn't much else for me to do tonight, and I needed to rest my body after using so much magic to restore myself. I'd have to be mindful of exerting too much magic without any means of gaining it back from my court. Like all Princes of Sin, my power was fueled by the sinners of my circle. Without them, I'd eventually weaken.

In the morning, I'd hunt for food and gather more firewood.

I closed my eyes, listening to the rhythmic sound of Lore's breathing.

I had no intention of sleeping but must have dozed off.

Something prickled my senses, rousing me.

My eyes snapped open, and my hand shot out for my dagger, my fingers closing around the cool hilt.

I paused as the figure backlit by the fire slowly came into focus.

Lore laid sprawled on her side, head propped on her fist, watching me with one brow arched high.

Firelight cast her mostly in shadows but gilded her curves.

My focus traced the golden edge of her body before I realized what I was doing and wrenched my attention back to her face.

Amusement lifted the corners of her lips.

"Sorry, I'm not into knife play, Sociopath."

My gaze narrowed. It *sounded* like Lore, but even though I'd only known her for a short amount of time, something felt off.

I scanned her, searching for any hint of dark magic, my senses warning me of unseen danger again.

It wasn't medically possible for her to be healed enough to sit up or joke.

Even if I *had* fallen asleep, it had only been for a minute or two.

My pulse quickened and I didn't release my grip on my weapon.

Her mouth curved wickedly as she let her attention roam over me, pausing first on the dagger, then on my tattoo, before dipping lower.

Heat flared in her eyes.

It took a moment to recall I was naked, and that she must have tossed the blanket aside when she got up, leaving me as exposed as she was.

No matter what my brothers claimed while teasing me throughout the centuries, I wasn't modest and enjoyed taking my share of lovers, so Lore's nudity along with mine didn't faze me.

Love, lust, infatuation; all could be weaponized in the right hands. They were among the easiest emotions to prey on, to exploit. Which was why I avoided such trappings.

Some of the most logical beings I knew became unhinged when their loved ones were threatened.

I'd seen what happened to Pride and Gluttony when they focused more on romance than their courts. Even Wrath and Envy had been preoccupied for a time, and it almost cost them everything.

Greed had his own casual liaisons that were whispered about, but his primary focus remained on fueling his sin above all else.

And Lust...he was caught up in idiocy every other week, always lounging around my House of Sin, seeking out advice he never put into practice.

I refused to end up in such a loathsome predicament.

My affairs were simple exchanges of mutual need and release based on physical desire, not emotional entanglements. I also needed a strong mental connection above all else. If my mind wasn't engaged, my body would never be.

Remaining single was a choice many of my sinners also made, though some decided to marry for—if not love—practical reasons and to form familial bonds.

So, as Lore leaned closer, her nakedness proudly on display, it wasn't her body that gave me pause.

It was the soft glow of my tattoo that was unsettling.

That hadn't happened earlier.

My attention flicked back to hers in quiet assessment.

A hungry expression crossed her face, one I couldn't imagine her wearing in reality. Not because Lore didn't strike me as a sexual being, but because this look spoke of darker, twisted cravings. Pain without pleasure.

Suddenly I realized my mistake.

I hadn't enforced my own mental shields before I fell asleep, and now the land of dreams and nightmares was toying with me. Or, more specifically, the goddess who ruled over slumber was.

Nyantha had found her way into my head.

I was still asleep, trapped in a dream, aware but unable to wake.

The goddess looked like Lore but didn't exude that undimmable sunshine she radiated.

There was an edge of darkness in this version. A twisted cruelness that felt ancient and utterly wicked.

I kept my suspicion from showing.

I knew better than to take anything at face value in Somnia.

This was the land where dreams ruled, and the goddess who presided over it toyed with those who dared to slumber in her domain.

The nightmare goddess wearing Lore's face cocked her head, the move more animal than human.

"You don't scare easily, do you?" she asked, never taking her predatory gaze from me.

I said nothing, knowing my body's lack of reaction would speak for me.

There was little I truly feared.

Not from hubris, but from arming myself with knowledge.

The more mentally prepared I was for any situation, the less my emotions interfered and distracted me.

The nightmare goddess inhaled deeply and closed her eyes.

I considered using my blade on her, but I wanted to know why she'd sought me out in my dreams. It was too good an opportunity to gather information to pass up.

The second the thought crossed my mind, her eyes shot open, glowing red once before fading to Lore's normal chocolate brown.

I sensed more than saw victory flash in her face.

The monster *liked* violence.

"Go ahead and stab me. See what happens." In the next breath, the goddess pretending to be Lore straddled me, offering up her throat. "I know you want to."

I stared at the expanse of flesh waiting for my blade. This dream felt so real. The weight of her pressed into me, her body now warm and enticing.

It was tempting.

My grip tightened on the hilt, my focus sliding from the artery pulsing gently in false Lore's neck to her heart. The goddess hadn't dressed, allowing my weapon complete access to her body.

Dark desire swept through me.

As if in some trance, I watched myself reach out, watched as the tip of my dagger skimmed the side of her neck, her shoulder, then lightly continued along her arm before shifting to her chest.

I ignored the way her nipples tightened as the icy metal kissed the skin between her breasts.

If Nyantha were actually straddling me now, I'd shove my dagger through her heart and be done with her. My House dagger was made from material that not even the gods could heal from. The only ones immune to its power were my brothers, the same way their blades couldn't end me, either.

With more effort than I realized it would take, I fought against the overwhelming craving for violence and dropped my weapon.

The blade hit the ground with a defiant clatter.

I would not be manipulated by anyone or anything.

The goddess pretending to be Lore growled at my look of dismissal.

But I was bored of this nightmare.

"What do you want?" I asked.

The nightmare smiled.

"That's a loaded question. I want vengeance. I want you to know the desperation that comes with losing your power, with being at the mercy of others."

"Your actions put you in this position."

She smiled, a small, cruel twist of her lips. "And you were self-righteous enough to believe you could be the judge, jury, and executioner to a god. Using a *druid* spell."

"I was asked for intel. I provided it. After observing reports of every twisted thing you were doing. You want to blame someone? Start with yourself. Take accountability and maybe your brethren will hear your case."

"Mm. Accountability is something I agree with. You used magic to escape my wards. Now I want something from you in return."

"I—"

The goddess lunged forward, pinning my hands at my sides, her strength taking me by surprise as she locked me in place. Not many beings could cage a Prince of Sin. I wondered fleetingly if it was a subconscious fear of mine and if the nightmare goddess had plucked it from deep within my head.

I also realized too late that while this might be a nightmare, the goddess pinning me down was very real.

She leaned close enough that I felt her warm breath on my neck.

"I want your fear, princeling."

I gave no reaction to her bastardization of my title.

The real Lore didn't know I was royal, which validated my suspicion that this was the ruthless goddess in disguise.

"I want your nightmares served to me like a feast."

False Lore's tongue flickered against the pulse point in my throat.

"I want you to question that cunning mind of yours. Who is really in control now? Maybe you aren't the hunter; maybe you're the hunted. Is this your Trial? Is this hers? Or have the real games not even begun?"

A wave of revulsion warred with a twist of desire as she closed her lips against my skin and sucked hard enough to leave a bruise. I got hard instantly.

Before I could analyze my horrific reaction, the goddess moved again.

She snatched my dagger from where it had fallen and drove my blade up and through my ribs, puncturing one of my lungs with expert precision.

I gritted my teeth to keep from crying out as she twisted the blade, but a wet wheeze rattled deep inside me, spurring her on.

An expression of pure bliss crossed her face as she gazed down at her work and shoved again until the blade hit bone.

I turned my head to the side and coughed up blood.

How a nightmare could cause physical harm was beyond me. But this was Nyantha and even without her full power, she was still a god.

"How?" I coughed.

The nightmare knew what I was really asking.

How had the goddess usurped Lore's body?

"She is but a vessel. I am a god. Do not ask foolish questions; it is far beneath you."

The sadistic goddess's eyes blazed with triumph when I said nothing. She bent down and slowly licked the blood from the corner of my mouth.

"Your defiance amuses me." She brushed her lips against mine. "But I told you, I will have your darkest fears in payment for your visit to your realm. I've been waiting centuries for this. Now you'll learn what I have; when the true nightmare begins, then we shall really have fun."

It was the last thing I heard before the world went dark.

I thrashed as the dreams overcame my consciousness, growing darker and more twisted with each cruel new vision forced into my mind.

It felt like my fears were being confused with someone else's memories, but I couldn't fully distinguish the two.

My library burning, hundreds of thousands of books consumed by flames in a raging inferno that destroyed a millennium of knowledge in moments.

My court falling into chaos, traitors rising among my most trusted, voices lifted in cries of betrayal and death.

The old gods waking from their slumbers and setting their sights back on the Underworld. Or were they here, in Somnia?

War and bloodshed reigned.

Not even Wrath, the prince fueled by war, was left unscathed. Eventually, each of the courts of sin fell, turning the Seven Circles into a true vision of hell.

And throughout it all, Lore sat beside the goddess in the throne room of what could only be the Court of Fear, her eyes black as pitch, lost to the pull of the book, crafting wicked tales to amuse them all as the realms burned.

I fought to get to her and failed every time, seeing my end play out over and over in a never-ending loop of destruction.

Every dream was a new nightmare, a new way for the world to end, and I was powerless to stop it.

If this was only the beginning of what the Book of Nightmares could do, we were in for the fight of our lives.

Our odds of surviving weren't favorable.

Fear finally sank its claws in deep and ripped into my mind, wrenching a scream from me that was immediately lost to a void as the next nightmare began.

A phantom chill slithered down my spine, leaving a trail of ice in its wake.

Shadows twisted and writhed inside my mind, hungry for my sanity, and whispers clawed at my ears.

I couldn't tell if the noise was coming from inside my head or not.

The boundaries of what was real and what was fantasy collapsed, leaving me to drift in a world without anchor or reason.

It was the most frightening reality for someone like me; to be out of control, to have my mind shattered, and to be ruled by baser emotions.

Fear guided me deeper, to a place where light could not penetrate the darkness, and with every step into that abyss, I lost another piece of myself.

"Sweet dreams," a cruel voice taunted, "*Prince Sloth*."

NINE
Love

WHEN I WOKE up, the first thing I noticed was the strong, tattooed arm draped over me. Which was rather disturbing since I had no recollection of falling asleep or, more importantly, falling asleep with a man possessively holding on to me, even in slumber.

I blinked until the early morning bleariness faded, wondering if I was somehow dreaming.

Had I *finally* had an unforgettable night of passion and lost my memory of it?

That seemed like the sort of thing that could happen to me. Well, maybe not the night of incredible passion, unfortunately. Or maybe this was a trap and at any moment I'd have to free myself from this captor. Luckily, I'd been preparing for this twisted scenario for years. I was almost excited. I didn't dare hope it was the beginning of my own reverse harem story and that there might be more heavily muscled—and tattooed—men lying around nearby.

Honestly, it could be a scene out of a dark fantasy *or* romance, and I was slowly realizing I might have questionable taste in fiction.

At least the members of my book club were on the same dark descent to literary hell—the novel we'd voted to read next was so wrong it was right. Agatha and Blake would positively lose their minds if I managed my own harem. Needless to say, our monthly discussions were very fun.

I made a mental note to have some *Team Morally Gray & Fictionally Depraved* tunics embroidered for our meeting the following month.

Gold ink shimmered in the darkness, drawing my attention back to the stranger's arm.

It was no dream.

Before I completely panicked about who the arm belonged to and how I ended up tucked in beside him, the events of the previous day came crashing back.

The old woman and her quest from hell, the shadows, the giant spiders, the goblin cannibal.

And my strong, silent, reluctant partner in crime. If he didn't tell me his name today, I'd have to give him a temporary one soon.

Maybe Zephyrus. Or Charles. Or even Bradford St. Germaine the third.

Obviously, I'd have to think on that more. Bradford wasn't the sexiest name. He needed something befitting a supernatural villain archetype.

If he was uncooperative, I could always just call him Blondie.

I smiled, imagining his scowl.

He would positively hate being called that.

Naturally, that was now his new name. At least until he started consistently calling me Lore; then we could revisit our stance on pet names.

I pumped an imaginary fist in the air, already claiming victory in our war. Long live my revenge for Peaches. I couldn't wait to unveil it when he woke up.

Hopefully he'd be in a good mood and wouldn't strangle me.

I peered at the ink on his arm through slitted lashes, admiring how lifelike the feathers were.

I wanted to see if they felt as downy soft as they looked but kept my hands to myself. The sociopath probably wouldn't appreciate channeling his inner house cat, so I refrained from petting him like one.

His sparkling tattoo was one more glaring indicator that he was not exactly what he appeared to be.

I'd never seen glowing ink before; maybe *he* was the one who'd made a bargain.

Hope bloomed like a spring flower in my chest.

If a thundercloud like him could manifest a bit of magic, my deal had to be on the horizon.

Unless he was the one doling out bargains; then that might get tricky. But I was positive we could work out something mutually favorable.

I closed my eyes again.

It was so warm I debated whether I should pretend to still be sleeping, or if I had to do the responsible adult thing and get up.

The thought of having to face the uncertain reality of this strange new world was a tad overwhelming. What little energy I'd recuperated overnight vanished and laziness won.

I burrowed against the assassin, seeking out more of that delicious warmth he radiated. For a stone-cold killer, he really was exceptional at cuddling.

I released a contented sigh as I wriggled into the perfect nook between his arm and body. Surprisingly, he didn't protest.

He must be in a deep sleep; otherwise, I imagined he'd be grumbling as I fluffed his arm like a pillow and stuffed it under my head.

Today was already off to a *much* better start than yesterday.

I wouldn't mind spending the rest of the day like this, lost in my own little daydreaming bubble, far from all the creepy things that went bump in the night here. Alas, my drowsy stupor didn't last.

The more I focused on trying to fall asleep again, the more my mind revolted. Someone needed to remind it we were on the same team and to stop internally fighting me.

My extremely valid argument with myself was simple: The more rest I had now, the more physically and mentally prepared I'd be to face whatever ghoulish delight awaited us. But my brain was a stubborn mule, and I slowly became aware of the other things it had been alerting me to.

Like the assassin's hard, *naked* body pressed against mine.

That couldn't be right. There was no chance Lord Serious slept nude.

I shimmied against him, expecting to feel the leather of his trousers. But no...that was bare skin.

All thoughts emptied from my head when I realized *I* was also completely nude and was still rubbing up against him.

He might be asleep, but parts of him were now very much awake.

I should have been more scandalized, but I was honestly a little disappointed I couldn't recall the details of him ripping his clothes off.

I imagined the assassin would be the type to set that brooding stare on me in challenge as he disrobed.

Confident but not arrogant that I would like what I saw.

He wouldn't be wrong. Even being wildly unfriendly, he was physically attractive and knew it.

I gave myself a mental slap.

Drooling over him when I had more important issues to solve was absurd. I'd definitely need to evaluate my priorities once I returned to Bellington.

I had been with a few lovers before, but I always remembered the getting-naked part. Now I drew a complete blank on how we ended up in this...position.

I swallowed thickly, trying to calm my racing thoughts and think beyond the sensation of his body molded to mine.

Logically, I knew he had to have a good reason for undressing us.

He didn't strike me as the kind of person who did something extreme without exhausting all viable options first.

Which didn't necessarily ease my worries.

I inhaled and slowly exhaled, attempting to calm myself.

If we were in a romance novel, he'd undoubtedly nuzzle into my neck, unaware of what he was doing, then jolt backward as he woke up and realized he was a little *too* happy, given the circumstances.

Or maybe not, depending on what sort of romance we were in.

If it was a dark romance, maybe this would be the dubious consent scene and we'd both pretend we didn't *want* to give in to our desires while absolutely giving in to them.

Because avoiding reality for another minute seemed like the best path to take, and I was on the verge of completely shutting down, I amused myself by analyzing why that worked in some books but not others, finally settling on whether the characters were openly attracted *before* the questionable antics began.

I froze, recalling the strange details from yesterday.

After all the weird, magical things that happened, I couldn't stop wondering if I'd accidentally transported us into one such romance novel.

Maybe that was one of the things the portal stone did.

I'd definitely been the one to bring us to Jessa Maya's book. The assassin hadn't read it. And if I did somehow use the portal stone to bring that story to life, then I could be in a new book now.

Maybe this *was* a dark romance.

I tried to figure out if my heart was pounding in excitement or concern. Or maybe both.

Would I pretend to still be sleeping and bite my lip to keep from making any noise if the sociopath's hands suddenly strayed?

I suspected I knew the answer. I was a hussy through and through.

I needed to start designing a tattoo—maybe *Ruined by Romance* in pretty script with peach anemone flowers woven around my wrist like a cuff, letting the world know I'd happily be chained to the genre for life.

A few minutes passed with no questionable groping, and I released a breath.

At least that was settled.

Since we were *not* in a dark romance, he didn't stir.

Which was a good thing—I needed one less complication in my world until I figured out what the hells had happened.

Bits and pieces of the previous night slowly came back.

Being strapped to a tree, the icy rain, the cold. The wolves.

I took a deep breath and slowly exhaled.

Were there wolves aside from the nightmare creature Jessa Maya rode? And if there had been, how did we end up in this... my attention swept around the dark chamber.

The primitive fire pit, small stack of twigs, the animal scat in the far corner.

The naked murderer had brought us to a cave.

I vaguely recalled him scouting the area for a warm, dry place to shelter for the night.

Given my memory of feeling frozen to the core, I imagined I'd been hypothermic, which finally explained the lack of clothing.

Something aside from the obvious—waking up naked in a cavern with a stranger who probably had an entire graveyard of dead bodies he was responsible for and being a *little* turned on anyway—was bothering me.

It took another second to realize what: my companion hadn't moved or spoken.

By now he should have definitely figured out I was awake and might have some questions about how we ended up twined together like two longtime lovers in this fine establishment.

Gods. I sincerely hoped neither the cannibal nor hypothermia had gotten to him. If I was cuddling with a corpse, I might lose my mind.

Horny horror was a genre I did *not* want to know existed or accidentally create.

I twisted in his arms, which proved to be exceptionally difficult.

His weight was leaden.

I elbowed him a little, fighting the frantic feeling building inside me.

He *couldn't* be dead. Could he?

"Wake up, Blondie."

He didn't. Another oddity. From our limited time together, he didn't seem like the type who would be a heavy sleeper.

Now that I was fully awake and alert, I listened closely, noticing the wet rasp of his shallow breaths for the first time.

As carefully as I could manage, I moved his arm off me and slipped out from under it, making sure to keep the blanket in place over his lower half.

Modesty was clearly important in a potential life-or-death situation.

I turned around and finally got my first good look at him since last night. I stilled as I discovered why my spider-killing-savior was silent.

Above his ribs the blanket tented out.

I must have made some sound of alarm, because the assassin's eyes slowly blinked open, and I nearly collapsed with relief.

That cool, beautiful stare narrowed on me, and I got all warm and fuzzy inside. Lord Stoic would live to torment giant spiders another day.

Praise be to the gods who watched over sinners.

He studied me for a silent moment, seeming to come to some satisfactory conclusion, then closed his eyes.

I might not be well-versed in medical thrillers but had read enough to know that I had to keep him conscious.

"Is that a dagger in your chest or are you just happy to see me?"

He groaned as if the joke pained him more than the blade in his ribs. But it served its purpose. He was now alert. Which was incredible and hard to fathom.

"Grab the hilt and pull it out at the angle it went in."

Correction, he was now alert *and* bossy.

I swallowed the lump in my throat at his command.

I was not equipped to remove deadly weapons.

Mostly because blood made me squeamish.

Also due to the small fact that I had no medical background, and it seemed like the sort of thing where experience was required.

His pale gaze held mine.

"You're stronger than you think, Peaches."

Sweet, delusional soul.

I wasn't worried about my emotional strength.

I was concerned about possibly puking on him or passing out or worse, puking and passing out in *it*.

Since he'd assumed I was a damsel in distress for all the wrong reasons, he would have to find that out on his own.

Some lessons were best learned through experience, anyway. I imagined getting vomit in a wound would be an event not easily forgotten. One day he might even thank me for instilling such valuable insight in him.

"You're just buttering me up to avoid the 'cuddling naked in a cave without buying me dinner first' discussion we're about to have."

I swore he almost grinned before his expression tightened again.

"Next time you're close to death, I'll be sure to court you properly first."

"See that you do."

Channeling my best impression of a main character who wouldn't pass out at the sight of blood, or care that she was butt naked with an assassin she'd accidentally dry-humped a few minutes before, I wrapped both hands around the hilt, closed my eyes, and tugged.

And tugged.

And *tugged*.

I opened my eyes and glared at the dagger. It was really stuck in the bone.

"Wretched, cursed thing. Who stabbed you? The god of war?"

"More like a goddess," he mumbled.

I glanced up, pausing my very important work.

"Are you telling me you experienced a real-life knife-to-the-throat scene? And I missed it?"

"Lore…"

"Oh, my gods." I leaned forward, mindful of not pushing the blade in. The extraction was difficult enough as it was. "Did you *like* it?"

I assumed the combination of heightened emotions mixed with danger could be an intoxicating aphrodisiac in the right circumstances.

Personally, I wouldn't be thinking sexy thoughts if some random lunatic accosted me with a blade in a shadowy location.

However, if my known enemy—who happened to look like a demigod—decided to lean in all slow and sensual…I might feel otherwise.

Briefly.

Then hate myself for it for at least a chapter or two until our next charged encounter.

I studied the assassin carefully, trying to dissect his thoughts.

His expression went completely blank. Not because he didn't understand what I'd meant, but because he *did* enjoy it. The fiend!

I stared at him like I was seeing him for the first time.

The quiet ones really were freaks in the bedchamber.

Who would have thought Lord Stoic would be turned on by violence? Actually, that sort of tracked, given his proficiency for killing.

Not to mention, he'd said the dagger was wielded by someone he'd called a goddess, so no wonder it had turned him on when she'd stabbed him.

I all but rolled my eyes at the predictability. Stupid, immortal were-god. Of course he'd fall for another inhumanly beautiful mate.

An uncomfortable feeling settled in my stomach.

One I refused to analyze too closely.

"Well," I said brightly, "I'm sure she was stunning, so a physical reaction makes sense."

He looked at me like I might be a little crazy, but my answering look reminded him I wasn't the one who'd gotten all hot and bothered while getting stabbed. I was simply being supportive of his obvious depravity.

Until we figured out how to get back to Bellington, we were stuck working together.

He wrapped one calloused hand around mine and nodded for me to pry the blade out again.

This time he helped.

"She looked like you."

TEN
Lore

I WAS SO shocked by his casual admission, I jerked back, finally tugging the dagger free like a true chosen one, and fell on my bare bottom.

The assassin didn't seem to notice. He released a sigh of relief, then lay back, covering his wound with one hand.

His face was perfectly calm and peaceful, as if we didn't just rip a blade from his chest and there wasn't now a disturbing amount of blood pooling at his side.

Before I could scramble to grab some leaves or moss to stuff into his wound, the blood trickled to a stop.

A few seconds later, it completely vanished.

There was no mark, no scar, no indication he'd been injured at all.

If there was any question left about whether he was mortal, that just answered it. I don't know why this surprised me.

After yesterday, my suspension of disbelief should have been more open. I should be used to the idea that magic was real, monsters roamed some worlds, and whatever Lord Stoic was...that was also real.

I crossed my arms over my chest and looked him over.

We would circle back to the whole goddess-who-looked-like-me-stabbing-him-and-turning-him-on story after we sorted a few important things out first.

"Well, I'd say it's obvious you're not human. You haven't asked for my blood yet, so I'm assuming you're not a vampire. But what, exactly, are you?"

He glanced up at the cavern's ceiling and sighed.

"At the moment? I'm a little sore. And tired."

I gave him a flat look. "Funny."

"Glad you noticed."

I grabbed his pants and threateningly held them over the fire. "These are now my hostages until you start talking, Blondie."

"Burn them." True amusement flickered in his eyes now. "You don't need to manufacture an excuse to keep me naked, Peaches. I *know* you like it."

I'd never been particularly good at lying, so I ignored his comment. He also seemed confident in his deduction, and I didn't want to poke at it.

His focus drifted down my body.

Partly to divert my attention, but I suspected now that I wasn't almost dead, he didn't hate my lack of clothing either.

I highly doubted he'd looked at me anyway, other than in a strict medical assessment earlier.

There was nothing cool or detached in his expression now.

I was surprised something actually made him thaw, until I remembered I was standing there, scowling, without a stitch of clothing on.

It wasn't my finest moment of intimidation tactics, but I had a wicked sense of false bravado that came in handy.

I gave him a haughty look and adopted my most unconcerned attitude as I flipped my tangled hair over my shoulder.

The perfect portrait of cool, calm, collected.

If I had pants on, they'd be in flames from the blatant lie.

I also realized too late that my hair had been keeping me partly covered. I acted like it wasn't cold and certain parts of my body weren't reacting accordingly.

His attention unapologetically roved over me again.

He was trying hard to distract me and he was doing a decent job of it, but—diamond-hard nips or not—I wouldn't be deterred that easily.

I ignored the crackle of the fire, mocking me for the fact it wasn't *actually* that cold in the cave, and my body might be reacting for very different reasons.

Namely, the brooding, sexy demigod staring at me.

I really, really needed to keep the portal stone tucked away. I glanced around. Speaking of the stone...

"Please tell me the portal stone is still in my dress pocket."

"Why don't you go check?"

His look dared me to bend over and rummage through my clothing. And that did terrible, terrible things to my imagination.

I focused on not thinking of any sexy stories now, lest the stone's magic latch onto it and we started rolling around the cave floor like two wolf shifters in heat.

One side of his mouth quirked up like he'd read each of my thoughts.

Unless he'd also devoured the Moonlight Mistakes series, he had no idea.

And I'd prefer to keep it that way.

I tossed the pants at his smug face and grabbed my dress. Blessedly, it was dry. Even if it wasn't, I would have put it back on anyway.

I quickly tugged it over my head and shimmied it over my hips.

I stuck my hand in my dress pocket and was relieved to feel the stone's smooth surface. I swore it hummed a little in hello.

It was much better to have a serious discussion while properly clothed.

And after the increasingly weird events of the last twenty-four hours, it was high time we ironed out some facts.

If I was coming to terms with being on a quest in a new realm that hosted nightmares, I needed to establish some framework.

I pulled my stockings on and quickly donned my boots, feeling warm from head to toe for the first time since we'd been ripped from Bellington.

I fluffed my skirt out and faced my companion.

The assassin had gotten up so silently, I hadn't realized he'd moved, let alone already finished getting dressed.

At least he wasn't trying to convince me he was mortal.

Though, after surviving a dagger *and* being impaled by a spider all within twenty-four hours, that would prove rather difficult.

He'd also turned his back, giving me privacy, which was both cute and absurd since he'd not only seen me in all my glory but held me in it for hours.

I was positive he felt my attention on him, but he was lacing up the front of his tunic like it held the answers to every question in the universe and he was a curious student taking notes.

Typical avoidance technique.

I admired him and his futile effort for a minute before getting back to the matter at hand. I wouldn't leave this cave until I had some answers.

"If you and I are going to be stuck together, I have a right to know what you are."

He turned around, a frown tugging at his lips. He was quiet for so long I started to worry that the dagger had hurt him more than he'd let on.

I raised my brows, and he finally relented.

"I am a male who will ensure your survival and return you safely to your home and family. I will kill or maim anyone or anything that attempts to harm you. And I'll stand by your side, through any nightmare that comes your way, and remain until it fades. Can't that be enough?"

My brows must have hit my hairline now. That was... intense.

Be still my fiction-loving heart.

If only life could be so simple.

I reached over and awkwardly patted his shoulder.

"Let's just start small, Blondie. I need to know who you really are, where you came from. We can discuss maiming my enemies later."

Mostly I wanted to rule out if he wanted to eat my aforementioned heart or drain my blood, or whatever other nefarious acts villains in my favorite books did.

He might have kept me alive, but I still didn't trust him. I suspected whatever his goal was, whatever he was after, he needed me in one piece.

"I'd rather keep things uncomplicated between us," he countered. "I'll be your guardian. You'll be my charge. Simple. Efficient."

I glanced down at the dagger he'd returned to the sheath on his hip. Perhaps if I stabbed him, he'd be more agreeable.

"I want to trust you," I said, wrenching my focus back to his face, "but I can't do that until I know more about you. If I'm constantly thinking you're a vampire, or weregod, things won't be simple or efficient."

He didn't seem wholly convinced.

Or maybe he was puzzling out the meaning of *weregod*.

I decided to go with my big finish.

"This might come as a shock, but I've read some interesting fiction and if I was able to bring one of the books I read to life with the portal stone, things are going to get *much* more complicated from here. Especially if I'm focused on figuring you out."

That seemed to do the trick.

I could almost see him replaying the goblin cannibal situation and then amplifying it by a thousand.

He'd still be off. I read *a lot of* disturbingly fun fiction.

"Very well." His icy gaze clashed with mine, almost in a dare. "I am known as the Prince of Sloth."

Silence followed his statement as I processed what he'd admitted.

Everyone in Bellington heard the stories of the Wicked. They were just tall tales, mere myths and legends we entertained ourselves with.

Or so we'd all believed.

Standing before me, that cold, hard stare still fixed to mine, he was very real. And not at all what I'd imagined when I'd listened to those stories as I was growing up.

How foolish I'd been to think he'd be lazy or apathetic. Or that he'd somehow look ancient. He appeared no older than thirty.

My mind spun with facts.

There were seven immortal princes who ruled seven courts of sin. They called themselves brothers but there was no proof they were blood related or even had been born. When I was younger, I'd been fascinated by them, researching as much as I could. Though, admittedly, there wasn't a lot of information available.

No one was really sure *what* they were, but there were plenty of rumors.

I swallowed hard. "You're one of the Wicked."

He inclined his head but remained silent, letting that sink in.

Blood and bones. My assassin protector was truly Prince Sloth.

Not much was known of him or his court, which, having now met him, I knew was by design. Prince Lust toyed with pleasure on all levels.

Prince Wrath stoked warlike emotions like anger and aggression; Prince Envy liked games that manifested his sin of choice.

Greed had infamous gambling dens to fuel his magic, Gluttony indulged in all manner of debauchery, and Pride had a gilded court rumored to have a hall of mirrors that allowed his courtiers to feed his sin with their vanity.

But Prince Sloth... I wasn't sure how his sin worked.

Whispers suggested that his power came from books and that his castle was a giant library. I'd dreamed of seeing it but had never been sure if it was even real.

Being an enigma among his brothers gave him an advantage—if someone didn't have readily available information on his court, they couldn't plot or plan a strategic attack.

Because of that, he might just be the most frightening of all seven princes.

And I'd been contemplating petting him like a cat earlier.

"What are you?" I repeated.

He expelled a long breath.

"Mortals always ask the wrong questions. Who are you, where did you come from, where are your families. They cannot accept some beings simply *are*. Not born but created. Our past is of no concern for the present or the future."

Finding out he was manifested into being, fully adult from the sound of it, was a lot to absorb on an empty stomach.

"But you *did* come from the Great Beyond, correct?"

His eyes twinkled. "If that's your belief, yes."

"Are you saying there is no such place?"

"I'm saying most realms believe in a location like the Great Beyond.

Some call it heaven. Others say it's a place called Valhalla. Whenever there are similar stories spread throughout regions and cultures, there's usually a grain of truth to it. Some texts would say it's simply a higher frequency."

"You're demons, though."

"Are we?"

"If you're a fallen angel, then history would call you a demon. Are you claiming you're not?"

He gave me a look long.

"We're whatever mortals need us to be. My brothers and I have taken to calling ourselves demon princes because that is what the majority believe, so it lends an air of truth we can utilize. But I can promise you that demon blood doesn't run through my veins. Once upon a time, we were considered heroes."

I snorted. Fine. He might not *technically* be a demon since he was created as an angel and I imagined that didn't change on a molecular level, but it was a nebulous gray area he was dancing around.

"I'm pretty sure all the folktales agree that you and your brothers are fallen angels. And are deceivers."

Which made them the ultimate villains.

He took a step closer. "Do I really look like someone who fell? Or do I strike you as someone who has a duty to uphold?"

My gaze narrowed in disbelief. "You have a job?"

"In a sense. We are to the Underworld what wardens are to prisoners."

"Meaning?"

"Do you put other criminals in charge of keeping the peace in jail?"

"So *someone* had to hire you for the position."

He snorted. "We all answer to a higher source at some point, Lore."

My brows tugged together.

What he was saying made perfect sense, but it twisted everything I'd read or heard about them.

They were the Wicked, soulless immortals so wretched they were kicked out of the Great Beyond. Enemies of all that is good and holy.

"But you're a Prince of Sin. And you do engage with your court. You need them and their sins to fuel your magic. Hence the whole Wicked thing."

His smile was positively filthy. Now he stepped close enough for me to breathe in his scent; leather, parchment, and something spicy.

It was like being curled up by a crackling fire with a favorite book. I resisted the urge to bury my face in his chest and breathe it in again.

"And why does that fact make your pulse race faster, Peaches?"

Because I clearly had some personal issues I needed to work out.

I inhaled deeply, ignoring the devilish gleam in his eyes that spelled disaster for me. I'd heard it only took one kiss to become addicted to the Wicked forever.

Somehow, out of all the rumors and stories, I believed that one to be true. Now, more than ever, I needed to keep a careful distance between us.

I gave him a dubious look.

"You don't expect me to go around calling you Your Highness or bending the knee to your court, now, do you?"

His laugh was a most unexpected delight.

"You're welcome to get on your knees whenever you like. But I'd prefer if you called me Lo while we're here."

Ignoring his innuendo for the time being because *oh, my gods,* having Prince Iceman Sloth thaw enough to flirt was as magical as having a jaguar playfully roll over and offer its belly for a rub. I considered his name.

There was nothing wrong with it, but it simply wouldn't do.

From what I'd read, the princes rarely gave out their true names, so I'd keep calling him Lord Stoic or Sloth until I figured something else out.

We couldn't be Lo and Lore and risk being known the realms over as LoLo.

There was nothing fearsome or wicked about that moniker, and the scandal sheets would be relentless if they ever caught wind of it.

"I'm surprised you don't use Akedia. Or something like Cassiel. Is Lo shortened from Sloth or Harlow?"

The humor vanished from his features at once.

One minute he was standing beside me, the next he'd caged me against the cave wall, his blade kissing my throat.

It glowed like a fallen star.

Holy gods. My heart pounded a violent beat.

The prince had gone from harmless flirt to supreme predator faster than I could blink.

And I had no idea what had happened to cause such a dramatic shift.

His eyes flashed with an emotion I couldn't decipher as he leaned in.

"Who the fuck are you?" he demanded.

ELEVEN
Prince Sloth

PREDICTABLY, MY QUESTION went unanswered.
 I pressed Nightmare Lore harder into the stone, annoyed I hadn't noticed the goddess's dark power seeping in.

I'd allowed myself to get distracted by flirtation of all things.

It was a mistake I wouldn't make again.

Nightmare Lore trembled against me.

"Is there a problem?" I asked.

"This isn't quite as thrilling as I imagined," she said, sounding disappointed of all things.

I moved back enough to glare down at the deceitful goddess in my arms. My magic hadn't clicked with the telltale signal that she had lied.

It had to be an anomaly.

There was no way that Lore could have guessed my true name if she hadn't plucked the knowledge from deep within my mental wards.

And that was not something a dreamweaver was capable of, no matter how trained or powerful.

Which indicated this was another realistic nightmare and I'd yet to wake.

"What isn't?"

"Dagger to the throat. Obviously. Were you not paying attention earlier? I expected it to be...a little more intoxicating."

She looked me over, a crinkle forming in her brow.

"You need to work on your seduction methods. Which reminds me.

We never finished our discussion about the goddess who looked like me and stabbed you."

Her attention dropped to my trousers, a frown tugging at her full lips.

"I don't see how you enjoyed it."

"Am I not feeding into your fear fantasy enough?"

She released a long-suffering sigh as if explaining this would be more tedious than being trapped between me and the stone wall.

"It's the romantic tension that's appealing, not fear."

That hadn't been true in the last nightmare. The goddess had desired the fear above all else.

Using the flat part of my blade, I tilted her chin up.

Her breath caught as I held it there, forcing her eyes to meet mine.

I waited, knowing the monster couldn't resist violence.

If this nightmare followed the same sequence as the one from last night, it wouldn't take long for her eyes to flash red, alerting me to the fact this was just another elaborate dream.

Her eyes didn't change from their normal warm brown, but she was definitely having a reaction.

I kept her pinned to the wall, satisfied by the swift flow of her pulse.

I felt it everywhere we touched.

Her tongue swept across her lower lip, wetting it in invitation, and my body responded against my better judgment.

It was just a physical reaction, so I leaned into it, using it to my advantage as I took the upper hand in this nightmare.

I brought my mouth close to hers before slowly trailing it along her jaw, noting the shiver that rolled through her as my lips lightly brushed against her skin.

Desire slammed into me.

Not my own, but hers.

I sensed how her body reacted to the contact and adjusted my strategy accordingly, aiming for optimum success.

I wanted the goddess to show herself so we could end this charade.

She reached out, clutching my arms as if to pull me closer instead of pushing me away.

But I would not be directed in this dream, not even by the goddess who ruled over slumber.

Using one hand, I pinned her wrists above her head and leaned in, erasing all distance between us.

Her breaths turned shorter, her desire spiking higher.

She truly enjoyed the sense of danger.

She had to know I could just as easily end her life as I could kiss her. Yet she didn't fear me when so many others would.

I stared into her dark eyes, keeping my blade at her throat the whole time. From this close, I noticed little starbursts of gold flecked in the brown.

She swallowed audibly, and I still didn't detect fear.

Anticipation thickened the space between us.

She wanted more.

If the nightmare wearing Lore's skin wished to play this game, I would win.

I'd studied seduction texts combined with psychological studies and memorized them, and that knowledge combined with my ability to sense emotions gave me an edge most couldn't resist.

They were useful tools in my arsenal that my brothers had teased me about, but none of my lovers ever complained.

Nightmare Lore's heart thundered so hard that I felt it pounding against my own chest and the sensation stirred a strange, primal need within me.

It was an ancient call I couldn't stop myself from answering.

I drove my knee between her thighs, and they parted without resistance, welcoming me as she submitted to my advances.

I paused to ascertain the goddess's reaction.

She tilted her face up to mine, and the molten look in her eyes told me she wanted me to keep playing out her dagger fantasy, to push the limits.

I shifted, pressing my hips against hers, and her breath hitched.

"Is this more thrilling, little nightmare?"

Her desire suddenly vanished, and I let her arms go at once.

She might be a monster wearing Lore's face, but I was not.

She mumbled something unintelligible as she peered over my shoulder, seeming dazed for only a second before shouting, "Get down!"

I hesitated. If this was a trick...

She shoved me hard to get my attention.

I immediately dropped my dagger from her throat and stepped back, watching as she swiftly sank to the ground and covered her head with both hands.

I had no idea what to make of this nightmare.

If its purpose was to confound me, it was working.

Nightmare Lore tugged at my shirt, attempting to drag me to her level.

"Duck, Blondie!"

TWELVE
Prince Sloth

THE CURSED NICKNAME gave me pause—the monster had never called me that.

A beat later, a hard object broke against my back.

It stung more than it should have, and my focus shot to the splintered wood as it clattered to the ground. It wasn't from the branches I'd collected for the fire.

As I stared at the ground, shadows I hadn't noticed dispersed, and the stone slowly morphed into worn hardwood planks.

I twisted on my heel, taking in our surroundings as more shadows faded to reveal a new scene, and the noise hit me a fraction of a moment later like the volume had suddenly been turned up.

We weren't in the cave anymore. We were in a crowded—

Another wooden stool careened across the...tavern, heading straight for us.

I grabbed it in midair and flung it aside, then glanced down at Lore.

She was still huddled against the wall, shielding her head. And her eyes were wide with alarm, but one that seemed turned inward. Which was strange.

I had no time to ask her what had happened.

The shadows streamed back into the stone she held, and something about the action didn't sit well with me. Dreamweavers ought to create reality from fantasy using their minds, not via the shadows. As far as I knew, anyway. There had to be some piece I was missing...

A beast of a mortal fell onto the table nearest us, shattering the old wood with his bulk and drawing my attention back to the issue at hand.

I had neither the time nor the patience to deal with this.

Lust would happily toss himself into the fray, taking pleasure from the fight almost as much as Wrath would.

Though Wrath tended to curb himself more.

Lust had no such restraint. If he were here, I'd turn him loose while I got Lore to some quiet place where we could figure out how her magic and the phoenix tear worked and uncover how she controlled the shadows.

I scanned the tavern.

Dimly lit, ramshackle, deeply scarred wooden walls and floors, with at least a dozen mismatched tables and chairs peppered throughout the midsized gathering room, the space had clearly seen its fair share of chaos.

I suspected brawls were more common than not.

We were standing on the edge of one such fight now; a crowd of about thirty were bashing into one another and anything else they could get their hands on.

Some were even throwing their heads back and howling at the swaying chandelier like wolves worshipping a full moon.

I didn't scent shifters in the crowd, which meant they were simply morons.

The main exit was blocked by a crush of bodies struggling to take the fight outdoors, but thankfully it wasn't the only way out of this charming establishment.

My attention landed on a staircase located in the back left corner.

So far, no one paid it any mind.

That was where we needed to go. I bet there were rooms we could rent, and the faster we could work on Lore's magic, the better.

I quickly assessed the best path and decided diving straight in would be the quickest route. There was always a lull located in the eye of any storm.

We just needed to make it there.

Ale mugs crashed into targets, the muffled sounds of fists smashing into soft flesh, and glass breaking added to the growing cacophony erupting around us.

I inhaled deeply, then slowly exhaled, missing the quiet peace of my library.

I cursed Xavier again for the role he'd played in forcing me to this realm.

If he hadn't stolen the book, I would be at my court now, reading and not having my sense of serenity tested every other minute.

Perhaps my brothers were correct about my antisocial tendencies.

Another table, already creaking under the immense weight of several large men climbing onto it, finally succumbed to gravity's pull and crashed to the floor with a deafening thud.

The men tumbled down with it, but their fall only added fuel to their fight. They grappled and clawed at one another amid the freshly splintered wood and spilled beer.

Clearly driven by too much alcohol and not enough brain cells, two of them seized the jagged remains of the table and used them as improvised weapons, bludgeoning their foes with merciless abandon.

Chairs toppled next as the tavern exploded into a full-on disorderly riot. The violence kept spreading like an uncontrollable blaze, and soon every corner teemed with drunkards engaged in primal warfare.

Gods only knew what had started this battle. I'd seen true wars that were fought more honorably and sensibly.

This could very well be part of the Trials—but whether Lore was being tested for heroics or fear or anything else was anyone's guess.

Rivers of beer sprayed the walls and soaked the floor, and the now empty bottles were quickly transformed into deadly missiles soaring through the air. Honestly, I was impressed they'd had the wherewithal to use them as projectiles.

Glass shattered and rained down across the floor.

These drunken fools would tear the whole rickety structure down at the rate they were going. And that would be inconvenient.

I didn't want to traipse around what promised to be a *lovely* village in search of different lodgings to begin our training.

Lore released a surprised squeal as I scooped her up and attempted to shoulder my way through the fight.

"Put me down, you oaf!"

Her fists pounded against my back, and she kicked wildly at the air. She was like a feral cat that had gotten tossed into a bath.

What a violent little ray of sunshine.

I set her back down.

"See those men?" I jerked a thumb toward the nearest group of brawlers.

Just then, a lone fighter barreled into the column where we stood, his body colliding with a dull thud before he crumpled to the ground.

One would imagine it would have knocked him out or slowed him down. But normalcy and reason had left this establishment several moments ago.

Dust swirled up from the impact, but the fallen man was undeterred; he immediately began pounding the floor like it was his worst enemy.

I cast a meaningful glance in her direction, eyebrows raised in silent commentary.

"Do they look like they'll care if they hit you? They're so drunk they're dueling the hardwoods, Lore."

She pursed her lips. Clearly at an impasse. It was hard to argue with the grand show of absurdity taking place at our feet, though.

"Fine." She cringed as another man hit the floor near the previous idiot, and the two began rolling around like pigs in muck. "But I'll ride on your back. I want to be in on the action."

I released a deep sigh, turned, and squatted down so she could leap up.

And leap she did. Lore took a slight running start and catapulted herself onto my back, nearly knocking us both to the sticky ground.

My hands shot out, fingers slipping through what I hoped was only beer.

"Oof. Sorry. That was a tad exuberant."

I straightened up and her arms locked around my neck.

She had the audacity to kick her heels into my sides like I was a horse and she was a general riding into war.

She thrust an arm straight out and pointed into the chaos, her excitement barely contained.

"Charge!"

I was clearly being punished for previous sins.

At least one of us was enjoying the mayhem.

If my brothers could see me now, feeding into this lunacy…

She nudged me again with her heels and I aimed for the stairs.

Within the first few steps I was greeted with several punches.

I gritted my teeth against the hits.

Pain was temporary, and it was best to not engage if I could help it.

Fists and elbows pummeled into me with brutal force as I strode into the heart of the brawl.

Each blow landed like a sledgehammer against my kidneys, sides, and spine, sending sharp waves of pain through my body.

Lore rounded a swift kick to someone's head.

His eyes widened with the same shock I felt, his body swaying for a split second before he crumpled to the ground, dazed and defeated.

She let out a triumphant whoop that carried across the room.

"Did you see that?" She practically squeezed my air supply off. "He tried to punch you in the throat! And then bam! Went down like a sack of potatoes."

"You are far too excited over violence."

"Violence? I am *exuding* some epic main character energy. No sword-training montage required."

I twisted and dodged a flurry of incoming flying limbs.

"If you're the main character, who am I?"

"My dependable sidekick, obviously."

Lore's other leg swept out, catching another would-be attacker in the face. His head snapped back and down he went, his expression slack. He'd wake up from the blow but would have one hell of a headache.

She really was quite good.

Her victory cry was so loud this time that I imagined people in the next realm heard her.

"Debatable." I twisted for her to land another blow. "Sidekicks don't fight like I do. I'm at least the wise mentor."

Someone attempted to break my shin with a hard kick.

I stumbled, nearly losing Lore in the process. Pain radiated up my leg, and I staggered another step before realizing I was in trouble.

Lore slid off my back. "Are you okay?"

"I—"

Out of the corner of my eye, I caught a blur of motion, but before I could react, a fist slammed into my face.

My head snapped to the side, and the metallic taste of blood filled my mouth as I stumbled backward, trying to regain my balance.

Lore grabbed the back of my tunic to steady me. "Holy gods!"

My attacker wasn't finished, but the element of surprise was gone.

I saw the second blow coming, and I caught the man's hand in a vise-like grip.

My fingers dug into his skin, and I squeezed until I heard the satisfying crack of his bones under pressure.

But he wasn't tapping out just yet.

Without missing a beat, he shifted his weight and delivered a powerful kick to my stomach. The impact knocked the wind out of me, and the unexpected pain had me doubling over.

It shouldn't have hurt that much.

"Behind you!" Lore shouted.

I swung around and punched the man in the face, sending him sprawling to the floor unconscious, then paused to collect myself.

Cold, efficient, analytical.

I had to mentally remind myself who I was.

Tinges of that same odd magic from the temple riled my emotions.

But with or without any magical prodding, my tolerance was wearing thin.

I stared down the nearest brawlers, then motioned Lore closer. "Hold on to my tunic and stay as close as you can."

"Your face is bruising."

And swelling, from the feel of it.

"Let's worry about it later."

"Total sidekick energy," she muttered.

I gave her a flat look that indicated *she wished*, then resumed my trek toward the stairs. I didn't hold anything back when I defended us from the next set of brawlers bold enough to cross my path.

Bodies of my would-be assailants flew across the room, crumpling to the floor in unmoving heaps. If they were lucky, they'd get up to torment more unsuspecting barstools in a few hours.

If they were less fortunate, they'd be meeting the goddess of death.

I didn't care one way or another.

We resumed our slow march through the chaos, and the next time someone ran at me, I bared my teeth and he stumbled away, a wet stain forming on his pants.

Lore's attention whipped up to meet mine.

"Did you just *growl*?" she asked, incredulous.

"I stepped in piss."

"Next time try not to make someone wet themselves."

My mouth curled at the edges. "Caught that, did you?"

"Very intimidating."

"Comes with the whole Wicked package. Intelligent, almost impossible to kill, and proficient in making mortals piss themselves."

"How humble."

"I think you mean honest."

Lore snorted as I kicked a table out of our way to clear the path and guided her over the rubble.

We finally stopped where the barkeeper was leaning against the wall behind the long, scarred partition, a damp rag tossed over his shoulder, watching with a detached calm as his tavern was ripped apart.

I dropped a small coin purse down before the barkeeper.

Gold was gold in any realm.

Before I'd left my House of Sin, I'd packed some for the journey as a precaution.

The man glanced at the coins, then back up at me.

"I need a room. Preferably one with a bathtub."

He pocketed the coin purse and grabbed a brass key off the wall, which he tossed at me.

"Your lucky day. We've got our best room left. Top floor. Attached bathing chamber, one bed. Food will be sent up"—he dodged a barstool that flew over his head—"shortly."

I scooped Lore up and managed to carry her halfway up the stairs before she demanded to be put down again.

I set her on her feet and watched with banked amusement as she gripped the railing, peering over it as she drank in the melee below.

It looked much worse from this vantage point.

Blood splattered against the walls, dripped down tunics. Men smiled with missing teeth as they rammed into one another.

Lore stared down, unblinking, her wide gaze taking it all in.

Bellington didn't strike me as the sort of place where brawls were normal.

"Is this really the kind of book you enjoy reading?"

Her attention flicked to mine. "Action-packed, filled with tension and romance? Who wouldn't love this book?"

"Surely it's not as appealing in reality."

She cocked her head, thinking.

I waited for the horror, the fear, the tremble in her voice... Seeing the scope of the brutality from up here would likely impress her that we'd made it relatively unscathed.

"You should make sure the bartender sends lager up to the room."

My gaze narrowed on her.

"You want me to go *back* into a brawl to request ale?"

She looked at me like I was quite possibly the dullest companion she'd ever had to be saddled with.

"If this is the lager from *Black Wings, White Bones*, it's legendary. It would be a crime to visit this story and not try it. Blake and Agatha will murder me if they find out I visited this book and didn't see if the lager lived up to the hype. I'm tempted to run down there and drink straight from the tap."

Somehow, I could envision her doing just that. Still, her reaction to the whole scene was concerning. Anyone would be nervous or stunned by the violence.

I filed it away for further inspection.

"Should I have any idea who Blake and Agatha are?"

"Oh, my gods."

She clutched my arm with a surprisingly strong grip, and I tensed for an impending attack. I opened my senses up, searching out the danger.

Nothing stood out.

"What is it?"

"I bet Logan Blaze is down there somewhere. Do you see anyone with an alarmingly sexy chest tattoo breaking bones? He'll have irresistible dimples."

A dreamy, hopeful expression crossed her face as she scanned the room again. I had a sudden, irrational urge to find the man and break some of *his* bones.

Must be the dark influence of the book.

I handed her the room key. "Lock the door and don't open it for anyone."

A mischievous gleam entered her eyes, and I realized my mistake.

"Anyone other than *me*," I amended.

She muttered something about Lord Stoic, and I waited until she'd climbed the stairs and entered our room before heading back into the fray.

THIRTEEN
Prince Sloth

THE BRAWL HAD shifted like a restless tide to the other side of the tavern, leaving only a few stragglers for me to push out of my path.

I dodged a flying barstool, narrowly avoiding a hit to the head, as it crashed into a window on the opposite end of the room.

Perhaps this *was* some new hell realm. One where drunks remained locked in a never-ending battle at all hours of the day. With luck, they'd pummel each other into unconsciousness and things would be quiet soon.

I avoided more flying furniture and made it back to the bartender without engaging with anyone else.

He raised his brows, probably surprised I'd waded back in this soon. He wasn't the only one.

"Room not up to your standards?"

I slapped two extra gold coins down, not in the mood for small talk.

"The lady is thirsty. Send extra lager up with our meal."

He scooped up the coins, then jerked his chin at me.

"Give me a minute."

I exhaled. Now I was to be a guard *and* a barmaid.

This had to be a waking nightmare tailored specifically for me.

My brothers would tease me for the next century if they ever caught wind of this.

I wanted to find a quiet corner to meditate on the events of the evening but refrained. A strong pulse of magic slammed into me, followed immediately by a hunger for power, desire, darkness, and chaos.

I went on immediate alert. I knew that feeling.

My attention swept across the room and halted. A man with dark hair and a familiar build shoved his way toward the back exit of the bar.

He held an object to his chest. Something that looked like an old book.

Xavier.

I charged across the space, dodging a few errant blows, but he darted out the door before I could get a good look.

The remaining fighters successfully blocked my path for a moment, and I shoved my way through, swearing.

I didn't see his face clearly, but with the number of people in this cramped space standing in the way, that wasn't surprising. I didn't need to see him to recognize that dark power calling to me like a beacon.

Xavier wouldn't get far unless the book masked his escape.

I finally elbowed my way to the door and burst onto the street.

It was quiet. Unnaturally so.

Lanterns flickered a few blocks down, but no pedestrians were out.

I stared at the empty street, the fine hair along my body rising. I sensed there was someone there, but I couldn't see them. The Liber Noctem was cloaking the area. It had to be.

I inhaled deeply, allowing my heightened senses to search for Xavier's scent. But if he was still here, I found no trace of him.

I tried to summon my own power, but even with my heightened senses, I couldn't see through the glamour the book cast. Still, it had to have made a mistake. No illusion was perfect.

I knelt and scanned the path for any clue to the direction Xavier had run, but the cobblestones gave no secrets away.

I strode along the empty streets for a while, but my master librarian was well and truly gone. The book must have wanted me to know it was near, for what purpose, I wasn't sure. But it succeeded in unsettling me. It had just upped the game, and for the first time in my life, I was hunting a worthy foe.

THRONE OF NIGHTMARES

I headed back to the tavern, feeling that peculiar simmering rage igniting once again. The Book of Nightmares had been close.

And now all that was left was its dark, twisted magic taunting me.

Most of the fighters had worn themselves out, so I had less trouble entering the tavern now. By the time I crossed the room and made it to the bar, my cold, emotional shield was firmly in place.

The bartender plopped two frothy mugs of golden ale on the counter before me, the foam cascading down the sides.

It smelled surprisingly good, so I didn't comment on his atrocious manners.

With a slight nod of thanks, I collected the beer and headed back up the stairs, bypassing a floor with two more rooms, both occupied by either lovers or more brawlers, judging by the sounds and grunts coming from them.

I kicked at the door. "It's me."

Instead of footsteps crossing the room, I heard a splash and a muffled curse.

"It's open!"

I closed my eyes, set a mug down on the ground, silently counted to ten, then opened the *unlocked* door.

I bent down to retrieve the second lager and forced myself to remain calm. Anyone could have snuck into the room and slit her throat, even her beloved Blaze with the dimples. Now that I was certain the Book of Nightmares had tracked us to this story, we needed to remain on guard.

"I thought we agreed that you would lock —"

A small copper tub greeted me in the center of the small room along with a cheerful-looking Lore splashing around in it.

Water steamed from a brass tap that I wouldn't have expected in a place like this, and the crisp scent of neroli and basil soap washed over me.

Lore had pinned her hair up and was soaking up to her neck, her mouth curving in delight when her attention landed on the drinks.

"You got some! Is it the most delicious lager you've ever tasted?"

Her hands shot out of the water in a not-so-subtle request, and the bar of soap she'd been holding went flying over the side.

She didn't seem to notice the sudsy projectile as it bounced and slid under the bed, then rocketed back to the tub.

I stopped it with the heel of my boot.

What an utterly ridiculous sight.

I quickly schooled my expression.

"You realize how vulnerable you are in the tub with the door open, correct?"

She shot me an exasperated look. As if my preparedness was tedious instead of practical.

"The door was unlocked, not open. And you were right downstairs, probably glowering at everyone. Try not to worry so much or you'll get wrinkles."

Ignoring the fact that I was immortal and wouldn't age, I released a sigh. At least she was making use of the tub I'd paid extra coin for.

She gestured impatiently at me again and I handed the lager over.

The carnal sound that came out of her after that first sip made the slumbering sinner in me sit up and take notice.

After my aggravation at losing Xavier and the book all over again, her antics were almost a welcome distraction.

"That good?" I asked, arching a brow.

She closed her eyes and sank back, letting the water slosh over the sides of the tub again.

She was a complete menace to the hardwoods.

I fought the urge to grab a towel and clean it up.

"Definitely worth braving the brawl and goblin cannibal for."

"You were hidden behind me," I pointed out, "almost the entire time."

"Don't dull my sparkle, Blondie. I landed a few impressive kicks."

"If you're this impressed by this lager, you should try the winter ale in my brother's court."

She gave me a devious smile. "Inviting me to meet your family already? And here I thought you barely liked me."

"You're impossible," I grumbled.

"Impossible not to like." She waved a soapy arm around, sending more suds flying. I eyed up the linen towel again.

She narrowed her gaze on my face.

"You're going to have a black eye. Why aren't you healing as fast as you did before?"

I reached up and winced. My face was still tender from the hit.

"I don't know."

And that was grating.

I didn't know if it was being in Somnia for an extended period of time that was starting to negatively impact my magic, or if it was the influence of the Trials.

No matter what the cause was, I'd need to pay close attention to it.

I scanned the small room.

Aside from the tub and comically small bed, a lone window perched high in the peaked ceiling and there was an attached room no larger than a closet that I imagined was for relieving ourselves.

Bathing chamber was a generous term.

I was starting to think I'd overpaid in gold.

Lore seemed perfectly content, though. She hummed to herself as she sipped lager and bathed. My attention drifted around the space again.

The pathway between the bed, tub, and watering closet was a mere foot or so, leaving no room for me to sleep on the floor later.

Not that that mattered after how we'd spent our previous evening.

Though it wasn't exactly the same since she'd been unconscious and dying and I'd ended up run through with my own blade.

It was an issue for later.

I grabbed my lager and moved to the mattress, its edge dipping low and creaking in protest as I sat and finally took a sip of my drink.

A rich vanilla flavor burst over my tongue.

I didn't mimic having an orgasm like Lore, but it was remarkably good. Gluttony would order several pitchers and down them in moments.

Lore watched me with wry amusement as she sipped hers again.

"What's so funny?" I asked, taking the bait.

"For a sinner, you sure do avoid any signs of pleasure. I bet your brothers tease you relentlessly." She studied me again. "You probably bring books to parties and spew facts instead of making small talk."

It was rather chilling how accurately she'd nailed me. I loathed the banality of small talk.

I leaned forward as if I was about to impart a great secret.

Lore couldn't resist. She drew closer, her attention rapt.

"Thinking of my brothers so soon after our exciting morning, Peaches?" I tsked. "And here I thought I was special."

A pleasant flush spread up her neck and face.

"I have no idea what you're talking about."

My magic buzzed. She knew exactly what I was referencing.

Teasing her was oddly pleasurable, but there were more pressing things for us to discuss, like the sudden reappearance of the Liber Noctem and what that meant. And what had happened right as we'd shifted into this new story.

But instead of doing that, my mind suddenly began replaying the way I'd awoken to— I smothered the rest of that thought and envisioned myself in a room without windows or doors.

No emotions reached me there. No desire.

I focused on the goals: winning the Trials, securing the book, returning home.

I took another sip of my ale.

"When we first arrived here, you looked like you'd seen a ghost."

"Did I?" Her gaze darted away. "Maybe it's just jarring to suddenly have your surroundings magically transform."

My magic clicked with the lie. I strummed my fingers along the side of my glass. It was time to change tactics.

"What do you do in Bellington?"

Her brows drew together at the sudden shift in our conversation, but she didn't comment on it. "I'm a librarian."

My interest was piqued further. I could see her tending to books. Which was perfect in her world but would complicate things for us here.

"Any husband, or consistent lover?"

"Does that matter?"

The question was curious, not sharp.

"The more I know about you, the more adeptly I can tailor your training to succeed against the Liber Noctem. If you feel deeply for someone, it could either anchor you or work against you. I'd prefer if we prepared for both instances."

"Slow down, Blondie."

She held up a hand, splashing more bathwater onto the floorboards.

I made a mental note to send for more towels immediately.

"Training me." She stared at me like I might have downed a barrel of ale before returning to the room. I waited patiently for her to digest what I'd said. She filtered through her emotions remarkably fast. "And the Liber *what*?"

"The Liber Noctem."

She gave me a blank look. This was clearly the first time she'd heard of it, so Xavier hadn't conspired with her. Some of the tension I'd still been carrying around her eased a fraction.

"Is that the name of the quest we're on?"

Now it was my turn to give her a blank look. "No. It's an ancient text that contains the magic of a goddess named Nyantha." Lore went pale. "Have you heard of her?"

"I know a little of the old gods, but not much."

There was no lie, but I sensed *something* off.

"Nyantha is the Goddess of Night. Being the physical manifestation of her power, the Liber Noctem is as wicked and cruel as she is."

I gave her a moment to absorb the information.

"How does a book possess those traits?" she asked. "I assume magic, but I don't understand."

"Nyantha was punished by the other gods. They drained her power and locked her away here, in Somnia. But the spell on the book can be unbound under certain circumstances."

I nodded to her.

"Which is where you come in. I suspect you are a dreamweaver. I don't know how that's possible, but it's the only thing that makes sense since you can use the phoenix tear. As far as I've read, only someone with that kind of god magic can wield the stone to its full potential."

"Phoenix tear, like the mythological bird? You can't mean literally."

I nodded at the stone she'd laid carefully on top of her folded dress. "That stone is the phoenix tear. There's only one in existence. And the fact you can use it indicates you have god magic running through your veins."

Lore was already shaking her head. "That's not possible. I would have known if I had magic from the *gods*. Maybe it just likes me. I swear I sense its feelings sometimes."

I gave her a sharp look. "You can sense emotions in the stone?"

"Can't you?"

No, I couldn't. And I didn't think she should be able to either.

Unease trickled in again. Lore *had* to be a dreamweaver. And her imagination was probably anthropomorphizing the stone.

"Impossible sounding or not, that's the best explanation for your ability to wield the phoenix tear. A dreamweaver can also be drawn into something called the Trials of Unbinding."

"Skimming over how insane it is that you think I'm a dream*whatever*, what are the Trials, exactly?"

I scratched the side of my neck. I didn't want to alarm her, but I had no good answer. And my sin was... agitated.

"No one is entirely sure. This is the first time they've ever been activated. I do know that you're basically acting as Nyantha's champion during the tests. And legends speculate that if you lose, the book will slowly manipulate you into creating mass destruction, the likes of which haven't been seen in eons."

She inhaled deeply. "And the prize behind door number two? If I win the mysterious Trials? Will the goddess gain her power back and just... send me on my way?"

"*When* you win, I have a spell to permanently rebind her power to the book before she gets it. Then the book will be rendered inert, Nyantha will continue to be powerless, and we'll return to our homes, where I'll lock the book in my collection, spelling it so it can never be used to cause harm again. If we locate the book before the Trials end, I believe I can spell it and the risk of failure is significantly reduced. Technically, it shouldn't count as interference." I hoped.

She stared at me for a long beat.

"I'm still not understanding what you mean by my magic. I don't *have* any magic. I've only used the stone to shift stories."

It was certainly starting to *look* that way, but it wasn't possible.

"We'll test some theories tonight, but I'm fairly confident you're a dreamweaver and the stone is simply channeling your power."

She stared at me like I was some alien life-form.

"Even if I was a dreamweaver, I have no idea how to use that power."

"I believe if you concentrate on a story hard enough, you can use the phoenix tear to help direct your power and shift the world around you to make it become real, especially here in Somnia, the land of dreams and nightmares. This tavern and the fight are both part of a book you've read, correct?"

"Yes."

"And the same was true for the goblin's cabin. Which indicates you are the one creating our reality."

Lore searched my gaze, likely trying to find some hint of amusement. She wanted this to be a joke. It was far from it.

She swallowed thickly.

"Have you ever met someone with my... abilities before?"

I shook my head.

She nibbled on her lower lip. "If I really am a dreamweaver, wouldn't the rest of my family also have this magic?"

"I have no answer for you. Dreamweavers are all but extinct. From my limited understanding, their magic had been directly tied to the Goddess of Night, and after the years of torment she inflicted on humanity, many stopped having children to let the bloodlines die out. They'd also been...hunted."

Lore splashed some water on her face and exhaled.

Her fear flashed out, but it wasn't as potent as it could have been. I watched her closely. Her reactions were definitely not meeting my expectations. I had no idea if it was a result of her magic or if there was some other reason behind it.

"I guess we should start making a plan to win. Where do we begin?"

She slowly glanced up and met my gaze. If I hadn't felt the brief fear, I would never know she'd felt it. Her face was set with determination.

"We'll start with your magic. Ideally, I'd like to locate the book so we have access to it before Nyantha. You mentioned yesterday that when we transported to the goblin cannibal's story you wanted to feel safe. What about this one?"

"I'm not really..." Her gaze turned inward. "The only thing I can think of is possibly danger or...I'll have to think more about it. But I wasn't really thinking about either story."

I sensed a partial lie there but let it drop. Lore was an expert at keeping her secrets and I'd need to figure out a more effective way of getting her to open up.

I sipped my lager.

"I've read a few theories that believe the Liber Noctem skims your mind for your worst fears and then adjusts the original plot to test you on it. Have you noticed anything different about the stories so far?"

Lore analyzed that for a moment.

"I need to be in the scenes longer, but so far each one has been slightly different from the books I've read. If I'm being tested now, nothing stands out. The tavern fight was directly from the book, but Logan Blaze wasn't there. Which was the only oddity."

"We'll figure it out."

She downed the rest of her ale in one go.

"The Trials are more of a mental challenge, then?"

"Yes and no. Think of it like you would any story. Each chapter is a new trial for the characters to overcome, right? Sometimes the heroes win, other times they face setbacks. You've already faced physical challenges," I said. "The spiders, the goblin and her wolf. The brawl. You will pass whatever comes next."

She gave me a disbelieving look but didn't comment on it.

"I imagine I can't simply refuse to participate."

"Unfortunately, that's not an option. The Trials have already begun."

Dread permeated the space between us, the emotion cold and coiling like a serpent. It was the strongest feeling I'd sensed from Lore since we'd arrived here.

"I'm not the save-the-realms-hero type. You know we're all doomed, right?"

I shook my head. "You'll be fine. I'll teach you how to use mental shields, and we'll figure out how your power works."

She studied me for a long moment.

"How did you get involved in this mess?"

I ran a hand through my hair.

"I made a terrible mistake many years ago, and I've been hunting the book ever since to study it and find a way to undo it."

It was as much as I'd admit to for now.

While she was focused on winning the Trials, I'd continue to search for the Liber Noctem. If I could just get ahold of it to see what the old gods had done, I was confident I had a way to spell it so it couldn't ever be unbound.

It would be difficult to accomplish and we'd have to get to the book before Nyantha did, but I was up for the challenge.

"Have you ever seen the Liber Noctem before?"

I inhaled and slowly released my breath. "Yes. I found it in a temple in Bellington. Right before my master librarian, Xavier, betrayed me by taking it here, to Somnia."

Lore closed her eyes, then opened them. I saw acceptance and determination in them, even through the lingering uncertainty.

"What if I can't figure out how to use my magic or survive the stories? I lose? And you'll return to your court?"

I slowly shook my head.

"We both need to survive the stories, or the Book of Nightmares will overtake you completely, and I'll die."

"But you're immortal."

I gave her a sad smile. "The magic that fuels the Trials is divine power. I'm strong, but without fueling my magic through my court, I would be weakened enough to potentially lose my life."

If I died, my circle would fall, and that would set off a chain of events that would destroy the Seven Circles and each of my brother's courts.

Our realm was based on balance. If one circle went down, the others would eventually follow.

And once the Underworld fell?

Then Nyantha would be free, powers fully returned or not. I had little doubt that she'd cause mass destruction with or without winning the Trials. She was a god. And no realm or dimension would be safe from her wrath.

There was nothing more dangerous to humans and supernaturals alike than a forgotten god who sought vengeance against us all.

PART II

Dark Night of the Soul

FOURTEEN
Lore

Prince Sloth, king of brooding, assassin of fun, enemy of a good time, certainly knew how to slaughter the mood.

The famous—and mind-blowingly delicious—lager I'd downed suddenly didn't make me feel so relaxed, and my bathwater sent shivers racing along my spine.

I wished he'd saved his "end of the realms and portent of doom" speech until after I'd finished soaking.

I was having a really difficult time accepting this twist.

My muscles were wound tighter now than when I'd first gotten into the tub.

"To sum this up, you're saying the old gods punished one of their own by binding her magic into a book, banished her here—to this realm where she can still manipulate dreams and nightmares—and if I don't somehow manage to beat it in Trials that test my darkest fears—with magic I had no idea I had—then you'll die and I'll what? Be stuck here like a mindless puppet for the goddess and or her dark book to use to create more nightmares to torture humanity with?"

The grin he flashed reminded me why I initially thought he was a sociopath, especially with the addition of his black eye.

"More or less."

"Try not to look so excited about mass casualties; you'll scare the children."

He chuckled softly.

The sound was deep and rumbling and perfectly distracting.

Gods. There was something different about him tonight.

He was not quite so cold, and the fact that he was capable of having a real conversation and *joking* was messing with me.

I knew he was trying to distract me, probably because he thought I might drown myself in the tub after the revelations, but still.

The sociopath was, dare I say, pleasant when he smiled.

He was either about to turn into the villain or I was fast approaching a different kind of danger.

I *really* needed to stop thinking about romance novels during inappropriate times, but the more I tried to ignore them, the more my devious mind sent images from my favorite books waltzing through my brain.

They were my preferred form of escape, so it made sense that I'd keep latching onto them while under so much stress. And I was wildly stressed.

I pressed the heels of my palms against my eyes, begging my brain to take a day off. The traitor would do no such thing.

A parade of debauchery marched by with me proudly twirling a baton in the lead. I prayed to whatever god watched over lunatics to end my suffering.

"You're intelligent and quick-witted."

Sloth's unexpected compliments yanked me straight out of my spiraling thoughts.

"You have a keen understanding of books. And you have an exceptionally sunny disposition, even under duress. You'll be a force to be reckoned with once you've harnessed your power."

I wasn't sure if the rumors about the Princes of Sin not being able to lie were true, but I comforted myself by believing they were.

Bolstered by my newfound praise kink, I sat straighter in the water.

I loved stories with my whole heart and soul. And if that played a key part in winning these Trials, maybe I *could* succeed.

I would do *anything* to keep my family safe. My village. My beloved library and my book club. Blake and Agatha, Fable... I couldn't imagine a world without them in it. That would be a true nightmare.

It was time to stop panicking and doubting the strange new circumstances I found myself in. On second thought, this seemed to dovetail with the quest the old woman had offered me. Regardless of who was pulling the strings, the fact remained the same: I needed to overcome my fears and then life would be good.

Where Lord Stoic failed at gently passing along bad news, he gave an exceptionally good motivational speech.

I felt like a soldier ready for war, as long as I ignored the fact that I had no uniform or weapon.

"So... how do I make a mental shield?"

He gave me an appraising look.

"Imagine your mind as a fortress with an impenetrable wall around it. Some envision building a wall of water instead of a stone wall—it's ultimately about creating a barrier. It will come naturally to you. You just need to seek out the divide and reinforce it. The trick is believing in it, wholly. No doubts, no distractions."

"Build an imaginary wall. Have complete faith in said wall. Simple."

The lies I told myself were truly astounding. But I decided it was best to fake it until I believed my own tall tales.

Sloth arched an imperious brow.

Right. Time to make my mind a fortress. Possibly one with a moat.

I closed my eyes, forcing my thoughts to still.

It took longer than I'd anticipated to center myself.

I hadn't realized how much my mind constantly spun with images and daydreams and random information. But once I did, it was much easier to picture the divide the prince had mentioned.

I'd always had an active imagination.

Something that would've been a glaring indicator I was a dreamweaver if my family had known to look for the signs.

Which made me wonder again how in the realms I ended up with this power and they didn't. Fable seemed like he would be much more capable of slaying the dragons of the world. Or even my parents. It was hard to fathom that I was the one with a secret power. That this adventure was, for better or worse, my chance to live my best main character life.

I thought of the old woman at the caravan again.

How had she known magic flowed through my veins when the people I was closest to had no idea? And did she know if my quest and these Trials were linked?

That had been quietly bothering me, but the mystery would need to be solved after I learned to shield my mind. Sloth hadn't seemed fazed when I'd mentioned a quest, and he seemed to know a lot about this realm and situation.

I forced myself to focus on the task at hand.

I used my innate skill at daydreaming to visualize a pile of smooth, flat stones.

I figured they'd be easier to stack, and I was nothing if not practical.

Step one in building an imaginary wall complete; I now had supplies.

I hefted the first stone and laid it where I was pretty sure my natural barrier began.

For some reason, I pictured it like a wall surrounding a stone country house with a large yard of wildflowers and dreamy pale blue shutters.

Very provincial.

At the last minute I added a tower to each side since the sociopath seemed to feel strongly about it being a "fortress."

I bet there was a library inside one of the turrets, complete with a rolling ladder and spiral staircase.

Before I decided to check out the nonexistent books, I wrangled my thoughts back to the wall outside.

Mass casualties. Complete destruction of the realms. It was amazing how fast that reminder put pep in a girl's mental shield-building step.

Without further distraction, I added stone after stone to the wall around my mind, working as quickly and diligently as I could.

I was wholly focused on my task, determined to succeed.

If I paused for even a minute, I feared I'd start panicking about the stark reality we faced. I couldn't be the reason my family or world met a horrific end.

When the pile of supplies grew small, more stones magically appeared.

It took a while, and I swore I mentally broke a sweat by the time I finally added the last stone in my modest wall, but it was done.

Fists planted on my hips, I spun in a slow circle, taking in the new barrier that surrounded the entire perimeter of my imaginary country estate fortress.

I prodded the nearest section with the toe of my boot, relieved when it didn't topple.

Thank the gods that was done. I might just survive the evil book's power and save the day after all.

I opened my eyes and blinked back my surprise.

Outside the world had darkened and a single candle flame danced in a sconce I hadn't noticed mounted on the wall by the door.

Shadows stretched from the corners of the small room, spreading inky fingers across the floorboards.

I must have been lost in my daydreams of wall building for hours.

My attention drifted to the bed and halted.

The prince was lying back on the mattress, his arms folded behind his head, his focus resting solely on me. His eyes glinted from a swath of moonlight that carved him out of the darkness like a silver blade.

He was so breathtakingly...dangerous.

To avoid accidentally dragging us into a romance novel, I skimmed over the triangle of tanned skin peeking out from where his tunic had been loosened.

I definitely didn't notice how hard his tattooed chest appeared or think about how safe I'd felt when he'd been wrapped around me last night.

He was a master at masking his expression, but I noticed a few details that hinted at his mood.

His pale hair was tousled more than it had been during the spider attack, like he'd been running his fingers through it the whole time I'd been playing build-a-wall in my brain.

To an outside observer, his position would probably seem relaxed, but I sensed an undercurrent of tension roiling through him as he kept that sharp gaze locked on me. He was wound so tightly I feared he might snap.

I pretended like his worry didn't worry *me*.

"Done?"

"Done." I tapped my temple and offered him a wide smile. "I bet even you can't get past this mental roadblock."

A devilish spark ignited in his eyes, banishing some of the tension from his body in an instant.

"Are you inviting me into your mind, little dreamweaver?"

Absolutely not. It's a terrifying place.

"Like a vampire? Sure, come on in. If you can."

I could seriously kick my own overconfident mental ass.

Taunting a Prince of Sin to magically invade my mind wasn't one of my finer ideas. But—like I'm sure he'd intended it to—his newest pet name got me all riled up, and I'd decided to dive headfirst into his villainous clutches anyway.

"Do you need to hold my hand to form a connection or—"

An electric bolt shot through my body, making me suck in a sharp breath.

I jolted forward, splashing water onto the floor, and scowled at the deviant.

That was not at all how I'd pictured things going.

The diabolical prince hadn't moved from his sprawled position at all. He watched me through slitted lids the way a cat watched prey.

I had the distinct impression he was about to toy with me before going in for the kill. There was a reason he and his brothers were known as the Wicked.

I should have expected that he wouldn't play nice.

I braced myself, wondering if I could picture more stones—or better yet, dozens of knives—to throw at him.

As if sensing the violent twist of my thoughts, the next time he tried to enter my mind, his approach changed.

The soft tingle of his power was more seductive, more tangible.

It rolled up and down my back, like it was erasing all the tension and worry from my body, before slowly traveling higher, massaging my neck, then my head.

I almost groaned from how good it felt and began relaxing into it.

A moment or two passed before his power paused, then shifted.

Now it was just beyond my shield, an apparition flickering between physical form and its ghostly essence, and it felt like he was slowly stroking a finger along that stone wall, testing it.

Each pass of that mental finger grew more tangible, becoming more solid, more substantial.

It didn't feel like an invasion.

It felt like an invitation that promised all kinds of wonderful delights.

All I had to do was welcome him in.

My tenuous hold over my emotions slipped further.

I no longer had the urge to force him out of my mind. I couldn't remember why he needed to remain on the other side of that wall.

To my horror, I felt myself doing the mental equivalent of arching my back into his strokes. I wanted to experience more of that delicious magic of his rubbing against mine, rife with promises of removing each of my fears from me.

The second my thoughts faltered, the instant I craved more, my wall vanished, and I felt him *everywhere*.

I was his and his alone.

It was a simple fact: the sky was blue, the grass was green, and I was bound to this male for eternity. The thought and finality of it should have been terrifying, but it...wasn't. I was at total peace with the absurdity of the claim.

He would protect me until every star and moon in every universe ceased to burn, and even then he would stand guard over my soul.

And in return I would become the darkness itself if anyone dared to harm him.

Mine.

The single word had been whispered in my mind in *his* voice.

It was the purest form of domination I'd ever experienced. Every cell in my body became electrified. Magic suffused me.

There was no fighting back against the sheer might of him. No one existed before him, and no one would come after.

I could accept it or fight the will of the stars themselves. Dramatic, perhaps, but I'd never been one to run from the idea of destiny.

Acceptance rolled through me and my magic gave in.

He might have entered my mind and laid claim to it, but he was now *mine*.

Something rushed below the surface, some thread, twisting and tugging…

Just as suddenly as he'd overpowered me, his presence in my mind was gone. I heaved myself over the lip of the tub, panting from exertion.

Cool water dripped onto the floor.

I focused on the patter, counting each drop as I tried to collect myself.

Holy gods. That was intense.

It felt like I'd run for my life for hours when in reality his magic had only held me in its grasp for mere seconds.

To say he was powerful was an understatement.

He *was* power.

I had a newfound appreciation for how much control he wielded to keep it in check.

No wonder he was so serious and reserved—he could probably break worlds if he had a bad day. That was a lot of pressure for anyone.

The fact that he hadn't torn this realm apart made me think he might be more caged here than I'd thought.

Movement brought my attention up.

I lifted my head and stared, unblinking, as the prince shoved himself into a sitting position. I noticed his own chest rising and falling rapidly as he leaned against the headboard. I had never seen him out of breath before.

Not even when he'd fought those giant spiders. Something had rattled him. Badly.

My attention finally reached his face, and I shivered.

His glare was as cold and fierce as an arctic tundra. Gone was any hint of the teasing prince from before. Whatever happened...he despised it.

"The first rule in protecting yourself is to *never* invite other magic in, no matter how good it makes you feel. With one caress, I *owned* you. Body and soul."

Wonderful. That wasn't embarrassing at all.

"How silly of me to not shield against magic, tingly fingers. Don't villains bash into walls, not try to make love to them?"

If he was amused, it didn't show.

Faster than I'd ever seen someone move, he swung his legs over the edge of the mattress, planted both feet on the floor, and clasped his hands loosely in front of himself.

Probably so he wouldn't be tempted to strangle me.

With his sleeves pushed back, I noticed a vertical tattoo that extended from his left wrist to his elbow. *Libri Ante Vir.*

I scrambled through my limited Latin and settled on *Books before man*. Cute.

He leaned in, invading my space like his magic had just invaded my mind.

"Enemies don't always come pounding at our doors, Lore. They don't hold daggers to our throats or threaten bodily harm. The cleverest use our own emotions and desires. Slipping past mental defenses is easier when you *want* someone to."

His penetrating gaze pinned me in place.

"Most seek to please those they hunger for, not fight or question them. And seduction is often the most effective means of accomplishing that."

He leaned in even closer and delicately traced a small circle on my chest.

His fingertip glided over my bare skin with precision, never straying from the area right above my heart.

An area that was now pounding with an intensity that felt almost explosive.

His touch was as soft as a whisper, but it managed to unleash a cascade of electric sensations that rippled through every nerve in my body.

Heat pooled low in my belly, and a fire slowly ignited in my veins. I hoped he somehow couldn't tell how much a simple caress was affecting me.

"Guard your heart as well as your mind, Lore. Or it will be the undoing of us all."

He withdrew his hand, and I instantly felt colder.

I shook myself out of the daze.

Basically, he was saying my mental shield was as much of a hussy as the rest of my cursed brain.

I blamed it on the fact that I hadn't courted anyone in a while.

And *maybe* it had a little to do with all the aforementioned romance novels I consumed.

A ruthless alpha starts dominating my brain, I start panting like a beta in heat. Smutty shifter fiction truly would be my downfall.

Prince Sloth observed me intently, his expression an enigmatic mask that revealed nothing.

His blue eyes were like deep, bottomless pools, giving away no hint of the thoughts swirling beneath their surface.

I longed to pry open the vault of his mind and decipher every secret hidden within its depths.

I suspected that would be an effort in futility unless he chose to grant me access, like a locked diary that only opens with its owner's consent.

And that would never happen.

I tugged myself from the vortex of his gaze and glanced around the room, pausing on a linen towel and change of clothing folded neatly beside the bathtub.

For one frantic moment, I thought he'd misplaced the phoenix tear. Then I saw he'd laid it on top of the new dress, just as I'd placed it on my dirty one.

He must have sent for the clothes while I was lost in make-believe.

Something warm and fuzzy took up residence in my chest.

I snatched the towel and wrapped it around myself like a prim and proper noble lady as I stood, flashing him in the process only a little.

The prince offered a hand to help me out of the tub and I graciously accepted it as I climbed out then plopped onto the bed next to him.

I glanced down at myself, frowning as I wriggled my fingers.

"How am I not pruned? I must have been in that water for hours."

"I spelled the water to keep you comfortable."

I jerked my attention to his.

He lifted a shoulder and dropped it.

No big deal. We were facing an enemy of epic proportions, and he'd simply used some magic to ensure my bath remained perfect while I trained.

It was...kind, thoughtful.

And absolutely could *not* happen again.

He wanted me to guard my heart, but whether he realized it or not, he was starting to become the biggest threat to it.

He was inadvertently channeling some serious main love interest energy.

Unlike the heroes I swooned over in my books, he was all too real.

And I knew that based on previous experiences, if I allowed myself to feel anything, it would be unrequited.

We needed to draw clear lines—we would work together to stop the dark book from giving Nyantha her power back. Save the realms. And I'd go back home to my family, my life, and with my heart intact. End of story.

"Thank you, but please don't trouble yourself again. I can take care of myself."

His mouth opened, but before he could object, I clapped my hands once.

"Okay! Let's try again."

My towel slipped and I paused to secure it in a tight knot. Best to keep my bits and pieces to myself in light of our new boundaries.

"I bet I can shield against your mental massage now. Hit me with your worst, Mr. Magic Fingers."

The new look he leveled me with made my pulse race for much different reasons. His unwavering gaze held mine, forcing me to meet it or forfeit this match. I wasn't a quitter but wished I was.

His expression said he'd happily accept the mental challenge I'd thrown down between us.

The air thrummed with the tension of it, taut as a drawn bowstring.

"Ready?" he asked.

"Game on."

I pretended I didn't instantly regret my words and prepared for the complete and utter reckoning his smile promised.

FIFTEEN
Lore

False bravado was not doing me any favors in this instance.

I absolutely did *not* shield against the prince's next mental seduction.

Or the one that followed directly after.

We spent the next two hours locked in one mental skirmish after another. I suspected it was way more exhausting for me, but I didn't give up.

No matter how hard I tried to bluster my way through this experiment, I failed.

After our first encounter, the prince didn't appear tired in the slightest.

It made me want to leap across the bed and strangle him.

And if straddling him with the intent to kill didn't pose a risk of me transporting us to a more volatile type of story, I would have done just that.

Instead of attempting to murder an immortal, I focused on my shield, giving it my all. I poured my whole soul into it. And it wasn't enough.

Sloth continued to easily batter my defenses, seeming no more affected than someone casually swatting away a fly.

Meanwhile I kept gasping for breath, my mind and body both growing more limp with every failed attempt to keep him out.

He was persistent and infinitely patient.

Victory wouldn't be handed to me; he'd make me earn it.

No matter how often I silently cursed him, he never held himself back, using the full might of his power each time.

It reminded me of a waterfall located high in the mountains of Bellington. The water cascaded down the cliffs with punishing force, a force that became even more dangerous in the spring when the snow and ice melted and joined the already raging waters in the pool located below.

When I was younger, I used to hike up to the grassy knoll located at the bottom of the falls during the summer to read, enjoying the cool mist that blew over me, banishing the heat.

Not once had I ever attempted to enter the water. I valued my life too much for that.

Now I felt like I was trying to swim up those cursed falls and kept getting knocked down and drowned every time.

Whenever I opened my eyes, the prince would nod in encouragement and say, "Again."

I'd never despised *and* appreciated someone more.

Maybe this was the start of my villain origin story.

I was frustrated. And under that, afraid. I hadn't admitted it to the prince, but something odd did happen when we left the cave and entered the tavern.

I had the most horrendous vision. It had almost felt like a memory, but it wasn't mine. I had no doubt the book had made me see what it wanted. And it was cruelty and horror and terror. Humans drowned in their own tears. Others were torn apart by all kinds of nightmare creatures.

I *needed* to shield myself from the evil book. If only to never see those images of death again.

And that wouldn't be possible if I couldn't master holding my wall in place.

The prince made it seem so effortless, as natural as breathing, but I failed to maintain it whenever he switched tactics.

We tried again.

And again.

Each time I lasted a little longer, until he changed his method of attack, and his magic overwhelmed mine again.

Sometimes his magic was a whisper, a tantalizing caress, other times it was like a tidal wave. One minute we'd be mentally dancing and the next we were brawling before he'd magically pin my barrier down and I'd tap out.

Every time I thought I'd mastered one move, he'd come at me with another.

He'd just sent the equivalent of a mental tsunami at me.

I slapped my palms against the mattress, fighting the urge to cry.

Tears wouldn't keep the Liber Noctem out of my head, and I already felt bad enough, so I shoved the urge down, wrapped heavy chains around it, secured it with a lock and silently screamed into the abyss.

"That's enough."

Lord Stoic was back, his gaze as cool and calculating as ever as it roamed across my face.

"Eat."

He pushed a covered tray of food at me.

I hadn't even noticed it had been delivered.

When I stared at it blankly, he yanked the cover off and set the tray on my lap, then grabbed a second tray and tucked into it.

After a few bites, he paused.

"*Eat*, Lore."

Finally, a bit of my fire returned.

"Your manners truly are exceptional, Your Highness. Did they teach you that when you attended royal pain in the ass academy?"

He glowered at me but said nothing.

I accepted the food because it smelled delicious, and I was starving.

Thick beef stew, freshly baked bread smothered in herbed butter, and a cold lager to wash it down with.

But his commanding attitude wasn't something I'd accept now or ever. I might choose to be cheerful and positive, but that didn't mean I was a doormat.

"Are you married?" I asked.

He looked me over before answering, a slight crease in his brow.

"No."

"Courting someone?"

"Not recently."

I flashed him a knowing grin. "Unsurprising."

His jaw tensed and I got the impression he was trying very hard to not ask the question I could see churning in the depths of those blue eyes.

One point to me. I took a bite of my food to hide my smile.

I'd realized one thing about him; he did not like questions without answers.

He would not be able to let it go, and I suspected it somehow played into how his sin worked.

From the corner of my eye, I saw him trying to piece together his own conclusion, but that would only be a guess.

He needed facts.

I gave him all of five seconds before he caved.

Five. Four. Three...

"Why isn't that surprising?"

I took another mouthful of stew, enjoying the savory flavor and the way the delay made him squirm. Who knew I had a sadistic side?

The sociopath truly brought out the best in me.

I made him suffer for another moment before putting him out of his misery. I was a merciful sadist.

"No one likes to be bossed around outside of the bedroom. Therefore, I'm not surprised you're unattached. While you clearly operate best by using your head over your heart, you lack the simple logic of catching more flies with honey."

He stilled.

I felt his attention shift to me — *all* his attention.

Holy gods.

Having the entire force of his focus directed at me was almost powerful enough to knock me over, but I pretended to not notice.

"Perhaps you ought to practice saying please," I added. "You might be surprised with the results. Maybe you'll even make a friend."

I kept shoveling food into my mouth and sipping my beer, completely relaxed despite the apex predator studying me with the intensity of a thousand burning suns.

I'm sure I was breaking all sorts of royal protocol, but I didn't care.

I was doing my best under the worst circumstances, and I didn't need to be treated like one of his royal hounds.

"You're right. Dealing with emotions is not my area of expertise." He exhaled. "I apologize for offending you. You didn't want to cry, so I attempted to divert your attention. My delivery could use some refinement. I will work on adjusting my methods so they're more agreeable in the future."

I dropped my spoon in my empty bowl and swiveled to face him.

"How did you know I was close to tears?"

He pinched the bridge of his nose. Apparently, that wasn't a secret he'd meant to share. "Because I sensed your emotions."

I took a long sip of my lager, needing time to let that sink in.

He collected our empty dishes and returned them to the tray, stacking everything in an orderly pile before sliding it across the floor.

He could sense emotions. At first that didn't seem *so* bad, then I started running a mental tally of everything I'd felt over the last two days and halted.

Dear gods.

"Like magic?"

He shook his head. "It's similar to other senses like taste and smell."

"You can sense *all* emotions?"

He scanned my face, the beginnings of a small smile playing at the corners of his mouth before he banished it.

I had a feeling the bastard knew exactly what I was asking.

"Yes. Fear. Sadness. Elation. Desire. *Anything* you feel, I sense. I don't always know the root cause, but sometimes I can accurately guess based on other factors." He hesitated. "I also know when you lie."

"That's...wonderful."

So those rumors were true. I'd *really* hoped they weren't.

A glimmer of hope sparked.

"If my mental shield improves, will that help?"

He shook his head, eyes glinting with the mirth he'd been suppressing.

"Not with emotions, especially ones that are more heightened than others."

He didn't have to elaborate on what kind of emotions were stronger. I could add two and two together on my own like a mathematical prodigy.

Passion. Desire. Hate. Things my book-addled brain excelled in.

Maybe I should let the Liber Noctem come swallow me whole to put me out of my misery.

I blew out a breath and set my empty lager glass aside.

Time to master my shield and stop thinking of my favorite romance tropes.

I had a sinking suspicion *that* might prove more difficult than beating the Book of Nightmares but put on a brave face and tried anyway.

Finally, when dawn broke and its candy-colored shades of tangerine and pink shattered the darkness of night, I managed to keep my mental barrier in place.

I flopped onto my back, staring at the ceiling.

I was completely and utterly spent but also buzzed with energy.

Even after all the training, it was still hard to wrap my mind around the fact that I was a dreamweaver and had magic.

I wanted to tell my parents and Fable all about it.

Some of my elation dulled. I needed to get back to them. With so much at stake, I couldn't stop the twinge of doubt that crept in.

Had I really done enough to enforce my shield?

Would I really be able to win the Trials and face my fears? I still didn't know why my fears were being tested. Shouldn't the cursed Goddess of Night be the one proving herself worthy of her magic?

I was just a book lover from a small village who had terrible luck, apparently. Maybe this was a test—facing my fears of inadequacy.

I felt a prickle of awareness and flicked my attention to Sloth.

His focus was already fixed to me in a quiet assessment that seemed to peel back layers and delve into the very soul of my being.

He sat on the edge of the mattress, looking as reserved as ever, but there was a lightness about him now too.

He'd been *really* worried.

I supposed that was due to the small fact that the fate of the realms rested on me figuring out my power, and up until a little while ago, I'd only mastered the art of creative—and highly expressive—mental swearing.

"We'll practice daily to keep your shields strong, but you did well, Lore."

A smile curved my lips.

Partly from the praise, but also because while I was more tired and drained than ever before, and while a sliver of doubt crept in, I also felt *good*.

I'd done it!

I'd kept a Prince of Sin from breaking through my mental shield.

In theory, if I could withstand his power, I should be able to keep the Liber Noctem out as well. Then I might really be able to direct which stories we ended up in. I'd take anything that could give us an edge.

I desperately wanted to help find the Book of Nightmares and give Sloth a chance to spell it forever. Then I wanted to go home and hug my family.

My victory was extra sweet since I knew Sloth hadn't held back; he'd given it his all. While his power was still overwhelming, I'd finally reinforced my own magic enough to withstand each of his attempts to infiltrate my barriers.

I'd also sensed the first trickles of power that didn't belong to me before he'd fully stepped into my head and immediately slammed that wall into place, effectively blocking him from invading, no matter how clever his tactics were.

Now it only took minimal effort to keep the barrier up while I focused on other things. He was right—it had been natural, and once I'd gotten enough practice, it was like working out certain muscles. I could flex it at will.

"If you sit up, we'll start testing your dreamweaver magic."

I rolled to my side and buried my face with a pillow.

Maybe if I smothered myself a new dreamweaver would magically appear and become the champion. Being a main character was exhausting.

Sloth plucked the pillow off my head and tossed it to the side like the wicked prince he was.

I was more drained than I cared to admit, so I just lay there and pretended like his gaze wasn't burning a hole through me.

The sociopath reached over and flicked me, not hard enough to hurt, but enough for me to realize I'd drifted off and had started snoring.

I groaned.

"It's dawn." I flung an arm over my eyes in a sorry attempt to block the light. "Don't you believe in the restorative power of sleep? You're the Prince of *Sloth;* try to behave more accordingly or your court will launch an uprising."

He was undeterred.

"My court doesn't act out of emotion. They are preoccupied with their own academic pursuits and will have the knowledge and power to maintain the status quo while I'm gone."

Honestly, I would love to be a member of his court. Reading my chosen genre all day was definitely an appealing sin.

"We've been in this story for hours. If the Book of Nightmares hasn't begun twisting it yet, it will soon. We need to figure out what your test is."

I dropped my arm from my face and peered up at him.

He was right. No matter how physically exhausted I was, we needed to keep forging ahead while we had some respite.

I pulled the phoenix tear from my pocket and held it tightly.

It was still hard to believe it came from a mythological creature, and I had such an odd sense of sadness for this bird I didn't know. It must have been heartbroken to cry magical tears. I swore a slight hum went through the stone, but other than that, it remained inert.

I really wanted to try to overpower the Liber Noctem before this test began. If this story followed the main plotline, then I had a growing fear about what the test might involve. Or rather, who.

I tried to remember what I'd been thinking or feeling back in Bellington. There had to be some spark, some trigger.

I closed my eyes and let the worry and pressure slip away.

We sat quietly for a while, and I pretended not to notice the tension building in the room as the minutes ticked by.

I poked and prodded at my mind, searching for any part that felt different. It wasn't like building a mental shield, and aside from allowing myself a few moments to daydream and see if that worked, we remained in the inn.

I exhaled, centering myself again.

I tried to imagine a channel or thread that bound me to the phoenix tear, allowing it to help guide my power.

But whatever made me a dreamweaver didn't respond.

I glanced over at the prince.

"Nothing is happening. I can't seem to feel or identify anything that triggers my power. Or the phoenix tear."

He stood from the bed and began pacing in the small space between the bed and the copper tub. "You *should* be able to shift us. Try manifesting a small change here. Maybe turn the glass into a mug."

I gave him a dubious look but focused on the empty lager glass.

I held the phoenix tear tightly, envisioning my mother's favorite "one more chapter" mug, which Fable and I had made her when we were children.

I could see the chip, the stained enamel. I could even smell her favorite rose hips tea. I opened my eyes and...nothing. The lager glass hadn't changed.

The prince pressed his lips into a tight line and remained silent.

He was doing his analytical mind thing again, flipping through catalogues of information he kept stored there.

He started pacing again and cut a few glances my way, his brows tugging closer and closer together. My magic clearly wasn't meeting his expectations, which made me more nervous. I'd told him I wasn't a dreamweaver. And now we were in serious trouble.

He finally stopped moving and peered down at me.

"The first use of your powers came when we were under attack. Which could indicate a fear of death. Then you shifted us again when…"

I fought my smile, waiting to see how he finished *that* sentence.

He cleared his throat but was obviously at a loss.

The fearsome prince could handle giant spiders and bar brawls, but sharing his emotions was the one hurdle he couldn't leap over.

I began mentally designing a tattoo for him, *Felled by Feelings*.

All my favorite love interests had unique tattoos, and it was something I liked to imagine to bring some normalcy back into my life.

The typeface would need to be bold, no-nonsense, and in a blue that matched his eyes. Maybe with some decorative icicles dripping from it as an ode to his chilly personality.

After another silent minute passed and he seemed no closer to expanding his thought, I decided to tease him.

"Are you talking about when you held the dagger to my throat?" I adopted my most innocent expression. "Or when you did some *very* interesting moves with your hips after you pinned my arms above my head?"

He shot me an unreadable look.

"Fear seems to be the common thread for your magic. Which makes sense, given how much the goddess thrives on it."

I wasn't as sure.

I thought back to when he'd pressed me against the wall and had leaned in.

I'd been convinced he was about to kiss me, and if the hungry look in his eyes was anything to go by, it would have been the sort of kiss I'd sell my soul over.

Obviously, fear had been the last emotion I'd felt.

Even if *he'd* looked like he hated the idea of losing control.

I was momentarily spellbound by the flicker of desire I'd seen in him, the passionate blaze he hid so well beneath that frosty veneer.

I never thought he'd be capable of such warmth or feeling, especially when it came to me. I suspected he'd been unaware his mask had slipped.

When he'd lifted my chin using the flat part of his blade, my brain promptly short-circuited, and I'd thrown common sense out the window.

Ready, willing, and able to sign on the dotted line and give myself over to the Underworld.

Apparently, a knife to the throat *was* appealing in the right circumstances.

"Not exactly fear-based."

Unless I was afraid of admitting my desires.

I pushed myself into a sitting position when he finally stopped pacing and sat next to me. I rubbed the phoenix tear, hoping it would wake up now and get me out of this conversation.

"I was afraid you were dying with the spiders, but... I wasn't scared in the cave."

He cocked his head to one side.

"What were you feeling then?"

His expression remained an inscrutable mask, giving nothing away, but I could have sworn his eyes held a spark of intrigue.

I couldn't tell if he was genuinely seeking the answer or simply wished to gauge my reaction, but either way, the atmosphere slowly became charged with a different kind of tension.

I suddenly realized we were alone. Sitting on one small bed.

As if he was just noticing the same thing, he shifted a little, his leg pressing firmly against mine. Gods. Maybe this was my test. My fear of rejection.

The heat of his muscular thigh warmed me through the fabric of my new dress. The dress he'd sent for while I was practicing my shields.

He glanced down, and I wished I could decipher his expression.

He'd asked me something, but I was struggling to recall what.

My feelings. He'd wanted to know what I'd felt when he'd thoroughly knocked me off-kilter back in the cavern.

"With the dagger or the hips?"

Energy crackled between us as he leveled me with his full attention again, the force almost palpable as his cool gaze locked onto mine and remained.

"Both. Either." He lifted a shoulder, then dropped it. As if he didn't care one way or another, but then he abruptly stood and took a few steps away from the bed. "If you weren't scared, were you angry?"

I narrowed my eyes at him.

He'd admitted to sensing emotions; he knew what I'd been feeling.

He was most definitely messing with me.

Suddenly, I wished I hadn't poked fun at him. He had obviously sensed my desire and now I had to figure out how to play my hand.

My throat felt parched.

There had to be a simple way I could talk my way around what I'd felt without setting off his lie-detecting senses.

It wasn't like I was withholding important information that would help us. He already knew I'd felt desire, not fear.

I wasn't sure what his game or angle was, but I refused to submit.

If he wouldn't admit that he'd been considering a kiss, I wouldn't admit how much I'd wanted him to. In that moment.

I chalked it up to TICS, temporary internal conflict syndrome. Never mind it was a completely made-up ailment.

"I—"

He stepped closer and loomed over the bed, enjoying every second I squirmed under that penetrating stare.

"You?"

I inhaled deeply, searching for the first, most ridiculous thing I could say...

The prince was really getting me flustered.

I rubbed the phoenix tear like it was a worry stone.

An enormous shadow flew past our window, eclipsing the light of the sun.

Whatever caused the momentary blackout circled back and hovered there, blanketing us in thick shades of gray before moving on again.

I released a dramatic whoosh of air.

I'd never been more relieved at an ominous interruption before in my life, even if it meant this was the testing portion of this Trial.

"Saved by the...Oh, gods."

This was bad.

If the shadow belonged to what I feared it did, then I needed to suddenly figure out my magic and overpower the Liber Noctem to get us to the next story.

Immediately.

Otherwise, I was pretty sure I knew what this test would be.

I *really* didn't want the prince to witness my complete and utter ruination. It wouldn't be at the hands of someone else; I suspected it would be my own undoing.

SIXTEEN
Lore

I WRACKED MY brain for another explanation for the giant shadow.

It couldn't be Logan Blaze; he wasn't downstairs in the brawl—my internal doubts cut themselves off as another massive shadow soared gracefully by the window. Its serpentine silhouette stretched across the walls, dancing and flickering with the shifting light.

On second thought, it looked like it very much *could* be who I thought it was.

I swore using one of my new creative expressions.

Sloth was near the door in an instant, his dagger in hand as he cut a sharp glance in my direction.

"You know what that is?" he asked. "This is part of your book?"

I cringed internally.

"Yes. To both." I might as well rip the bandage off my soon-to-be-wounded pride. "Remember Logan Blaze, the man with the dimples?"

The room temperature seemed to drop a degree or two.

I glanced at the window to see if it had blown open—it hadn't—and fought the urge to rub warmth into my arms.

"How could I forget?"

"Well...he's a dragon shifter. Specifically, he's the alpha of the Black Wings dragon clan. Hence the 'Black Wings' part of the title."

I pointed to the window as the shadow blotted out the sun again. This time, I heard the swoosh of wings as the creature surged by.

"I'm pretty sure that's him."

Sloth looked like he was mentally counting until he'd gotten himself under control. He was either wildly impressed by my taste in books or was wishing he'd gotten stuck with a more boring partner in dream-weaving crime.

I didn't delude myself into thinking it was the former. And he should be so lucky to end up in my twisted tale.

"And?" he asked. "Does he attack the main love interest?"

I snorted.

For all his vast knowledge, Blondie clearly hadn't read any shifter romances. Otherwise, it would have been obvious.

"Don't be ridiculous."

Relief was short-lived for my companion.

I hadn't finished explaining the plot.

"He kidnaps her from the man who tried to enslave her. She turns out to be Blaze's fated mate, but we don't learn that until the second book. Though the author gave so many hints that I'm not sure how anyone missed that plot twist."

The prince glanced up at the ceiling, his lips moving in either silent prayer or colorful cursing.

"Anyway, if that's Logan, then I'm positive he's hunting for his mate. He probably senses her somewhere and is narrowing down her location."

The dragon shifter flew back across the sky, this time low enough for the building to shake from the force.

Logan Blaze would rip the roof off soon to collect his prize.

We should be safe as long as we didn't catch his attention.

If we posed a threat, then he'd unleash his dragon flames on us. I really didn't want to end up as barbecue because of my top fictional crush.

I scrambled to think of how he might be used for my test.

The most enticing idea was also the most unlikely. I doubted *the* Logan Blaze was going to attempt to seduce me.

In the book, Logan only had eyes for the woman he'd felt compelled to protect. That was the first flicker of the mating bond snapping into place.

He'd followed that insistent tug to the tavern.

Then he'd swept in with his giant black bat wings, broke an obscene number of bones, grabbed his mate from the clutches of the man who wanted to cage her, then, well, technically he'd kidnapped her from her kidnapper and chained her in his cave, where they—

Footsteps pounded up the stairs.

Before Sloth could heave the sturdy nightstand in front of the door to barricade us in, it burst open with a thunderous crash.

That was roughly about the same time my jaw hit the floor.

Standing there, dark wings beating like bad omens, was the dragon shifter of legend. I now completely understood how it was possible for characters to release a breath they didn't know they were holding.

It felt like he'd sucked up all the oxygen in the room and I'd been too overwhelmed by his presence to notice.

Logan Blaze's golden gaze skimmed over the prince, then fixed to me.

Hunter meets prey.

I swallowed thickly.

"Logan Blaze."

My voice was barely above a whisper, but he heard me.

"In the flesh."

His voice was a deep, sensual rumble that resonated like a distant storm. It sent a flurry of butterflies fluttering in my stomach.

By the gods, there was undeniable power in an alpha's stare, a magnetic force that seemed to reach out and ensnare my very soul.

Even though I didn't know him, I had an overwhelming urge to submit to his every demand, as if his presence alone commanded unwavering obedience.

If he told me to get on my knees and crawl, I'd weep at the honor.

Definitely not the kind of main character energy I wanted to channel.

I gave myself a mental beating and snapped out of it.

I was correct with my first, seemingly impossible assessment: This test was centered on desire. I just had to resist lusting after my number one fictional crush and calmly switch to a new story without giving in to his temptation.

I wasn't deluded into thinking that would be easy.

This was *Logan Blaze*. In the flesh. I was ready to praise the dark gods who made such a magnificent specimen.

Sloth moved with his supernatural speed and placed himself in front of me, shielding me from our intruder.

And possibly those potent pheromones.

Gods, I needed a fan or less clothing.

Sloth stood so close my chest pressed into his back with each of my breaths. His proximity combined with the heat in Logan's gaze was making my mind spin wildly out of control with some creative scenarios.

Even knowing I was being manipulated with magic, I couldn't stop myself from reaching over and running a hand down Sloth's back, craving some sort of physical connection to take the growing edge off.

He went completely still but didn't step away from my touch.

Which wouldn't go over well if we were following the storyline.

Dragon shifters were notoriously possessive.

Only trusted members of their clan could go near their mate during the bonding period. Everyone else was collateral damage.

I halted at that. I wasn't the shifter's mate, and unless the Liber Noctem had made that happen, we should—

Fury rolled off Logan as he tucked his wings close and took a step into the room. Naturally, like all proper love interests, he wasn't wearing a shirt.

I tried, gods did I try to avoid looking, but I was weak when faced with something so godlike in its perfection.

I cursed the authors who dreamed up the dark, brooding bad boys with ill-fitting clothes that showed off their decades of hard training.

Really, it would be rude to not acknowledge such dedication, though.

I peered over the prince's shoulder and reminded myself that panting was for cats, not humans. And I refused to be reduced to baser instincts.

The primitive little monster part of my brain cackled.

I was just a beast standing upright, wearing a pretty dress.

Logan's trousers were slung low enough to send non-shifters into heat.

Muscles surged with each of his movements, the dark, swirling tattoos on his chest and abs seeming almost alive, undulating with that raw, masculine power he exuded.

His whole presence was like a vortex that threatened to consume the room. Well, it *would have* been consuming if it didn't brush up against a more chilling, powerful presence.

Blondie was pretty darn impressive.

Then Logan moved again, drawing my attention back to him.

A knowing smirk played on his lips when he caught the direction of my gaze. I couldn't even pretend like I wasn't drooling.

To be fair, the way his carved muscles tapered to that V with a light trail of dark hair leading to the promised realms was unreal.

Even my nan would have stared.

His grin widened when Sloth cleared his throat in a failed attempt to wrench me out of my lusty daze.

And there were those dimples.

Goodbye, panties.

The shifter could have his way with me. Right here. Right now. Up against the wall, on the floor, the bed. Beggars couldn't be choosers. But I'd beg for him to choose a starting position before I combusted.

I was suddenly very motivated to fail this test. No one had mentioned anything about me needing to pass them all to win the Trials. That seemed like a pretty critical piece of information to have.

Surely, if I had to lose one round, this would be the one to do so. Death by orgasms was preferable to death by any other means.

Logan crooked a finger in my direction.

"You're coming with me."

Absolutely.

Sloth's entire body tensed.

Absolutely not, then. Spoilsport.

The dragon shifter probably wasn't talking to me anyway.

I glanced over my shoulder, wondering if Logan's mate had somehow slipped into our room while we'd been practicing with my mental shields.

Nope. Just an empty bathtub and bed.

And one pissed-off Prince of Sin.

It took only a second more to register what was happening.

"Oh, no."

I finally understood a basic fact of how the Trials worked. The Liber Noctem created our reality from stories I read, but it also made me assume the role of the main character from each book. Since it twisted the plots to meet its tests, I had no advantage.

This wasn't good. Well, it was actually pretty amazing for living out my fictional dreams, but for practical purposes, it was very bad.

And I needed to live in the world of logic, not fantasy, right now.

No matter how difficult said fantasy was making things with those half-lidded bedroom eyes.

"Oh, yes."

The dragon shifter flashed me a look that said *no* wasn't on the menu.

If this was how the Liber Noctem planned to seduce me to the dark side, we were royally screwed. It was much more devious than simply attacking my mind.

I'd fantasized about meeting Logan Blaze from the moment he first appeared on the page in his story. He was everything I secretly wanted. Brave, bold, and completely ruthless when it came to claiming what was his.

He was definitely the type to burn the world if it meant saving his one true love, and he wouldn't think twice.

And while I wouldn't want someone in real life to break worlds for me, it would be nice to have someone who looked at me like I was one of the best things *in* the world. At least as far as they were concerned.

What reader didn't want to be the object of their fictional crush's obsession? This realm really was cruel. But I was thankful that this was a test I knew I could pass...if I could just stop being mesmerized by his eyes.

Or the way he was looking at me like he was about to pin me down and devour me right there in front of the prince.

I felt myself straining toward him, like the temptation to go to him was indeed being fueled by forces greater than myself.

Not even Sloth could stop me if I decided to go to Blaze.

My hands curled into fists, my nails digging into my skin.

This test was more than simply about desire; if I looked deeper, it was actually tapping into my fear about ever truly being loved.

If I chose Logan, it wouldn't just be the physical element. It would be the promise of forever, of pure devotion.

A new fear pressed in, nearly choking me.

The Liber Noctem was pumping more magic into the scene. I closed my eyes and saw images of my future if I walked away. Loveless. Solitary. Forever cursed to live out my days without companionship.

The book made it seem inevitable, like it would cast some dark spell and make that my reality, Trials or not. If that was my fate by choice it wouldn't be terrible, but I sensed the decision would be taken from me. And that was a true nightmare.

A single tear streaked down my cheek.

If I was an antihero, the choice would be easy.

But I wasn't a villain.

At my core, I wanted to be a hero. Tragically so.

I would never be selfish enough to damn the people I loved. And maybe that wasn't romantic love, but that didn't diminish its power.

I thought of my family and any hold the book had on me vanished.

"There's been a terrible mistake, Mr. Blaze. I— Well. I think I dreamed you up and this isn't exactly real. I mean, it is, but it's...complicated."

His amusement grew. "I dreamed of you too."

The way his eyes darkened hinted that his dreams were filthy.

"Unlikely," Sloth snapped the same moment I said, "That's not—"

I shook my head, hoping to clear it.

My hold on my resolve was tenuous at best.

There was way too much male energy in this tiny room, and I was getting really flustered as some of the scenes from Logan's real book made a sudden reappearance in my mind.

The alpha had stamina.

And a dirty mouth that should require a warning label.

I needed to stop being influenced by the Trials and take control of my emotions before I stripped off my dress and things got weird.

I didn't think Sloth would want a front-row seat to the debauchery I knew Logan Blaze could bring in the bedroom.

"The prince and I were just leaving…"

Logan's focus snapped back to Sloth with a hardness that could cut through steel.

"Not a fucking chance."

Murder flickered through those gold eyes as they locked on his perceived enemy, and a deep, menacing snarl erupted from his chest.

Perfect. I could check peace negotiator off the list of any future employment options. I'd accidentally just made things ten times worse.

Because if I was playing the role of his fated mate, that meant Sloth was the kidnapper he intended to steal me from.

As a shifter, Logan was probably an equal match for the prince.

If they began fighting…

Sloth's dagger started to glow. "Now would be an ideal time to think of another story, Lore."

Yes, it would be. Ten points to Lord Obvious. I gripped the phoenix tear in my fist. "I'm trying…"

"Tell me the first title that pops into your mind."

His voice was cool and controlled. The perfect balm to my flames.

Oh, gods. Blaze took another step into the room.

His black wings flared wide, forcing Sloth to retreat, which made me stumble back onto the bed.

Logan's hungry gaze landed on where I was sprawled on my back. He looked ready to pounce. I wish I hated it. Instead, I found my fingers curling at the edge of my hem, slowly tugging my skirts upward.

"Lore…"

I shoved myself back up, avoiding the bed and all the images flashing in my mind as the two males squared off.

I held the stone tighter, begging it to help me out.

"Pick a title, Lore!"

"*Silverbeak's Wrath*!"

Shouting probably wasn't necessary, but both males stopped posturing to glance at me. Blaze looked baffled, but Sloth simply shook his head. Same carnival, new act.

Literary snob.

I ignored them both.

Screwing my eyes closed in utter concentration, I kept silently repeating the title. I didn't even open my eyes when I heard the first sounds of their fight.

Logan must have pulled a weapon from somewhere.

The clash of metal against metal was distracting, especially when it was accompanied by grunts as they traded blows.

I ignored the way the floor vibrated as they grappled closer, then charged away. I mentally begged my powers to just...do something.

Silverbeak's Wrath. Come on, *Silverbeak*!

Footsteps thundered beside me.

I was yanked off my feet and whirled around so quickly that my head spun, leaving me disoriented and breathless as I struggled to regain my balance.

My eyes snapped open, and relief speared through me when I realized that Blondie had gotten me out of harm's way from a falling chunk of the ceiling. He pivoted and surged ahead, gaining precious ground against Blaze.

He rammed into the dragon shifter and shoved him out the door.

Logan stumbled into the corridor, his big muscular body crashing hard into the wall.

"Try to think of something that anchors you in the story!" Sloth shouted, dodging a very wicked punch from the dragon shifter.

Right. Anchor. Oh! Anchors. Ocean.

I drew in a deep breath, closed my eyes again, and emptied my thoughts.

Just like when I'd built my imaginary wall, I *finally* found that creative part of my brain that desired to paint a vivid picture for me.

I snatched onto it, pouring all my energy into it. I let my imagination run wild, the same way I daydreamed the scenes from the books I read.

There was nothing I loved more than fully immersing myself in a story.

It felt as intrinsic to me as breathing. It gave me peace and joy. A release whenever life got too stressful. Books were my one true love.

The moment I cracked open a spine, I was transported to some wild new adventure. Filled with romance and danger and mystery.

I would be the fated mate of a wolf shifter, or the daughter of a king with a plot to rule the world who was sent to my family's enemies, or a pirate on a doomed ship.

I found nothing more thrilling than reading those first few chapters of a book I just immediately connected with.

And when someone came into the library, asking for a book recommendation, it felt like I was handing them the keys to their very own castles when I told them about my latest obsession, and they came back the next morning after staying up all night to finish and were just as excited to borrow the next one.

I lived for those moments, the absolute certainty I'd found my next favorite read, and our love affair had just begun.

Maybe I would never marry, or fall into a wild, passionate courtship with someone, but that was okay. I loved a hundred characters and would never be lonely with them by my side. I didn't need someone like Logan Blaze to make me feel desirable.

Suddenly, a small trickle of magic flowed through me and into the phoenix tear, or maybe the opposite was true. Whatever it was, it was fueled by my pure devotion to stories.

I felt the rolling waves beneath my feet.

Smelled the brine of the ocean. Heard the far-off sounds of gulls as we sailed farther from the safety of the shore.

"That's it! Keep going, Lore."

Thank the gods. I imagined the creaking planks, swore I really did feel the undulating waves beneath us. Rolling and swaying.

Someone grabbed my hand, and from the way my heart skipped a beat, I knew it was the prince.

Not even Logan Blaze—my top fictional crush—could wreck my pulse with a simple touch the way the sociopath could. No dark magic required.

And then, just as suddenly, the swaying stopped.

We were still shifting stories, but instead of hearing the rolling waves and gulls, new sounds emerged. A sea of surprised gasps...

No, not surprised. Scandalized.

"*Lord Winters, I beg your pardon!*"

The older woman's chiding tone snapped me out of my post-story-shifting confusion; I couldn't believe the Liber Noctem had taken over so easily.

One moment I'd felt the waves and smelled the ocean, and the next we were hauled out of the scene and dropped into a new one before I fully grasped what was happening. It was like something triggered the shift, and it had nothing to do with me.

I kept my eyes squeezed shut for another moment before finally braving our new reality.

I wished I hadn't.

I found myself standing in only my unmentionables in the middle of the modiste's shop, while several horrified noblewomen stared first at me, then at the man towering beside me on the dressmaker's raised platform.

The prince wasn't scantily clad, I noticed crossly.

He looked as fine and dapper as any high-society man out for an afternoon jaunt.

He wore a deep blue tailcoat, tan trousers that showed his muscular form, a starched white shirt, a perfectly tied cravat, and a pair of Hessian boots that gleamed.

I caught sight of myself in the mirror across from where we stood, and I decided right then and there I hated the Book of Nightmares.

I was wearing nothing but soft lace and ribbons and looked like a present waiting to be opened.

Garters held cream thigh-high stockings up that also featured little ribbons tied in neat bows.

Sloth peered down at me, his attention roaming all the way to my stockinged feet before he dragged it up and slipped his hand out of mine.

His mask of indifference settled firmly into place.

"And *you*."

The woman swung those shrewd eyes to me; then she shoved her way between me and Sloth, holding up a swath of fabric she'd wrenched out of the dressmaker's hands to shield his prying eyes from my nearly naked form.

"Cover yourself at once, my lady! What on earth will your fiancé think if he hears of this? And right before the betrothal ball tonight too! Lord have mercy, this is a scandal in the making."

The other women all clucked their tongues in agreement.

I wrapped myself in the bolt of fabric. This felt like punishment from the Liber Noctem for passing the last test and denying Logan Blaze.

"I—"

Apparently, the woman wasn't finished scolding me.

She wagged a finger in my face.

"Mark my words, if the marquess finds out, someone's head will roll. To think you allowed that libertine to stare at you so thoroughly. One would even believe you enjoyed his attention like some common harlot."

I took a deep breath to center myself.

I was feeling... strange after this story shift.

I wasn't sure if it was because the magic that created the stories was becoming more powerful, even with the dark book twisting it, as evidenced by our change in clothing this time. Or if there was some other force at play.

Whatever the cause, the more the woman insulted me, the darker my thoughts became. The phoenix tear warmed in my hand, like it knew I might call upon it again and was letting me know it was ready.

Part of me wanted to lash out, to set my magic on anyone who dared to reprimand me or attempt to shame me. I did not like when women were called harlots for the simple fact that they had physical desire.

Darkness swelled up, eager to do my bidding. Shadows seeming to uncoil like a nest of vipers ready to strike.

I blinked as horrific images flashed across my mind.

Blood splattered across the fine silks. The bodies of the women in this room lying in unmoving heaps.

Their eyes unfocused and lifeless.

I could end them all, trap them in nightmares until their minds shattered, and go about my day. My hand tightened on the phoenix tear.

For some reason, I knew it would be so easy to direct those thoughts, to punish and seek vengeance right now.

My parents' worried faces suddenly crossed my mind.

They would be *horrified* by my twisted thoughts.

And rightfully so. They'd raised me to be loving and kind.

Not...some callous murderess. That thought was enough to wrench me out of whatever had overtaken me.

The prince shot me a concerned look.

I offered a slight shake of my head; we'd discuss it when we weren't surrounded by members of high society who loved to gossip.

I exhaled slowly, the sensation calming. That was...intense. I was starting to worry that I was teetering close to a nervous breakdown. My thoughts had never been so...twisted. I was a dreamer by nature, and wherever those images came from, they felt *wrong*.

Sloth had stepped down from the platform at the woman's insistence, but he arched a brow in my direction.

His mood was getting downright stormy.

I didn't need any psychic abilities to see he was close to reacting to the woman's proximity to me and whatever dark feelings he likely sensed that she was stirring within me.

Being the supreme sociopath he was, I knew he wouldn't hesitate to make my bloody thoughts reality.

I needed to figure out what this next test was before someone got hurt. Possibly by my own hand if I was playing the part of noblewoman who moonlighted as a killer.

Or, more likely, a dreamweaver being manipulated into some casual murder by a dark book of magic.

I scrambled to think of which historical romance this was, but it was difficult to do when I was standing in a few scraps of lace and had just daydreamed a massacre that felt like a memory more than simply the Liber Noctem's newest interference. But that couldn't be true.

Unless something else was slowly taking over me.

When faced with the possibility of losing my mind in public, I did what any main character would do.

I pasted on a bright smile and batted my lashes like everything was completely fine and I hadn't been envisioning their murders in graphic detail.

"No one's head will roll, my lady." Unless, of course, the Liber Noctem came out to play. I shoved that thought aside.

I had no idea who she was, but that didn't seem to land since I'd called her a lady and I assumed that was a sufficient honorific for the time period.

"You know Lord Winters enjoys chaos," I guessed based on all the historical romances I read where a rake or rogue was often at its center, stirring up all sorts of fun drama.

These women seemed well acquainted with his debauched ways.

A ripple of irritation went through me that I promptly ignored. I wanted Dark Lore to stay locked away.

"You ought to have known better," the chiding woman sniffed.

"You're absolutely right. But we have a betrothal ball to prepare for. I'm sure we can keep this minor hiccup from my wonderful husband-to-be." I turned my charm up a notch and faced the prince. "Isn't that right, Lord Winters?"

Sloth leveled me with an icy glare.

He looked like we'd entered his own personal hell.

I'd already guessed that social gatherings were his least favorite things. Second only to playing nice with others.

"Your secret is safe with me, *my lady*."

That sounded like a threat more than a promise, but my heart gave an extra pitter-patter all the same.

This time when I smiled, it was genuine.

As far as Trials went, how bad could attending one little ball with a grumpy prince be?

SEVENTEEN
Prince Sloth

DESPITE MY URGE to remain close to the dreamweaver, I left Lore in the dressmaker's shop and stepped onto the sidewalk. Separating now, when the stories were unpredictable, wasn't ideal by any means. But with this cursed propriety getting in the way, there was little choice but to go along with it. Still, unease trickled through me at the thought of letting Lore out of my sight for long.

Horse-drawn carriages and buggies clattered by the bustling street where rows of businesses catered to the upper class.

Men in top hats tipped their brims in my direction, while ladies in their finest day dresses blushed and giggled as they passed by me with their chaperones trailing on their heels.

My scowl deepened.

Being trapped in a historical romance was low on my list of enjoyable ways to spend my time in this cursed realm.

I had no use for the strict society rules that would make things difficult for me and Lore to work alone on this next test.

I already wanted to strangle the woman who'd all but shoved me outside for her interference. At least we'd successfully moved past the last Trial. I would have liked to speak to Lore about it, to glean any information from her about what she'd felt. Clearly, that had to wait.

I glanced back into the dressmaker's boutique. I knew by my blatant dismissal that I was expected to leave but couldn't bring myself to move just yet.

Lore had gone unnaturally still for a moment, and when I'd tapped into her emotions, it felt like an ancient void had opened inside her.

One that had beckoned to me.

It was...unsettling.

Then it was gone, and she was as effervescent as ever. And I was left wondering if I'd imagined the dark tug I'd felt.

I couldn't escape the sense that I was still missing an integral piece of the puzzle when it came to her and her magic. By now, if she was a dreamweaver, she should be able to at least change small aspects of the stories we were in. The unanswered questions about her power reinforced my hesitation to leave her, no matter what propriety dictated.

An invisible tether seemed to go taut in my chest.

I rubbed my sternum, brows tugged close.

"Winters!"

I briefly shut my eyes, praying I hadn't heard my fake name being shouted. I wasn't that fortunate.

A mortal who looked to be around thirty waved at me from across the street. The only reason he hadn't reached me yet was because of the parade of carriages rolling by.

I ignored him. With luck he'd be waylaid by the traffic.

Footmen carried packages and boxes to waiting carriages for their mistresses, all of whom were giving me a wide berth.

I was thoroughly disappointed when the mortal who'd been shouting dodged the next wave of carriages and clapped me on the shoulder like we were the oldest of friends.

He clearly didn't understand the concept of personal space.

"Didn't expect to see you out and about." He scrutinized me. "Thought for certain you'd still be with Nadine until one of us dragged you out tonight."

I gave him a blank look.

He stared at me for a solid moment, then doubled over, laughing.

"You dog! You didn't remember her name?" He shook his head. "That singer has been after you for an age. She'll kill you if she knew."

That at least confirmed Lore wasn't an opera singer named Nadine I'd apparently taken liberties with. I glanced back into the dressmaker's shop where she was still milling about with the other women before returning my attention to the exuberant man. Thus far, all seemed well.

If I was forced to participate in this conversation, I might as well learn all I could. Any information might be useful for the Trial.

"I didn't take Nadine home."

I scanned the street again, feeling someone's attention on me. No one was looking our way. Still, I knew I'd felt a prickle of unease.

Which I was starting to associate with one thing.

I stole another subtle look at Lore, then glanced back at my companion.

"I ended up looking for Xavier instead."

It was a gamble. I had no way of knowing if my former master librarian would be known in the stories we visited, but the man standing beside me took it all in stride.

"That prick?" he scoffed. "I thought he left the country after stealing Autumntide's prized book."

That caught my attention. "Did Autumntide get it back?"

"Don't know. You'll have to ask him tonight. If he did, I'm sure he'll let you look it over. You know how prideful he is over his collection."

"Remind me where we're meeting him, again?"

He narrowed his gaze on me.

"His engagement ball. You know, to Lady Brimstone? The woman you loathe more than cheap wine?"

I kept my reaction minimal.

Lore's name didn't change from story to story.

I don't know why that surprised me, but I supposed I couldn't blend in by maintaining my royal title.

"Queen's tits, Winters. You sure you're not still knackered after all that bourbon last night? You were the one who sent the marquess after Xavier as an early wedding gift. To make up for all the unflattering things you had to say about his bride being the dullest, plainest woman in Season City. You told him to his face his beloved was only good for her coin purse. And to get the heir and the spare taken care of and then send her off to their country seat."

My hand curled into a fist at my side.

I was spared from knocking him out by an unlikely source.

"Oy!" A bulky man who looked to be an enforcer of some sort shouted from down the avenue. His furious gaze was locked on my companion. "Midsummer! Time to pay up."

My acquaintance's attention whipped to the angry man shoving his way through the busy streets, ignoring the shocked gasps of the ladies and the clearing of throats from the highborn men.

He swore roundly and clapped me once more on the shoulder.

"See you tonight, old fellow!"

Midsummer disappeared around the corner, and I welcomed the peace for all of one moment before a footman waved me down.

If I didn't unleash my magic and kill everyone in this story, it would be a miracle.

"Yes?" I gritted out once I realized he wouldn't speak unless I acknowledged him first.

"My lord, shall we be getting back to Snowdrift House to get you ready for tonight? You're expected at Autumntide's by nine sharp. You asked that I remind you..."

I glanced in the window at Lore. She was now fully dressed in what I assumed her character had been wearing when she'd entered the dress shop.

I wondered if she'd kept those stockings with all the tiny ribbons on. Then I immediately banished the thought.

As if she felt my attention though the window, her gaze found mine.

She looked me over, then tipped her chin, letting me know she was well and to play my part. The story seemed to be going smoothly, but I didn't trust it would last.

I stared for another moment, hesitating, then nodded back.

I'd meet her at the ball and then we'd search through her fiancé's home

for any signs of the Liber Noctem. And no matter what society deemed proper, I wouldn't be leaving her side again.

I stood in a shadowy alcove on the upper level of the Marquess of Autumntide's estate, waiting for Lore to arrive at this obnoxious party. I'd left her before but hadn't gone too far for too long.

I'd quickly discovered that our fictional townhomes were only separated by a few blocks, so I'd lingered in the shadows outside her family's home until I'd heard her carriage rolling to the front entrance, then made my way back to mine.

I'd only been here for a short time but already grew restless.

Thus far I'd avoided running into Midsummer for another inane chat, and I'd expertly dodged a few marriage-minded mothers as they vied for my attention near the punch bowl.

Apparently, in this story, I was a known rogue, but I had a title, and my sins were easily overlooked on the marriage market.

A champagne flute dangled from my grasp, near to spilling.

I held it for appearances only.

If Midsummer had been correct, if the Book of Nightmares had indeed found its way into the marquess's private collection, I wanted to be primed and ready to grab it without anything dulling my senses.

Not that one drink would impact me. Princes of Sin burned through inebriation much faster than mortals.

While I waited for Lore, I'd scouted the upper floor of the sprawling townhome and found two locked doors.

I'd guessed one was the private study of the marquess, and the other I'd wagered was his library based on the scent of leather and parchment that permeated the corridor outside the door.

It took an enormous amount of restraint to not slip inside and search it while I waited for the bride-to-be to arrive.

It would be easy enough to break into the rooms, but I held off on making a move until Lore was accounted for.

Best to not get kicked out of the ball before I had a chance to search for the dark book, especially if my character had pissed the marquess off by slandering his bride the night before. I didn't sense any dark, pulsating power coming from the corridor or home, but I wouldn't give up hope just yet. The book *had* to be close.

I suspected it would want to remain near Lore so it could accurately twist the stories as needed. Which meant Xavier had to be on the grounds.

I did a slow sweep of the first floor, then crossed over to a balcony that looked out onto the gardens. No shadows lurked, no signs of dark magic. Still, there was a growing restlessness inside me. I suspected it was mostly from the forced separation from Lore and any complications that might arise from the dark book's meddling.

I wouldn't relax until the dreamweaver was in my sight.

I returned to my position on the second floor, and the ballroom doors were suddenly thrown open. My attention fell to the herald as he cleared his throat for the announcement.

"The dowager countess Brimstone, Lady Brimstone, and the Earl of Brimstone."

A knot loosened in my chest.

I moved from the shadows and paused at the railing, watching as Lore entered the ball on the arm of the man I imagined was her fictional brother.

She looked like she'd stepped from the pages of the novel.

I had to admit that she made a striking noblewoman.

Her dark hair had been curled and pinned up, showing the long line of her elegant neck. The gown she wore was one of the palest shades of peach I'd ever seen and made her seem ethereal.

I was surprised at the deep sense of satisfaction I felt at her color choice. Though I was less surprised that her husband-to-be strode over to intercept her immediately, then pressed a chaste kiss to her gloved knuckles.

Excited titters went up around the gathering. Apparently that one pathetic act was worthy of high praise. Murmurs of how attentive he was sparked even more gossip over their union being a love match.

Even from where I stood, I saw the slight flush of her cheeks.

My hand tightened on the stem of my glass.

The marquess escorted her onto the checkered dance floor and a waltz promptly struck up.

Lore's gaze subtly darted around the ballroom.

I wondered if she was looking for me or simply taking in the sight of another one of her stories come to life.

I ignored them and scanned the crowd for Xavier again. I didn't think he'd be bold enough to show up, given the falling-out he'd had with this group, but it was best to remain on alert. He would likely sneak in and try to blend in.

Perhaps he'd come in disguise. I watched all the footmen and staff coming and going, searching for any signs of nervousness.

I slowly took in every nook and corner, then allowed my senses to spread out, searching for his familiar aura, the same way I'd done over the last half hour.

He still wasn't in attendance.

My attention settled back on the waltz that seemed to be never ending.

As the couple of the hour swept around the floor, the marquess's hand slowly strayed lower, his palm laying a possessive claim as he pressed Lore closer.

They were skirting the lines of propriety.

And the crowd couldn't get enough.

Lore peered up into his face, a bright smile lifting the edges of her full lips.

I downed my champagne.

This song had to be nearing its conclusion.

I slowly made my way to the first floor, slipping between members of Society who were openly watching the couples spinning around the dance floor, and ignoring others who tried to catch my eye.

Most were gossiping about the betrothed marquess and his lovely lady, who were dancing scandalously close.

I prowled around the ballroom, keeping them in sight.

The last thing we needed was for the marquess to attempt a private interlude and waste more of our precious time.

I waited until the song almost ended before striding over to Lore.

A few shocked gasps followed in my wake. But if I was to play the role of unaffected libertine, I'd own it.

I stopped close enough to the happy couple that Autumntide was forced to step back. He stiffened when he realized who'd approached.

I summarily dismissed him and inclined my head at Lore.

"May I have the next dance, Lady Brimstone?"

"Winters." A deep frown formed on the marquess's face before his years of good breeding kicked in and his expression smoothed out. "Of course. So long as you take care with my lady."

My jaw tensed as I held my hand out, palm up, waiting. I wasn't asking for his consent. "Lady Brimstone?"

Lore's brows hit her hairline, but she quickly schooled her features and curtsied. "My lord. I'd be honored."

The marquess didn't seem pleased to relinquish his partner to me, but there was nothing he could do without causing a scene.

A fact I was well aware of, given the historical setting.

I might not be an expert with Regency-era romances, but I was well acquainted with mortal history, especially involving the peerage.

Dancing two songs in a row would cause a scene, so he couldn't claim the next dance. And Lore hadn't had time to have her dance card filled out before her so-called fiancé had swept her away. There was no good reason for either of them to deny me the dance. Which would serve as a way for Lore and me to finally speak again.

I slipped an arm around her waist and placed her hand on my shoulder, then led us through the next dance.

"You're glowering like a sociopath again," she said, her smile still in place. "Try not to look so pissy."

"I find ballrooms and dancing abhorrent. Along with idle gossip."

"So you mean to tell me your court never hosts balls or parties?"

I bristled at her tone. "Occasionally. For practical purposes."

"Such as?"

"Marriages. Or other ceremonial unions." I thought of the last ball I'd hosted for my court. "They're mostly used for networking. Though when we do throw an event, it's normally bookish in nature. We tend to decorate based on themes. The last wedding was between an astronomer and astrologer, so we turned the castle into the cosmos."

"That sounds rather romantic."

I almost missed a step and corrected our movements before answering. "Practical. My court doesn't feed into frivolous emotions."

Lore shook her head.

"Don't any of you believe in the magic of falling in love?"

"Not particularly. Romance has devolved into performance over substance. It's become less authentic and therefore odious to deal with at best; my court prefers direct honesty over anything that feels...transactional. Why play a coy game when both parties want the end result?"

"Perhaps the so-called game is simply a method to establish a foundation built on effort and balance." She narrowed her gaze on me. "You think true love is transactional?"

I felt Lore's attention boring holes into me but pretended not to notice.

"I think romance, at its heart, is essentially an act of pomp and circumstance. It can become...distracting."

Unlike my brother Envy's former one-night rule that he'd used to stoke jealousy in his lovers, I had no qualms about bedding the same partner more than once. Things only ended when emotional attachments formed.

They tended to create an imbalance and complicated matters.

My circle was very much of the mind-versus-heart mentality.

Since my court dealt with things in an intellectual manner, most parted ways amicably as soon as they recognized the signs of emotional bonding. They, too, wanted to spend their time holed up reading—focusing on academic pursuits.

Science, mathematics, medicine, astrology, astronomy, philosophy, architecture, the occult, art, and history were only some of the scholarly focuses members of House Sloth dedicated their lives to.

Along with most of my court, I avoided inviting unnecessary drama and conflict into my life whenever possible. Though some texts I'd read on relationships indicated I simply hadn't met my match yet.

It was one subject I didn't care to pursue, so I left it be.

She sighed. "You could at least tell me I look pretty."

I glanced down at her, drawing my brows together. "Why would I do that?"

"Forget it."

We moved effortlessly across the marble floor, silent until I brought my lips close to her ear and murmured, "You don't look pretty. You look like complete and utter ruination, Lore."

She drew back to stare up at me.

"You really need to work on compliments, Blondie. Being called a pretty disaster won't win you any hearts."

A smiled tugged at the corners of my mouth.

"You misunderstand. Causing ruination is far more dangerous than simply being pretty. You are intriguing and therefore wholly captivating. Men go to war over less."

I jerked my chin at the edge of the dance floor.

"Your fiancé is ready to murder anyone who comes too close. He's danced with you once and he's already out of his senses. Which is a problem since I need to steal you away unnoticed."

Lore's expression shifted. "You found something? About the book?"

I gave her a sharp nod of assent. "Top floor."

Other couples were straying too close for us to speak more.

She nibbled her lower lip.

I inadvertently pressed her closer and her attention shot up.

"Step on my hem," she demanded. When I didn't immediately catch on, she sighed. "Getting it mended will give me an excuse to disappear for a while."

I gave her an appreciative look. She was cunning in all the right ways. I spun us around then made sure my boot caught in her skirt.

A loud ripping noise drew several pairs of eyes our way.

The scowls shot at me were filled with loathing. One would think I'd kissed her senselessly and impugned her honor right there in front of the whole crowd instead of accidentally tearing her skirt.

"Apologies, my lady." I escorted her off the dance floor and leaned in. "I'll be waiting upstairs."

I'd been standing behind a potted fern for only a few moments when I heard soft footsteps coming my way.

I reached out and yanked Lore into the alcove, then held a finger to my lips. Her fiancé had been trailing behind her until he'd gotten waylaid by Midsummer. I wanted to ensure he was truly distracted.

A beat passed and I slowly became aware of the fact that Lore was pressed against me, her warmth enticing…

I gently pushed her forward and silently indicated for her to move down the corridor. She shot me a questioning look but didn't comment.

We got to the end of the hallway without being intercepted by any stragglers or servants and I let my senses filter out, searching for anyone approaching. I heard nothing but the sounds of the party downstairs.

I closed my hand over the doorknob and released a tendril of magic; the lock clicked open.

I ushered Lore inside and didn't speak until I'd closed and locked the door behind us. I waited a beat, hoping I'd sense the wrongness of the Liber Noctem's power seeping into the room. There was nothing. If Xavier had been caught and handed the book over, it wasn't here. I would feel that dark magic anywhere.

I gave the library a perfunctory glance to be sure we were indeed alone, then I peered down at her.

"Are you all right?" I asked.

Lore gave me a bemused smile. "If you keep fussing, I might think you're starting to like me, Sociopath."

"I was talking about the Trials."

"Oh." She lifted a shoulder. "I think this test might be patience."

"And the last one?"

She didn't meet my probing gaze. "Desire."

"Interesting." I rolled my shoulders back, noticing the tension in them for the first time. "Based on a conversation I had earlier, I think the Liber Noctem might be somewhere close by. If not this estate, someplace the marquess frequents. Have you sensed anything...odd?"

I still didn't feel the dark, raging power I normally did. So if it was on the grounds, I wagered it wasn't even on this floor.

Lore began walking toward the nearest bookshelf, her gloved fingers trailing over the well-oiled spines.

She paused at a shelf with a rectangular box and snapped the lid open. She plucked a gilded stiletto dagger up and admired it.

"Well, there was one odd thing that happened. In the dress shop...I had a vision." She finally turned to look at me. "I'd been daydreaming about graphically murdering the women. But the daydreams were strange; they almost felt like memories. Not mine, someone else's. Which is why I think this might be about patience. I was close to snapping when the dowager countess kept tossing around insults."

I schooled my features.

The Liber Noctem had impacted both Xavier and me when we'd been near it, stirring up dark emotions.

It didn't surprise me that it made Lore feel the same way.

But the visions were troubling. In all the texts I'd read on the Liber Noctem, that possibility was never mentioned. Maybe it had to do with being Nyantha's champion.

I motioned at the leather settee. "Sit."

Lore made an incredulous sound then swiped a pillow off a nearby high-backed chair and tossed it past me. "Fetch."

I stared at her for a moment, then couldn't stop the bark of laughter from escaping. I was thankful she hadn't flung the stiletto at me.

She crossed her arms, careful to not stab herself with the blade she still held, her expression less than amused.

I shrugged off my tailcoat and tossed it over the back of the settee and loosened the cravat at my throat.

She watched me without uttering a single word.

"Please, sit. I'm going to attempt to bring you to my library. I need to be comfortable, and you need to be near if it's to work. Physical contact is probably best."

Her scowl disappeared.

"If we're trapped in this realm for the duration of the Trials, how are you going to take us there?"

"Come find out."

I took a seat and spread my arms across the back of the settee, waiting. Curiosity got the best of her, and she slowly approached.

"There's not much room for—"

I reached over and dragged her onto my lap. Her body molded against mine, warm and inviting, and I was noticing far too many other details for either of our own good.

For a second, neither one of us moved. I recovered first.

"Empty your thoughts, relax, and let me in."

EIGHTEEN
Lore

Lowering my mental shield seemed like a *very* bad idea at the moment.

For starters, my heart was pounding so hard I knew the prince felt it.

And second, I was having some wildly inappropriate thoughts that I did not want him to be privy to.

When he'd pulled me onto his lap, all quiet confidence and brooking no room for argument, I quickly discovered I might have just developed a new library fantasy. Starring him. It was terribly inconvenient.

"Lore?"

"One second. I'm trying."

He released an amused huff and reclined, his movements lazy and unbothered. The complete opposite of how I was feeling.

I wondered how much practice he had to be so at ease.

I told myself to get a grip. Nestling against his hard chest while being perched on his lap was completely normal.

"Easy."

Sloth's hands came down firmly on my hips, holding me in place.

I hadn't realized I was fidgeting. Unfortunately, the prince *had* noticed. And he'd... reacted.

I froze.

I tried not to think about the hardness pressing into my backside.

Or the tense way the prince held himself perfectly still behind me, his grip tightening ever so slightly on my waist.

For a fleeting moment, I convinced myself he ground against me.

All thoughts fled as my focus narrowed to where we touched.

His body was so warm and firm against mine.

Maybe I'd been wrong about the dragon shifter test; maybe *this* was desire or seduction. If Sloth moved his hands up, if he skimmed them along my silhouette, I might combust.

My mental shield dropped faster than my inhibitions, and the next thing I knew, his presence filled me.

Relax, Lore, he said directly into my mind. *Let me lead.*

Relaxing while he was hard as granite beneath me and inside my head seemed fairly impossible. Especially when I started picturing him on his knees, slowly undoing the ribbons on my garters.

He groaned.

"I'm doing my best to get it under control," he said. "But you might want to focus on something else."

I couldn't tell if he'd spoken aloud or in my head because I was too busy being mortified that he'd heard my thoughts.

I tried to focus on the Book of Nightmares, the Trials, the danger that was pressing in. Then I forced myself to think about this story, and if my patience wasn't being tested, try to identify what was.

For his part, Sloth kept his thoughts from me and didn't speak in my mind again until he'd...recovered.

Once he had, we both relaxed. Marginally.

A moment later, it felt like he'd wrapped my essence with his and then we were funneling through time and space.

When we stopped, I sucked in a sharp breath.

We were no more solid than ghosts, but that didn't matter.

Oh, my gods, I thought, glancing around.

A giant tree with multicolored leaves filled the space, the towering shelves all around it filled with books that gleamed. A faint glow threaded through the branches, sending shifting colors across the shelves.

The prince stepped back toward a table stacked with texts, but I couldn't tear my gaze from the chamber. It was pure magic, and the tree was its heart.

Its leaves rustled like pages being turned in books.

The shelves stretched higher than seemed possible, vanishing into starlight overhead, and ladders drifted smoothly along rails, guided by unseen hands.

The air itself smelled of ink, parchment, and something older—like the weight of every story ever told pressed into the space around me and created its own magical aroma.

How I could smell in this form was a mystery I didn't care to solve.

The walls seemed to be carved from shadow and moonlight, arching up into a domed ceiling that allowed the night sky to peek down into the room.

I slowly spun in place.

Between the shelves, alcoves invited readers to come in and explore. There were cushioned window seats tucked beneath the stained-glass windows, armchairs angled toward the tree's otherworldly glow, and small tables scattered throughout.

The chamber felt vast but welcoming. It was the kind of space where time fell away completely, and someone could lose themselves in a book and never mind being lost at all. This was only a fraction of House Sloth, and I was hopelessly in love.

"It smells divine in here," I said aloud.

Sloth shot a look over his shoulder, his brows pinched. Whatever he was thinking, he didn't share.

This is the most beautiful library I've ever seen, I thought to myself.

I was suddenly aware of another presence. One that felt like it preened at my comment.

You are a most unexpected delight. And clearly of superior intelligence. The prince should study your charm. He clearly has much to learn in that area. Though I suppose he has his own gifts.

My ghostly form shot an incredulous look at the prince. He rolled his eyes.

Library, this is Lore. She's a dreamweaver and we're in need of information that can help us with the Trials and her magic.

My eyes rounded. He had a library that *spoke* to him and was not afraid to sass him. I never wanted to leave.

In fact, this was where I lived now, even if that meant staying a weird apparition. I wondered where the essence of the Library was and if I could give it the equivalent of belly rubs. It had a strange combination of dog and cat energy that just begged to be loved on.

Sloth gave me an exasperated look, and I realized he was still very much connected to my thoughts, and I might as well be shouting them to him.

The Library took on an air of gentlemanly charm.

It is a great honor to host such an esteemed guest. I am but your most humble servant. Whatever you need, simply ask and it shall be yours, O mighty one. And, no—it paused for dramatic effect—*I am not speaking of you, Prince.*

Duly noted. The texts, Library...

The one I'd pulled for you last is still on the research table. Make haste and finish the passage I pulled.

Sloth released a long sigh, as if the Library's attitude was tedious, but I had never been more entertained in my life.

I strode over to the table where the prince was and scanned the title before the book magically flipped open and the Library resumed whatever research the prince had last left off on.

Philosophy of Sacrifices Throughout the Ages

A case study of points and counterpoints in the quest to determine if good versus evil exists beyond theory in mortal trappings.

It's not easy to maintain the lies we tell ourselves while still hiding behind the pretty masks of deception we wear. When concealing our ugliest truths is no longer an option, that is when the ultimate test of mettle begins.

When we're pushed to our limits, when we're forced to break, do we become the villain, or do we choose to be the hero?

Some scientists wonder if genetic makeup impacts the outcome.

Does the child nurtured turn evil when pushed into darkness, or does it remain good?

Madness, sanity, one coin, two sides.

Is a simple toss all it takes to determine the victor?

The pages flipped until they neared the middle of the text.

If I lived forever, I would never get over how incredible it was to have an enchanted library.

Some scholars wonder if the essence of life can be transferred or trapped. What is immortality? Can that which lives ever truly die? Or does it simply change forms? Historical documents indicate even mortals never cease to exist; they simply exchange one state of being for the next.

Is it magic? Is it alchemy? Or is it simply the desire to live on that drives the evolutionary process? What is the catalyst for change?

Sloth stared down at the page, his jaw tight. *Library, bring me anything you have on dreamweavers and their magic.*

There is only one small text.

The leaves in the tree rustled again, the pages flipping through until a book flew off the shelf and landed gracefully on the table.

I watched, spellbound, as the pages flipped open and the Library stopped on the section it had been searching for.

Dreamweavers are blessed with the ability to create fantasy from reality. The changes can be small — altering the color of a rug, or curtains.

Sometimes they shift the color of their hair or eyes. The magic comes from their imagination. Not much is known about how it manifests.

Sloth slanted a glance my way. I had a feeling we'd be trying to change my hair or eye color soon to test my power.

I need the legend of the lost phoenix. Flip to the section on the phoenix tear.

The Library muttered something about manners, but in the next instant, the requested book was there, and I was completely taken with how beautiful it was.

The pages were illustrated, the chapter headers works of art. It looked to be an illuminated manuscript, and I couldn't begin to guess its age.

> *…after its mate was killed via a creature born of nightmares, the phoenix flew across the realms, crying tears of sorrow. As they fell, they exploded, creating craters that later became hot springs.*

The pages flipped…

> *The Goddess of Night caught the final tear in her palm, and instead of exploding and maiming her, it became imbued with her own power.*
>
> *The great goddess never forgave herself—it was her nightmare magic that created the monster that slayed the phoenix's mate. Both the phoenix and the goddess became consumed with darkness.*
>
> *It is believed—*

I'd barely finished reading when we were yanked out of the Library and funneled back into our bodies.

I blinked slowly, readjusting to the abrupt shift. That was…peculiar and amazing and a little hard to reconcile. One would think I'd be used to magic by now, but I could live a hundred lifetimes and would still be just as awed.

Sloth shifted beneath me, reminding me of our current seating arrangement, and I felt the prince's mind slip from mine.

I promptly erected my mental shield again before I shot any unwanted thoughts his way.

I thought about the last text, the phoenix who'd lost its mate. The story struck a deep chord of sorrow in me. I couldn't imagine losing my love and having to go on. Especially as an immortal. What kind of monster would it take to kill a phoenix, which shouldn't be able to die? I wanted to find the lost phoenix and share its burden.

A fissure of sympathy worked its way in for Nyantha, too. The guilt she must have felt...I couldn't fathom it. It didn't excuse her actions after that, but it certainly gave me a little more understanding of how she might have dived fully into the darkness to avoid feeling those emotions. As a god, it must have been foreign to experience something so powerful.

"What do you—"

"I *knew* I couldn't trust you."

Sloth and I both jerked our attention to the open door. The marquess stepped fully into the room, and I glanced down, noticing the pistol in his hand.

I tensed.

"*Murder and the Marquess*," I said, finally pinpointing the book.

Sloth's arm tightened around my waist.

The Liber Noctem had gone deep into the archives of my mind for this story. I hadn't read it in ages. I tried to remember what I'd been feeling when I'd read it, what had been going on in my life that stood out to the dark book.

Then I remembered. And I wished I hadn't.

The plot slowly came back to me, and as it did, a deep sense of dread settled in. I believed I knew exactly what this test was. Loyalty.

It was the only time in my life when I'd felt betrayed by someone close to me, and the memory of it made me relive that horrible time as if it were happening right now.

"Autumntide, be reasonable," Sloth drawled, yanking me back to the here and now. I knew he wasn't as calm as he sounded. He was a coil ready to snap. "It's not what it seems."

The marquess's face turned an angry shade of red as he lifted the gun.

"Oh? So you're not, in fact, taking liberties with my fiancée? In my personal library? During my betrothal ball like the cad you are?"

"She fell. I was just helping her up."

It was one of the most insincere-sounding excuses and I wondered if Sloth was trying to get himself shot. I was stuck somewhere between the memories of my past and the scene playing out before me. It was such an odd sense of déjà vu.

"Do not insult my intelligence. Anyone with eyes could see the way you were watching her tonight."

"You're overreacting."

"Like hell I am. Do you actually want her, or are you just interested in taking what's mine?"

I flinched at that.

When I'd read that line in the original book, I had felt it with my whole soul. I'd been in the marquess's shoes, and it hadn't felt good. One of my best friends had kissed the boy I'd been courting at a festival.

We were still in school, in that age between full adulthood and late childhood, and it had felt like the worst sort of pain when they'd come out of the woods, hand in hand, cheeks flushed, lips swollen. I'd tried to get past it, but our friendship never recovered. I never spoke to the boy again, but that wasn't what tore my heart in two. I missed my friend and our easy laughter and the fun we'd had. The trust had been broken, though, and no matter how hard I tried, I couldn't get back to that time before.

"Put the gun down before you hurt her or yourself."

My fake fiancé knocked the hammer back on the pistol.

"Darling, get up and leave the room while I restore your honor."

My heart was beating so fast I thought it might stop. The moment I got up, he was going to shoot the prince. I had to do something...

"My lord, it isn't what it appears. I really did trip—"

"*Don't.* It's bad enough you're here, with *him*. Unchaperoned. I'd thought you were above the common whores he surrounds himself with."

Sloth made to get up, but I dug my heels in.

The marquess didn't misread the action for what it was.

As far as he was concerned, I'd protected the enemy.

His arm jerked to the side, and I saw the moment he decided to pull the trigger. He was going to put a bullet in Sloth's head.

Something violent stirred deep within me.

I didn't think; I acted. I let the stiletto dagger I still held fly with far more skill and precision than I knew I possessed.

It hit him directly in the eye.

He collapsed before he had time to cry out, the life instantly blinking out of his remaining eye as it stared upward, unseeing.

Dead. The marquess was very much deceased. By my hand.

For a moment, Sloth and I both sat motionless.

I couldn't believe I'd done that. I'd really killed the marquess.

And I had no idea how I'd managed to throw the dagger with such ruthless skill. I'd never done something like that in my life.

The fact that I was thinking of that after taking a life sent me teetering closer to the edge. This was clearly the start of hysterics.

It didn't matter that he was a character in a book—in this realm, in this reality, he had very much been a living, breathing person. Filled with hopes and dreams, and I'd taken that from him. Without one ounce of remorse.

What kind of monster did that make me?

"It's okay." The prince ran a soothing hand down my spine. "He would have shot us. You did the right thing."

The contact broke me out of my shocked stupor.

I glanced down at my hands, wondering at the lack of trembling.

Then I promptly shot up off Sloth's lap and vomited onto the expensive woven rug.

And that was how the marquess's best friend found us. Me, dry heaving onto the rug, and Sloth towering over me.

His gaze dropped to the man bleeding out, his face awash in horror.

"What have you done, Winters?"

I went to open my mouth, to proclaim his innocence. But he stepped in front of me and casually tucked his hands into his pockets.

"He tried to shoot me." He flicked his attention to the corpse. "He missed."

Before we could plan an escape, the lord started yelling for help. Within moments staff came running and Sloth was hauled out, shooting one last look at me over his shoulder, before he was gone for good.

I don't know why he didn't fight back when he could have easily taken them. And a trickle of fear found its way to my heart.

Maybe the Liber Noctem hadn't allowed him to. Maybe this was where the story was about to go horribly wrong for us and the real test was about to begin.

"I say, what a tragic turn of events."

The dowager primly sipped her tea in our parlor.

"Winters was always prone to scandal, but murder?" she tsked. "What will become of his estate? He's the last of his line. Maybe one of his harlots will rise above her station after all. Wouldn't that be something? If he left his fortune to that *actress*?"

"*Mother.*" I was aghast at my fake parent's callousness. "Is that all you can think of? The man is set to die."

I tore my attention from the window to stare at the woman who was my mother in this story. She could not be more different from my real mother if she tried. My mother was kind, empathetic. Someone who always chose to see the good in others and knew flaws were simply places waiting for growth.

This woman was superficial and downright joyful over someone else's misfortune. It rankled me to my core. And not simply because it felt like the walls of fate were closing in and I could barely draw a deep breath.

They'd been building an execution block all morning and I was scrambling to come up with a way to get us out of this nightmare before it got worse.

The trouble was, I didn't want to risk shifting stories and leave Sloth behind. And they were guarding him in some dungeon and refusing all visitors.

My fake mother lifted her chin imperiously.

"You're fortunate that no one is looking too closely at you. And you better hope his death proves to be the biggest scandal of it all. Otherwise, one might question how you were found with the body of your beloved and his estranged best friend. *Alone.*"

I kept my eye roll internal. "I already told you. I was stealing a few moments of peace in the library. Winters happened upon the open door. And then before he left, Autumntide barged in. He drew a pistol and…"

And then I'd murdered him without a second thought.

The darkness lurking inside me seemed to thrill at the memory; meanwhile the part of me that wasn't completely deranged fought to keep the few sips of tea I'd had down.

The dowager's gaze narrowed on me. It was the same story I'd given to the police. It would be difficult to prove otherwise.

Only the prince and I knew the truth now that the marquess was dead.

I faced the window again, mind racing with the same plan I'd been working out all morning. I would have to wait until Sloth was brought out from where they'd been holding him and then make my move.

It wasn't ideal, but there were no better options I could think of.

I didn't want to leave him behind. He was a good ally to have. And if I was being completely honest with myself, I might be the one being tested, but I couldn't imagine going through this nightmare world alone.

A short while later, we got word that the execution was set for noon.

The trial, if they'd even *had* one, had been some swift meeting that was closed to the public.

Sloth's fate had been decided in less than an hour. And now, as my pretend mother and brother stood in the growing crowd, getting jostled closer to the looming execution block, my nerves were almost entirely shot.

Pretend Fable gave me a concerned look that I waved away.

The silk gloves I wore were damp with my sweat.

I'd checked and double-checked the phoenix tear and had tucked it inside one of my gloves while dressing.

I wasn't entirely sure if it needed skin contact to work, and I didn't want to risk not getting the tight gloves off in time if it did.

I swore I felt the stone humming against my skin, primed and ready.

The crowd seethed with impatience, growing more irate the longer we all waited for the prisoner to be hauled out. I stared at the block.

I'd thought he was set to be hanged. I'd been wrong.

They were going to *behead* him.

He might be immortal, but I wasn't sure how that would hold up to having his head sliced from his shoulders. And I didn't want to find out.

I glanced down, my pulse racing. A few shadows seemed to stream out from my glove. I shot a nervous look around; no one was paying any attention to me.

Until that suddenly changed. Recognition hit a few of the nearest attendees.

They unnecessarily shoved into my family and leered.

"Stand back."

Our footman shielded us from more errant hits.

But it wouldn't be enough if the crowd turned on us. I hated the idea of anyone else ending up in harm's way because of this cursed Trial.

I ignored the panicked feeling spreading.

I reminded myself this realm thrived on fear, and I was unintentionally feeding it in gluttonous amounts.

The midday sun beat down on us and I cursed the layers I was forced to wear for propriety's sake.

Then, when the shouting and shoving had been stoked to a fever pitch, the guards made their entrance. Twelve heavily armored men strode out, six in the front and six behind their prisoner.

Sloth was bound and chained. His face was bruised and his hair mussed.

He scanned the crowd, his face a cold, ruthless mask; then his gaze found mine. All other sounds vanished as he held my stare.

There was no panic. No silent pleading.

Just a slight incline. As if the idiot was saying goodbye and good luck.

That strange pit of darkness writhed in annoyance.

I remembered what he'd said back at the tavern, that we could still be harmed in the stories. And that if he died here, he would actually be killed.

I exhaled a shaking breath, feeling less certain of my plan.

If I miscalculated, I could end up sending him to his death.

I cursed the damn prince for taking the blame.

"On this day, by order of the king and the magistrate of Season City acting on his behalf, we have found one Lord Ashmore Winters guilty. As such, he is hereby sentenced to death by beheading. At once."

The man kicked the back of Sloth's knees out, forcing him to kneel.

"Any last words, scum?"

The sociopath was back. The prince glared over his shoulder and the look he flashed was so filled with malice, the crowd stopped chanting for his death.

"Right, then. Executioner, at the ready."

Sloth exhaled and glanced back at me.

His expression was completely closed off. If he knew I was planning something, he gave no indication of it. I really, really hoped this worked.

As the executioner slowly took the stairs, I made my move.

I raced forward and hoisted myself up, rolling and tangling in my gods-damned skirt before reaching the block.

"You bastard!" I yelled, drawing a hand back as if I was ready to slap him. The crowd cheered for the dramatics. "I'll kill you myself!"

The guards were shocked by my outburst but also seemed sympathetic to my cause. The bride whose beloved was slain. No one made a move to stop me.

I'd been hoping for that. I wrapped my hands around Sloth's neck, and his brows hit his hairline as I squeezed a little for dramatic effect.

"You're going to get yourself killed, Lore."

"Hush, villain!"

I concentrated on the stone in my hand; this time I would manifest the gods-forsaken ocean if it was the last thing I did. We needed to be as far away as possible. I swore I felt a ripple go through the stone when I made contact with the prince. Like whatever fueled its power was *excited*.

This time, the phoenix tear didn't hesitate to meet my call.

Apparently, it didn't want to lose our Prince un-Charming yet either. Later, I'd have to consider why, but for now, I was too thankful to worry.

I held on to Sloth and felt the rolling waves as I ignored the shouts from the guards, the cries for us to be slain as witches.

I sent my shadows out with a mental plea to save us, unsure if it was working until I heard the screams and sounds of people running from us.

I widened my stance so I could lean into the rhythm and not lose my footing.

I kept my focus turned inward, until I actually felt the salty mist of the sea on my face.

When I finally opened my eyes, we were exactly where I'd envisioned.

The ship—*Silverbeak's Wrath*—was still covered in ribbons of shadows, but the cerulean ocean to our left was unmistakable.

There was no longer any bloodthirsty crowd; Sloth was unchained, clad back in his fighting leathers.

I was still in my day dress, but I didn't care.

We'd survived the execution block. And I knew it hadn't been patience like I first thought. It was definitely loyalty I'd been tested for.

I didn't leave the prince when it would have been easy to do so. I stayed and plotted his rescue. And not just for selfish reasons. I couldn't bear the thought of him being killed because I'd taken the easy road and left him.

Suddenly, another vision crashed through me.

This time there was no mistaking what they were; they were memories that weren't mine but felt so visceral, so real, that I wanted to scream.

I saw reassuring hands reaching out as a friend dangled from the edge of a cliff, but instead of helping her up, I watched in horror as the woman slowly ground her heel into the other's fingers, letting her fall. The memory expanded and I saw another person hanging on to the cliff; his eyes widened as his devotion for whoever he stared at twisted into betrayal.

Feminine laughter rang out, sharp and delighted, as her lover begged, only to realize the one he'd revered had damned him. His shock, his heartbreak, seared into me as if *I* had been the one to betray him. I wanted to cry out, to save him, but it was too late. He fell into the abyss. Then I was yanked out of the vision and stood blinking in the rays of the sun off the ocean.

I wondered if I was losing my mind, or if the Book of Nightmares was punishing me for winning the last test. The vision only lasted a few seconds, so I ignored it for now and focused on claiming my small victory.

"I did it!" I tried to banish the dark cloud still hanging over my thoughts, but the falseness in my tone was hard to disguise.

Sloth was stoic as ever, but when I glanced up into his face, I knew he was thrilled. It was that slight twinkle in his eyes that gave him away.

"Is this *Silverbeak's Wrath*?"

The shadows were still slowly streaming back, but I didn't read many pirate books. "I'm pretty sure."

"Another shifter story?"

I gave him an indignant look.

"I'll have you know, I read more than shifter romances. As was clearly evident by the historical murder we just escaped."

He shook his head. "And this delightful tale features..."

"A pirate king. More of a fantasy adventure. And he's obsessed with booty. Be thankful you're not about to lose that pretty head."

Blondie's eyes skimmed down my frame in cool assessment.

If I were being delusional, I'd almost swear a muscle ticked in his jaw. By the time I blinked again, his expression was unreadable.

"We'll see."

I grinned.

"While it's flattering that you think my bottom is a treasure, I meant gold and jewels. The pirate king is hunting the ultimate treasure in the story. A sea serpent–octopus–unicorn hybrid. Its scales are worth a fortune."

I tried to recall the name.

"Serp-i-corn. Uni-pus? You get the idea." I waved my hand around in dismissal. "It's a giant sea monster with a horn, basically."

"Let's not be too hasty, darling," an unfamiliar voice purred from behind us. "I'd consider parting with some coins for time with you alone."

Before I could turn around, the man who'd spoken with that low drawl grabbed a handful of my butt and squeezed.

I yelped, more from surprise than pain, but his grip hadn't been gentle.

"Your ass is treasure enough for my tastes. And we've been out at sea for too many lonely nights. Ain't that right, boys?"

Shouts rang out in agreement and my blood turned to ice.

I'd done it, all right.

I'd *finally* used my magic and brought us to the story I'd been imagining.

But with Sloth's life hanging in the balance, I hadn't had the time or the space to think it through.

This might not be the best book for us to be trapped in.

I spun around.

The shadow ribbons had fully receded into the phoenix tear, and I was able to take quick note of the leering crew before settling my attention on the pirate king.

Theo Saint Elliot, known to his crew as the Devil of Dark Water, was exactly how I pictured him.

Windswept dark gold hair fell to his shoulders in unruly waves, a well-trimmed beard accentuated a cut jaw, and—

The prince stepped around me and seized the pirate king by the neck with one hand, effortlessly lifting him off his feet as if he weighed nothing.

With his other hand, Sloth forcefully clamped down on the pirate's chin, his grip unflinching as he held him in place.

I watched in stunned silence as the prince twisted sharply and violently.

A loud, bone-chilling snap reverberated across the ship, instantly silencing the raucous hoots and jeers from the crew, leaving only the haunting sound of the sea lapping against the sides of the boat in the background.

Dozens of wide eyes drank in the sight of their leader, now limp in the prince's hands, a puddle of urine pooling at his feet.

My heart thudded against my ribs.

The prince dropped the pirate and stared coldly at anyone stupid enough to hold his gaze.

His low voice sent a ripple of fear through the crowd.

"*I'm* the king now. Any objections?"

NINETEEN
Prince Sloth

My declaration swept over the deck like a strong gust of wind, capturing the attention of every crew member as it traveled from bow to stern.

The instant I hurled the pirate king's lifeless body to the deck and gazed at the crew, an oppressive silence fell.

The pirates' eyes locked onto their vanquished leader, then slowly rose to meet mine. For a group of roughened mortals who likely caused their own fair share of violent endings, they were surprisingly shocked.

They would either bow to my authority while we were stuck in this scene or share his grim demise.

This wasn't like the tavern or the cave, or even the last historical novel.

We were trapped on a vessel in the middle of an ocean with potential enemies all around us.

If I didn't assert dominance, they would've been trouble.

The captain could have chained me and then gods only knew what could have happened to Lore.

After my fight with the dragon shifter, I realized I wasn't healing the way I should be. His hits had been hard, but normally I'd shake them off.

I'd healed well enough before the betrothal ball had begun, but something had closed off my magic when I'd been captured.

It was back, but now that I knew that it could be stolen so efficiently during the Trials, I could no longer trust I would have it.

If I'd waited to see what the pirate king had planned, it could have been a costly mistake.

The fact that he'd grabbed Lore without permission at all, let alone hard enough for her to cry out, might have also played into my decision.

I would have killed him for that reason alone.

I was quite thoroughly over this adventure from hell.

Fierce winds howled, dragging storm clouds across the sky.

The crew seemed to grasp that the true threat wasn't the tempest looming on the horizon. It was their new leader. I allowed my heightened senses to drift out, testing them. None indicated they were foolish enough to seek vengeance. Yet. But I'd stay on alert.

I sensed a storm growing inside me, and I shuddered to think of the destruction that might follow when my control finally snapped.

This realm, the Trials… *something* was taking its toll.

I felt Lore's attention on me and debated whether I should ignore it.

I imagined I'd see fear or disgust in her eyes. She teasingly called me a sociopath often enough, but she hadn't truly witnessed me take a life. And even though she'd just killed a man herself, that had been different.

We'd been in true danger, and she'd acted.

I still wasn't sure how she'd managed to throw a blade like it was second nature. That sort of precision took years to perfect.

My attention swung to hers, ready to accept her trepidation or scorn.

Once again, she surprised me.

She wasn't scared or trembling.

She was furious.

Her expression was filled with a dark rage that she was directing entirely at me.

A beat later, her emotions slammed into me like a tidal wave.

Her glare was not merely fearsome; it was a blazing inferno that threatened to consume everything in its path.

It was an impressive sight to behold. A strange part of me wanted to push her to see how high her temper could be stoked. I fought the peculiar urge.

"Something you'd like to say, Peaches?"

"As a matter of fact, yes." She crossed her arms. "You just killed the man we needed to strike a bargain with to get off this damned ship." She toed his unmoving body, then shot me another angry look. "Are you planning on killing all my favorite characters?"

My brows rose.

"Only the ones who touch you without permission and talk about bedding you. It's crass."

Whatever she'd been expecting me to say, that clearly wasn't it.

Her mouth dropped open before she snapped it shut. Most of the fire extinguished from her expression, replaced by an almost inquisitive look.

I didn't want her deciphering emotions that were a tangled mess even to me, so I carefully composed my features into a mask of neutrality.

"I like neither the sea nor pirates." I spoke low enough for only her to hear. "Now would be a good time to practice using your magic again. Take us someplace more pleasant, or I might kill everyone on this cursed ship, favorite characters or not."

I straightened and gazed down at the dozens of men still watching us.

"Where are the captain's quarters?" I demanded.

A man sporting a wicked black eye—who also happened to be missing his front teeth—motioned toward the back of the ship.

"I'll show ye, Cap'n."

I flashed Lore an incredulous look.

How she suffered through novels with pirate speech was beyond comprehension.

She rolled her eyes as if she'd understood my silent judgment and made a crude gesture in return.

Despite the events of the last few days, I felt my lips curve.

She couldn't care less what anyone thought of her reading choices, myself very much included.

It was refreshing.

Being a prince often led to people telling me what they thought I wanted to hear, always searching for threads of commonality to bind us.

Members of my court might choose to remain single more often than not, but there were always nobles who sought a crown.

I could imagine Lust quipping about how Lore was the sunshine to my storm. And the most aggravating fact was he wouldn't be wrong.

She never allowed negative emotions to dampen her spirits.

And she never let anyone's opinion sway hers.

It spoke of a steel-like inner strength. One I couldn't help but grudgingly admire.

Lore followed who I imagined was the first mate as he parted the crowd and led us belowdecks.

I trailed a few paces behind, meeting the eyes of any man who dared to glower at me or show any sordid interest in the woman making her way past them.

I felt the sharp gazes of the crew drilling into my back with every step, the tension thick enough to carve through as I moved deeper into the crowd. Still, none of them seem poised to strike me.

I strode down the stairs toward the captain's quarters.

As we descended into the belly of the ship, the air grew thicker and carried the faint scents of oak and salt.

It was far more pleasant than I'd imagined.

I scanned the rooms lining the wide corridor, noting the details that whispered stories of their life at sea.

The crew's dorms featured rows of narrow bunks; each was neatly made, their rough woolen blankets folded with military precision.

It was not at all what I would have expected from pirates.

As we continued down the corridor, we eventually arrived at the end, where a pair of intricately carved double doors waited.

Lore paused to take in the artwork. And I couldn't help but admit it was impressive. The artist's skill was evident in every groove and curve.

The wood almost came alive with fantastical creatures.

Mermaids with flowing hair, sea serpents coiling through the sea, and majestic whales breaching the surface; all carved with such accuracy that they seemed to leap from the panels into the corridor.

The first mate glanced over at me, his eyes flickering with a hint of unease as he pushed the doors open.

"If yer needin' anythin' else, give ol' Kensie a holler."

His voice wavered a little.

He was treading very carefully after my display. If anyone was to launch an uprising, I suspected it would be him. And that seemed... unlikely.

Lore gently took the man's hands in hers, her expression a serene portrait of composure and gratitude. I'd never seen her look so earnest.

She was really taking her role as pirate queen seriously for this test.

"Thank you so much for the tour, Kensington. This one needs a nap"—she stuck a thumb in my direction—"he gets rather murderous when he's tired and cranky. But I look forward to meeting more of the crew later."

His face flushed scarlet as he dipped his chin and hurried off. Lore might have just inadvertently swayed him to our side.

I gestured for Lore to hold back as I made my way into the room, my senses on high alert for any potential threats lurking within its seemingly innocuous walls.

I didn't sense the Liber Noctem on board but wondered if it could somehow mask itself from us.

While I scanned every corner and crevice for hidden compartments or traps, Lore let out an exasperated sigh.

A hint of amusement came from her that indicated she wasn't as put off as she'd like me to believe.

"It's safe."

"As long as we're not counting the threat *you* pose, Lord Neck Snapper."

Her quip held no bite, and she quickly forgot all about me as she swept into the room and immediately squealed with delight.

"It looks just like I imagined it in the book!" She paused. "Probably because of my magic. But still. Look at all the gold and treasure! We're filthy rich. Do you think we can take this back to Bellington when I kick the dark book's ass?"

"You can certainly try."

Now that I wasn't searching for danger, I actually took in the chamber. The captain's quarters exuded opulence and elegance.

The room was adorned in rich crimson velvet and had several gilded sconces set into the walls that had been cast in mermaid shapes.

Dark, polished wood panels made up the interior walls and reflected the ambient light of the sconces. A plush king-sized bed dominated the left side of the chamber, and its covers were a deep scarlet that surprised me.

I would have imagined the former pirate king choosing to dress the room in blues or greens, something more befitting the sea. Perhaps he enjoyed sleeping on sheets that reminded him of the blood he shed to gain such riches.

A finely woven rug spread across the hardwood floor, its whirling patterns and intricate design making it a statement piece on its own.

The pirate king had impeccable, if not a bit gaudy, taste.

On his desk sat a quintessential treasure trunk.

Several carvings were etched onto its sides that told tales of the distant lands he must have stolen it from.

The chest was filled to the brim with shimmering gold coins. Nestled among the coins were resplendent jewels. Strands of pearls spilled over the sides of the chest, each bead perfectly round and gleaming with a soft, opalescent sheen.

"A treasure chest is a bit trite. You need some better books."

"It's not my fault you read boring nonfiction. Who rolls their eyes at a real-life pirate horde?" Lore plucked up a strand of pearls to admire it, then tried on a few jeweled rings before moving on to the next treasure.

The former pirate king must have raided the best ships and lands for the bounty of riches displayed in this room alone.

He put Gluttony to shame with the sheer grandeur of the space, and that was quite a feat, to outdo the prince of overindulgence.

Lore drank it all in before turning to me.

She crossed her arms and scanned me from head to toe, her expression guarded.

"Are you feeling all right?"

Clearly, she wasn't asking after my health.

"Yes. Why?"

She moved over to the bed and dropped onto the mattress, bouncing a little as she did.

"The punishment didn't fit the crime back there." Her dark gaze narrowed on me. "You seem more murdery than normal."

"Murderous."

She heaved a sigh.

"Lighten up, Blondie. Not everything needs to be so literal." She flashed me a teasing look. "These accommodations are definitely an upgrade from the dungeon you found yourself in last night. Try smiling for once."

I bared my teeth in an approximation of a grin, and she shook her head like I was a lost cause.

"We'll work on that. I wanted to know how you felt after the dungeon and almost beheading."

A real smile ghosted across my lips before I caught myself.

I rolled my neck from side to side and exhaled slowly.

"You passed the Trial, clearly, or else one of us would be dead. So there's no need to discuss what might have been."

"Still, you seem off."

"Maybe because I'm trying to puzzle out what you're hiding."

"I'm not hiding anything, per se. It's just...complicated." She spun the stolen ring on her finger. "I'm trying to figure it out."

I arched a brow. "How fortuitous that my sin is tailored to working complications out."

She half-heartedly rolled her eyes.

"Okay, then. Let's see your deductions in action. I had another vision after we escaped the chopping block." Lore looked uncomfortable, which made me home in harder on every detail. "I watched as someone betrayed their loved ones and sent them to their deaths. It was...brutal."

"And?"

"Whoever's memory that was, she *liked* it. Their fear, their hurt. It was beyond terrible to sit through, let alone to live through. I couldn't imagine ever being that cold or cruel. To anyone, let alone someone I loved. Their expressions will haunt me forever."

I let the information settle into the vault of my mind and turned it over, examining it from all angles.

I was growing more confident that there weren't any mentions of visions or memories being part of the tests. It was clearly emerging as a pattern, though.

It was possible Nyantha's power was slowly being unlocked from the book and was somehow corrupting Lore's mind. It was a variable I hadn't accounted for.

But Lore was also getting stronger with her dreamweaving, as was evident by her shifting stories before the Liber Noctem could. I had begun to doubt whether she was a dreamweaver, but that fear was now laid to rest.

"We should focus on your magic," I said. "Maybe better control over it will help block the visions."

And if it was Nyantha's power seeping in, it would hopefully prevent it from getting worse.

After studying me for long moment, she fished around inside her dress and pulled out the phoenix tear. It emitted a low hum, like a cat purring for its favorite person. It almost made my skin crawl.

I moved away from where I'd paused by the window, my focus locked on the object in her hand.

"Has it always made that sound when you hold it?"

She shook her head. "I felt it more than heard it before. This is definitely new."

My gaze narrowed as I tried to sort out why that might be.

Thus far, none of this was following any of the myths and legends I'd read about the phoenix tear or the Trials. Or her dreamweaver power.

Unease worked its way back in. There was another anomaly I couldn't account for—the Liber Noctem. I'd assumed it would remain close to the dreamweaver while the Trials were in play. That it would want to closely monitor the situation to twist it as needed. Xavier wasn't on the boat, so how was the book still digging its claws into Lore? I wondered if it could move from host to host, then promptly dismissed the thought. I had to believe I'd sense that dark power.

"Try to shift us to a new story."

She closed her eyes, then snapped them open again.

"Shouldn't you...hold my hand or skirt, or something? What if I go flying through another portal?"

I crossed the chamber and knelt before her, offering my hand, palm up. "Scared you're going to lose me, Peaches?"

She rolled her eyes, but I didn't miss the way her skin flushed.

"Just take my hand or I'll leave you with the pirates as punishment."

I swore under my breath and her delighted laughter caused one thread of worry to loosen. Somehow, that created a new set of strain.

One I refused to delve into, for fear of what it might reveal.

TWENTY
Prince Sloth

ALMOST A FULL day had passed without any changes, and Lore's frustration grew.

"I can *feel* the magic, but it's like it's in a deep sleep." Her focus slid to mine. "It was eager to help when you were about to lose your head. Now it feels more dormant than it did in the beginning. Is that normal?"

I rubbed my temples. I had no answer. As a dreamweaver, she should be able to access the magic at will.

"Try coaxing it awake."

"What an inspiring idea." She gave me a flat look. "Why didn't I think of that?"

The air grew thick with tension, like a taut wire ready to snap.

We'd been trapped on the ship for less than a day, yet the walls already felt like they were closing in on us.

It could be the dark book working its magic for whatever this test was, but it could also be the circumstances. Lore was remarkably optimistic, even during the worst of times, but dreamweaver bloodline aside, she was human.

I kept reminding myself that her entire world had flipped on itself; she'd been ripped from her family, her life, her home.

I pinched the bridge of my nose, hoping to relieve the pounding ache that pulsed behind my eyes, a painful reminder of our predicament.

"I'm going topside." I studied Lore. Exhaustion was apparent in the redness of her eyes. "Try to sleep for a while. We'll practice later."

"I thought you said we needed to shift stories now."

It would be ideal to get us off the ship and somewhere we had a better chance of hunting the book, but we'd make do. It also gave me another excuse to keep an eye on the crew in case anyone decided to attempt to overthrow me.

"Rest. A few hours won't mean the end of the realms."

I strode out of the room and into the dimly lit corridor, the wooden floor creaking gently underfoot. A few rugged and weather-beaten pirates crossed my path on their way to their evening meal, and their boisterous conversations came to an abrupt halt as their attention landed on me. They were wary but not exuding any murderous intent. It was a small mercy.

I ascended the narrow staircase to the main deck, where the open sky greeted me, and I immediately felt more grounded.

The sun hung low on the horizon but still managed to break through the gathering clouds.

I inhaled deeply, and the crisp, salty scent of the sea filled my lungs.

It felt invigorating and fresh after being locked belowdecks for so long.

I slowly ambled across the deck, logging different areas where someone could lie in wait, for future reference.

When I'd done a full loop and reached the railing on the starboard side, I paused to take in the vast expanse of blue surrounding us.

The ocean spread out before me, waves rising and falling rhythmically, the speed slowly increasing with each passing moment.

It was another foreboding sign that a storm was brewing on the horizon. I hoped we'd be off the ship before it reached us.

With enough distance between myself and any other crew member, I enjoyed a few moments of uninterrupted solitude to gather facts and plot our next moves.

I turned over the events of the last few days, beginning with a troubling personal issue. I needed to pinpoint when my powers started to show strain.

The tavern fight actually left bruises for several hours, but I'd really felt the drain when I'd fought the dragon shifter. And then of course when I'd suddenly found myself without *any* magic after Lore murdered the marquess...

My thoughts kept returning to Xavier's betrayal. To the temple.

I couldn't escape the feeling that something had happened there, something far more detrimental than I'd first thought.

But *what*? What piece of the puzzle was I overlooking?

I'd believed the temple had been warded *against* magic, but now I wondered if that was entirely true. Was there a spell in place, a trap I'd walked into?

I replayed that day over and over. The only thing that stood out was when I'd held the Liber Noctem.

That seemed like the moment it all went horribly wrong.

I still couldn't work out why or how the tattoo had manifested itself on me. Or what it meant.

I shoved a hand through my hair.

It was a mystery I needed to solve, sooner rather than later.

There were no such things as coincidences during the Trials. And I was starting to question if anything I'd read about them was accurate.

The old gods could have spread lies to keep their secrets to themselves. It made me want the Liber Noctem even more.

If only I'd gotten to examine it in the temple, I might have unraveled the truth of what they'd done. I needed to locate the damned book before it was too late. But there was little chance of me hunting it while we were trapped at sea.

The sky was now streaked with more shades of gray than gold and seemed to mirror the turbulent waters below.

And, oddly enough, my own darkening emotions.

I pushed off the railing and headed to the quarterdeck, where the first mate stood at the helm. His knuckles turned white as his grip tightened on the wheel, the only outward sign I made him nervous. I still didn't pick up on any deceit or treachery from him. And I suspected I had Lore's personable nature to thank for that. She'd smoothed things over expertly.

"Yer needin' an'thing, Cap?"

A steel beam to the temple.

I gave Kensington a polite shake of my head. Then thought better of it.

"I'll need a change of clothes for the young lady. Trousers, shirts, a weapons belt with a pouch if you have one."

A flush crept up his neck.

"Leave it to ol' Kensie. I'll have it done w'thin an hour."

My lips twitched upward.

That erased any lingering doubts about the first mate's loyalty. Lore had truly worked her magic and won the first mate over. I wasn't at all surprised. It was hard not to fall under her spell.

"Where were you headed before we arrived?"

He nibbled on his lower lip, his gaze darting around the nearly empty deck.

"The Isle of the Damned."

His words were barely audible and carried a heavy, ominous weight that hinted at more trouble than the island's dark name.

"What were you looking for there?"

"Fortune an' glory." He steered the ship into a wave, then noticed my raised brows. "Legend claims the island has a host o' treasure, waitin' t'be found. Magic compass. Riches. If ya survive the specters."

"Ghosts?"

Kensington shook his head.

"Ol' Kensie hears whispers from distant shores. Specters isn't spirits, they're creatures. Stand about yea high—" He indicated about three feet. "Skin and hair as white as snow, eyes as red as blood. Distant relations to vamps, if stories can be believed."

The ocean lapped at the side of the ship, the soft, rolling waves a sharp contrast to the eerie tale he'd just shared.

I glanced out at the endless expanse of sea, half expecting to see the island he'd mentioned looming in the distance.

All was quiet, peaceful. The proverbial calm before the storm.

In the short time we'd been talking, the sun had set.

Moonlight glimmered on the water's surface, and the wind rustled softly through the sails.

I *really* didn't want to fight any miniature second or third cousins to vampires, distant relations or not. They would be monstrous given our location.

"Might wantin' t'be gettin' belowdecks." Kensington jerked his chin toward the racing clouds. "Storm'll be 'ere soon."

It was exactly what I was afraid of.

I stopped by the galley before heading to our room, hoping to select an assortment of food items to arrange on a small tray to bring back to Lore.

I was surprised by what I discovered there. The ship was far from the scurvy-ridden historical accounts I'd read of other long voyages.

I walked along a buffet-style table laden with food.

There were ripe fruits, and the aromas of warm freshly baked bread and savory meats mingled in the air as I gathered the peace offerings.

I almost walked by the dessert station before I halted and turned back.

I carved a thick slice of chocolate cake and added it to the tray.

As was the case with everywhere I went on the ship, conversations halted as I passed by the tables of pirates lingering over their dinner, but no one sent any glares my way.

Once I'd made it to the corridor, the chatter started up again.

Someone loitered outside our door and my hand was on my dagger before I took in the scene and slowly released it.

Alongside the meal, the items I'd tasked Kensington with procuring for Lore arrived. He'd come through well.

A timid young man was standing outside the captain's quarters. He'd brought me the bundle of clothing.

"'Ere ya go, Cap'n. Got ev'rythin' you asked fer."

"Well done."

I handed him the tray while I took the clothing and inspected it.

I was pleased with the quality.

There was a pair of finely crafted leather trousers, their supple texture promising comfort and durability, a fitted tunic woven from soft linen, and a sturdy leather belt equipped with pouches for carrying essential supplies.

I took the tray back from the young man and sent him on his way.

He hurried off without a second glance.

I nudged the door open and closed it with my boot, then crossed the room, feeling Lore's gaze burning into me and my overflowing arms.

I placed the bounty of goods on the desk with a gentle thud, finally meeting her wide, astonished eyes.

"Did you rob a small marketplace while I was sleeping?"

"I wasn't sure what you liked to eat, so I got a bit of everything." I gestured to the varied selection before her. "The clothes will allow you to move more freely, and the belt is essential in case we have no time to gather supplies. You should be able to keep the phoenix tear in it safely."

Her attention shifted to the tray, then back to me.

"There's enough food to feed a family."

"Not quite that much."

I held out a plate and fork for her, hiding a grin as she rolled her eyes at my literal nature. It was far too amusing to get a rise out of her.

She hopped off the bed and crossed the room to accept the plate and peered into the dishes I'd uncovered.

Stewed meat, fried potatoes, some vegetable mash laden with butter, dinner rolls, sautéed greens with almonds, and dessert.

"Chocolate cake? Bless you, Wicked thing."

I watched in bemused silence as she grabbed the dessert first and tossed a few other dinner items onto a smaller dish.

Her priorities were horridly skewed yet somehow endearing.

Once we'd piled our plates high, we sat cross-legged on the floor and placed our meals haphazardly before us.

She practically bounced in place.

"Are you about to combust?"

"Maybe. How many people get to say they've had a pirate picnic? This is much more fun than our last meal together at the inn. Mental shield building was interesting, but it doesn't really stand up to this."

I snorted. I'd never met someone who could find thrills and adventure simply by eating on the floor of an old ship.

She made the mundane magic.

"If we survive, we'll send letters to all your fictional friends to share the news."

"Even Logan Blaze?"

She was baiting me, and even being fully aware, I still glowered.

Cursed dragon shifter and his dimples.

"Only if I get to deliver it personally to him."

"Mm."

Her mouth curved in wicked delight. *Point one to Lore.*

Outside, the storm that had been threatening finally howled, and the ship rocked with the rhythm of the waves, making our little dining area feel like a teetering stage. At least neither of us appeared to be seasick.

A hint of laughter danced in her expression as I tried to skewer a runaway potato that rolled dangerously close to the plate's rim.

I swore and stabbed down, finally spearing the cursed thing.

I shifted my gaze to her, one brow arching in playful challenge.

"Something amusing, Peaches?"

"Not in the slightest."

My magic clicked with the lie.

Her eyes twinkled with mirth as she eagerly dug into the rich, velvety slice of chocolate cake before her, leaving her dinner untouched.

I was glad the food and her "pirate picnic" brought her a bit of happiness. She needed to maintain that lightheartedness, or the dark book would eventually obliterate all that was good in her.

A flash of my nightmares crossed my mind.

Lore's eyes pitch black, the realms burning…

Worry dug its claws into me. While we'd received some news of the Liber Noctem in the last story, this one had no new leads.

I loathed sitting still and waiting for it to come hunting us.

Xavier was not on the ship, and I felt trapped here. An overwhelming sense of claustrophobia rose inside me, one I'd never felt before in my existence.

I needed to—

"Oh, my gods." She took another bite and danced in place. "This is the best thing I've ever put in my mouth."

The room suddenly felt stuffy.

I tugged at the collar of my shirt, feeling the fabric cling uncomfortably to my skin. As a Prince of Sin, I wasn't prone to illness, but I almost swore I was feverish.

Lore took another bite and moaned.

I flicked my gaze toward the window. Its panes were sealed tight.

I released a sigh. I'd need to endure the stifling warmth that seemed to intensify with every passing moment.

I shifted my attention back to my own meal, analyzing the same worries I continued to cycle through from earlier, when Lore released another sound of pleasure.

I stared as she licked the frosting from her fork, her eyes closed in rapture.

Cake was certainly good, but I'd never had something *that* good.

I forced myself to slice into the meat, ignoring the show. I turned my attention inward, still mulling over the tattoo.

If the Liber Noctem—

"Mm. Gods. It's *so* good."

Lore tossed her head back and seemed to have an out-of-body experience.

Whatever I'd been mentally sorting through vanished as my focus zeroed in on the dreamweaver.

My attention skimmed down the long line of her neck, arched elegantly. The position made my mind spin with other scenarios, far less innocent in nature.

I had no business looking at her, but every time she made that cursed sound, it did something to my pulse.

I imagined an ice bath, a frozen lake, a room with no windows.

Lore scooped another bit of cake onto her fork, and the way she licked the frosting shattered my control.

Her attention flicked to mine as she repeated the motion.

She had my undivided attention.

The air around us seemed to thicken, becoming almost tangible.

I breathed in deeply to steady my pulse, and the aroma of cocoa and sugar that enveloped the room added to the already intoxicating atmosphere.

My blood heated as she moaned again, louder this time.

The crew would think all sorts of lurid things were happening in here if she kept that up.

I'd have to ensure she had baked goods when she returned home. Though I'd need to have her house soundproofed first.

"I had no idea I'd be having dinner and a show."

She rolled her eyes but kept the charade up.

It wasn't my finest attempt to lead us away from dangerous waters, and Lore seemed only too pleased that she'd distracted me so thoroughly.

"Don't be boring, Your Highness."

I raised a brow as she dug into the rich chocolate cake with abandon.

She took another bite, slowly savoring the creamy frosting and moist layers before letting out another soft groan of pleasure.

It took me far too long to realize she was doing it to distract me from my darkening thoughts.

And I'd only just caught onto her little game.

"Here." She scooped up a generous portion with her fork and held it out to me, chocolate smudging her fingertips. "Taste this."

Her gaze sparkled with impish challenge, daring me to break my rigid nature for once. I might be analytical, but I was far from *boring*.

I leaned forward, accepting the offered bit of cake as she watched, a mischievous smile playing across her lips.

The cake melted on my tongue, decadently sweet and utterly delicious. It really was damn good.

"Was that an actual groan of pleasure, Lord Stoic?" she teased. "Should we throw a party and invite all one of your friends to celebrate?"

"Bold of you to assume I have *any* friends."

She barked a laugh, then clapped a hand over her mouth and snorted. The sound was filled with unmitigated joy, and I couldn't help but laugh too.

I leaned in closer, feeling the warmth radiating from her as I gently swiped my thumb across her soft, inviting lower lip.

Her breath caught in her throat, the sound a subtle gasp of surprise mixed with anticipation as her gaze cut to my mouth and lingered.

With a wicked smile of my own, I revealed the smudge of rich, dark chocolate I'd stolen from her lips, holding it up for her to see before slowly sucking it off my finger, savoring the sweet taste that lingered there.

She tracked the movements intently, her throat visibly moving with each swallow, clearly caught off guard by my unexpected response.

She wasn't the only one who could employ distraction tactics.

"Well?" She finally managed to wrench her attention back up to my eyes. "What do you think? Is it the most delicious cake you've ever had?"

"It tastes divine, but I prefer peaches."

A hint of pink crept into her cheeks as I watched her struggle to regain her composure. A wave of satisfaction surged through me with her flustered reaction.

She'd started this, and—while she'd bested me for a while before I'd caught on—I'd finally matched her wit for wit.

Just when I thought I'd won...whatever this game was, she swiped a bit of frosting off the cake, then planted a dollop on my lips.

With lightning-fast reflexes, I held on to her wrist and licked the rest of the frosting off her fingertips. Her breathing turned short and ragged.

She was right where I wanted her.

We *should* focus on the practical issues we faced, but I found my gaze drifting to the mashed vegetables on my plate.

Before I could think twice, I scooped up a spoonful and launched it across the short distance between us.

She let out a high-pitched squeal, instinctively ducking, but not fast enough—the greenish mush splattered against her cheek.

A thick glob clung to her skin before slowly sliding down, leaving a trail on the front of her dress. "Ugh!"

I pointed my spoon at her in challenge.

"If we're going to play this imprudent game, I promise you, I *will* win."

She gave me an exasperated look.

"Only you would sneak *imprudent* into the same sentence as *game*," she quipped, then jumped to her feet and returned fire.

A buttered roll hit me in the chest and slid down my fighting leathers. I stared at the greasy streak and slowly lifted my gaze to the beaming woman before me.

"This means war, dreamweaver."

Before I could get to my own feet, Lore lobbed an herbed potato at me.

I swore roundly as she raced across the room and dove behind the bed, taking cover.

I was a patient male. The moment she popped her head up, I slung another spoonful of mash at her, the hit landing directly on her other cheek. She was a formidable opponent. I dodged around the desk, mindful of the treasure chest, and took another hit.

Soon we were both covered in mashed vegetables, and I couldn't remember a time I'd had half as much fun.

Hours after our food fight, after we'd cleaned up and practiced Lore's magic and tried to figure out what this test could be, she'd fallen into a deep sleep.

She curled up on her side on the large bed, her dark hair spilling over the pillow. One arm was folded beneath her cheek as she slept.

Her chest rose and fell with each gentle breath.

She looked so peaceful, so free of the worry we'd felt earlier today.

I didn't usually wish for things, finding it foolish and not practical, but I found myself hoping it wouldn't be the last time she'd look so at ease.

I took the soft comforter from the end of the bed and draped it over her, feeling an odd tug in my chest.

There was no use in denying that her presence was magnetic, not just to the first mate of this ship. It also drew me in with an inexplicable pull.

Even if I decided to invite Lore into my bed, she would not be satisfied with keeping our emotions out of the equation.

She would want the fairy-tale ending like the heroines in her favorite romance books.

And that was a life I could never offer her.

With a sigh, I shook my head to clear those thoughts and reached for a spare pillow, tossing it onto the hardwood floor.

There was no logical reason for me to be thinking of anything other than passing this current Trial and trying to locate the Liber Noctem before the Trials ended.

When I returned home, I'd need to find a physical release. It had been far too long since I'd engaged in any carnal activities.

I lay down beside the bed, the coolness of the floor seeping through my tunic, and tried to quiet my mind.

I focused on the rhythm of my breathing, willing myself to think of nothing at all. Sometimes my thoughts were too loud, too complex.

It was a downside to my sin—the unquenchable thirst for knowledge that was never sated.

I'd had to work hard over the years to fortify my mental shields to avoid getting lost in too many theories and facts.

Yet Lore had managed to tear her way through those walls.

With chocolate cake, no less.

She was my opposite in all ways, except when it came to our love of books.

I rolled onto my side.

I should be focusing all my efforts on tracking Xavier and the Liber Noctem through the stories.

And yet my mind refused to relinquish its hold on the mystery of the dreamweaver. My sin languidly turned over every interaction, searching for clues to my strange behavior around her.

Did the tattoo and whatever magic the ink contained somehow bind me to her and the Trials? I wasn't sure that was even possible, but I was desperate for any excuse.

I was caught in a vexing web of uncertainty, unsure if my emotions were stirred by the nightmare realm itself or if there was a more innocent explanation for my muddled feelings for her.

Perhaps I simply needed to take a dip in the cold ocean to clear my head.

With that settled, I forced my mind to empty and drifted off into a dreamless slumber.

I'd left a breakfast tray and note for Lore and left our room by dawn.

The morning sun poured its intense heat onto the ship's deck as I pushed through a rigorous workout, my skin glistening with sweat.

I gripped the coarse, weathered ropes and hoisted myself up into the rigging, feeling the strain in my arms and shoulders.

The burn felt good, distracting. It was exactly what I needed after last night.

The ropes creaked under my weight, and the salty breeze brushed against my face. Climbing took all my focus, my mind blissfully distracted with the physical exertion of the workout.

Reaching the top, I paused to catch my breath and study our surroundings. The horizon stretched endlessly before me, still with no island in sight. Frustration built inside me again. The Liber Noctem had to be out there, close by. I swore it was toying with me, stoking my emotions. Thankfully, it hadn't caused any unrest on the ship, though. The crew was still cautious around me, but they were treading carefully, not plotting a revolt.

I swept my attention across the ocean one more time before letting myself down in a controlled descent.

My muscles ached with each climb, but a sense of satisfaction pulsed through me as I repeated the cycle, savoring the challenge and the rhythm of my movements. Sweat dripped from my brow, and I shook it from my face.

I'd just pulled myself up into the crow's nest when a hush fell over the crew.

I glanced down to see what had caught their complete attention.

Lore strode onto the deck with confident steps, her new leather trousers hugging her frame. I couldn't help but take in the full effect of her new clothing.

She'd tucked the shirt in to grant her more freedom of movement, but the sleeves fluttered slightly in the breeze, giving her a decidedly feminine touch.

The curved sword in her hand caught the sunlight, but it didn't feel half as dangerous as the woman holding it.

Her dark hair was tightly braided and intricately pinned to her crown, adorned with glittering jewels from the treasure chest she must have raided from the captain's quarters.

She looked every inch the pirate queen from her story.

Instead of appearing absurd, she exuded an undeniable authority and charisma.

One that appeared to be contagious, as the crew all respectfully bowed their heads. She sauntered across the deck, adding an extra swagger to her stride.

I'd never been more intrigued by a pirate.

My heart thumped wildly in my chest.

I took a deep breath to gather my wits, but the salty air suddenly seemed to cling to my skin, and it was far more irritating than refreshing as I tried to steady myself.

She caught sight of me and raised her curved blade, its edge gleaming dangerously in the morning light.

Her voice carried over the sound of the waves, loud and commanding.

"We need to talk, Blondie."

Some of the crew snickered at the nickname.

I arched a brow. She was enjoying bossing me around and using that horrid name way too much.

And yet, I found myself wrapping my fingers tightly around the ropes and descending swiftly from the rigging without complaint or protest.

The ropes strained against my grip as I maneuvered down, my muscles taut under the effort.

I released my hold and dropped the last few feet, landing with a muted thud on the weathered deck before her.

Straightening up, I noticed her eyes were riveted to my bare chest, her focus as sharp and unwavering as the blade she held.

"Did you summon me here just to stare, Peaches?"

She wrenched her gaze to mine. "We're supposed to be a team, but you left me."

I motioned to the rigging. "Only to work out."

"What would have happened if I suddenly shifted stories, or faced a test, and left you here?"

"I would have tracked you down."

I wasn't sure why I knew, without any doubt, that I could. But it was a certainty I didn't question.

She shook her head. "Really? You would have escaped this story and somehow found a way into the next?"

I would have cleaved the realm apart if I must.

I opened my senses to glean why Lore was so upset, but she'd somehow managed to lock her emotions away.

Or I was suddenly unable to use that power.

I was at a loss. Clearly, there was some emotional component I was missing.

"What are you really upset about?"

She gave me a look that said I was an idiot but changed the subject.

"Your tattoo is glowing again." She slid her gaze from the ink to my eyes. "Why?"

My jaw tensed. I loathed the foreign power claiming my body and at the same time felt strangely attached to it. Shaking that dichotomy away, I was starting to have a pretty good theory about why it reacted.

I debated my next move. I could shrug it off or be truthful.

I leaned in and pressed my mouth close to her ear.

"Because your imperious commands are making me plot wicked things, when I should be focused on more immediate threats, Peaches."

"I'm not following."

My magic detected a partial lie, but if she wanted me to lay it out there to avoid any misunderstandings, so be it.

We needed to cut this beast's head off before it grew worse.

"When I remember all the clever, wicked, ridiculous things you say, I start thinking about your mouth. And my sin demands I analyze *why* I'm fascinated by it."

I stepped back slightly, allowing myself a clearer view of her face.

Her brows were arched high, her lips parted in surprise.

I shouldn't reach out but found myself doing it anyway.

I traced my thumb softly along the curve of her lower lip, feeling its smoothness and the subtle warmth beneath.

"Is it the shape? The fullness? The way you playfully taunt me at every turn? Or is it simply your mind that's ensnared me?"

Her gaze flicked to my mouth and lingered there.

The inquisitiveness in her eyes called to my sin, a silent language that spoke of mutual curiosity and something more.

It was a dangerous thing, that gaze, as if it could unravel my secrets and stir emotions I'd locked away for safekeeping with just a look.

I threw all caution to the wind and laid it out for her, being far more forthright than I'd ever been with anyone. Maybe it was magic egging me on, maybe it was part of her test, or maybe I just *wanted* to.

"I believe the tattoo reacts to any surge in my emotions. Last night, I realized the chocolate on your lips wasn't the only thing I'd wanted to taste. So, Peaches, once I start thinking of your mouth, eventually I imagine all the ways I'd put it to use. And that is a line we cannot cross."

TWENTY-ONE
Lore

For a moment, it felt like the sea itself held its breath.

Sloth, the cool, calm, collected Prince of Sin, just fed into one of my favorite romance scenes. And I was too damned annoyed to fully appreciate it.

Or his beautiful, shimmering, sweat-slicked muscles.

There really was no justice in this nightmare realm.

"Don't try to distract me with fun tropes." I pointed my blade at him, impressed I held the sword steadily. It was much heavier than I thought it'd be. I seriously needed to work on gaining some upper-body strength. "Are you saying the tattoo is manipulating your emotions?"

"No." He gave me a flat look. "I'm saying I left our room because if I stayed, I would have been tempted to climb into bed with you. And I'm…frustrated."

Which didn't actually rule out my tattoo theory.

It was taking much longer to process his admission. I blamed the aforementioned sweaty muscles of wonder. Training montages were a weakness.

And intentionally or not, he'd put on one heck of a show.

He might have been the one working out, but I was the only one breathless.

Once I got beyond that distraction, I figured he wasn't talking about sleeping. And that fact made my heart do a series of strange gymnastics in my chest.

Of course, being the kind of secret deviant I was, I'd let my thoughts wander. Having Prince Sloth in my bed would probably ruin me for life.

Before I could respond or stop thinking about creative ways of using the rigging in my daydream, he continued.

"You and I are partners for the duration of the Trials only. I don't want to confuse the issue and create distractions by giving in to passing physical desires."

Ouch. I rubbed at my chest, wondering if he'd somehow snagged my sword and pierced my heart with it.

Lord Killjoy wasn't done.

"You're pleasing to the eye and, more importantly, to the mind, but I'm not looking for love or romance. It's best to understand that now. Being tempted to relieve stress is logical, considering the circumstances, and it would undoubtedly feel incredible, but it's a complication we can ill afford."

I narrowed my gaze on him. The prince doth protest too mucheth.

"You put an awful lot of thought into something that's *never going to happen*. If you haven't noticed, I haven't tried to kiss you, you overconfident ass. But you certainly stood in the way of my top fictional crush kissing me. Do you have any idea how hard it was to walk away from *Logan Blaze*?"

Seriously, if I was facing almost certain death with the book of doom, the prince could have at least let me have one last kiss.

A girl needed a little something good to cling to in the darkest hours.

Suddenly, my chest brushed against his, the thin fabric of my shirt grazing his bare skin.

His eyes locked onto mine with a force that made my heart race.

"Next time one of your crushes tries to bed you, I'll give you space."

The air between us crackled with tension, a charged energy that left me uncertain if he'd actually managed to lie.

I wondered if he knew that not only had his mask of cold indifference slipped, but his face was wholly unguarded for once.

The prince wasn't looking at me like he wanted to braid my hair and talk about boys like we were the bestest of friends.

He looked like he wanted to tie me up in the rigging and make me beg.

And that made heat pool low in my belly.

I seriously doubted he'd be fine with leaving me alone with someone like Logan.

Maybe this was part of my test, somehow. I certainly wanted to push him.

"Good, try not to kill them either."

I couldn't decide if the heat in his gaze signaled his longing to lean in for a kiss despite all his *many* reasons to avoid one, or if there was a darker, more troubling intent lurking beneath the surface.

He stared down at me, a storm brewing within his eyes.

"As long as we're both on the same page."

"Same book, same scene," I said sweetly. "If Logan appears again, you'll give us time alone. They say an alpha's kiss is almost as addictive as one from the Wicked. What do you think, is there any truth to that?"

He jerked back as if I'd slapped him.

I raised a brow at his visceral reaction. He didn't care, my booty.

"I've always been curious to test that theory. Since you don't want to indulge me, I'll just have to hope Logan comes back."

Before I could decipher the new flash in his gaze, he leaned in swiftly, and his mouth descended on mine with an unexpected intensity.

His kiss was scorching, a stark contrast to the icy demeanor. And by the gods, it lived up to every rumor ever spread about the Wicked.

I should not be kissing him back after his lovely happily-never-after speech.

But my resistance crumbled faster than some third-act breakups, and I found myself melting into the fervor of the moment.

I kissed him back without limits, unleashing all my romantic cravings.

His hands were strong and steady as they cupped my cheeks, tilting my face upward to meet his. He knew exactly what he was doing by angling my mouth for better access. He didn't plunder or commandeer.

His tactic was much, much more enticing. The kiss wasn't fast or brutal; it was a controlled, languid, maddening descent into overwhelming desire.

My entire body responded. My fingers slid down his sweat-slicked chest, and the heat in my belly grew.

His tongue traced the seam of my lips, finally coaxing them apart, and I opened up, inviting him in with a breathless sigh.

If I was drowning in desire before, I was wholly consumed by it now.

His kiss was unlike anything I'd ever experienced.

It was an education in seduction, as if he were savoring every moment of the lesson while simultaneously driving me insane.

A tingling sensation spread through me, like a warm current coursing through my veins. His lips moved against mine with a practiced grace, and the world around us faded away.

There was only the prince, standing before me, and this earth-shattering kiss that seemed to suspend time itself.

He kissed me like it was the beginning and ending of the greatest love story ever told, like he'd live and die in the span of this one moment.

Then, just as suddenly as it had begun, it was over.

He stepped back, his chest rising and falling as hard as mine was.

For a moment, silence reigned, enveloping us in a cocoon of stillness as we stared at each other. That was the most intense experience of my life.

Then, like a wave breaking against the shore, our surroundings crashed back into focus with a cacophony of sound.

The pirates erupted into a chorus of whistles and hollers, their voices clamoring for an encore, their raucous laughter echoing across the deck.

I'd forgotten we had an audience.

Whatever impulse had driven the prince to kiss me seemed to evaporate into the humid air, leaving no trace behind.

"I apologize for my actions," he stated, his tone clipped and formal. "It won't happen again."

With a swift turn on his heel, he snatched his rumpled tunic from the planks and strode purposefully toward the captain's quarters, his footsteps echoing with finality.

I stood there, fingers pressed to my swollen lips, the warmth of his kiss still lingering. I hadn't even caught my breath yet, and he was almost gone.

My mind spun in a whirlwind of confusion, trying to grasp what the hells had just happened.

He'd given a million reasons why we could never happen.

Then he'd gone ahead and kissed me anyway.

And, quite infuriatingly, it was the best kiss of my life. At least until he'd *apologized*, then walked off like it was nothing special.

Total villain behavior.

Or *maybe*, a darker voice whispered, maybe it had been part of the test. And he'd had no more control over his actions than anyone else at the Liber Noctem's mercy.

Kensington approached slowly, his expression filled with sympathy.

I glanced up at the sky, wondering why there was no black hole swirling overhead to suck me into the abyss.

There was never a decent plot twist when it would be highly beneficial.

"Eddie o'er there offered t'teach you to wield a sword." He grinned a toothless smile that warmed my heart. "Stabbin' things always makes us feel better."

I inhaled deeply, letting the briny air fill my lungs, and then slowly exhaled.

My emotions were all over the place.

Either I was going to march after the prince and demand he do that again to prove he'd been in control and wanted to, or I was going to dive headfirst into the ocean to put myself out of my misery.

Neither seemed like the most prudent option.

Perhaps Eddie was right.

Maybe if I learned to wield a sword, I'd feel less rejected.

Or, at the very least, I'd have better aim.

"Okay," I said with cheerful determination, "let's go stab things."

Training with a pirate was an unforgettable adventure.

One I wasn't sure I ever wanted to repeat. Training always seemed fun in books, but the reality was much less thrilling.

My shirt clung to me, my skin itched from the sweat and sunburn I was getting from being out on the water in full sun, and I was pretty sure I pulled a few muscles I never knew existed before today.

Eddie didn't instruct me in the art of fighting with any sense of honor or decorum; instead, he was a gritty brawler, unafraid to employ any tactic necessary to win.

It didn't matter that I had no experience. In fact, I got the impression he might be a bit of a sadist himself. He certainly seemed to enjoy my suffering.

He lunged forward, his sword reflecting the sunlight so harshly that my eyes teared up, then made a quick, deceptive motion as if to strike on my left.

Just as I braced for the impact, he pivoted sharply, his foot whipping out in a blur, and took my legs out from under me.

I barely registered the move before feeling the unexpected force against the back of my legs.

My balance wavered, and the ground rushed up to meet me as I landed hard on my backside, the shock of the fall vibrating up my spine.

I stared at him, and he smiled brightly.

The fact that I was a woman didn't faze him in the slightest. I was grateful for that but also silently cursed the day he was born.

I wondered if this test was for endurance. If so, I was about to lose this Trial in a very pitiful manner.

"Up yer go."

He tugged me to my feet and started in again.

"You, sir, are a savage."

"Aye. An' proud of it."

With a sly glint in his eye, he demonstrated several more techniques for disarming an enemy, each one more cunning than the last.

None of his methods were gentle or polite, but they were undeniably effective. Next time the sociopath kissed me with reckless abandon and stormed off, I'd trip his ass. It was hard to pull off a dramatic exit when you face-planted.

Not that it seemed like there would be a next time.

"Watch yer feet." Eddie gave my boots a gentle tap with the flat of his sword. "Keep 'em firmly on the ground. And stop lookin' fer yer fella."

"He's not my—"

Eddie's sword swung toward me in a swift arc, and I instinctively stepped back, my heels skidding slightly on the dusty floor in my haste to keep my head attached to my body.

"Or you'll lose yer balance." Another devious grin played on his lips.

He really was a sadist.

I brushed a stray lock of hair out of my eyes, feeling the dampness of sweat on my forehead. Perhaps I was not cut out for the pirate life.

"You are a beast, Eddie," I muttered, trying to catch my breath.

"Aye," he replied with a hearty chuckle, the lines around his eyes crinkling. "And with some practice, you will be too, lass."

After another hour, I finally called it quits.

Main characters put a lot of effort into fighting. I'd seriously need to rethink my stance on how bad it was to be a secondary character from here on out.

Eddie handed me a frosty glass of water, the condensation trickling down my fingers as I leaned against the wooden railing.

I had no idea where he'd procured ice from but decided it was one of those fantasy elements I'd happily suspend my disbelief for.

We stood in companionable silence for a few minutes.

And no matter how hard I tried to not think of the prince, my thoughts kept going back to our kiss. Which was *really* inconvenient when I needed to figure out what this test was and how the Liber Noctem might have twisted the plot.

The ship rocked gently with the rhythm of the ocean, but within me, a storm of unease brewed. I'd expected the prince to eventually come back and resume his workout. Or scowl from across the deck.

Or give me a well-rehearsed dissertation on why the kiss was a mistake.

For the hundredth time, my attention moved toward the narrow staircase leading belowdecks.

Lord Stoic hadn't come back up since he descended it earlier.

Hours later, and the memory of our kiss still felt as real as when it first happened.

I couldn't shake off the worry that either he regretted it, or worse yet, he'd somehow been influenced by the dark book.

Maybe he was belowdecks trying to figure out a nice way to let me know he hadn't been in control of his actions at all.

That would be a nightmare in a sense. Finally getting the kiss from the wicked prince, only to discover he'd been forced into doing it.

Paranoia was clearly getting to me. But since I couldn't figure out what this test was focusing on, it seemed like insecurity or heartbreak was reasonable.

Eddie stood quietly by me, then finally said, "Can't hide up 'ere all day."

I looked out across the vast expanse of the sea, where dark clouds gathered, bruising the horizon with their deep, menacing hues.

The wind whipped at my clothes, carrying the heavy scent of rain.

Another storm was brewing, and its approach felt inevitable, much like the confrontation I dreaded.

No matter how much I'd like to stay up here, I couldn't keep hiding from the prince or delay honing my magical abilities. I needed his help.

Eddie was right. It was time to face the tempest—both around and within.

As dramatic as that sounded, it was necessary. If that didn't mark some decent character growth, I wasn't sure what would.

With a deep breath, I straightened from the railing and let a warm smile stretch across my face as I faced the grizzled pirate.

"Thank you for the lessons," I said. "They've been most illuminating."

He chuckled, his eyes twinkling, and leaned in closer.

"If he gives you any trouble, just aim a good kick at his balls," he advised with a wink. "Less messy than stabbin'."

I grinned back at him. That it certainly was.

Adopting my best pirate queen visage, I made my way across the deck and slowly descended the stairs. Once I was belowdecks, it took far longer than necessary to arrive at my destination.

I'd never been one to delay a conversation, no matter how awkward, so this was a new and unwelcome feeling.

I lingered outside the carved wooden doors to the captain's quarters, my knuckles hovering just above the surface as I debated whether to knock politely or burst in unannounced.

Gods. Why was a simple kiss making us both act so strange?

It certainly wasn't his first kiss, nor was it mine.

I'd had several different first kisses, some chaste and innocent, some after a few too many glasses of ale that were just okay. But very few had been soul shaking.

And the kiss earlier had been in a class all its own.

I exhaled and squared my shoulders.

Even through the door, the tension between us hung heavy in the air.

It wasn't natural or normal.

It definitely felt like some sinister force was at work, weaving dark magic to drive a wedge between us, and we both seemed to be playing into its devious hands. Maybe this was tied into my test. How, I wasn't sure. But my emotions were definitely being toyed with.

Blondie was far less scary than the uncertain reality we faced, and it was time to shelve those personal emotions for a different day.

It was easier said than done, but...false bravado was a hell of a thing.

My heart pounded as I finally mustered the courage to push the door open.

The hinges creaked softly, and my attention immediately fell on the prince, standing near the window.

He twisted to glance my way, and it felt like the world stopped.

His piercing gaze locked onto mine, a mix of emotions flickering across his face. None of which I could read or decipher.

He stood like a statue, tension coiled tightly within his broad shoulders, as I stepped into the room. There was no sign of the male I'd laughed with last night.

The one who'd cracked himself open a little for me and offered a few hours of normalcy when I'd needed it the most.

We both had, actually. He'd been lost to stormy thoughts, and I'd dragged him out of that, trying to get him to focus on other things.

Prince Sloth, the most logical, practical, no-nonsense being in existence, had a pirate picnic food fight.

And he'd *laughed*.

Then, when I'd been teetering on the verge of darkness, he'd been the light guiding me back. Now he was colder and more remote than ever.

It stung.

I walked over to him, stopping just inches from his rigid form.

His eyes flickered with a brief, intense warmth, before the familiar frosty barrier slid back into place, masking any trace of his feelings.

"Are we all right?" I asked, pointing between us. "Or are you going to keep acting like the abominable snowman because of one kiss?"

His brow furrowed slightly.

Great.

He'd gone into a fugue state and completely blocked the kiss from his mind. What a confidence booster.

He opened his mouth, then closed it.

I waited for another minute, secretly hoping he'd confess his undying love and we'd ride off into the sunset after we'd survived the Trials and slain the proverbial dragons keeping us apart.

But his lips pressed into a firm line.

Apparently, I'd misread the situation.

"Never mind." I waved my hand around, dismissing the conversation before I took Eddie's sage advice. "I want to know what's really going on with your tattoo. You can't just think it's reacting to your emotions. And it's the only thing you're not forthcoming about when I ask. What are you scared of?"

TWENTY-TWO
Prince Sloth

I STUDIED LORE CLOSELY, my focus tracing every subtle shift in her expression as I tried to decipher the emotions hidden behind her calm facade.

The moment lingered between us, heavy with my unspoken words.

I couldn't sense her emotions, and I wasn't sure if it was another symptom of my dwindling powers or if she'd somehow blocked me.

Very few beings in any of the realms had that power.

Dreamweavers, to my knowledge, weren't among them.

I'd come here to visit my library and do some quick research but couldn't. Either my power was severely drained now, or something was preventing me from using my magic to get there. I was unable to replenish my magic from my court, and stoking sloth in someone wasn't ideal given our surroundings. My frustration had grown tenfold.

I'd crossed a line I shouldn't have when I kissed her, but she dismissed it with a nonchalant wave, as if it hadn't stirred anything within her.

It was far from insignificant.

Something awakened in me. Something I was having a difficult time wrangling back into submission. I'd been grappling with it ever since.

I would blame my reaction on this peculiar dream realm, but I suspected it had little to do with it. And now that my library was taken from me, I had no text to pull to help decipher what the hells I'd felt.

If Lore wanted to move on from it, I wouldn't press her into a discussion.

All the reasons I'd sketched out earlier for why we shouldn't give in to temptation remained. More so now than before if that single kiss was anything to go by.

"Sometimes I think the Liber Noctem's magic grates on me."

Her brows pinched together. "How?"

I turned back to the window, running my hand along the drapery as I watched the storm clouds gather.

Lightning whipped across the sky.

Ten seconds later, thunder clapped.

It wouldn't be long before the storm hit us.

"I believe it has something to do with the tattoo. I also think that might be interfering with my powers, but I haven't had time to analyze it fully, so it's just a working theory. I normally replenish my magic through my court, so it's also possible this realm is simply taking its toll. There was no need to discuss it when you have so much else to be concerned with. I might not even be right."

All of a sudden, I felt Lore's emotions again. They were like a tsunami.

I squinted into the darkness.

I could have sworn I'd seen a glint below the water.

"You mentioned a sea monster yesterday. Does it attack the ship in your story?"

I watched Lore's expression in the window's reflection.

Her gaze moved from me to the storm, a furrow in her brow. She hadn't tamped down her emotions; if anything they seemed to rise higher. It seemed extreme. I suspected the Liber Noctem was close and ready to act.

"It does, but it's not until the end of the book and it's not very big. This is, by all accounts, too early for that to happen."

Unless the Liber Noctem was running interference.

I saw the exact moment horror dawned as she came to that same conclusion.

She smothered her fear an instant later.

"I'll try to get us to a quieter story before—"

Her words were abruptly silenced by an eerie, mournful wail emanating from the depths of the ocean just outside our window.

It was a haunting sound that lingered in the air, sending chills along my spine. I pivoted to face her.

The column of her throat bobbed visibly as she struggled to swallow the next wave of fear I sensed coming from her.

"Dear gods." She tore her attention from the window and looked at me. "In the book, the monster eats a few crew members, but it's killed with a harpoon."

Whatever made that noise sounded much larger than something easily dispatched by that sort of weapon. Ten harpoons wouldn't likely have enough firepower to stop it.

Her fear was growing.

"Do you know what this test might be now?"

She nodded. "I have a slight phobia of drowning."

I drew in a deep breath. Then the dark book would definitely attempt that. We'd simply keep her belowdecks and out of harm's way.

"Grab the phoenix tear. Try to visualize another story. Just like you did before I was almost beheaded."

Lore closed her eyes, her chest rising and falling as something brushed up against the side of the ship, forcing us to sway wildly.

I felt her fear grow impossibly stronger.

Something deep inside me twisted. My hands flexed at my sides.

It took a moment to realize what it was, a protective urge.

My instincts demanded I grab her and run. The almost overwhelming *need* to do just that pounded in time with my heart.

I struggled to rein myself in, completely out of my element as I tried to take in whatever was happening with me. I breathed out, keeping myself centered.

I watched her hands curl into fists as she concentrated on channeling her magic into the phoenix tear.

She moved to the bed and sat down, her eyes closed in concentration.

Another wail went up outside.

Seconds later, the ship lurched violently, caught in the turbulence of the monster's wake. It hadn't even attacked; it was just languidly circling us, a predator toying with its prey.

When another moment passed and Lore showed no signs of manifesting us into a new scene, I shifted to our next best option.

I strode to Lore and squatted before her.

None of the earlier tension between us remained.

"I'm going topside for a few minutes. Gather as many supplies as you can safely carry on your person."

Her panicked gaze shot to me. "You're leaving me alone? What if I shift stories without you?"

I suspected that *couldn't* happen, not that she wasn't capable. Somehow, someway, the Liber Noctem had to be blocking her power. It could be part of the tests. Otherwise she would have been able to dream up new scenes.

"If that happens, I *will* find you."

"You can't know that."

I tucked a strand of hair behind her ear.

"I'll be back before you finish gathering supplies. Then we'll make a plan when I return." I stood and backed up a step. "Try not to miss me too much, Peaches. Or I might think you actually like me."

Before she could respond, I whipped around and bolted for the door.

The crew buzzed with frenetic energy despite the rain now pelting down. They were a hive of movement as they braced for the impending attack.

I paused for a moment to assess the situation.

Pirates swung agilely from the rigging, their feet barely touching the ropes as they maneuvered with practiced ease.

Their grim faces were set with determination as they hefted massive harpoons and carefully positioned them for the strike, the metal flashing dangerously with each whip of lightning that cracked overhead.

The very atmosphere itself was charged with tension.

Not a single glance of suspicion was sent in my direction as the crew scrambled across the deck, their focus set entirely on their defensive preparations.

We had a common enemy now. Which made us allies.

I spotted the first mate near the spyglass and aimed for him.

"Kensie! Any eyes on the beast?"

"There, Cap'n!" Kensington shouted. "Starboard side, comin' in around fifty knots!"

I followed the line of his outstretched arm and swore.

Amid the howling winds and crashing waves of the furious storm bearing down on us, a monstrous sea serpent emerged from the ocean.

It was unlike anything I'd seen in the Underworld. A creature that could only be born of this nightmare world and Lore's colorful imagination.

Its massive body rivaled the size of our ship.

It looked like the nightmare creatures had come to us after all.

As it sliced through the turbulent waters with fearsome grace, I finally saw the spiraled horn crowning its head that Lore had described.

It glistened with seawater as the monster banked toward the ship and aimed that deadly horn our way.

If it hit the hull of the ship with that weapon, we'd suffer a devasting blow.

I followed it from one side of the deck to the other, planting my feet wide and gripping the railing as the next surge of water tossed us around.

A violent surge of dark magic hit me a beat later. Somehow, someway, the Liber Noctem was with the beast. My skin prickled as I searched the waters.

There was no sign of Xavier. Which meant if the book was here and he wasn't, he'd been eliminated. I had no time to dwell on that.

The creature circled closer, the power of the Book of Nightmares pouring from it undeniable. I needed to kill the beast and claim the book.

The serpent's scales shimmered like wet obsidian under the flashes of lightning, and each time it breached the surface, the sea around it boiled with fury.

My dagger would cut its flesh, but I'd need to land a direct hit to its eye or heart to kill it. And I'd need to get close for that.

I swept a hand through my wet hair, pushing it out of my face.

My tunic was soaked through, the material sticking like a second skin. I ignored the discomfort; it would not be ideal for fighting, but I'd manage.

This might be the only chance I had to secure the book.

The pirates closest to the creature scrambled across the deck, shouting in panic as it reared up, ready to strike with its powerful tail and razor-sharp teeth.

It rose like a hell beast from the water, its body far larger than I'd first thought. It towered above us, and I noticed it wasn't exactly a serpent.

Tentacle-like appendages, grotesque and leeching, sprouted with force from behind the monster's jaw. It dove down, wrapping that hell mouth around one of the ship's masts in a vise grip and snapping it with ease, like a twig underfoot.

It happened from one breath to the next.

The crew tried to swing the harpoon around, but it was too late.

The monster sank back into the waters before lashing up again, attacking the second mast with the same brutal violence.

That last mast splintered into jagged shards that rained down on the deck. Crew members scattered, their cries swallowed by the roar of the sea and the beast.

The monster rose from the water and dove for us again.

It crashed onto the deck, tentacled mouth snapping, searching for prey.

"Arm yourselves with swords!" I yelled, rolling to the side, narrowly missing a crushing blow.

The ship shuddered under the weight of the attack.

Beneath the monster's massive, armored underbelly, thousands more tentacles, slick and sallow, unfurled in a frenzy.

They were the size of human arms, and they writhed in savage unison, ravenous and agitated, helping the beast skid over the deck like a centipede as it slithered through the ruin it had caused.

The beast shoved its spindly arms into the giant cracks it had made with its thrashing, searching out victims to yank into their watery graves.

"Weapons at the ready!" I yelled. "Attack!"

Swords glinted in the flashes of lightning.

I gripped my dagger in my fist and raced for the monster, intent on landing a kill shot while it was distracted. The Book of Nightmares would be *mine*.

I flung myself onto its back and slid off—its scales coated in some slick oil-like substance. I regained my footing and dodged a swipe of its tail.

The pirates were slashing at it, hacking away, but it wasn't enough. However the Liber Noctem had unified with the beast, it was in control.

The monster retreated from the deck and sank back into the water, circling us from below again.

I followed its massive wake as it swam under the boat, trying to figure out a way to work around the slick scales.

When it emerged on the other side, it had a new trick.

One I was not at all prepared for.

Its singular crystalline horn seemed to vibrate with an ominous glow now, generating an eerie harmonic sound as it pierced the water's surface, resonating like an otherworldly siren.

The air was alive with the haunted melody, and the sound swirled around the ship, shaking the very planks beneath our feet.

It was loud enough that it could probably be heard several realms away.

A ghostly fog emerged, following each chilling note, and shrouded the men with its cold embrace.

The Book of Nightmares had called in the storm.

Lore hadn't mentioned that—which meant we were now fully under the influence of the Liber Noctem. I was glad she was belowdecks, safe, for now.

I had little doubt it would do everything it could to make her fear come true. The siren's call grew to an unnatural pitch.

A paralysis gripped the crew, a terror so profound that even their shouts were silent, swallowed by the relentless ringing sound.

I scented blood on the air. Some of the crew were bleeding from their ears and noses, the noise too powerful for their mortal bodies.

This was unlike anything I'd ever faced.

But even nightmares could be slain.

The monster flew up from the water, swaying like a giant cobra.

Its serpentine body shimmered with an otherworldly brilliance, each bioluminescent scale flaring violently with every lightning strike, carving a haunting and spectral silhouette against the churning, malevolent storm clouds.

Gripping my dagger with white-knuckled intensity, I glared at the monster as it coiled back, poised to unleash its next brutal assault.

The serpent's milky eyes were a chilling, sightless white, yet it eerily tracked my movements with an unerring precision that defied logic, as if it hunted by feeling every tremor and vibration rippling through the ground.

The dark book had to be in its gut. I'd need to tear open its belly to be sure.

"Distract it!" I shouted.

The crew jumped into action, fighting to ensnare the monster's attention, but the beast's resolve was growing more determined, more vicious by the minute.

It craved death and violence and would not rest until it was sated.

Its tentacles ripped through the crew and the ship, winding around it in a deathly embrace. The creature lurched and tensed, its muscular body wrapping around the ship's hull with shocking speed, and applied such a massive force that every wooden plank strained against the others.

The Liber Noctem would not be taken easily.

The timbers creaked beneath the immense pressure, each one bending to the brink before the vessel gave a horrifying shudder.

Then, as if in a violent crescendo, the boards began to split and fracture, snapping sharply and sending splinters into the air like a volley of jagged arrows.

It was a scene of utter ruin.

The crew staggered under the sudden jolt, their shouts drowned out by the terrifying symphony of cracking wood.

The sound of the crushed boat carried across the water, a brutal testament to the creature's devastating might.

It was going to rip the damn ship in half.

Fuck.

We needed to retreat, but a quick glance indicated that the dinghies were destroyed. We'd need to swim and pray there was a shore close by.

I did not want to get Lore into the ocean without a life raft, nor did I want to leave the Liber Noctem behind, but I couldn't ensure her safety if I stayed.

Cursed Liber Noctem.

Wood groaned as the ship buckled, decks beginning to collapse upon themselves while the creature's tentacles tightened, leaving the vessel gasping under the strain.

We had moments left before we capsized.

"Retreat!"

The crew started abandoning the ship, knowing it was a lost cause.

I raced toward the end of the deck, sliding over the slick wood.

I needed to get Lore before we went down.

The ship seemed to scream as the beast's grip shattered all hope of its survival and the front half exploded into dust.

A new scream sounded that stopped me dead in my tracks.

I swung around, searching for the woman who'd made the noise.

There.

At the far end of the ship, like a distant, unreachable shore, was Lore.

And right behind her was the Liber Noctem in its nightmare creature form.

Her eyes locked onto mine, a storm of fear and apology swirling within them. She was saying goodbye. She knew the book was orchestrating her worst fear and she didn't think she'd pass. We'd been wrong. It wasn't the fear of drowning that was being tested. It was hopelessness.

The realization shattered something deep within me.

A thread I had only started to sense vibrated with tension.

"Lore! Run! The creature, it's the book!"

She didn't hear me over the howling wind.

I sprinted toward her with every ounce of strength I had, my heart pounding like a war drum, each beat mimicking the sudden desperation coursing through my veins. I couldn't lock my panic down.

The book could not have her.

Rain lashed at me with brutal force, driving our failing ship sideways as Lore desperately clung to the frayed rigging.

I was still too damned far away.

The ground was slick and treacherous beneath my boots, and for the first time in my life, I stumbled. My heart seized in my chest. Every moment counted and I'd lost one. Possibly the most important second in the realms.

I pushed on, cursing the elements and the dark book and the emotions I normally suppressed that were boiling to the surface.

If Lore died... if I failed to keep her safe...

She slid down the ship's tilted deck, her legs flailing over the jagged edge where the tumultuous waves seethed in a frothy cauldron of chaos and death.

I watched as her fingers struggled to maintain their grip and the creature lunged for her. The Liber Noctem almost had her.

An icy dread gripped me as I realized I was too far away to help her, even with every ounce of speed I possessed.

With a primal roar, I hurled myself at the beast, my outstretched hands grasping at empty air, missing it by mere inches.

I landed hard on the deck and rolled to a stop.

Lore's terrified gaze found mine right as she was yanked into the churning ocean below. There was one solitary beat where I was frozen to the spot.

Then I snapped back to myself.

All my control vanished.

In the next instant, I detonated.

Without hesitation, I clenched my teeth around the cool metallic hilt of my dagger, then plunged headfirst into the water after Lore and the Book of Nightmares.

TWENTY-THREE
Lore

A TORRENT OF icy water surged over my head, its chill biting into my skin like a thousand needles. Or perhaps those were teeth.

Dear gods. Did the tentacles have actual teeth in them? What kind of monster lived in my brain to dream up something like that?

Those horrific arm-sized tentacles coiled tightly around my middle, constricting my lungs so hard I couldn't breathe, let alone scream.

And now was very much a time for screaming.

This was my absolute worst fear come to life. If I allowed myself to think about it, to sink into that fear, I would lose.

I thrashed and writhed in a frantic attempt to break free, but each movement only caused the creature's hold to tighten further.

I might as well be trapped in an iron vise, its grasp was that secure.

I barely managed to gulp down a final breath before I was dragged beneath the surface. The icy grip of the ocean tightened around me almost as hard as the creature's tentacles did. Soon I was struggling against both forces.

The monster's slick, sinewy body cut through the water, pulling me in an endless downward plunge.

The deeper we went, the colder it got.

My muscles seized up and my lungs burned with the desperate need for air.

I clawed at the tentacle, my fingernails barely breaking the strange surface of its skin. Some areas had scales; some reminded me of a whale.

And every part when combined was terrifyingly alien.

My lungs burned with desperation, each second underwater stretching into an eternity. If I didn't get air soon, I was going to drown.

I had no sassy quips, no books or tropes to compare it to.

Only a growing terror that my life was coming to a violent ending.

This had veered wildly off course from the original story, so I had no idea what would come next. But being on the water, knowing how much I feared drowning, I should have known the dark book would pluck that from the deepest recesses of my mind and toy with me.

It was too late for *if only*s.

Now was the time to come up with an exit strategy from this terrible death ride on my own.

I did not want to go out with a whimper, but fighting the monster wasn't getting me anywhere except winded faster.

Bubbles escaped my lips, spiraling upward in a frantic dance toward the surface that seemed now to be impossibly distant.

Dear gods. I was seconds away from complete and utter panic.

I had taken a slim dagger from the pirates' stash, but it was in an ankle sheath I couldn't reach. That option out, I focused on the next.

I tried to latch onto my magic, thinking I might be able to twist the story enough to give me an advantage without leaving the prince.

Maybe I could dream up a mask or set of gills to breathe underwater.

Or even imagine the monster as a fierce, sassy guppy. Instead of whatever peculiar amalgamation this serpent-unicorn-octopus from hell was.

Obviously, this was another nightmare creature from this realm that was only inspired by the original story.

But as I finally felt my powers awaken, I couldn't go through with it.

If I accidentally shifted to a new story, then I'd be leaving Sloth in the middle of a stormy sea with a monster.

He was confident he'd track me, but he'd need to get out of this situation first. And then what if he *couldn't* find me?

It was a gamble I refused to take.

I hoped my decision didn't come back to haunt me, but something about this moment, this choice, felt like the true test. Would I leave him behind to save myself? Or would I fight for us both?

My mind raced with any other ideas. If there was ever a time to step into some epic main character energy, this was my moment.

But the only thing epic about it was how hard I was failing. Stupid adventure stories and the unrealistic expectations they set.

The pressure mounted around my ears, and the dim light above faded into an inky darkness. Death loomed closer. This was worse than any nightmare I'd ever had about drowning.

Even if I broke free, I'd have to hold my breath for several moments to reach the surface.

My airways felt like lava.

I remembered the time when I was little, the time my fear began. I'd been with my family on the beach; Fable was collecting polished glass with our mother. And my father and I were walking in the water, kicking at the waves.

Every Sunday after we'd visited the library and had come home to cook as a family, we'd venture out to the beach and take an evening walk. It was one of my favorite childhood memories. That Sunday had been different, though; there'd been a storm blowing in, making the sea churn.

One small wave knocked my feet out from under me, and while I wasn't ripped out to sea, my father couldn't get to me right away.

It had felt like this. Like my lungs were heaving and my heart might burst.

Panic sank its claws in deep. I wanted to *survive*.

I thrashed against the monster's impossible grip, and the icy water pressed against my lungs, urging me to kick harder toward the distant surface.

Fear like I'd never known consumed me.

I was going to die.

And the prince... He said we both needed to survive, or he'd die too.

A surge of desperation had me fighting harder, battling the monster with my bare hands.

I would not go down quietly.

I would curse this realm and the Book of Nightmares and the cruel goddess with my last breath. I would never lose hope. And that had to be what this test was centered on—trying to take my hope from me. I would never give that up.

Ever. I would rather die than lose myself to hopelessness.

Suddenly, a brilliant streak of light sliced through the murky depths, illuminating the shadowy expanse of water around me.

It moved too swiftly for me to make out what it was, but the monster wasn't happy with this new development. I couldn't help but wonder if I had just passed the test.

The creature's massive jaws parted, unleashing a deafening roar that sent harsh ripples coursing through the water.

The sound was so intense that it reverberated along the ocean floor, causing schools of fish to scatter in panicked swirls and the seaweed to sway in turbulent waves. Salt stung my eyes as I blinked rapidly, trying to focus.

And there he was, my prince of icy rage.

He'd come for me. His blond hair was a radiant beacon, slicing through the endless dark water like a golden blade.

He looked like an angel of vengeance, a celestial warrior descending into the abyss with a singular purpose. To free the heroine from the monsters he'd slay.

Just like the heroes in my stories.

Now I couldn't tell if it was the water stinging my eyes or the sudden prickle of tears. Sloth would hate being called a hero.

But neither one of us had given up hope. I knew with certainty that was the crux of this test. Now we just needed to survive.

As he grew closer, I noticed the ice-cold fury etched into his handsome features. He'd never looked more beautiful or more terrifying.

The prince plunged through the water, his form cutting through the darkness with determination. His dagger glowed like a shard of starlight clenched tightly in his fist as he aimed for the sea monster.

With a swift, forceful strike, he slashed at the tentacle that was coiled around me, squeezing the air from my chest.

Though the creature's hold remained impossible for me to break, a stronger flicker of hope ignited inside me.

I was not alone.

Somehow, with my valiant sidekick here, this seemed less impossible.

I kept my attention locked on the prince but continued to wriggle, hoping with two of us, the monster might lose some of its focus.

All I needed was to get my hips free; then I could kick myself to the surface.

Instead of attacking the monster like I had been doing, I pushed myself against the tentacle like it was a small window I was attempting to squeeze out of.

I managed to gain a few inches.

The creature let loose another roar.

Sloth propelled himself through the water with powerful strokes, determination on his face as he closed the distance between himself and the monster.

His fist connected with the beast's slick body, sending a tremor through the water. Instead of letting go, the creature's grip tightened around me, its scales suddenly slicing into my palms like it had activated armor.

I gasped involuntarily, the last bubbles of air escaping from me.

In a blur of motion, the prince was suddenly in front of me, his eyes intense and focused. His hands cradled my face, and before I could comprehend what he was doing, his lips met mine, not in a tender caress but with a sense of urgency.

It wasn't a kiss of passion but of necessity, a desperate act to save my life.

I parted my lips, feeling the warmth of his breath as he forced life-giving air into my lungs.

He drew back slightly, his gaze tracing every contour of my face, as if he was committing each detail to memory.

Then, without hesitation, he kicked up through the water, swimming toward the monster's massive head, his dagger gleaming in his clenched fist.

The creature's horn lashed out with deadly speed, inches away from striking him, but he twisted his body just in time to evade the lethal attack.

He surged forward again, his muscles straining as he launched himself faster through the water.

On the next pass, he crashed into the back of the serpent's head and reached around, driving the dagger deep into its eye.

The sea monster's tentacles finally loosened their grip, and I tore myself free, my heart pounding as I kicked desperately, slicing through the water, trying to distance myself from the creature's writhing form. The belt and little pouch I'd secured the phoenix tear in were still in place and I thanked whatever god was looking out for me that it hadn't been lost in the attack.

I paused, squinting through the murky water, horrified to see the prince still fighting valiantly, his dagger flashing as he slashed at the beast's other eye.

He was using himself as a distraction to give me a chance to escape.

I wanted to scream at him. Didn't he realize the damned hero always died?

A pang of fear twisted within me, urging me to stay, but his eyes locked onto mine, silently begging me to go.

Against every instinct screaming inside me, I spun around and swam toward the surface, my legs and lungs burning with the effort.

I hesitated only once, glancing back over my shoulder.

Sloth was now wound up in one of the tentacles, but his expression was anything but defeated. He looked like he was exactly where he wanted to be.

My heart pounded wildly, a deep, unfamiliar terror clawing at my insides.

I couldn't bear the thought of losing him.

Why the hells wasn't he trying to escape?

Before I could grab my own blade from my ankle sheath and swim to him, the beast yanked him downward, vanishing with my selfless, idiotic prince ensnared in its death grip.

"No!" I let out a garbled scream, draining the last of my breath, but I didn't care. I was no longer terrified of drowning. Something far more powerful gripped me as I searched for the prince.

I plunged deeper into the inky water, the coldness enveloping me.

Sloth and the monster were nowhere in sight; they'd been completely swallowed by the darkness.

I pushed myself forward, my arms slicing through the water with desperation, but my lungs burned for air, and I had to propel myself upward, breaking the surface, gasping for breath.

As I bobbed on the waves, a hollow ache spread through my chest, as if I had left a piece of my soul behind in the sea. And then, as if it knew the perfect time to strike, the Liber Noctem showed me another horrid vision.

I wanted to scream at the dark book, but suddenly, I wasn't just on the water; I was watching from some higher land while someone thrashed in the water. In my vision, I had no emotion. Nothing but a dark sense of pleasure as I watched the man struggle for breath. His pain amused me. But only slightly. As if whatever had taken control of me had long since lost the ability to truly *feel* much of anything.

I shuddered at the thought of being so empty, hollow. Void of emotion. Void of all hope of finding something better.

Just as suddenly as the vision appeared, the book released me and I was thrust back into the middle of the ocean.

I bobbed around, disoriented for only a beat. Sloth was still missing.

I kicked through the water with all my strength, my limbs aching as I plunged beneath the surface time and time again.

He'd chosen to go with the monster. And I couldn't understand *why*.

My eyes stung from the salt, scanning frantically for any glimpse of them. But the ocean stretched vast and empty around me.

The ship was gone, the pirates either dead or too far away for me to see, and the frigid water wrapped around my body like icy chains, each second more punishing than the last. Still, I couldn't abandon him, not like this.

Whatever his plan, whatever his motive, he should have surfaced by now.

My heart hammered as I gulped another breath and submerged once more, driven by the refusal to accept that he might truly be lost forever.

Eventually, my body shook too hard, and I risked hypothermia again.

I had to stop searching.

As much as leaving without him felt like I was tearing out my own heart, I refused to let his sacrifice be for nothing by dying.

He would be highly annoyed.

I could picture him storming the gates of the Great Beyond just to throttle my soul. Or maybe he'd battle the Underworld god himself to take me back just to torment me with an entire encyclopedia of reasons why I made the wrong move.

Anything was possible when it came to my favorite sociopath.

I spotted a smudge of darkness in the distance and used the last of my strength to get there.

Maybe Sloth had already swum ashore.

It was the little lies we told ourselves that could do the most damage. But I kept telling myself he was okay, he was waiting for me, we'd find each other and our adventure would continue. If he wasn't there... I couldn't finish the thought.

So I swam, one agonizing stroke at a time, focusing on that little spark of hope in my chest, and prayed it wouldn't betray me.

TWENTY-FOUR
Lore

I DRAGGED MYSELF across the rocky beach, each pebble and piece of driftwood digging into my palms and knees, as I fought the receding tide.

Being attacked and nearly eaten by a serp-i-corn wasn't one of the fears I'd had while living in Bellington.

Now I had a new nightmare to add to my growing collection.

I also really needed to reconsider what I read from now on.

Maybe adding some boring fiction wouldn't be the worst idea.

I doubted Lord Stoic would have had to worry about the uni-pus.

Pain shot through me that had nothing to do with the cold or the rocks.

I still couldn't accept that he was gone. I knew he was immortal, but the last conversation we had kept nagging at me. Was his immortality tied into his ability to wield his powers? Could he somehow survive without breathing underwater?

He'd admitted that his magic wasn't behaving normally.

But he hadn't told me how bad it had gotten. Knowing Lord Stoic, he probably kept the worst of it to himself, trying to sort out the facts on his own.

He was absolute crap at being a team player.

It was possible that the Liber Noctem had waited until he was drained to use the serp-i-corn to defeat him in an attempt to get me alone for the next test.

A powerful wave surged over me, its force sending me tumbling once more as it broke against my body.

I blinked rapidly, trying to clear my vision, but the sharp sting of the seawater made my eyes water and burn. Cursed ocean.

My trousers, sodden and heavy, clung to my legs like seaweed. My cream-colored tunic was now translucent and revealed exactly how cold I was.

And I was fairly positive sand had found its way to places it had no business exploring without a proper commitment first. The only positive was that the belt and the phoenix tear contained within the pouch had survived.

I felt raw on all levels. Physical, emotional, and definitely psychological.

If this was the Liber Noctem's dark magic at play, I hated to admit it was taking a toll. But I couldn't let it dim my light, no matter how dark and dreary the path got. And this path was definitely dreary.

I needed to work extra hard to find a silver lining.

I closed my eyes and could almost hear my mother pressing me and Fable to find the positive. I pretended they were all here now, and it gave me an added boost of determination and strength.

I heaved myself up onto my elbows and scanned the horizon for any signs of life. Beyond the strip of shoreline where I was gracefully sprawled like a beached whale, the land was dark, the kind of deep, enveloping darkness that swallowed all light and sound.

The water's icy chill seeped into my skin, but that wasn't what made me shudder. The moonlight barely illuminated the deserted shoreline, casting long, creepy shadows that danced with the rhythm of the waves.

It was horribly eerie.

I pushed myself to my feet, my boots sinking into the cool, damp sand, and felt the oppressive emptiness around me.

Sloth's energy had been palpable and without it I felt like I was missing a part of myself. It was strange how quickly we adapted to someone else's presence.

With him by my side, it had been easier to ignore the fact that we'd traveled to a realm literally built from nightmares and were embroiled in a deadly game that could unleash them on the world. My family. My friends.

I squinted into the night, desperate to spot a familiar shape against the crashing waves. But there was nothing—no shadow cutting across the moonlit sand, no outline of a figure moving toward me with reassuring strides.

My chest tightened with a painful throb of fear and denial.

The haunting lullaby of the ocean was broken only by the wind's mournful whistle, but no sounds of the prince emerging from the darkness joined the song.

I scanned my surroundings, but it was useless. I couldn't see more than a few feet in any direction and had no idea what waited for me above the shore.

It was best to hunker down until daybreak.

Shivering, I padded across the beach and dropped onto a fallen log.

I stayed like that for hours, shuddering in place, watching the waves ebb and flow, and there was still no sign of my faithful companion.

Total secondary character behavior. He'd hate that.

But I had few options without light. It wasn't prudent to go racing into a dark... forest? Vegetation? Jungle? Portal into some new fresh hell?

I had no idea. Which was why staying put was the wisest decision. I'd had enough excitement for one night anyway.

I kept replaying the last moments we were together, trying to pick it apart. He'd clearly been pleased to stay with the sea monster, but I couldn't understand why. If he hadn't solved some clue, then maybe the Liber Noctem had twisted his thoughts, so he'd welcome death instead of fight it. It was an abysmal thought.

When I'd exhausted every reason why he'd choose to stay with the monster, I tried to think of stories to entertain myself, to stop the fear from invading my senses, and failed.

I *was* frightened.

And it was exactly what the Book of Nightmares thrived on.

I wanted to be brave and fearless, but I was just a librarian who never expected to end up *in* a story.

Let alone create one. Not that my magic was behaving the way Sloth had believed it would. That kept nagging at me, but it was hard to know what was odd and what wasn't when I didn't know I'd even *had* magic a week ago.

In all my fantasy adventure stories, this was around the time the characters faced their inner fears. And that took some serious self-awareness.

Temet nosce. Know thyself.

Fable and I had more than one lively debate with our parents around the dinner table regarding the power of knowing thyself in fiction.

It was where true growth began after false starts.

To really know oneself, the character had to acknowledge every dark, mangled part of themselves as intimately as every light, joyful aspect.

That was when true mastery of introspection happened.

If we remained unaware of our faults, we could never hope to improve or grow. Perfection was not only impossible; it was boring.

Why live up to impossible standards set by others?

Or feel bad for not achieving something no one can?

I was always a fan of imperfect characters; it made their pursuit of either learning to change or accepting their flaws all the more interesting.

I knew what I feared and what I needed to face.

My fear of never finding true, passionate love. Never being loved wholly by someone else or giving that kind of love *to* someone.

Maybe the biggest romances in my life would always be fictional.

I had to trust that *I* was enough, that I didn't need fighting skills to win this battle. Or a grumpy, immortal prince to slay all my dragons for me.

I could depend on the strength of my mind.

I just had to have complete trust and faith in myself. I was the heroine in my story, and I was more than enough.

It was much easier said than done. Especially while stranded on an abandoned beach that I was pretty sure was known as the Isle of the Damned.

Pushing that sparkling nugget of joy from my mind, I scanned the shore again. Ever hopeful.

Nothing changed.

I pulled the phoenix tear from the belt pouch and closed my fingers around it.

The stone warmed under my touch.

Closing my eyes, I concentrated, trying to establish a deeper bond with the stone, hoping to awaken the magic it held.

Time seemed to slip away, the world around me fading until I felt the first gentle stirrings of my magic flickering within.

It felt like tiny sparks igniting in the dark.

Instead of letting my power surge forward all at once, I carefully imagined a thin tendril separating from the main flow, a delicate shadow ribbon unfurling from the rest of my power. I was a dreamer; I had to remember that above all else.

Anything I imagined could be real. I just had to believe hard enough.

I didn't want to shift stories; I only wished to call forth a single shadow.

When I finally opened my eyes, excitement bubbled within me.

In the center of my palm, a small shadow creature squirmed and twisted, its form reminiscent of a baby snake made of pure darkness.

There was a playful energy about it, almost like it was wagging a tail that wasn't there. I instantly fell head over heels in love with the peanut.

"Aren't you the cutest," I cooed to it.

The little shadow creature coiled itself around my wrist, its touch as light as a whisper. I laughed as it wriggled over my palm, loving its personality.

I swore I heard a soft, contented purr emanating from its ethereal form as I hugged it close. I wondered if it was born of my loneliness or if I'd had the power to draw it forth all along. No matter the how, I was thankful for its company.

After teaching it some tricks, like bolting down the shore to spy for me then racing to report back, I decided to name it Theodore, Teddy for short.

We practiced controlling my magic for hours.

I'd send Teddy back to the rest of my magic, then I'd call him out again. By the end of the night, I felt more confident in my control over my magic. There wasn't a lot of it, but I had enough to aid me.

I just needed to work with it instead of fighting against it.

And one of the biggest hurdles I kept facing was not fearing it.

Teddy was helping more than the little shadow pet could ever know. He was opening a true bond between myself and my magic.

It was hard to be afraid of the shadows when they purred.

I was in no way a master dreamweaver, but I had more basics down, which was more than I could claim a few hours ago. Now I just needed time to practice.

Together Teddy and I sat and watched for any movement along the beach.

"Sometimes I used to walk to the cliffs back home," I said. Teddy curled around my wrist, excited for a story. "I'd go right before twilight, when the sun was sinking low on the horizon, casting a golden glow across the water."

Our family called it magic hour and it felt like it truly was just that.

"I'd watch the sunset, and I'd dream that one day I'd go on a quest of my own." Teddy wriggled excitedly, wanting more. "Not like this one. I'd just thought maybe I'd get the courage to travel to the capital city. Visit Fable. Fall in love with the kind of man who thrilled me on all levels."

Except now I'd ended up on a quest that was centered on my worst fears, and I doubted Prince Sloth would permit himself to ever follow his heart, especially after what he'd confessed about how his court viewed love.

"I'm happy you're here with me, Teddy. I don't suit being all alone. Which might come as a surprise, considering how much I read."

We sat quietly for a few hours.

Then, as dawn crawled itself out from the cover of darkness, a figure emerged.

Followed by another.

And another.

"Gods' blood," I swore, jumping to my feet. "Will this nightmare ever end?"

I probably shouldn't ask that sort of thing out loud, lest I accidentally manifest more dark fun.

I'd forgotten all about the cursed specters.

It seemed like I was about to be reacquainted with them soon enough.

"You better hide back with the rest of my magic, Teddy."

The little shadow seemed agitated to leave me alone but dutifully vanished back to wherever my magic lived.

I set my feet the way Eddie had shown me, preparing myself for the fight that was fast approaching.

The specters moved in a disjointed rhythm, their tiny feet floating a few inches off the ground, red eyes gleaming, and something inside me snapped.

"Nope."

I wasn't even remotely prepared to face off against those eerie creatures. They seemed to be slightly different here, thanks to the nightmare realm's influence.

My survival instincts kicked in, and I spun around to flee, only to collide with an unyielding wall of muscle.

A flicker of hope ignited, my heart racing with anticipation as I drew back.

"You're—" I began, my words catching in my throat as I choked on my emotions.

But the figure before me was not the prince.

He stood over six feet tall, his broad shoulders straining against the fabric of his tunic. His jawline was sharp, and his piercing gaze brushed past me with a look that bordered on disdain.

I glanced over my shoulder and noticed the specters had vanished.

Wonderful. If the vampire cousins feared this man, I needed to get away from him as soon as possible too.

I stumbled back and he moved with me. I hadn't expected that.

Maybe I'd imagined it. I moved again and he did too.

Every step he took was deliberate, as if he expected the realm itself to bow before him.

I stopped trying to escape and held my ground.

I did not do well with bossy men. Prince Sloth excluded.

My gaze roamed over the stranger's perfectly defined features, the deep emerald eyes, the burnished auburn hair, then lingered on the pointed tips of his ears. They extended beyond those of any mortal I'd ever known.

I swallowed hard.

He wasn't human.

He was Fae.

His attention swept over me with a deliberate slowness, his gaze as sharp as a blade. There was no warmth in his expression, only a cold scrutiny that lingered on the sheer fabric of my top, the dim morning light accentuating its translucence.

"Do you mind?" I crossed my arms.

"Not in the slightest."

His voice carried a lilting accent I didn't recognize. Probably because I'd never met someone from Faerie.

Finally, his gaze snapped back to my face with a dismissive flick.

I returned his stare with a hard glare of my own, my jaw set in defiance.

"Follow me," he commanded, his voice carrying an authority that would brook no dissent.

That was definitely sexier in books. In real life it made me want to stab him.

Repeatedly.

He was out of his mind if he believed I'd meekly trail behind him into some secret Faerie lair after that level of rude scrutiny.

And insane he must be.

Without another word, he pivoted and began to stride away.

What an arrogant ass.

He only managed a few steps before realizing I hadn't budged.

His shoulders stiffened as he turned back to face me, a scowl carving lines into his forehead. How dare a lowly mortal not fall at his Fae feet.

"Is there a reason you're not doing what I said?" he demanded, his voice dripping with irritation.

Several.

I met his gaze steadily.

"Probably because I'm *not* going to follow you. Which you would know if you'd bothered asking."

His jaw tightened, the muscles twitching under his bronze skin.

With a predatory grace, he marched back toward me.

But I was prepared. In one fluid motion, I unsheathed my blade, holding it firmly in front of me in the defensive stance I'd practiced with Eddie.

Bless that pirate.

If the Fae had been irritated before, his expression now twisted into something far more menacing.

He muttered something in a language I didn't know, but from the gist of things, I imagined he was cursing.

Frustration obviously transcended language barriers.

He advanced until his chest pressed against the tip of my blade, the cold steel barely indenting his tunic.

"Unless you've got an iron dagger, you're only aggravating me."

To drive home the point, almost literally, he leaned in, the tip of my dagger piercing his skin. I sucked in a sharp breath and dropped my arm.

Only a complete lunatic would voluntarily stab themselves.

Or, I supposed, an indestructible, pompous Fae.

He gave me a mocking grin.

"Follow me now," he said with a threatening edge, "or I'll *make* you."

I had a sinking suspicion that hadn't been an empty threat. I'd read plenty of books with Fae who would enthrall mortals.

A few quick words and gods only knew what this beast could make me do. If our introduction was anything to judge by, it wouldn't be pleasant.

He gave me a long look, then turned and stalked away.

As I plodded along behind my new best friend, I tried to figure out what book he was from. With such a charming personality, I should have recognized who he was immediately. But, then again, I read so many books about arrogant Fae, they tended to blend together after a while.

I needed more context clues to sort out who he was.

Unless this was some weird hybrid of two stories.

I shuddered at the thought. Given how things were going, I wouldn't be surprised if my magic was now piecing together a weregod of a tale.

I wondered if my subconscious could activate my dreamweaver power and change stories without me sensing any shift consciously. And if that was the case, then maybe I didn't need the phoenix tear to help me wield it at all.

It was a scary thought. I felt possessive of the phoenix tear, but more in a way that I wanted to keep it protected.

If the stone wasn't activating my magic, what, exactly was it for?

Aside from when I started practicing my magic, I struggled to recall if I'd seen any telltale signs of my powers when I'd first washed ashore, but the whole beach had been shrouded in shadows so thick I wouldn't have noticed my magic swirling around in them.

Sneaky ribbons of doom.

I daydreamed so often, I couldn't definitively say I *hadn't* summoned a new story as I swam to shore either.

There hadn't been any Fae in the pirate book, only the creepy specters.

And if I hadn't seen the mini-vamps at the same time Mr. Tall, Rude, and Brooding appeared, I would have thought I'd shifted stories completely.

Which meant it looked like this really was a hybrid story and I had no idea what to expect from him or wherever he was leading me.

But I knew I really didn't want to find out.

The plot was certainly thickening, and not in a fun way.

My one consolation was that if Sloth had survived the monster attack, there was still a chance we'd be reunited.

Sooner rather than later, I hoped.

Given how poorly things had been going of late, I figured that might be the biggest daydream of all.

TWENTY-FIVE
Lore

I TRAILED A few steps behind the surly Fae male, my attention sweeping over every inch of our path through the island.

It was much larger than I'd realized.

After only walking for a solid thirty minutes or so, I no longer heard the waves crashing against the shore.

I was hoping to find some way to leave a few markers for Sloth, so I stomped on a few patches of wildflowers, saying a silent apology, and accidentally tripped and snapped a twig off a branch or bush here and there.

My tour guide was more observant than I liked.

"Unless you wish to be chained to my side, stop that."

"Stop walking?" I shrugged. "Fine. Please feel free to continue without me."

He shot a glare over his shoulder.

Then his lips curled upward, revealing a grin that immediately set me on edge. He really needed to work on his friendly face.

He summoned several ropes of vines. "Attempt to leave a trail again, and these will be your new accessories."

Wonderful. He was a gardener from hell with a bondage kink.

He resumed his unforgiving pace across the island, and as much as I hated to admit it, the landscape unfolded like a scene from a fairy tale, with ancient trees stretching their limbs skyward, their leaves a vibrant jewel-toned green.

It felt like a whole new world from the one I'd washed up on.

Giant ferns unfurled along the trail, and rocks blanketed in velvety moss dotted the ground.

Of course, there was the occasional skull, which I studiously ignored.

After what I estimated to be an hour or possibly even a month of more walking, and absolutely no polite conversation, we approached a babbling brook.

Its melody was a soothing backdrop to an otherwise tense journey.

The whole time we'd been walking, I couldn't help but think of those skulls, picked clean to the bone, and wonder if I would be next.

As we got closer to the stream, I nearly dove in.

I hadn't had anything to drink since the battle with the sea monster and the exhausting swim to the shore, and my throat ached from how dry it was.

I dropped to my knees, cupping my hands to scoop the pristine, ice-cold water into my mouth, feeling the refreshing liquid quench my desperate thirst.

Normally, I'd be worried about ingesting bird or bug poo, but desperate times called for desperate measures.

It was like the nectar of the gods.

After I'd slaked my thirst, I splashed a bit of water on my face.

My skin stung and itched from the dried salt, and I was seriously considering jumping into the stream, when the Fae decided to dazzle me with more of his signature charm.

"Enough," my best friend snapped. "We're going to be late."

I was obviously destined to fall in love any second now.

Hopeful suitors the realms over would weep in jealousy at my good fortune.

"Perhaps if you were a decent tour guide, you'd share basic information on where we're going, what to expect, maybe inform me if I need to be presentable."

His teeth ground together so loudly, I heard the sound over the running water. If he wasn't careful, he'd crack a few of them in half.

Then he'd *really* have something to glower about.

"Maybe you'll find that out when we get where we're going. Or maybe I'll snap your neck and end our mutual torment. Now, move."

My gaze narrowed on him.

"If this is the beginning of some enemies-to-lovers romance, it seriously fails in reality. There is nothing remotely appealing about your attitude."

He gave me a look that said he had no idea what I meant and didn't care to find out, then abruptly turned on his heel and stormed down the trail.

I fantasized about tripping him for a solid twenty minutes. Much to my dismay, my magic didn't help that daydream manifest into reality.

Though I suspected if I called Teddy back, the little shadow would happily do my bidding. The thought warmed me. It was nice to have a diabolical shadow pet.

As we ventured deeper into the enchanted forest, the path began to gently slope upward. The ground here was almost completely covered with a soft carpet of moss and fallen leaves, and the air smelled of the earthy scent of the woods.

For a few blissful seconds, I forgot I was forcibly being escorted to a secret Faerie lair.

Birds called to one another from the treetops, and if I closed my eyes, I could pretend I was on a pleasant hike through the woods with a bag of books and picnic supplies. Like dark chocolate raspberry jellies.

I would commit homicide for one.

Preferably, the Fae male would be my victim and I'd live happily ever after once I'd disposed of his corpse.

Honestly, I'd work up an appetite after all the grave digging and would demolish the whole bag of jellies. I hoped daydream Lore had the foresight to pack a fizzy pink drink to quench my thirst.

A strawberry lime spritz would pair nicely with the raspberry jellies.

The slope's incline became more steep and less gentle and drew me back to the here and now, though I still had graphic thoughts of murder flitting through my head.

The dead Fae walking glided effortlessly up the terrain, his boots barely making any noise, while I trudged behind him, my mind conjuring images of him tripping over a hidden tree root and tumbling to his doom.

A girl could dream.

Sunlight filtered through the dense canopy above, dappling the ground in contrasting shades of light and shadow that grew brighter as we approached the forest's edge.

Once we arrived there, a breathtaking sight awaited us.

I stood there, mouth agape like a true mortal peasant, and stared at the aching beauty.

A hanging bridge woven from thick, twisting vines and rope spanned a deep ravine that led to a castle unlike anything I'd ever imagined.

It was a colossal structure grown from the heart of a tree that looked like it was as old as time, its bark walls spiraling upward, blending seamlessly with the branches and leaves high above. Each giant branch had a balcony that was partly covered with a leaf roof.

I would love to have a room with a balcony where I could sit in the sun and read to my heart's content.

I had no idea how the Fae had managed to build the castle, complete with turrets and battlements, from a tree, but I figured magic was involved.

I attempted to sidestep the Fae to get a better look, but he swiftly yanked me back by the fabric of my tunic, the sudden force making my heart skip a beat.

For a second I couldn't tell if he was about to toss me into the ravine.

Now *really* would be a wonderful time for my magic to make him sprout a tail for me to strangle him with.

"This way."

His voice was as hard as his grip on my poor shirt.

With increasingly violent thoughts filtering through my head, I followed my lovely companion down a serpentine path that meandered through the dense forest and skirted the edge of the ravine until I no longer saw the giant gash in the earth.

After a few minutes of brisk walking, the trail finally opened to reveal a waterfall cascading into a steaming-hot spring.

It was another undeniably beautiful sight.

Mist hung in the air, and the sound of rushing water echoed against the cliffs that curved around the falls.

My gaze shifted from the sparkling water to the Fae, who wore a stonelike expression. I'd never met someone more unpleasant.

It was obvious he hadn't brought me here to discuss our favorite anti-heroes. I needed to bathe before being presented to whoever ruled the tree castle.

The ultimate in Faerie lairs.

No matter how appealing the idea of getting clean was, the thought of doing so under his scrutinizing glare sent a shiver down my spine.

"Strip," he commanded.

Romance truly was dead.

"Are you capable of speaking in full sentences?"

His lips curled into a cruel, mocking smirk.

"Take off your clothes. Or I will be forced to do the task myself."

I took a step back, wondering what circle of hell I'd fallen into now.

Thankfully, the look he leveled me with was not remotely sexual, but still, there was no way I would do what he'd demanded.

"I'm not getting undressed with you standing there staring like a serial killer who's imagining flaying my skin off."

He advanced toward me, each step more menacing than the last.

"If I answer one of your questions, will you get in the damned water?"

Honestly, I'd be getting in either way because I was uncomfortable, but if he wanted to offer up information, I wasn't about to turn it down.

Plus, this established that I wouldn't simply roll over and heel every time he tossed an order out.

"You'll answer truthfully?"

"Yes."

I considered what would give me the best clue about which story we were in. He hadn't offered his name yet, and I figured he wouldn't.

Fae, like the Princes of Sin, were touchy about that sort of thing.

I needed to figure out what this test was and do everything I could to mentally prepare for it.

"What am I getting ready for?"

His smile raised the hair on the back of my neck.

Apparently, he'd been hoping I'd ask that particular one.

"You'll be participating in a hunt, darling. Now, bathe quickly. We have much to prepare for and the fun begins at midnight."

"An actual hunt?" I asked.

He inclined his head.

Oh, crap. His horrid personality, the haughty disdain, the hunt. The tree castle was different from the original story, but I knew exactly what book this was.

Hunted by the Horsemen.

It was an interconnected story set in the same universe as *Silverbeak's Wrath.*

I flipped through my memories of the plot. I'd read it a few times, but on my rereads I usually skimmed until I got to War's point-of-view chapters.

He was everything right about morally gray love interests.

Confident, just shy of arrogant, dominating in the bedchamber, and completely unapologetic about his very skewed moral code. He was driven and goal oriented. Never mind that those goals could destroy realms.

I stopped myself from internally swooning and focused.

In Faerie, the four horsemen hosted an annual hunt to welcome in the spring. The prey represented winter, the horsemen and their chosen hunters represented spring, and a mock battle ensued between the seasons.

Basically, its purpose was to welcome in the harvest season.

Once the hunters captured their prey and the spring was victorious over winter, there was dancing and drinking and lots of frisky behavior because somehow a bunch of horny villagers made the crops grow more plentiful.

Briefly, I wondered if that was where the expression *sowing his wild oats* came from, then dismissed it. Those were musings for another time.

As my attention drifted back to the Fae who still stood across from me, I realized he'd been watching me closely.

His eyes gleamed with a hint of amusement as I processed the truth. Part of the hunt was an ancient ritual, a raw and visceral offering to the harvest goddess, meant to honor her with the thrill of the chase.

"This is to celebrate the harvest season?"

"Your one question is up. Now, get in the springs."

His lips curled into a knowing smirk, the expression confirming that I had connected the dots.

He was one of the hunters, and I, with a sudden chill creeping up my spine, realized I would be one of the unfortunate souls who'd be the prey.

Damn. I'd really wanted to play the part of fearless hunter.

My heart started trotting through my chest as I took him in again. The green eyes, tanned skin, and that dark auburn hair: one character came to mind.

I had a feeling he was none other than Prince Leif Saxon, or the horseman known as Conquest.

If the hunt he mentioned remained true to the main plot of the book, then I was in more trouble than I thought. The four Fae princes were legends.

Despite the danger looming, my traitorous pulse sped with the thrill of being in this book.

If I managed to elude all four of the horsemen and their chosen hunters during the hunt, then I could claim a favor as a prize.

It was their way of bribing the last of winter to relinquish its hold over spring.

But if I failed...

I inhaled.

I simply wouldn't let that happen.

No matter if the horseman known as War was sitting *just* below Logan Blaze on my list of fictional crushes.

Sloth would absolutely lose his stoic cool.

And if anything could motivate the prince to hunt me down himself, it would be the possibility of a fictional crush batting his seductive eyes at me.

This might be the best way to get my favorite prince back.

My earlier trepidation gave way to excitement. I was in one of my favorite books, and I was going to make the best of the situation.

The Liber Noctem was cunning at twisting tales, but it had no idea who it was up against. It might have taken Blondie from me and moved the pieces around to get me alone, but alone was where I thrived, even if I didn't prefer solitude.

I was no damsel in distress.

I was no warrior either.

But I was a reader and a damned voracious one to boot.

I read *everything* I could get my greedy little hands on, and my mind was a twisted pit of chaos waiting to be unleashed.

It was time to embrace my power and dream myself into victory, even if that meant I had to become a little wicked to achieve it.

A smile curved my mouth.

My villain era was about to begin.

Conquest jerked his chin toward the steaming-hot spring, a not-so-subtle demand to get in, and successfully broke me out of my dark plotting.

I couldn't deny that the prospect of washing away the stubborn salt water and gritty sand from my skin sounded like heaven.

But I didn't love the idea of one of the four horsemen peering down at me.

He advanced toward me, his gaze dark and unwavering, and I felt my resolve crumble. Bathing in a waterfall with Conquest standing guard wasn't the worst demand he could make, considering he was a harbinger of doom and all.

"Fine. Turn around, though. I don't need your murderous stare on me the whole time."

With a resigned sigh, he did as I asked. A true gentleman.

Once I was sure he wasn't some pervert with a peeping fetish, I unbuckled my weapons belt, which contained the phoenix tear, and set it on the ground, then peeled off my soaked tunic, the fabric clinging stubbornly to my skin.

I dropped it on the grass and squatted down to unlace my boots and kick them off. I tipped them over and shook out an impressive pile of sand.

No wonder my feet felt raw. I'd brought half the beach with me.

Next came the leather trousers, which proved to be quite challenging.

I cursed under my breath, hopping awkwardly on one foot while wrestling with the stubborn pants, which refused to let go.

Honestly, leather and pirates were probably the worst combination.

Water did not do that fabric any favors.

In a final act of desperation, I plopped back down onto the soft grass and yanked each pant leg off with determined tugs.

Thank goodness the Fae didn't turn around to watch my dignity wither and die in real time.

He would have had quite the entertaining show.

Finally free of my clothing, I waded into the pool. The water was the perfect temperature and fizzled lightly against my skin.

I wondered what Sloth would think of the waterfall and hot spring and imagined his stoic expression being less than impressed.

Secretly, though, he'd love it.

Under all those fortified emotional walls he was a real softy.

I ached at the thought of him being injured and forced myself to get through the present. He would find me.

Or maybe I'd try to find him with my power once I was alone. I was sure Teddy would comb the island for me if I asked. He hadn't been able to travel too far from me last night, but maybe we could test the distance today.

Not wanting to prolong this bath any longer than I had to, I swam into the heart of the waterfall, letting the water cascade over me as I sank beneath its soothing rush. It felt incredible to get the salt and sand off.

It also felt a *little* like I'd lost the upper layer of my skin in the worst exfoliation process of my life. However, it was also as soft as butter now, so there was my silver lining.

I worked my fingers vigorously through my tangled hair and scrubbed my head, silently wishing for something more luxurious to wash with—

A sudden splash interrupted my thoughts.

My attention snagged on a corked bottle bobbing in the water beside me.

Praise be to the gods of soap, I must have manifested...

I whipped around, my gaze narrowing in irritation.

"You promised you wouldn't look."

"I did no such thing." A genuine smile spread across his face for the first time, making me instantly wary. "Better catch the soap before it drifts away."

I hesitated for only a minute.

If he'd somehow laced the shampoo with a sedative, at least I'd get clean hair before he whisked me off and deposited me in the woods for the hunt.

I uncorked it and took a small whiff.

Maybe the soap *was* magic. It smelled like a blend of fresh florals and sweet herbs that floated in the air around me like a spell.

I dumped a generous amount into my palm and lathered it into my hair, then massaged it over my skin, enjoying the rich, creamy suds that kept releasing the captivating scent.

I dunked back under the waterfall to rinse.

The water was warm and soothing, a stark contrast to the chilling presence of my silent, watchful bodyguard, who hadn't bothered to give me privacy again.

Conquest really was living up to his reputation as the most unpleasant of the four princes. Even *Famine* was more liked.

I glanced over my shoulder, scowling.

"You really need to work on respecting boundaries."

"Are you done?"

Not at all, but I figured he wasn't asking about the mental list of complaints I was currently logging against him and was referencing the bath.

"Are you going to turn around so I can get out?"

He shot me a withering look—like *I* was trying *his* infinite patience by asking for basic manners and decency—before he pivoted on his heel and gave me his back.

He was a true delight.

I swam through the water and climbed onto the grassy shore, then stared down at where my clothes lay in a crumpled, filthy heap, cursing.

I'd been so excited about the prospect of getting clean, I hadn't thought about putting my sea-soaked clothes back on.

The shrunken leather was going to be one of the circles of hell to shimmy back on, but I never shied away from giving my all to seemingly impossible tasks.

I bent to grab my trousers, and a sudden, warm weight thudded against my face—a bunch of fabric.

I reached up reflexively, snagging it before it fell to the ground, and glared at the Fae standing a few feet away. Shockingly enough, his back was still to me.

And he was no longer wearing a shirt.

I gave him a cursory glance.

His toned body did nothing for my romance-addled mind.

The only thing I still fantasized about was stabbing him. Repeatedly. And not in the hot enemies-about-to-become-lovers kind of way. Sloth would be pleased. His sociopathic tendencies were rubbing off on me.

I looked down at the shirt in my hands.

In a rare act of consideration, Conquest had tossed me his tunic. I held it up to inspect it. It was a soft, thick fabric that would hang loosely to my knees.

It was fine, practical even, but I hesitated, holding it at arm's length.

It smelled like the Fae, an earthy, woodsy aroma that was distinctly his, and I felt a peculiar resistance to wrapping myself in someone else's scent.

I didn't think the prince would care for that at all.

Which was absurd.

I ignored the little thread inside me that vibrated madly in indignation and slipped it over my head.

Better to be draped in someone's scent than to prance into a castle filled with the Four Horsemen of the Apocalypse butt naked before a horny harvest festival. Sloth would surely come to the same conclusion.

Not that his opinion on the matter was important.

Gods. I needed to get a grip. One kiss really did ruin me.

I slipped my boots on, feeling the snug fit as I laced them tightly, then reached for the dagger I'd stolen from the pirate ship.

The blade glinted in the dim light as I slid it into its sheath and strapped it securely to my ankle.

Hopefully, I wouldn't accidentally stab myself.

I grabbed the weapons belt and checked to make sure the phoenix tear was still tucked safely inside one of the built-in compartments. All was well.

Conquest had finally turned around, and his attention fell to the weapon.

He studied it with a measured look, as if weighing my ability to wield it. I wouldn't be winning any competitions, but I knew to aim the pointy end at him.

His gaze traveled upward, tracing the curve of my bare legs, pausing briefly on the borrowed tunic that hit just above my knees, and finally rested on my face.

A slight nod accompanied his single word of approval.

"Better."

It was a miracle that I kept my eye roll internal.

"I'll sleep soundly knowing I have your blessing."

Without another word, he spun around sharply on his heel and strode back up the winding dirt path we'd taken earlier.

I kept pace with him, delighted about getting on with the hunt. I needed to think of a good strategy to evade capture and collect my favor.

The main character in the book hadn't been lucky; she'd gotten corned by Death and War. Personally, I was convinced she'd *hoped* to get caught by them.

The love triangle was one for the ages.

Pitting War against Death led to some epic tension. And lots of disaster.

Thankfully, I had no designs to meet either of them if I could help it.

Since the sun was still slowly slinking across in the sky, I had plenty of time before midnight to come up with something good.

They might be Fae legends, but I'd read their stories and knew all their tricks. I had to hope they translated to this realm.

We walked briskly up the path, and the towering trees on either side of us swayed gently in the breeze, their leaves whispering softly.

The forest buzzed with the sounds of small animals and birds rustling through the foliage. Thankfully, I didn't think any of the creatures scurrying around were the specters.

Those creepy vampires had taken one look at the Fae and vanished.

I imagined it wasn't the first time they'd encountered him.

As I strode along after Conquest, I concentrated on stepping lightly and silently, thinking there was no time like the present to practice for later.

I wasn't horrible at treading quietly, but I had also never *needed* to be aware of each footfall before.

Whenever I walked to the library for my shift, I was usually wrapped up in whatever book I'd just finished and had no need to focus on where I stepped or how loud I was. No one cared aside from a few annoyed squirrels, which would flick their tails and chitter at me as I accidentally disturbed their peace.

My heart pounded in anticipation as we reached the top of the hill, and the magnificent tree castle reappeared before us.

Its soaring wooden towers intertwined with the branches, making it the most magical sight I'd ever witnessed.

The only thing that marred the view was the hanging bridge, its vine-covered ropes creaking ominously in the wind.

I'd forgotten we needed to cross it to get to the castle.

Conquest approached the bridge confidently and extended his arm, gesturing for me to get on it first.

Of all the times for him to suddenly become a gentleman.

"So magnanimous."

"Feel free to thank me as often as you'd like. I enjoy a bit of groveling."

I shot him a glare, and he responded with a dark grin.

I ignored it and his glimmering chest and adopted my best fake-it-'til-I-make-it attitude to hype myself up.

Heights weren't my favorite.

Mostly because I was sane and valued my life.

The bridge looked ancient and weathered, and one wrong step would probably send me plummeting to my death.

"All this magic and you don't have a sturdier bridge?" I asked.

"Quit stalling."

The soft fabric of his borrowed tunic whipped around my legs as I hesitantly placed my foot on the first wooden plank of the bridge.

It creaked in warning.

I immediately stepped back.

The arrogant Fae jabbed me between the shoulder blades to prod me along.

"Start walking, or I'll carry you across."

Given his sweat-slicked bare skin, I might go careening to my death. If he didn't toss me over the side first just for fun.

Which, judging by the slight longing in his tone, was exactly what he'd want.

I was seriously surrounded by murderers and psychopaths.

I swallowed hard, ignoring the sudden lump in my throat, and gathered every ounce of courage I had.

To make things extra fun, the hanging bridge started to sway alarmingly fast from side to side, its wooden planks groaning under the mounting pressure of the gusting wind.

With a quick mental note to myself that plummeting into jagged rocks wasn't on today's agenda, I gingerly stepped onto the first plank.

The bridge swung harder, and my heart pounded like the most overused drum in existence. This next leg of our journey was off to a tremendous start.

I froze, waiting for the movement to settle, then began the world's slowest shuffle forward.

Behind me, I felt the horseman looming like a threatening rain cloud. My pace was giving snails a good name and he was muttering curses in Fae.

His lack of concern for our impromptu tightrope act was both impressive and irritating, and I not-so-secretly hoped the next gust of wind would knock him off it.

Alas, he stepped onto the bridge with a casual stride, completely indifferent to the precarious swinging we were doing over the deep ravine.

He leaned close, his breath warm against my ear, and taunted.

"Don't look down, little rabbit."

His unsolicited advice sent a shiver down my spine. He and Blondie needed to compare notes for their stellar motivational speeches.

I gripped the coarse vine-covered ropes on either side tightly, and with white-knuckled determination, I pressed forward.

Every time I faltered, I forced myself onward, one sluggish step at a time.

I kept my attention locked on the imposing silhouette of the castle at the far end, even if each step was a battle against the fear threatening to overwhelm me.

I really, really hated heights.

I cautiously made my way across the Faerie bridge from hell while the wind lashed at my hair and clothing with the fury of a displeased god.

I kept my gaze fixed straight ahead, refusing to look down into the dizzying depths of the ravine below, terrified of the drop that awaited if I took one wrong step.

The bridge swung wildly beneath us, the ropes creaking and groaning in protest with each gust of wind.

Only a few yards remained before we'd reach the other side.

I continued forward, carefully placing each foot on the weathered planks, conscious of their shifting beneath my weight. One step closer. And another.

My pulse raced, but there was an undeniable exhilaration coursing through me too, an intoxicating thrill that mingled with the fear.

I'd never been more afraid, but I'd also never felt more alive.

Every cell in my body was buzzing.

Probably in fear, but still.

Energy crackled through me with every step I took.

We finally reached the end of the ancient bridge, and I let out a sigh of relief. I managed to avoid the crabwalk of shame and retained all my dignity, or at least what was left of it. I counted that as a solid win.

Conquest reached around and placed his palm against the enormous arched doors, muttering something in what I assumed was Old Fae.

Words etched in an unfamiliar language shimmered into existence, glowing with an otherworldly, iridescent hue before gradually fading back into the wood.

With a deep, resonant creak, the doors swung open, revealing what was hidden beyond them and the hanging bridge of doom.

A courtyard. Cobblestones. Vendors setting up their stalls.

And more pressingly, a second horseman.

That was how I found myself staring directly into the enigmatic face of War.

"Hello, mortal."

So much for staying off his radar.

TWENTY-SIX
Prince Sloth

The last several hours solidified the fact that I did not care for the sea.

After I slayed the monster, the Liber Noctem never materialized. But I *felt* its power all around me, taunting, infuriating. Then it vanished as if I'd imagined it.

And if I never suffered through another pirate encounter, I would finally allow my brother Gluttony to throw one of his famous feasts at my House of Sin to celebrate.

I'd even make a concession to not sneak a book to the affair and to participate in their antics. Menu planning seemed far less loathsome now.

I squeezed the excess water from my tunic and took in my surroundings.

This had to be the illustrious Isle of the Damned Kensington had told me about, though he hadn't mentioned any inhabitants.

Other than the diminutive vampires.

But at first glance, the island didn't seem entirely abandoned.

On a jagged cliff a few miles from where I'd washed ashore, a crumbling lighthouse sent out rhythmic flashes that cut through the gathering dusk.

I watched it for several minutes, searching for any movement or clue about who might be running the old building. Or to see if I spotted Lore there.

No shadows flickered past the windows.

It appeared to be operating of its own accord.

I scanned the shoreline but didn't notice any footprints or signs that Lore had come this way. I moved purposefully across the rocky beach, each step crunching against the pebbles, my attention fixed on the beacon of light ahead.

I ignored the discomfort of my sodden clothes and the gash in my side.

The damned sea monster hadn't gone peacefully to its grave, and I wasn't healing properly. Soon I'd be no better off than a mortal.

I ascended a modest incline where a sandy dirt trail bisected a field of tall, billowing grass and halted to assess potential risks.

Conceivably, something could be concealed within the grass, poised to ambush me as I traveled deeper through the field.

I suspected the vampire-like creatures weren't the only things I'd like to avoid here. I moved as silently as my waterlogged boots allowed, attuned to any faint sounds that didn't belong to the natural landscape.

I didn't feel the telltale pressure of any hungry gazes on me but suspected the vampires wouldn't be too far.

If no other pirates had made it here, I would present an appealing target.

Unless they'd gotten to Lore first.

A quiet, simmering rage spurred me onward. The emotion was becoming familiar the longer I stayed in this nightmare realm, though still unwelcome.

I advanced along the dirt path, noting subtle rustling in the grass that might be the movements of something more nefarious than the breeze.

I tugged my dagger from its sheath and remained alert.

My focus shifted from one side of the hilly fields to the other.

I still didn't see anything that indicated Lore had passed through, no footprints or broken stems of grass.

Given the size of the island, it stood to reason she'd swum to shore elsewhere, though a sliver of doubt crept in. It hadn't looked like the island was terribly large, and I normally could pick up on some faint scents or emotions.

I'd search all night if I had to.

Each step made my drenched clothes cling uncomfortably to my skin and my mood darken. A sharp pain flared from the wound in my side, where blood still seeped through the torn fabric.

While I trekked across the island searching for Lore, my mind buzzed with unsettling thoughts of my weakening powers, and what the root cause was.

I kept coming back to the tattoo. I was starting to believe the ink from the design might actually be ink from the pages of the Liber Noctem.

The how or why was just out of reach, though.

It was a persistent worry I tried to shove aside.

I listened for the slightest sound of movement as the wind whispered through the grass, anything that might signal Lore was close.

There was nothing.

And yet...if I concentrated hard enough, I almost sensed *something* drawing my attention, a feeling I had no reference for. It wasn't as potent as the lure of the dark book; it was lighter, but more intense.

I wasn't walking aimlessly. I was following some subconscious drive.

I halted. Following an emotion I had no name for was a far cry from logical.

Indecision warred within me—I couldn't discern if I was picking up on a connection to Lore or if the dark magic was tugging me astray.

I could either trust that *feeling* or choose logic.

I glanced up at the lighthouse again.

It was elevated high enough on the cliff that Lore should have seen it from wherever she'd landed on the island. Even if she hadn't gotten there yet, it was the most promising place to start my search for her.

It was the only building I'd seen, and it would be the most appealing place for her to seek out and try to shelter in. Logically, it made sense, but this was the world of nightmares, and logic didn't always reign supreme.

Shoving the strange feeling aside, I opted to go with my head.

Every few feet, I halted, lifting my face to the salt-laden wind, trying to catch a trace of Lore's scent mingling with the sea air.

A coil of unease twisted tighter in my gut, a tangible knot of worry.

She was determined, resilient.

She had to have made it to the island.

I refused to consider the grim alternative...

The possibility that she might have drowned before she'd reached the safety of the shore, or worse, that she'd been attacked when she'd been most vulnerable.

The vampires with their insidious patience could have been lying in wait, ready to strike just as her strength waned from the desperate swim for survival.

I should have been there by her side.

I cursed the old gods for their cruel games. If they had let me bind the Liber Noctem for good, we wouldn't be in this situation now. Lore would be living her life, far from this realm and any danger. Nyantha would remain forever powerless.

I continued my trek across the island, the dirt path slowly giving way to a more rugged landscape. I kept my senses open to both the Liber Noctem and Lore.

Since I was fairly certain it had done away with Xavier, or he'd been collateral damage in this realm, that meant it could be with anyone. I would have preferred to find his mangled corpse, but if he'd been eaten by the giant sea monster, there was nothing to be done now. I would need to let it go and focus on the remaining Trials and securing the dark book.

Some mysteries would always remain unsolved, no matter how much that drove my sin mad. I hoped however Xavier died it had been with the same lack of mercy I'd have given him.

Not only had he put my court in peril, but he'd also endangered the entire universe.

My boots still crunched over the rocky terrain and dense underbrush, but the lighthouse remained a flashing beacon in the distance.

I slowed my pace and cocked my head to the side. I'd been walking for at least an hour, and the lighthouse was no closer than it had been.

I pivoted in a small circle. I'd definitely made progress—I could no longer see the ocean, and the island's vegetation had shifted from tall grass to lush forest.

And yet I could still see the lighthouse from my position, the same size and distance as it had been when I first started walking.

It made no sense. The perspective should have altered the closer I got.

I ignored the strangeness of it. I needed to search the island in its entirety anyway and didn't care if there was an illusion in play.

A cool breeze whipped against my face, but Lore's trail remained elusive as ever. I scanned the horizon, hoping for a clue, a broken twig, or a footprint in the dirt, but there was nothing. The sun dipped lower in the sky but hadn't fully set.

My gaze narrowed on that anomaly. It had been dusk when I'd first arrived.

By my estimation, it should have been full dark already.

Perhaps this was why it was called the Isle of the Damned. The very land itself tormented wayward travelers until they lost themselves to madness.

A new sense of urgency had me doubling my pace.

I came upon an unexpected fork in the trail and halted.

One path would likely wind its way toward the lighthouse, the destination I'd already decided was the most promising.

But the other path pulled at something deep within me, urging me to follow it. I studied it, trying to decipher *why* that direction appealed. I wasn't sure if I could trust any feeling, knowing it might be a manipulation from the dark book.

My gaze traced the narrow, winding trail that snaked into the dense woods.

Fallen leaves and twigs lay undisturbed, no indentations or broken branches to suggest recent travelers.

The other path was wide and well-trodden, still the obvious choice.

It should be simple, but I stood rooted to the spot, unable to make my feet move in either direction.

I shoved my hands through my hair and paced, conflicted.

Logic never failed me. But my instincts hadn't either.

"Fuck it."

I strode down the path on the right-hand side. Whether the book was manipulating my emotions or not, I'd comb every inch of the island to find Lore.

A few moments later I finally caught the faint scent I'd been searching for. Neroli and basil soap and some underlying sweetness that was entirely Lore.

Some of the tension in my body eased a fraction. How I'd innately sensed she'd come this way based on a feeling was troubling. But I'd known earlier; even on the ship, I'd felt entirely certain I could find her anywhere.

Maybe we'd forged some connection because of the Trials. Whatever the reason was, I was thankful.

My relief at her safety was short-lived when I picked up on another scent I didn't recognize. Someone else had found her first.

Male, judging from the musky undertone.

The river of ice that shot through my veins nearly froze me in place.

I imagined with clinical detachment what I would do if I found her harmed. The dark scenarios played themselves out in my mind in quick, brutal succession.

In one vision I administered hours of sadistic torture to whoever had harmed Lore, mentally rehearsing step by step the extraction of pain I'd employ. Each joint and tendon would become a target in a surgical procedure of vengeance.

No methods of violence were off-limits; restraints, medical implements, and weapons, horribly successful techniques I'd gleaned from case studies and forensic texts I'd read, the sorts of cruelty I'd once dismissed as the purview of lesser men.

I would have her back unharmed, or I would make this realm pay in blood.

I inhaled and let my breath out with practiced calm.

My emotions were clearly being stoked by the Book of Nightmares; the tattoo ink glowed as it burned on my chest and in my veins.

But even being aware of that fact, I couldn't extinguish the simmering wrath I felt each time I imagined Lore being hurt and alone.

It was primal, unhinged. And utterly foreign to me.

For once, instead of holding back, I unleashed myself.

I gave in fully to the dark fantasies plaguing me, letting my mind race with more twisted visions of vengeance. There was no scenario I dreamed up where I didn't become the monster required to unmake a monster.

If anyone so much as touched a hair on the dreamweaver's head, I would be the worst nightmare this realm had ever known.

I forced myself to breathe, to remember the rules I lived by.

Observe first, then act.

Behaving impulsively would only make things worse or tip my hand before I could plot the best path forward.

It took several moments, but I finally reined in my emotions, feeling the last vestiges of the dark magic release me.

My tattoo stopped burning and the ink slowly faded to a normal gold instead of the blazing glow it had been giving off through my tunic.

Gods-damned Liber Noctem. By the time the Trials ended I would intimately know each of my rival courts' sins.

I breathed in again, probing the air for subtler clues surrounding Lore and her companion. There was no evidence of violence, no traces of the coppery tang of blood or the telltale sourness of fear or sweat.

Lore hadn't run, nor had she fought the male.

Her scent was steady, the emotional undertones neutral.

Which meant whoever this male was, whatever his purpose, he hadn't frightened her—at least not yet. I almost swore I scented a hint of annoyance lingering, but it was too faint to be certain.

The absence of blood should have been reassuring, but it made the situation more ambiguous, more dangerous. Lore might have gone willingly with him.

And that...that disturbed me more than it should.

My mind reeled, spinning out different possibilities.

A new fictional crush? Another gods-forsaken shifter with dimples?

I halted myself there. That was skirting the line of jealousy far too closely and I refused to be influenced by my brother Envy's sin.

I calmed myself and focused. If not another character from her dreams, who would she have come across? A vampire, a recluse...

Or, worst of all, a predator from Nyantha's twisted world?

That thought made me want to lash out, but I channeled that energy into action instead, lengthening my stride, recalibrating my hunt.

Some of the icy rage dulled a fraction, replaced by a determination that felt as old as time. There was nothing for me to do but to follow Lore's scent, track it to its source, and deal with whatever waited at the end.

If I had to fight my way to her, so be it.

With newfound purpose, I pushed onward, my boots sinking slightly into the soft earth as the sound of rushing water greeted me through the trees.

The air carried the scent of wet leaves and moss along with Lore's fragrance.

I reached the stream, the water gurgling over smooth stones, and noticed fresh boot prints pressed into the mud.

The edges were still sharp and defined, which suggested they hadn't been left that long ago—perhaps just an hour or two at the most.

Some of my tension eased. My senses hadn't deceived me.

Lore had been here and she was able to walk on her own. It was a victory worth celebrating.

We'd both survived the sea monster attack and capsized pirate ship, battered but breathing. Everything else we could deal with.

I continued to hike along the narrow, winding path through the dense forest, relieved to find Lore's scent growing stronger.

I pushed aside a low-hanging branch and spotted a few broken twigs on the towering oak tree.

A faint smile crept onto my lips. Lore was clever. It seemed she'd been trying to leave a trail for me, subtle but unmistakable.

Knowing her, she probably pretended to trip and catch herself on the oak.

I moved with long, confident strides, ready to close the distance.

It shouldn't be too much longer now.

Several moments later, an unsettling sensation crept over me.

Fine hairs on the back of my neck stood on end, and a prickle between my shoulder blades signaled the presence of *something* tracking my every move.

I refused to turn, not wanting to let whatever it was know I'd sensed it.

I subtly scanned the undergrowth on either side of me, my gaze sliding off shadows that seemed to thicken the deeper into the woods I traveled.

A new scent drifted on the air, different from Lore and her companion—or more likely, her captor.

The odor held a familiar yet foreign combination of scents: the sour stench of rotting leaves, the bitter tang that collected in an old root cellar, and the sickly-sweet top note that signaled a body left out in the elements.

It was the unmistakable scent of decay.

Death was stalking me.

I should have known it wouldn't be easy. I braced myself for the telltale signs of the Book of Nightmares' dark power to seep in next.

I maintained an even pace, deliberately unhurried, my senses attuned to any subtle hints that might reveal how many adversaries I was about to face off against.

As I continued down the path, I felt it again, closer this time, the pressure of a cold, malevolent stare pressing against the base of my neck.

Whatever they were—vampires or some other nightmare creatures inhabiting this cursed realm—they moved on near-silent feet. The faint susurration of the foliage they passed was the only hint at their numbers.

I approached the next bend in the forest trail and smoothly dropped to a crouch, feigning the need to tie the laces on my boots.

Most predators couldn't resist easy prey.

I'd only just started silently counting when they lunged, swift and fierce like shadows come to life.

I spun around, my weapon poised for action, and stabbed my attackers with precision, taking one down instantly from the surprise burst of violence.

I drove my blade up and through its bony chest, piercing its unbeating heart in a clean motion, then wrenched my weapon out.

Unlike in fictional tales, the vampire didn't burst into flames or disintegrate into ash. Instead, it crumpled to the ground, its limbs folding awkwardly beneath it.

It lay there in a motionless heap, the eerie red glow of its eyes fading into a dull, lifeless gray. Black blood dripped from the tip of my dagger and splattered onto fallen leaves, the scent foul and pungent, as I took in my remaining opponents. A dozen miniature vampires hissed at me like a disturbed nest of vipers.

Their faces twisted into a seething rage as they flexed their claw-tipped fingers toward me. Their talons were as bone white as the rest of their bodies.

Kensington had called them specters. Now I knew why.

Ghostly white skin and hair contrasted starkly with the dark foliage, and their piercing red eyes shone with an insatiable hunger aimed solely at me.

I wondered if they were more of a Somnia creature rather than something inspired by the original book. They seemed like they'd been born of nightmares.

These were not even close to the vampires I knew from Malice Isle, the outwardly refined Underworld royals and nobles who were human in appearance, except for their crimson eyes and thirst for blood.

These smaller cousins were more animal in nature, seeming to act solely on their baser instincts. They didn't speak aside from the hissing and deep growls.

Which meant there would be no reasoning with them or threats I could make that would give them pause.

My wound from the sea monster attack probably drew them. Along with the assistance of the dark book. I swore I felt a faint echo of its power skirting the edges of the forest. It was hunting me along with these creatures.

For someone with such a sunny disposition, Lore certainly read a lot of dark fiction. It wouldn't kill her to read some poetry once in a while.

If we made it out of this cursed story alive, I would pen her letters every day myself. The least useful documents of all.

I widened my stance and prepared for the onslaught.

The nightmare vampires clocked my fighting position, and as though a silent command filtered through their ranks, they lunged at me in unison.

PART III

Happily Ever After?

TWENTY-SEVEN
Prince Sloth

All twelve of those monstrous creatures tore into my flesh with unnerving ease, using their razor-sharp claws and fangs to shred my leathers.

Their movements were wild and untamed, but the longer I dodged their worst blows, the more I recognized a chilling pattern to their ambush too.

Their feral hits were mostly aimed at the vulnerable spots of my body not shielded by my leathers, and that level of coordination revealed a cunning intelligence beneath their savage exterior.

The fact that they'd utilized such a strategic assault shattered any illusion of mindlessness their bloodlust initially suggested.

They were attacking with clear, calculated intention.

And they were gaining the upper hand.

They might be inspired by Lore's book, but they were more nightmare creatures from this realm than anything else. However the Liber Noctem was involved, I had little doubt it was feeding them strategies. The dark book wanted me out of the way.

I jerked back before one sank its fangs into my throat.

I slammed my dagger forward, striking flesh each time. Every swing delivered a lethal blow, but their numbers quickly overwhelmed my defenses.

Each time I took one down, several more appeared in its place.

There were too many to fend off without seeking higher ground.

I retreated a few steps, hoping to put distance between myself and the angry horde, but it was like the forest itself was spawning more of these haunting creatures. They emerged silently from the shadows, their pallid bodies multiplying in even larger numbers than should have been possible.

I dodged another blow and swung out, knocking my attacker back.

Then I felt it.

The ground itself rumbled.

"Gods' blood."

Realization hit me hard and fast. This was how the Book of Nightmares would twist this scene; it had just raised the stakes.

The entire island must be riddled with underground hives or nests of these creatures. I bet every burrow, fissure, or cave mouth in the forest was a doorway into and out of that subterranean hell.

There were far too many vampires to inhabit the upper portion of the land alone. They'd never survive daylight.

The ground rumbled harder, the force similar to an earthquake.

It felt as if thousands of creatures were charging through the tunnels, and it didn't take any sophistication to figure out where they were heading.

Based on the intensity of the vibrations beneath my boots, I imagined the labyrinth below was packed with the undead, all of whom hungered for fresh blood.

I needed to get out of here. Now.

I felt the first true stirring of panic, then banished it.

I would not feed into the Liber Noctem's fear-inducing nightmare. It wanted more power and I would not give in.

I spun slowly, taking in the encroaching horde.

Some floated an inch or two off the ground, and others moved with an eerie grace that didn't seem entirely humanoid.

Hundreds of eyes glittered in the woods.

In the space of a few seconds, the empty area around me rapidly dwindled to a small circle. I'd barely be able to extend my arms to fight or get any momentum.

Everywhere I looked, rows of ghostly vampires lined up, some snapping their teeth or clawing at one another to get closer.

I was surrounded.

The forest suddenly fell silent except for their eerie hissing; even the rumbling stopped. That couldn't be a positive sign.

"Shit."

I analyzed my best exit strategy.

Climbing a tree was not a viable option—they were already ascending the trunks with ease, their claw-tipped fingers allowing them to move faster than I could in my diminished state.

In every direction I turned, there were swarms of specters.

Their numbers would be difficult for a battalion of soldiers to fend off, which wouldn't normally be an issue if I was fully restored.

They were crammed together so tightly, they created an impenetrable wall. One with blinking red eyes and pale faces pulled into snarls.

It was as if the night itself had come alive with the specters, leaving me no easy path to escape or find any tactical advantage.

There was no way out but through.

And that was far from ideal.

With no better alternatives, I utilized my only option: taking them by surprise. I dove into the writhing swarm of specters, bellowing as I swung with both blade and fist, determined to escape this nightmare unscathed and get to Lore before I lost her trail. Or worse, before they got to her.

Their eerie gazes fixed on me, mouths agape with sharp, deadly fangs.

I couldn't afford to be bitten; even knowing that my magic would eventually purge my blood of their venom, the risk of infection was too great right now.

Something the Book of Nightmares had to know.

As if sensing my weakened state, two dozen of the closest vampires lunged at me, their icy fingers reaching out to pin my arms, but I refused to submit.

I refused to give in to fear.

I drove my blade into them, cleaving through the flesh of the undead writhing around me, their grotesque figures closing in on all sides.

Their guttural growls and hissing groans created a cacophony of horror that matched the chaos of the fight beat for beat.

I lunged forward, plunging my blade into the chest of the nearest vampire with a swift, practiced motion, and hit its unbeating heart.

The creature hissed, its eyes wide with rage.

I twisted the dagger, fighting the resistance of bone and muscle, then ripped it free. I didn't wait to see the vampire drop.

I was already on to the next.

With each swing, I aimed for vital spots—eyes, hearts—delivering lethal blows that sent the ones I'd hit crumpling to the ground.

I whirled in a circle, dispatching my opponents as they continued to move in, hindering my blows. My fist connected with the jaw of one vampire, sending a jarring shock through its small frame.

I spun and delivered a powerful kick, sweeping the legs out from under another, leaving it momentarily stunned on the ground.

With a fluid movement honed over centuries, I drove my dagger deep into the chest of a third, piercing its cold, lifeless heart.

Despite the efficiency of my strikes, the vampires kept surging at me with their fangs bared and talons out.

My muscles tensed with each swing, the effort sending a slight tremor through my arm as I focused on maintaining my fighting rhythm.

I swung my dagger in the widest arc I could manage, the blade slicing through the air with a sharp whistle from the velocity of my movement.

A taloned hand swiped at me, aiming straight for my throat.

I dropped low to the ground, feeling the rush of air as the claws narrowly missed their mark, then sprang back to my feet.

The gash in my side oozed, the wound fully reopening from the harsh movement. The scent of my blood permeated the space around us, sending the creatures into an impossibly wilder, maddened attack.

The specters lunged at me.

With inhumanly quick, agile leaps, they closed the distance. Their speed and dexterity left little room for escape, even for a skilled fighter like me.

I lashed out with my feet and fists, adrenaline coursing through my veins as I fought to keep those deadly teeth from sinking into my flesh, but with each punch or hit, I was losing precious energy.

I sank my blade into the chest of the next vampire, feeling the moment the vampire succumbed to its final death.

Another shadow loomed to my right, and I swung my fist with all the force I could muster, meeting the vampire's blow with a bone-jarring impact.

The fight was wearing me down, and fast.

I slowly carved my way to the outskirts of the vampire horde, my heart pounding in my chest. Each swing felt more laborious than the last, and sweat trickled down my brow, stinging my eyes.

My legs were leaden, and each step forward was hard-fought. But just beyond the gnashing fangs closest to me, the trail was empty.

I still felt the darkly amused power of the Liber Noctem around the periphery, but I couldn't ascertain its exact location.

Gathering the last reserves of my strength, I prepared to break into a sprint, knowing if I made it there, I had a chance to outrun them.

Out of the corner of my eye, I saw one of the vampires dive forward with a vicious, predatory snarl. The vampire's eyes glinted with hunger as it sank its razor-sharp teeth into my wrist.

I tried to wrench my arm back or dislodge it with a swift blow, but it latched on. Its fangs pierced my flesh like hollow daggers, sending a shock of pain through me as venom pumped into my veins.

Agony exploded through my arm as the venom barreled through my body like a volcanic eruption. In an instant, the chaotic assault ceased.

The vampire who'd bitten me unlatched its jaws and faded into the horde.

The specters hissed but didn't attempt to attack me again. They closed ranks, boxing me in as the venom worked its way deeper into my system.

I ground my teeth together; the sensation of the toxin was excruciating and alien. It felt like every fiber of my being was rebelling against its intrusion.

The spider venom had been far less horrific.

At least I'd retained my sense of self with that.

This...this was erasing my senses only to replace them with twisted, dark desires. This was what the Liber Noctem had been after. Or maybe it was Nyantha getting her wish from the cave—my greatest fear.

My vision wavered, shifting between my normal clarity and shadowy blurs.

With each fluctuation in my vision, my mind also turned into a battlefield where baser instincts clashed violently with reason in their own war.

A chill ran down my spine as my primal instincts began to claw their way to the surface, threatening to drown out any rational thought.

Was I monster or was I man?

It had been the same existential question I'd asked myself after what most thought of as our fall.

What my brothers and I had done... Most memories of that time were hazy, but one had always remained clear. At least to me. I wasn't sure my brothers had the same memory, or if it was simply due to my sin's affinity for knowledge.

Our greatest sin hadn't been desires of the flesh like most texts claimed.

From what I'd gleaned of my fractured memories, we'd been warriors tasked with observing and carrying out divine will to keep order among humankind.

We'd corrupted mortals by giving them angelic knowledge in an attempt to help them. Astronomy to aid them with counting the days to prepare their crops, art to separate them from animals, clothing. They'd started to think of us as gods.

We'd dissuaded them—that I recalled clearly—but it was too late.

Our sole purpose had been to remain emotionless watchers.

And we'd failed.

Good intentions were truly the pathway to hell.

That was how we'd ended up as the wardens to the Underworld.

Most of our memories were stripped of our time before, our orders shifted from watching mortals to now ruling over the sinners we'd helped to create.

It was not a punishment; it was merely a consequence of our actions.

I clenched my fists, trying desperately to hold on to a shred of lucidity. I couldn't allow the Liber Noctem to gain control of my mind or emotions.

But the vampire venom kept coursing through my veins like liquid fire, consuming the frigid, analytical persona I had always prided myself on maintaining throughout the most difficult times, melting it away with a vengeance.

Each corrupted heartbeat obliterated another piece of my fading logic.

My breaths turned ragged; I couldn't seem to get enough oxygen into my lungs. As I inhaled deeply, the most intoxicating scent filled my senses.

Lore.

Something ignited deep within me, a spark that quickly turned into a blaze, more consuming than the venom; this inferno of *need* overwhelmed me.

Protection. Possession. Desire.

But above all else, the fierce drive to care for her, seeing to all her wants and needs and comfort.

I inhaled again, desperate for another hit of that intoxicating sensation.

Then the second scent drifted in, turning my vision red.

It was the male I would kill with my bare hands.

But after that...

I had the urge to hunt her, to protect her, to claim her... to sink my teeth into her soft flesh and mark her as mine.

I curled my hands into fists.

My emotions weren't rational, it was the venom and whatever the dark book was forcing me to feel. And yet, underneath that, I wasn't quite sure those were the only factors in play.

Those thoughts faded away almost as quickly as they'd come.

Another wave of pain swept through me.

This time I did yell, but it wasn't in agony; it was in raw hunger.

And there was only one thing that would sate me.

I straightened from where I'd doubled over and bared my teeth at the horde surrounding me.

The specters retreated, their eyes gleaming with cruel anticipation as they watched the venom take hold, slowly turning me as feral as they were.

That had been their goal all along. To twist me into something wretched.

They'd wanted me to become a monster. And I knew it was because that was what the Liber Noctem desired.

My heart thudded against my chest. I tried to slow my breaths, to keep from being enticed by that aroma that called to the elemental fabric of my soul.

It hung in the air, taunting, teasing... a temptation unlike any other.

My control unraveled, the threads unspooling with each cursed breath.

I couldn't fight my instincts any longer.

Leaves crunched beneath my boots as I spun on my heel and sprinted through the dense forest, a ravenous, all-consuming desire coursing through me.

My need to hunt drove me forward as I navigated the narrow trail, my pace quickening with each stride.

Gone was any sensation of being tired or wounded.

I was brimming with power once again, my senses heightened.

The earthy scent of moss and damp soil called to my inner animal, but the distinct aroma of my prey fueled my pursuit above all else.

I ran and the forest blurred around me, a tapestry of vibrant greens and earthy browns flickering past in my peripheral vision.

The rhythmic pounding of heartbeats echoed through the trees, each beat pulling me farther into my chase.

With every inhalation, the scent grew stronger, intoxicating and maddening, guiding me like a beacon.

Mine.

I burst through the edge of the forest, skidding to a halt as I took in

the sight of a hanging bridge swaying over a ravine. Its weathered planks creaked under the gentle breeze, the vine-covered ropes fraying with age.

A second path twisted away to the right, carrying the elusive fragrance of my target. Despite the alluring promise it held, I knew I wouldn't find her there.

She'd come back this way; her scent was unmistakable—sharp and new, and layered, now, with the musk of the male who would soon die.

I took a deep, deliberate breath, to be sure. There was no doubt her sweet fragrance carried traces of another man threaded with it.

A protective rage roared to life, a fierce growl rumbling in my chest, fueled by a burning need to claim what belonged to me.

The thought of his hands on her ignited a new fire within me.

I exhaled, focusing on my goal. Soon, I would close the distance and end this torment. It wasn't just the desire to maim her captor that called to me.

It was her, always her. Like I'd been hunting her shadow through every waking moment and half-remembered dream since before I was consciously aware.

As if the venom opened the door to some emotion I'd locked deep inside. It had set me free.

I prowled forward with a predator's intensity, my gaze fixated on the structure looming at the end of the bridge.

A castle had been carved out of an ancient tree with a gnarled trunk and sprawling branches, its wooden turrets reaching toward the darkening sky.

I couldn't sense anything beyond the ravine.

I paced in front of the bridge, my senses finely tuned to detect even the slightest rustle of leaves or the whisper of footsteps.

I wouldn't hesitate to destroy anything that dared to stop me.

The vampire venom coursing through my veins clouded my judgment, reducing me to a single-minded creature driven by an insatiable urge.

Her scent called to me like a siren's song.

I couldn't resist its pull for another moment.

I curled my fingers around the first post, testing its give, unconcerned for my safety. If the bridge fell, I'd climb out.

Nothing would keep me from her.

I thought I felt an echo of dark power, but it was faint. I shoved it aside.

I eased onto the bridge, the boards bending beneath my weight, and found a rhythm that swayed with the structure's movements. Stealth was my focus.

Below, the ravine hummed with insect life, a song of hunger and raw need.

I sympathized.

With deliberate steps, I advanced across the bridge.

Each footfall I made had purpose, drawing me inexorably closer to that intoxicating aroma. To the one I hunted. Yearned for. Longed to possess.

The venom in my blood quickened, melting the edges of my thoughts into a silken, predatory clarity. The closer I got, the more fixated I became on my target.

Every part of me was attuned to her: how her scent tangled with the sweetest parts of the failing daylight, how her emotions drew me in.

Halfway across the bridge, I stopped in my tracks, my ears pricked with sudden alertness. What I initially mistook for the rhythmic chirping of insects resonated with a peculiar energy.

A tingling sensation danced along my skin, like tiny sparks crackling in the air. The primitive beast part of me recognized the potential danger.

The magic swirling around me was potent.

I gripped the frayed rope and let the bridge swing, testing it again now that I'd felt the power. When no defense magic swarmed up, I continued forward.

I was almost to the end of it, just a few yards from the tall, arched doors.

Almost to the one I'd stalk the ends of the realm for.

A few more strides and the towering wooden doors loomed before me, their dark grain swirling with ancient enchantments.

My prey was just beyond my reach, but I sensed her.

It was like a tether of magic tugging at me, guiding me, and not even my feral nature could ignore its summoning.

I pressed my palm against the rough wood, feeling the tingling energy seep into my skin. A slow smile spread across my lips as I tilted my head back to take in the height of the walls.

From here I couldn't see the top of the castle; the vast expanse was clearly meant to dissuade anyone from attempting to scale the sides.

One slip and death would be imminent.

But I didn't plan on falling. The old wood offered just enough divots and knots I could use as handholds for my ascent.

Once I scaled these weak barriers, the real hunt would begin.

Without delay, I reached for the rough, twisted wood of the castle walls, my fingers finding purchase on the aged knots and splinters.

Each pull upward brought me closer to my goal.

My heart raced in anticipation, matching the rhythm of the faint heartbeat I imagined just beyond the parapets.

Her presence was almost tangible in the cool night air, and I knew that soon we would be reunited.

And then she would finally be mine.

TWENTY-EIGHT
Lore

WAR WAS, IN a word, devastating. And, in another word, shirtless. Because *of course* that was how our introduction would go.

I blamed the id portion of my brain—that primitive, pleasure-seeking heathen had no self-control. My mind was utterly shameless.

And I was staring. Open-mouthed. Possibly with a hint of drool.

Like a true leading lady.

"Leif." War's voice rolled through the courtyard like distant thunder. "Why is there a mute mortal in nothing but your tunic?"

Conquest gave a casual shrug, as if the situation was beneath his concern, and I shot him a glare sharp enough to cut any normal person.

It had little effect on the arrogant Fae.

I hadn't exactly volunteered to be hauled across the island, forced to cross the bridge of doom, only to then be presented here like a prized calf at the village fair.

"She's joining the hunt," he said.

"Not by choice." My gaze shifted back to War, meeting his dark eyes with defiance. "Also, not mute. You just surprised me. Most people wear more clothes in public."

He arched a brow. "Good thing I'm not most *people*."

His fathomless gaze swept over me in a slow, deliberate sweep, like the shadow of a passing cloud. And I felt...nothing.

No spark, no warmth flowing through my veins, no heart-fluttering excitement. I stared at him, wondering what in the realms was wrong with me.

War stood before me, looking just like I'd pictured from the book I'd read—his eyes were pools of midnight, his presence commanding, and an aura of raw energy rippled around him like a living thing I would normally fantasize about taming.

He was tall and forbidding, dark-haired, brooding, obviously, because what sort of antihero would he be otherwise?

Given his half-dressed state and the weapon he held, he'd probably just finished training. My attention fell over him in another critical sweep.

His chest was sculpted, every muscle defined as if chiseled from stone, then inked with intricate tattoos that were both mysterious and enticing.

A fine sheen of sweat glistened on his bronze skin.

In one hand he gripped a rune-covered sword, its blade polished and ready for whatever challenge might come his way during the hunt.

His features were carved with a ruthless sort of beauty, sharp and compelling, *almost* impossible to look away from.

I waited for a spark to ignite in me.

This was feeding into one of my favorite scenes in romantic fantasy stories—the post-training, first, tension-filled, unexpected meeting.

He was shirtless, sweaty, heavily tattooed.

And, aside from my initial flash of surprise at his state of undress, I had nary a questionable thought.

I probably looked constipated as I concentrated, but I didn't care.

He was one of my *top three* fictional crushes.

Surely I could muster up a speeding pulse or small blush.

He arched a brow. "Like what you see?"

A confident gleam entered his eyes as I took him in again.

His posture turned relaxed and self-assured as he grinned at me. Clearly, he was someone who didn't face rejection often.

Must be nice.

I also noticed that *he* didn't look at me with interest at all, but there was a certain smugness in his expression that suggested he just assumed I'd fall all over myself to catch his attention.

Nope, not doing it for me at all.

Arrogance notwithstanding, I was as unmoved as a statue.

"Unsurprisingly, no. Main love interest looks aside, your personality doesn't do you any favors. In real life, you need more than a pretty face and cocky attitude; otherwise you're just rude and boring."

Conquest choked back laughter, his shoulders shaking with silent amusement. But for a few seconds, War's expression was a portrait of shock.

His eyes widened and his jaw dropped, betraying his disbelief.

To be fair, I couldn't blame him for his reaction; even *I* was taken aback by my words. But I meant them.

With his classic features and striking appearance, he undeniably turned heads wherever he went. But he did nothing for me.

I craved a mental connection. Someone I could talk to for hours and never get bored with or run out of things to say. Someone who adored me for myself, just as I adored him for who he was at his core.

An image of frosty blue eyes and hair as pale as moonlight danced through my thoughts. The prince was in a league of his own.

He'd had a food fight with me on a pirate ship, read everything he could get his hands on, made his entire home a library, danced like a prince, kissed like a sinner, fought sea monsters and giant spiders, yet he could just as easily nurse me back to health as effectively as he killed. He was ruthless and gentle.

Cold and analytical yet sometimes passionately hot.

He also held a world of secrets in his gaze that I'd give anything to unravel.

Too bad he'd already let me know in no uncertain terms that we had no romantic future. Even surrounded by leading love interests, none of them came close to making me burn like the prince did.

And now, faced with the horseman of war, I couldn't manifest one iota of attraction.

A mask of indifference slipped onto War's face.

But even as he feigned a lazy disinterest, the set of his jaw and the dark glint in his gaze gave away the truth he was attempting to hide.

That look was one of calculation and intent.

War *thrived* on the friction of conflict and drew energy from the very prospect of a *no*, leaning into a challenge the way a gambler leaned into the risk of reward by playing one more hand.

He hadn't been interested in me in the slightest, *until* I stoked whatever it was that made him crave battle.

He still didn't like me. Nor was this about romance or seduction for him. This was about winning a skirmish simply to prove he could.

I really needed to get a new hobby; alpha Fae were growing tedious.

Silence continued to spread between us, the air charged and tense.

He was quietly shifting tactics, searching for the angle to press that would change my mind. The true hunt might begin at midnight, but I had a feeling a different one had just begun.

"Well, then. It was a pleasure to meet you." He gave me a slow, wicked smile. "Until next time, prey."

I met his midnight gaze, determined not to flinch, but the intensity there made me want to look away. Or kick him.

Thankfully he broke our stare off before I got myself into more trouble by employing one of the pirates' favorite tactics.

He clapped Conquest on the shoulder, then strode confidently out of the courtyard, his footsteps echoing against the cobblestones.

Honestly, I'd barely registered our surroundings until War left.

He didn't spare me a backward glance, but I somehow *knew* his attention still lingered on me. It felt like a subtle tug at the edges of my awareness, alerting me to the danger he still posed.

My subconscious deserved a cookie for flagging the fact that the horseman of war posed a threat.

I inwardly sighed. A lifetime of never attracting the attention of any suitors and now I inadvertently drew all the wrong kinds.

My dream magic needed to take it down several notches. Or maybe this was just the dream magic from Somnia. Sloth had mentioned the goddess used to rule over dreams before she went completely dark and was stripped of her powers and bound to this realm. I paused at that... Had he told me that? I suddenly couldn't remember, but I was certain it was true.

Conquest leaned against the wall, a smirk playing on his lips as he surveyed the courtyard, which was slowly filling with vendors for tonight's festival.

"Things will be extra interesting later," he said.

I crossed my arms over my chest, my gaze narrowed on the Fae as frustration and prickling unease warred inside me.

"I hate you."

Conquest's grin widened, his teeth flashing in the evening light.

"Just wait until after the hunt." His voice dropped lower. "You'll positively despise me then."

He straightened and jerked his chin toward the castle proper.

"Time to meet the other prey, little rabbit. Better hope you make some friends or tonight won't be much fun for you at all."

I'd expected to be escorted to a room in the enchanted Faerie castle where I could plot and plan, and that was my first mistake: having any sort of expectations this far into the Trials with the dark book.

In the original story, the main character was brought to the most beautiful guest-room suite and given food and clothing and a piping-hot bath.

Instead of bringing me in through the magical doors made from flowering woven vines, Conquest led me down a narrow alley that stood in the shadow of the giant castle.

I glanced at the backs of the buildings we passed.

Some doors were thrown open to let out the heat from what I assumed were small eateries. The scents of savory meats and fried potatoes mixed with confectionaries and soon my stomach was grumbling.

Conquest shot me an irritated look, as if I had control over being hungry.

I considered calling my shadow pet to wreak havoc on the Fae but didn't want to put little Teddy in harm's way.

Inside the giant tree structure, I was surprised that it looked like any other small fortified village.

Cobblestone streets, tons of buildings crammed together made from pale stone with thatched roofs. Some were two stories high, others three, but none were as towering as the castle that loomed above it all.

As the bustling establishments thinned out, the delicious scent of food was replaced by a pungent odor of manure.

I crinkled my nose. The scent of hot, steaming crap really killed an appetite.

We continued down the narrow alley, and the vibrant chatter and clatter of the nearby streets faded, replaced by the sounds of our footsteps on the cobblestones.

Any lingering noise stopped completely when the alley ended, revealing stables at the far end of a flat expanse where no other buildings were located.

Wooden beams framed the structure, and horses whinnied softly within the straw-laden stalls I could just make out in the cracks in the side of the building.

Outside, a sprawling livestock pen gave me pause; its wooden slats were weathered with age but still sturdy-looking enough to prevent escape.

A group of men and women were huddled together inside it, their eyes downcast as Conquest and I approached.

I shot a wary glance at the Fae beside me, my heart racing with trepidation.

"You're not seriously leading me to that pen, are you?"

A sort of savage glee entered his gaze, as if my wariness was highly amusing.

"No, I've decided to escort you around the castle grounds, take you for a horseback ride through the country, then woo you with poetry by starlight."

His tone was so dry I could practically taste dust in my mouth.

I looked him over. "I liked you better when you barely spoke."

"Duly noted. Now get in with the rest of the prey."

I didn't move.

His hand landed on my back, guiding me the last few steps to the pen.

He jerked his chin at the gate and the small crowd inside cowered backward, as if they were terrified of drawing the Fae's wrath.

This was definitely not the same as the original story. People had fought to become prey, to catch the attention of the legendary Fae hunters.

In the book, they were treated like royalty before the hunt. Fed the finest foods, dressed in white linen to represent winter, and wore crowns made of holly.

They were admired and envied as they walked down the avenue toward the hills where the hunt began. Villagers not chosen all lined the streets, tossing white petals to mimic falling snow, and sang folk songs.

In that beautiful version, the prey had been courted like brides and bridegrooms, not corralled like livestock.

In this twisted version of the tale, their fear was palpable. I reminded myself that we weren't even technically *in* Faerie. This was still Somnia, still the land ruled by dreams and nightmares. And it was doing a heck of a job making me forget I had the power to change things...if I could only get my magic to cooperate.

Conquest gave me a gentle push and I stumbled forward, catching myself on the splintered wood.

The gate banged shut behind me, and I spun around, grabbing the handle and shaking it a little. Locked.

"Blood and bones."

This night had gone from bad to worse.

Once Conquest had stridden back down the alley and was out of sight, the other prey finally glanced up.

I smiled tentatively. "Hi. I'm Lore."

No one smiled back.

One of the men, who was barefoot, shirtless, and drooling a line of blood from the corner of his mouth, grunted and hid his head in the crook of his elbow.

A woman I'd guessed to be about twenty pressed her face so deep into the fence that the wood left indents in her cheeks.

The rest of them outright turned their backs on me.

Except for one woman, who narrowed her eyes.

"You'll be the lamb," she said.

She didn't have to elaborate on what she meant by that.

Before I could say a single word of protest, the others nodded—some with relief, some with resignation, none with any real enthusiasm.

Which honestly didn't make me feel better.

The woman was obviously their leader, or maybe just the last one brave enough to keep making decisions for a group that had clearly given up.

I had no idea what to make of this version of the story.

"While being the sacrifice sounds like important work, I'm afraid that's not going to happen. Does anyone want to brainstorm a better strategy?"

She cocked her head, her smile curling into something sharp. "Last in, first to die. Majority rules."

"Die?" If that was true, things had devolved majorly from the plot I knew. "I thought this festival is supposed to welcome in the spring. Being chosen as prey is an honor. And if we win, we're granted a favor."

The leader of the prey circled me.

"An honor? Is that what the honey-tongued Fae said to lure you here?" She pointed to the people crouched in the mud. "If sitting in our own shit and being starved all week is an honor, the Fae bastards can keep it. As for favors..." She shook her head. "You don't want to be in their debt."

I glanced at the hollow eyes and gaunt faces. The woman wasn't lying.

"Why don't you escape?"

"No one escapes."

Her voice hadn't been cruel, but she said it with enough finality that it momentarily dampened even my unending supply of hope.

"I've seen the unfortunate ones who tried. You start running, the Fae break your legs. Sometimes they don't even wait for us to try to flee. Sometimes they feel like playing early, prepping us for their games."

I studied the people around me again.

They were all haunted, defeated in a way I'd never known or seen before. These mortals didn't worship the Fae like the ones in my book had. They didn't dream of marrying into high Fae society and being granted immortality.

These people were terrified of the supernatural beings lording over them.

This was what happened when the Liber Noctem twisted the tale.

Almost everyone in this pen had accepted their grim fate and was simply waiting for the next time the door creaked open and their luck ran out.

I wondered if I could summon Teddy to pick the gate's lock...

"The hunters always want fresh meat." The leader gave me a pitying look. "You've got fresh clothes, fresh-smelling hair. That's what they're after. Something pretty for them to corrupt. That's why you're the lamb. They'll make an excuse to take you anyway. Might as well send you off and save ourselves."

Gods, this was truly starting to become a nightmare.

"I won't just agree to be the lamb," I said, firmer this time.

Her gaze dropped to the dagger sheathed at my ankle.

I didn't like the hungry look that crossed her face. She seemed like the sort who would stab me with my own blade and not feel an ounce of remorse.

"When they come just before midnight and cull more of us for the hunt, you will be the first to go."

She shrugged as if sending me off to potentially be slaughtered was of no consequence. Murderers and psychopaths continued to abound.

"You'll run, or you'll die," she continued. "Either way, you buy the rest of us another day before we're expected to be their prey."

My mind raced with this new information.

Conquest hadn't mentioned anything about the hunt taking place over days or weeks. This woman had to be wrong...

And yet, as my attention swept over the broken people shivering and afraid in this livestock pen, doubt crept in.

He hadn't *actually* said it was a festival. He'd only said *hunt*.

When I'd asked my second question, he hadn't answered.

The first stirrings of panic flickered through me.

I'd been counting on the fact that there would be several other people acting as prey, drawing the hunters away from me while I found a quiet place to hide and work my magic. If I was the only one running, then my odds of avoiding all of the four horsemen were not very favorable.

Conquest's warning came back, this time with a new, sinister meaning. *Better hope you make some friends or tonight won't be much fun for you at all.*

I certainly hadn't made any friends, and tonight wasn't shaping up to be fun. Rotten Fae bastard.

With a renewed sense of urgency, I strode over to an empty corner in the pen and pulled out the phoenix tear.

It was time to dream up something much more pleasant and I only had a few hours to do it. I first tried to summon Teddy. But wherever my shadow pet lived, he didn't heed my call.

My stomach pinched at that. He'd been there for me when I needed him before, keeping me company. Now I suspected the Liber Noctem was keeping him from me, and I hated how frightened and alone that made me feel.

I didn't want to admit it, even to myself, but the Book of Nightmares might be getting closer to winning after all.

TWENTY-NINE
Lore

Midnight came whether I was ready for it or not. I hadn't been able to access my dreamweaver magic, and I was beginning to piece together that meant the test was fully underway for this Trial.

It seemed like the Liber Noctem was able to shut my power down, trapping me in a story that tested whatever subconscious fear lurked below the surface of the test. Jessa Maya's cabin was my desire for safety and the fear that I'd never truly find that in myself or anyone. The dragon shifter test wasn't just about desire; it was about the fear of never being loved. The murder and the marquess was about loyalty and my fear of betrayal. The sea monster attack was centered on my fear of drowning, but when I looked deeper it was really about remaining hopeful. If this test was about survival, I suspected the underlying fear would be being alone.

"Who's our lucky rabbit tonight?" Conquest asked, unfastening the lock and swinging the gate wide.

I stepped forward without prompting. I might not be able to free the rest of the prey, but I would make sure none of them were taken. This was my test. No one else needed to suffer for it.

His gaze burned with amusement.

"How utterly shocking that you didn't make a single friend."

I pulled my shoulders back as I strode out of the pen.

His hand clamped onto the back of my ill-fitting tunic, the fabric stretching taut against my skin.

"Not so fast, mortal." A sly grin spread across his face. "Tonight my fellow hunters want to have some real fun."

I stiffened. I hadn't wanted anyone else to get hurt because of me.

"You stay there." He pointed at me. "And you four. Come."

The leader had been spared, but three other young women and one man were not as fortunate. I wished there was something more I could offer them.

We trudged along behind the Fae, and as we were herded out, nervous whispers started from the ones left behind. Mostly they wanted to know what dark games the Fae had in store for us tonight, but I didn't want to dwell on that.

With the Book of Nightmares twisting the plot, it wouldn't be fun.

Guilt coiled around me. I was the reason these people were trapped in this nightmare world. Even if the Liber Noctem was the true villain, it was my test that had brought this story to life, and the book was having a wonderful time torturing everyone in it. If the book was this terrible, I could only imagine how awful the goddess was.

I struggled to rein in my own darkening thoughts and mood; it was getting harder and harder to cling to that little flame of hope I'd always had.

No one in our group of five spoke, but everyone's attention was far more alert than it had been while we'd been trapped in the pen.

Hopefully that meant their survival instincts were kicking in.

We marched single file out of the city limits and eventually traveled through an old village, one that seemed to be more uninhabited than lived in.

There were no lights flickering in windows, no smoke wafting from chimneys or scents of food lingering in the air.

We passed crumbling stone cottages that loomed like gravestones in the moonlight, and even though there were no obvious signs of life, I swore I felt eyes watching us from those deserted homes.

We continued our silent march until we finally hit a dirt road that led out of the village and walked for another long stretch before we came to the bottom of a large hill. If the cursed Fae was trying to tire us out before the true action began, he was doing a wonderful job of it.

No food or water had been provided, we hadn't slept, and we'd easily walked a few miles. I was struggling to find my silver lining. My mother would encourage me to keep trying, to find that one spark of hope and cling to it.

Thinking of my mother made me think of the rest of my family. They might not be here physically, but not even the dark book could take them from me.

I pictured a familiar nightly scene from our worn wooden table: Fable and I had just cleared the dinner plates and my father sweetly demanded that my mother put her feet up after cooking the majority of the meal by herself. He'd pull out whatever book he was reading at the time, a paperback in which he'd dog-ear favorite passages or places he could ask us questions on the text. Mother would have a fit over his folding of the pages and Fable and I would grin as Father simply said, "Yes, dear. I'll take that into consideration next time." Knowing he'd never met a paperback he wouldn't eventually dog-ear.

We'd all sit around, bellies full, laughing and discussing whatever section had caught his fancy. We'd analyze it sometimes long into the night. More than once Fable and I had fallen asleep at the table and had been carried to our beds.

My father and mother both had such a strong desire to connect with our daily worlds, no matter how busy their days or weeks were. Their love and company had always been my guiding light, no matter the storm.

My father, mother, and brother were in my heart. My soul. And that meant I was never truly alone.

Conquest spared us one long, sinister look, then strode up the incline.

We slowly ascended the hill behind him, and in the distance a line of trees stood like soldiers at the far end of a field, their tall outlines darker than the night sky.

I wondered if the hunters expected us to run for the woods, and if the forest would offer any sanctuary at all or if I should seek a different route. Would it matter if we all chose different directions and forced them to split up?

Somehow, even if we'd planned our tactics earlier, I doubted we could have devised much of an advantage against immortal harbingers of doom.

It was hard to make out details, but shapes were moving up ahead.

As we drew closer, I noticed where we were heading: a rough amphitheater carved out of earth and stone, rising in tiers along the slope.

The seating looked ancient, as if it had hosted thousands of blood spectacles, and with all the dark stains splattering the stands, I imagined it hadn't been cleaned since the first ever hunt.

Some people enjoyed freshly cut flowers or beautiful art in their sacred spaces; others enjoyed decorating with the blood of their enemies.

Not my personal preference, but I doubted they cared.

My attention moved away from the blood-splattered gore and took in the spectators. Fae clustered in every row.

Some wrapped in silks and furs, some gleaming with bone jewelry and metallic masks, some barely more than shadows with glinting blades they kept raising toward the moon.

I swallowed the lump in my throat.

I wasn't sure if they were dressed in all black and armed to make a wicked fashion statement, or if they would be participating in the grand event tonight.

They looked like the grim reaper had a handful of bastard children and they wanted to gain his favor by bringing him tokens of death.

This was very, very different from the original book. My pulse started pounding and I tried to calm it. The immortals probably sensed my fear.

And terrified or not, I didn't want to give them any other free entertainment.

Hundreds of Fae turned toward us, sighing with the impatience of a bloodthirsty crowd waiting for the main act to get slaughtered and being forced to suffer for few more moments without any action.

A cold, ticklish dread ran over my skin. This was their Colosseum. My father was highly curious about mortal history and had read many tales of distant mortal lands where people were forced to fight to the death. He'd quiz me and Fable on the psychology of why those blood sports were so popular. And what it said about society as a whole.

If my magic hadn't been locked down by the dark book, now would have been a fantastic time for me to manifest a new story.

I held the phoenix tear and tried again to summon my power.

The stone remained as cold and distant as it had before. There really was no way out but through.

Conquest held a fist in the air, sending a signal to the spectators.

"Everyone, take your seats."

A hush swept through the stands as our group was herded onto a patch of bare earth at the center of the makeshift arena.

I tried to ignore the growing discomfort of hundreds of eyes boring into us, taking our measure.

The five of us prey stood in a loose circle, waiting for instructions.

"Welcome to tonight's hunt. As you can see"—Conquest swept his arm out—"we have an odd number of mortals. That was by design. One target per horseman, plus a bonus for the goddess of the harvest."

The crowd tittered and I knew whatever subtext he'd meant wasn't good.

I glanced around at my companions, trying to see them the way our enemies did. Each one was exhibiting their own signs of tension.

One woman was biting her lip so hard I thought it would bleed, her gaze darting nervously from Conquest to the stands of Fae; another shuffled her feet, unable to stand still.

The man wrung his hands together, sweat glistening on his brow. And the fourth young woman kept swallowing hard, trying to maintain her composure.

My own breathing was shallow, my chest rising and falling rapidly no matter how hard I tried to calm myself.

We looked like exactly what they'd called us: prey.

When I thought my heart couldn't pound any harder, the other horsemen of the apocalypse sauntered out onto the field with a ruinous sort of grace.

War's gaze locked onto mine immediately, his eyes smoldering with a dark glint that promised he was coming for me the moment the hunt began.

I tore my attention away, shifting it to the two imposing figures flanking him. Both were towering males with powerfully built frames and exuded an aura of danger that was palpable even from this distance.

I really, really needed to read some fiction with characters who didn't look like they could lift a thousand pounds without breaking a sweat.

Famine's golden-blond hair was braided tightly back, revealing a visage that seemed chiseled by conflict itself, each feature a testament to the chaos he embodied.

And Death...dear gods, he was a vision of haunting beauty.

Terrifying in his allure, his raven-black hair curled softly at the nape of his neck and his eyes were like clear blue ice that commanded attention.

Those eyes were the last ones countless had gazed upon, and I prayed I wouldn't be one of those unfortunate souls.

His full lips curved into a wicked grin as he inspected our group, a silent promise of the destruction he would unleash.

The air around them seemed to vibrate with violence, a dark energy that dripped from their presence despite their stillness.

A wild thrumming began, and I couldn't tell if it was the Fae stomping their feet in the stands, the pounding of our hearts as we stared at those who'd dole out our deaths, or the very ground beneath the horsemen trembling in anticipation of the devastation they heralded.

I was seriously starting to spiral. It had to be something with their magic. On top of the Liber Noctem's dark power, the horsemen made me feel helpless and alone and destined for death.

I distracted myself from falling into the trap of feeling completely doomed by plotting my best strategy.

If Sloth were here, that's exactly what he'd do: calculate his surroundings, search for useful tools, then carry out his plan without any hint of emotion.

I thought back to the spider attack, to our conversation.

He'd said the spiders wanted us to be afraid, that they'd use our emotions against us. These Fae were no different. And the same could be said about the Liber Noctem itself. In fact, this realm, this whole test, was really about pushing the limits of fear, seeing how long it took for me to break.

The horsemen were terrifying, no doubt about it.

Whispers of their names alone inspired dread. Everyone feared the horsemen of the apocalypse—they weren't known to usher in a good time.

But I needed to maintain my inner calm, to not panic. These were not the real horsemen of the apocalypse, these were characters from my book. And they *could* be defeated.

The amphitheater, the hungry gleam in their eyes, the weapons, all of it was meant to intimidate us, to make us easier to manipulate.

I inhaled and slowly exhaled. I wouldn't pretend like I had mastered my fear, but I would do my best to channel it into something useful.

A cool breeze lifted strands of my hair, and I smiled at the small gift.

The sky was a deep, velvety black, punctuated by a full moon that cast a harsh silvery light across the landscape.

Under any other circumstances it would be welcome, but tonight it signaled more bad luck.

The moon's brilliant glare illuminated the field, and from what I could make out of the forest, it was shining brightly there too.

With the fullness of the moon, the forest wouldn't provide much concealment in the shadows, but heading there was still better than running across the mostly empty field without any cover at all.

Conquest faced us.

"When the trumpet sounds, you have ten minutes to hide in the forest. Then we hunt."

My mind raced. Ten minutes. It wasn't the best head start considering we were facing immortal legends of the hunt, but it was better than nothing.

I tried to picture what the heroine in my second-favorite survival novel would do. Find high ground, locate water, avoid open spaces.

Water seemed less important at first, but then I remembered that it was harder to track prey if they ran through a stream.

"When you hear two more short trumpet blasts, that means the ten minutes are up. If you survive without being caught until sunrise, you win."

The lip biter raised her hand. A ripple of indignation went through the stands as if asking a simple question was the worst offense. Pompous Fae.

"How many are allowed to win?"

"All of you." He gave her that terrifying grin that made me wary. "But we've not been bested once. When we catch you, we'll drag you back here for the crowd to decide your fate."

What a tremendous pep talk.

Conquest was saying something else, seeming to play to the crowd, and I tuned him out, attempting to hear any subtle sounds of rushing water.

The moment that trumpet blared, I wanted to pick a direction and run like the devil was chasing me. I couldn't be sure, but I almost swore I heard the faintest hint of water flowing from the left.

Maybe that was just the sound of my pulse gushing through my veins.

My palms tingled and I bounced on the balls of my feet. I wasn't the best runner, but I'd had some practice recently.

Who knew I'd be thankful for the goblin cannibal and her death wolf?

The trumpet blasted and I sprinted for the tree line.

I made it there faster than I'd ever run before and dodged through the tangled vines of the forest, the ground trembling beneath my feet along with the vibrations of the others running close behind me.

I veered deeper into the woods, wanting to lose the other prey and find a quiet place to listen for water.

We couldn't stick close together or we'd be picked off in one swift group.

Twigs snapped underfoot and I winced at the noise.

Speed was my best strategy now; stealth would come later.

Thorned branches grazed my skin, leaving tiny trails of blood from my exposed legs and arms. I hoped that wouldn't prove disastrous for being tracked.

There wasn't anything I could do, my borrowed tunic only covered so much, and I had no time to slow down to avoid getting cut on branches.

My lungs burned, but I barely dared to inhale; behind me, the shrill whoops of the Fae spectators were still far too loud for my comfort.

If I could hear them that well, I needed to run harder and faster.

I jumped over fallen logs and stumbled a bit but kept moving.

The rules to winning the hunt were simple: run, hide, survive.

And no matter what, do not allow myself to wallow in fear or be fooled into believing I was alone forever.

I tuned out the fear, the worry, the anxiety, and just concentrated on placing one foot in front of the other. My mind was as sharp as a blade, focused on escape.

I kept running, my legs pumping harder and faster than ever.

I emptied all thoughts except the feel of my boots slamming into the earth, the wind tugging strands of my hair loose, and the steady beat of my heart.

Several long minutes passed, and eventually all other sounds faded. No other prey crashed through the forest, no joyful Fae calling for our deaths.

Unfortunately, I also didn't hear the trumpets. I must have gone out of hearing range, which was both good and bad.

I had to assume the ten minutes were long up and the horsemen would be prowling through the woods.

I didn't slow my pace; I kept sprinting as fast as I could through the undergrowth. I'd have to slow soon, but not yet.

A little while later, my muscles began to ache from exhaustion, and my mouth felt as dry as the desert.

I'd been running for what felt like ages on low energy, and I knew that in a forest this old, every step could be either the worst betrayal or the greatest salvation.

A betrayal by stepping wrong and twisting an ankle or breaking a limb, or salvation by providing a place to hide.

If I broke a bone now, I would have no chance to win the hunt.

The canopy above me suddenly pulsed with something that looked like a pale blue Fae light and made weird shadows flicker over the root-knotted ground.

Wonderful.

Conquest hadn't mentioned anything about Fae magic being permitted. I wondered what other surprises they had in store for us. Maybe this was a nightmare creature spawned from Somnia to keep things interesting.

I really hated this nightmare-inducing realm.

I darted beneath some low hanging moss, and the air underneath it thickened with a sweetness that immediately dulled my senses.

I had a sinking feeling the Fae or the plants were releasing some toxin.

I held my breath, trying to take in as little air as possible.

Gods only knew what it could do if I breathed in too much of it.

I might strip and start howling at the moon, or maybe I'd roll around in the leaves like some wild, untamed beast scratching fleas.

I cursed myself for silently asking the dreaded *what other fun surprise might come next* question. That never ended in cake or cocktails and a day off.

From somewhere to my left, the silvery laughter of another person echoed—much closer than I liked. It was female, so it wasn't one of the horsemen, and I doubted it was one of the mortals.

But that didn't mean this random Fae was any less lethal.

My heart jackhammered and my blood turned to ice.

I dove for cover, rolling silently into a tangle of brambles, the thorns snagging at my tunic and scratching my already battered arms.

I didn't so much as blink.

I waited, trying to slow my racing pulse. There were no other sounds. I wondered if it was real or if I could thank the Liber Noctem for a new mental assault.

I lifted my face and exhaled, slow and measured, then pushed myself up from where I'd crouched. I crept out from the underbrush and waited a few beats, listening to make sure I was alone.

Once I was positive there were no other Fae lurking, I walked briskly between the trees.

This wasn't a sprint anymore.

This was a dance, and the price of a single misstep was my life.

Survive the story or suffer your fate.

It was a charming mantra I couldn't seem to stop silently repeating. I wondered if the Book of Nightmares was hoping to twist my thoughts, to get deeper into my head to try to make me lose this test.

Then I wished I hadn't considered that. I needed to focus on surviving one mini disaster at a time.

I moved along an animal trail, the moss springy under my boots as it swallowed the sounds of my footfalls.

It was another blessing and a curse. The moss was helping to cover my steps but would be doing the same for anyone following me.

I listened for the telltale rhythm of pursuit.

The ground rumbling, branches shaking, the startled flutter of birds taking off, or the silence that indicated an apex predator had arrived.

Anything that might signal someone closing in.

I had never been more grateful for reading so much end-of-the-worlds fiction before—it prepared me for this moment.

The forest was alive with subtle sounds: insects thrumming, leaves sighing in the gentle breeze, the distant trickle of water.

I almost whooped with joy—the water source was off to the left. If I could make it there, I could get something to drink and cover my trail.

It would give me an edge I desperately needed.

Then I just had to wait until dawn. Hope kindled in my chest.

I went to move but halted, listening.

Some inner voice warned me to freeze.

I waited, wondering if I'd simply imagined the warning and had mistaken my fear for something it wasn't.

A moment later, a different sound caught my attention: something that was not quite a footfall, not quite a heartbeat, but some odd combination of the two.

I froze. Since when could I sense heartbeats?

That had to be the Liber Noctem interfering. I hadn't suddenly turned immortal in the span of a few hours. But my senses were slowly growing stronger. Maybe it had to do with my magic.

With the same increasing panic I'm sure most prey felt when a predator neared, I knew I was being tracked. I needed to seek high ground. Now.

As quickly and quietly as I could manage, I scaled the nearest tree, using the lowest branches and fallen logs for leverage.

I'd only made it a few feet off the ground when I felt a shift of energy through the undergrowth—an innate awareness that I was no longer alone.

All the hair on my body rose.

One of the hunters had found me.

Indecision kept me rooted in place.

I could either hope I hadn't been spotted, or, if I had been, pray that someone else would race by and prove to be a more tempting target.

But if War was this close, it wasn't an accident.

I squinted through the tangled branches, my heart pounding a frantic rhythm as I tried to catch any movement on the narrow path ahead.

The dense foliage formed a natural screen, and I hoped it was enough to keep me concealed. One moment turned into two. Then three.

A few more passed and I waited, ears straining. Still, nothing.

I slowly started to relax. Whatever I thought I'd felt must have moved on.

A twig snapped behind me, sharp as the crack of a whip.

The unexpected noise sent a jolt of fear through me, and my body involuntarily jerked. I slapped a hand over my mouth, smothering the sharp inhale.

I had been so sure the threat lay directly in front of me, I hadn't even sensed the danger lurking behind.

That meant there were two closing in.

Like the spooked prey I was trying *not* to be, I panicked. I jumped from the tree and bolted, blood pounding, and plunged through the thicket.

This part of the forest grew darker, tightly woven with twisted limbs of towering oaks and rambling bushes, rich with the potent scent of damp earth that smelled like it had been deprived of sunlight for decades.

A sense of dread gnawed at me as I ran; I couldn't decide if the thick shadows were shielding me or if they were the harbingers of my doom.

I tried to connect with them, but they weren't the magical ribbons of my dreamweaver power. That would have been far too convenient.

I sprinted with every ounce of energy I could muster, but the sheer number of branches forced me to slow, dragging myself over and through the suffocating thicket that seemed to conspire against my escape.

Stupid Faerie forest.

I swore the undergrowth was doubling before my very eyes, trying to trap me for the Fae who ruled this realm.

Since the plot was now nothing close to the original story, I had no idea what they'd do to me. Murder? Imprisonment? Force me to fight to the death without any weapons? Or worse...

I refused to find out, so I pumped my legs harder.

Branches smacked at my arms, my face, but I wouldn't stop. Not yet.

Not when every nerve screamed with the very real possibility that I was about to die.

I hurdled a fallen log, rolling to break my momentum, and skidded to a stop at the base of a huge old tree.

The bark was slick with dew, and the roots at its base were like a tangle of serpents trying to wrap around my legs as I stepped over them, but I scrambled up it anyway, my hands and boots somehow finding purchase in the trunk's deep grooves.

I focused on controlling my breathing while I listened for sounds of pursuit.

There was nothing. No crashing through the trees, no crunching of boots on twigs. It was like being stalked by a ghost.

I knew I didn't imagine the damn branch snapping. But that had been the only sound that had given the hunter away.

My pulse sped as realization dawned. That meant he'd *wanted* me to know he was closing in, and he'd wanted me to run.

He was enjoying the chase.

From my perch, I scanned the clearing below.

This part of the woods was secluded and hard to reach. Someone would have to make a real effort to find their way into this glen. Especially someone larger than me. The horsemen would certainly make noise.

The moon still barely reached this part of the woods, but what little light did slip through painted the scene in a spectral silver.

Nothing moved. Not even the wind stirred now.

But the hunter was close.

I *felt* him. It was like a gravitational pull growing stronger with every heartbeat. Instead of warning me to run, it tempted me to seek him out.

To run *to* him.

Which was *not* going to happen.

Cursed Liber Noctem, making me seek out the very source that could be my undoing. I would *not* fail this test.

I pressed my back to the trunk, chest heaving, and closed my eyes to ground myself for a moment. I waited, trying to hold on to the hope that I'd escaped, that I'd bested War or Death or even Conquest.

That my story was not about to come to some sudden, violent ending.

As the seconds stretched into minutes and no sounds reached my ears, I almost believed he'd lost my trail, that I'd earned this respite, this brief victory.

But just as I thought I was free, a large hand closed around my ankle.

The world spun as I was hauled out of the tree.

It happened so quickly I had no time to process that I'd been caught, let alone react.

A pair of strong arms shot out, grabbing me before I hit the earth, and pressed my back up against the trunk. He'd pinned me a few feet off the ground, ensuring my feet wouldn't gain purchase; then a massive wall of warm muscle stepped between my legs, locking me in place.

My body crackled with electricity from each point of contact.

I immediately began thrashing, trying to free myself.

"Lore."

I stopped fighting at the sound of that voice.

It couldn't be.

My heart raced for a whole new reason as I looked up into achingly familiar eyes. "You're alive."

THIRTY
Lore

I DRANK IN the sight of the prince I thought I'd lost forever and exhaled in relief. Sloth was unharmed, alive, and even more breathtaking than I remembered.

I threw my arms around him, squeezing tightly, feeling the solid, comforting mass of his body against mine.

Surprise flickered through me when he nestled his face into the curve of my neck, inhaling deeply as if memorizing my scent, his breath warm and steady against my skin. I swore an electric current passed between us.

Considering how tightly he held his emotions in check, that action was the equivalent of him falling to his knees and weeping for joy.

I *knew* I'd wormed my way under that icy exterior. *Felled by feelings* really came through.

We stayed like that for a few moments before I slowly drew back.

"You found me."

He stood in the shadows, so it was hard to make out his features clearly, but I thought I saw his mouth curve with a hint of amusement.

"Always."

I felt more than saw his attention slide from my face and trail down my body, and knew he was checking for injury and cataloguing anything amiss.

"I waited on the beach all night," I said while he continued his inspection. "When you didn't show up, I really thought the serp-i-corn killed you."

His teeth flashed in the darkness. He was *definitely* amused now.

"Have a little faith, Peaches. I'm trying to not be insulted. Suffering through more pirate talk would have been far more likely to kill me."

I gave him a flat look. "The uni-pus was larger than the ship. And you went after it like a madman."

He tucked a strand of hair behind my ear.

"Fortunately, I can swim."

He was clearly downplaying the situation—he hadn't simply survived because he'd been a good swimmer. He'd been trapped underwater for the gods knew how long. And he was not even at his full strength.

"But you did choose to go after the creature, correct?"

"Yes. I didn't think it was strictly from your story and wanted to test a theory."

"What do you mean?"

"I believe the Liber Noctem killed my master librarian and is somehow moving from host to host as the Trials draw closer to the end."

"Do you think it can inhabit anyone?"

"Or anything, given the last encounter was a beast."

It sounded plausible, but something about it didn't sit right. If I'd been that close to the Liber Noctem, wouldn't I have felt it?

I could consider all that later; right now I couldn't stop staring at Sloth.

His presence felt surreal, like a dream I was afraid to wake up from.

He stood there, holding me up, blond hair tousled and clothes torn in several places, indicating he'd had a long, rough journey despite his nonchalance.

But he *was* here and that was all that mattered right now.

Something deep inside me settled, like a weight was suddenly lifted.

Against all odds, he'd found me.

My heart swelled with disbelief and joy as tears threatened to spill over. I blinked rapidly, willing them back.

"Lore." He shifted his hold on me so he could use his thumb to gently wipe away the tears that escaped. "I promise it will take more than tiny hissing vampires and whatever that sea monster was to end me. Your

nightmares will not be my destruction. Give me your worst and I'll still be by your side. It's okay."

It was more than okay.

My romance-centered brain was having a complete meltdown.

This was far better than any story.

Sloth kept his promise. He'd stalked me across realms from the depths of the ocean, over an island of vampires, and through the forest of Faerie.

Never stopping, never giving up.

I didn't think his devotion was entirely related to the Liber Noctem or the Trials. This felt personal—like he would have come for me regardless.

The thought sent a strange shiver through me.

He went preternaturally still.

I froze too, bracing myself for a nefarious plot twist.

It took another few seconds for me to realize it wasn't because he'd sensed danger. He was taut for very different reasons. Ones I was now acutely aware of.

When I shivered, he'd *felt* it since his body was fitted to mine, pinning me against the tree. And he'd physically responded.

I dropped my attention to the area in question.

His bulge was impossible not to notice or feel, especially since I'd locked my legs around his waist when I'd hugged him. And I hadn't released him.

Now that he knew I wasn't injured, he seemed to finally notice my rising hemline. And the way our bodies were intimately pressed together.

My breathing sped up.

I was trying to think of a joke to lighten the mood, but the longer we went without speaking, the more a heated tension started to simmer between us, like one tiny spark would set off a fire neither one of us could put out or control.

Or maybe that was just my wishful thinking.

"Lore."

His hands gripped the back of my thighs where he still held me up, his fingers pressing into my skin like a brand.

My own hands rested on his broad shoulders, and his muscles tensed beneath my touch. I sensed it was because he was trying to rein himself in.

"I apologize for..." He trailed off as I shifted a little, hoping to ease the physical tension.

It had the opposite effect.

Our hips were now aligned in a way that left *very* little to the imagination.

When I wriggled up, I felt how turned on he was by the motion, and I'd unintentionally increased the friction between us.

I muttered an apology, and like the smooth seductress I was, I tried to make things less charged by moving again, the same way. Obviously, it had worked so well the first time. This was why I hadn't courted anyone in forever.

I'd now accidentally dry humped the prince on a few separate occasions. That had to set some record for embarrassing encounters in a nightmare world.

I stopped fidgeting and honestly wasn't sure if that helped.

His breathing slowed, and his gaze locked onto mine, a storm flickering in their depths. His expression was impossible to read, though.

I wondered if he was suddenly recalling our kiss, how it felt like the purest form of magic, and how I'd never be able to forget how perfect it was even if I lived for a thousand lifetimes.

Something seemed to shimmer around us, some magic locking us in this moment, safe from the nightmares for a little while.

For one wild, reckless second, I imagined him closing the remaining distance between us, his fingers plunging into my hair right before his mouth came down on mine in a searing kiss, ending this growing torment.

"We should hurry," I said, slamming the door on any romantic notions.

"Mmh."

He hadn't removed his attention from my lips.

And he looked ready to devour me.

I was fairly sure that was not wishful thinking on my part.

"There's a hunt and we really don't want to be found. I think War wants to either murder me or convince me he's not just pretty and boring. In the original story, he ended up in a love triangle with the main character. But I haven't really met Death yet, so I doubt we have to worry about that."

That caught his attention.

His gaze snapped up to mine. All ice and no fire now.

"If anyone tries to touch you, harm you, or take you in *any* capacity, I will destroy them."

I smiled.

Only a sociopath wouldn't bat an eye at the prospect of fighting literal harbingers of doom. "They're the Four Horsemen of the Apocalypse. You might be outmatched."

A dark shadow flickered over his expression.

"Fuck the horsemen. Anyone can be killed with the right knowledge and skill."

I cupped his face lightly. "There's my sunny sociopath."

With his face tilted upward, I finally got a better look at him in the sliver of moonlight. Something was wrong.

Sloth's pupils were blown wide, his nostrils flaring as he scented the air around us. This wasn't the cool, calculating royal I knew.

This was a male on the verge of turning completely feral. I had no idea how he'd managed to hide...whatever was happening. He'd sounded perfectly fine.

"Are you all right?" I whispered. "What happened to—"

My words cut off as I spotted the injury on his wrist: two puncture wounds.

"You were bitten." Ice flooded my veins. "By one of the specters?"

If that was the case, that was bad.

In the original story, their bites were known to drive their victims out of their senses, making them act on animal instinct.

A low growl rumbled in his chest, proving the point.

"Did any of them harm you?"

It sounded like he was trying *very* hard to speak around his anger.

My sweet, vengeful prince.

It really was good to have his murdering self back.

I shook my head.

"I'm perfectly fine. Aside from being locked in that livestock pen for a few hours." He looked ready to stalk into the forest and hunt the horsemen down for that. "Did I mention I missed you and your sociopathic tendencies?"

His grip on me tightened a fraction.

"You have no idea...When I finally tracked your scent on the island and discovered someone had intercepted you, I almost went mad."

"I hate to break this to you, Blondie, but I'm not sure you've got that impulse under control yet. You're looking a little feral around the eyes."

His gaze dropped to my lips.

"That mouth will be my undoing."

He leaned in so fast the movement barely registered until his breath tickled my neck. Sloth hesitated for a fraction of a second before his teeth grazed my skin.

He slowly dragged them along my throat, in a caress laced with promises of dark, wicked seduction.

The sensation sent shivers of pleasure down my spine before he tore his mouth away. His attention flicked up to mine in quiet assessment. Holy gods. That was unexpected, and I kind of wanted him to do it again. And again.

If he was expecting me to be upset or shove him away, he would be disappointed. This unleashed version of the icy prince set my blood on fire. So different from his usual detached, cool demeanor.

He was ruthless on and off the killing fields, and I might be in danger of developing a taste for darkness. I wanted him to kiss me hard and fast against this tree. Then I remembered with his powers, he'd *know*.

His gaze lingered on mine before dropping to trace the curve of my lips.

It continued downward, following the line where our bodies remained locked together, pausing briefly there before it slid lower.

As he continued to drink me in, his hands slowly began to glide along my bare thighs, his touch light and unhurried.

I didn't think he was aware of their movement. It was as if he was keeping himself so tightly wound that a few threads of his self-control had finally given way, but he was concentrating too hard on *not* breaking to notice.

I could feel the new tension in his posture, like a coiled spring on the verge of snapping. His Adam's apple bobbed visibly as he swallowed hard.

"You should tell me to put you down."

I *should* say something, break the spell, but I couldn't bring myself to.

The rough bark of the tree pressed into my back through my tunic, and I reveled in the sensation of the prince's strength, the way he held me captive against the trunk. The position was commanding and impossible to resist; the prince was an alpha in all the right ways.

I stared down at where he was slowly drawing little lines up the sides of my legs with one hand, feeling the delicious burn of being wanted in return.

"Lore."

My name almost sounded like a plea.

"Sloth." I tentatively reached for him, my fingers brushing against the defined angles of his jaw and the softness of his full lips.

I felt an overwhelming urge to pull him closer, to press my lips against his, then slowly trail them along his neck, down his hard chest.

I wanted him so bad I ached.

We'd been running from one battle to the next and I just needed a single moment of something good to cling to. Something not marred by nightmares.

I needed the magic of dreams. But mostly, I just wanted *him*. My cold, forbidding prince who secretly burned hotter than a raging inferno.

The world around us was on the brink of unraveling, and I wanted to seize this moment of respite before everything changed.

"Thank you for finding me. No one has ever..." I swallowed the sudden emotion down. "I've always wondered what it would be like, having someone stand by my side. Now I know."

He looked like he was on the edge of complete destruction.

"I swore a vow to you. Nothing but true death would see me break it."

My mouth curved from the memory.

He *had* actually done that—when he'd promised to stand by my side and maim all my enemies. I'd thought he'd been half-serious.

Clearly, he'd meant every slightly disturbing word.

His gaze was a smoldering fire that made my heart race in anticipation.

He wanted me. No matter what he'd said before about us being a bad idea, his expression told a different story. As did his body. The proof of his desire was still pressed between us, and I was trying desperately to not think about it.

Prince Sloth looked like he was just barely restraining himself from acting on his baser emotions by a crumbling veneer of self-control.

"What do you want?"

I wanted *everything*.

The press of his lips to mine, the brush of his knuckles against my inner thighs. I wanted his tongue and fingers to learn every curve and dip of my body, strumming me to the brink before he slowly thrust in, filling me completely.

I wanted to sleep in a tangle of limbs, spent from our many adventures. And I wanted lazy mornings by a fire, reading, with our future pet cat. And of course Teddy, my shadow pet.

The air between us crackled with tension now, and I knew that if I asked him to kiss me, the thin barrier of civility would shatter, and he would toss aside all restraint and claim me right now.

I managed to break the trance.

"Whatever you're feeling, it's probably just the venom—"

"It's *not* the venom." His breath was hot against my skin. "I can hear your pulse racing. Sense your desire. And I am trying very, very hard to not think about the fact you're covered in another male's scent. Or why it's affecting me this way. I do not get jealous—that's my brother's sin. But I can hardly think past the urge to cover you in *mine*."

Oh, gods. I was living out every jealousy trope I'd ever read.

And loving every second.

"I had nothing to change into," I said, trying to soothe the beast I sensed lurking beneath his hooded gaze. "If he tried touching me, I would have stabbed him." I nodded toward my ankle sheath. "Even when he didn't touch me, I wanted to stab him. You would have approved."

"I always approve of you. Your lightness, your darkness." The prince's lips brushed against the tender curve of my throat, sending a thrill of danger coursing through my veins. "And especially your intelligence."

I closed my eyes in an attempt to leash my libido. He wasn't himself.

In the original book, it took days for the venom's effects to dissipate completely. He might feel mostly better, but his pupils told a different tale.

Prince Sloth was still more monster than man.

"The venom..."

He thrust against me, once, and I saw the gods themselves.

"Has nothing to do with what I feel. I can promise you; I didn't get hard when I was bitten. Or when I tore through the forest hunting you. Or when I scaled the castle walls and stalked through the streets."

His teeth skimmed along my pulse point again. The risk of being bitten only heightened my desire for him, making him even more impossible to resist.

I really needed to seek a healer if we made it home. I had serious issues.

"It's you, Lore. You drive me out of my senses."

One of his hands left my leg only to curl around my waist, firm and steady as he anchored me in place, pressing me harder against the tree. He was careful to avoid the weapons belt I wore, but I almost thought the phoenix tear hummed in its pouch, pleased by our closeness.

"I have never been more frustrated, off-balance, or turned on in my life."

I shook my head, unable to hide my smile.

"For someone who lives in a library, you need to brush up on your wooing skills."

"Would you like me to pen you sonnets now?"

He gave me the sort of wicked grin that made my pulse race for all the right reasons. Then his hips moved again, hitting that little bundle of nerves with precision, even through his trousers.

I arched into him, my heartbeat drumming a feverish rhythm against my ribs. If this was only a taste of what he could do, I was in trouble.

Slayed by Sex might end up being the inscription on my tombstone.

"Or do you want me to fuck you hard and deep against this tree first?"

I was absolutely going to offer up my soul to this prince.

And all it took was one kiss, a little neck biting, and a few dirty words. I was weak but didn't care—there were far worse vices than being overcome by orgasms.

I moved a little and I felt every defined ridge of his body, each muscle coiled and tense beneath his shirt.

He was so close to losing control and I couldn't say I hated it.

Or his filthy mouth.

Gods, I seriously hoped this was not some figment of my imagination. That would be the upset of the century.

Barring my fears of being lost in a sexy daydream, I needed to at least *attempt* to be responsible once more. Then I'd have done my due diligence in being the voice of logic and couldn't be held responsible for any bad decisions.

"This is a terrible idea. For multiple reasons."

His low, dark chuckle sent delicious shivers of anticipation racing down my spine.

"Then, tell me to stop."

I remained silent as his mouth grazed my collarbone, then dipped lower; each gentle scrape of his teeth ignited a honeyed sensation that spread through every fiber of my being. He moved lower, pressing a chaste kiss over my heart.

My senses were heightened, hyperaware of every touch, every breath.

This was what being worshipped felt like. Adored beyond the physical.

"Do you want me to tell you to stop?" I asked. Maybe he hated losing his grip on his cold indifference; maybe he needed me to end this before it began.

He stroked the sensitive area of my inner leg. "No."

"Then, don't."

With a possessive growl, he balanced me on his knee, seized the fabric of my tunic, and pulled, the sound of tearing cloth echoing in the stillness.

Holy gods.

He'd torn the shirt in half down the center.

The shredded garment fell open, leaving me partly exposed. Only my weapons belt kept the shirt from falling open completely.

He drank me in, my eyes, my mouth, the expanse of bare skin from my neck to my navel, and I saw his beautiful mind kick into action.

I knew without a doubt he would put all his knowledge to use, wringing pleasure from me until I couldn't remember my name.

The anticipation had me squeezing my thighs together.

His gaze locked onto mine with a yearning so intense it mirrored the ache building within me.

"Put my tunic on, then tell me to put you down, Lore. If you don't, I'm going to make you come so hard you beg for mercy." He leaned in, brushing his lips against the shell of my ear as he whispered, "My House is not known for being merciful."

I heard what he *said,* but the prince's arms were ironclad around me, and the way his voice vibrated low and dangerous against my ear indicated he wasn't about to walk away unless I told him to.

The clipped, strategic prince I'd teased him for being was gone; this male was hungry in every conceivable way.

He was unpredictable and wild, and the effect on my romance-addled heart was positively catastrophic.

I wanted him to claim me in every way he'd laid out.

Be logical, Lore.

But that was not in my nature—I was a being forged of fire and emotion, of impossible dreams and a not-so-secret yearning for true, storybook-worthy love.

My hands flattened against his chest, but instead of pushing him away, I fisted the fabric of his shirt.

I wasn't sure who finally made the first move, but in the next instant, his lips crashed against mine, the kiss all-consuming.

My fingers sank into his hair, yanking him nearer until there was no space left between us. He growled with approval as I tugged his face toward mine and kissed him like my life and soul depended on it.

His tongue swept into my mouth, stroking mine.

The taste of him was intoxicating, but it still wasn't enough.

His hand inched upward, encouraged by the subtle rocking of my hips, and he groaned against my mouth.

Gods, I wanted his hands *everywhere*.

A warmth ignited deep in my belly, spreading through my veins as his fingers traced a deliberate path from my thighs upward, gliding over the curve of my hips and the gentle slope of my waist, before slipping under my fluttering tunic and grazing the sensitive skin just beneath my breast.

I threaded my fingers through his hair harder, gripping firmly as I rolled my hips into his, silently begging him to give me more.

He tore himself away from our kiss, then dragged his mouth along my throat.

"I want you. More than I've wanted anything. I could worship you for the rest of my life and it still wouldn't be long enough. Your mind." His right hand was making a slow, torturous path upward, skimming along my silhouette. "Your heart. You know what you like and don't care what anyone thinks. And there's nothing sexier or more interesting than that. You're fucking perfect, Lore."

He finally cupped my breast, kneading it as his tongue plunged into my mouth, claiming mine in a battle I was all too willing to let him win.

His thumb brushed against the sensitive peaks, playing and teasing until I could hardly think straight from the sensations.

"More."

My demand was met with fervor.

He gripped me by the back of my thighs and began to slowly grind his hips against mine in a tantalizing, rhythmic motion. It was a precursor of how it would feel with him thrusting inside me, and I was already close to the edge.

"Oh, my gods."

For a moment, I saw the stars and heavens and every realm in between. And that was with a layer of fabric between us.

When he finally drove inside me, I might combust. But what a way to go.

I clawed at the fabric of his tunic, gripping the woven material as I tugged it upward, inch by inch, over his head. I needed to see him, feel him without barriers.

I tossed his shirt aside and took a moment to drink him in.

His body was a work of art; his muscles were chiseled with precision, each curve and hard line a testament to years of rigorous discipline and dedication.

The gold phoenix tattoo glowed, and I couldn't stop myself from tracing its realistic feathers. I swore it buzzed beneath my touch, a little warning sign or something more innocent, I wasn't sure. But then my attention shifted back to the prince's face, and I forgot to breathe.

He was looking at me like I was his favorite story, and he was eager to read every word on the page.

It was the most unguarded he'd ever been, and I knew it wasn't an accident. He wanted me to see the depth of his desire, how it surpassed the physical.

I'd never seen someone more perfect; no character from any of my books compared to the prince and the sheer power he exuded in all ways.

But his mind captivated me the most.

Now that he had my full attention again, his seduction resumed with renewed determination.

He continued that slow, maddening movement with his hips, his focus set entirely on where our bodies met.

Every sharp intake of breath I made spurred him on. He cupped my breast and teased my nipples, cataloguing every nuance of how I responded, what I liked.

He was studying me like I was a text he was desperate to learn.

I'd never found something so attractive.

I glanced at his forearm, at the Latin inscription tattooed there.

Books before man.

This academic certainly knew what he was doing, and I sent a silent prayer of thanks to whatever he'd read that gave him an edge in the bedroom.

Then his mouth was on mine again, and there was nothing slow about it. This kiss was a claiming, a branding. A promise of passion untold.

I grew slicker with need.

He gripped my legs and thrust again, harder.

His tongue owning mine.

In a few short minutes, he'd already mastered what I liked and was now employing those tactics to wring pleasure from me.

I'd never had another lover be so in tune with my body, my needs. His desire to learn what turned me on was a seduction of its own.

The friction between us sent waves of heat coursing through me that intensified each time his arousal pressed against my core.

I didn't care about the hunters, or the Trials, or any other twisted thing coming our way. I was starting to lose track of the woods around us, my senses narrowed to a tunnel that led directly to the prince.

Nothing else existed outside our bubble.

The world was dark at the edges, except for our sliver of moonlight.

Each time his body connected to mine, my focus on him sharpened.

The next time he thrust against me, a deep, primal need rose, eclipsing everything else. It was ancient, demanding, and impossible to ignore.

I needed to claim the prince and be claimed by him.

I broke away from our kiss.

"Take your pants off." I drew back, panting. "*Now.*"

THIRTY-ONE
Prince Sloth

LORE'S FINGERS CURLED around the waistband of my fighting leathers, pulling me against her with a confident tug. As if I needed any further encouragement or prompting to give her everything she wanted.

I was barely maintaining my control now.

I couldn't seem to leash the growing need to protect her, care for her, claim her in every way.

When I'd finally tracked her down and wrapped my arms around her, it felt like a missing piece of myself clicked into place, granting me a sudden sense of peace amid the chaos.

The feeling hadn't subsided.

I hadn't experienced something like it before and couldn't quite pinpoint what the cause was. It was likely the result of several factors.

I ran my knuckles along her inner thigh, noting every breathy inhalation, ragged exhale, and flutter in her pulse the higher they roamed.

I wanted her dripping and half mad with desire.

After seeing the sea monster drag her into the depths, and the all-consuming terror that followed...I needed to erase that, replace the image of death and loss with its complete counterpart.

My attention flicked up as I finally brushed against her center.

Her eyes glazed with lust at the featherlight touch.

I'd never seen someone more beautiful.

"For the love of the gods." She tossed her head back. "What are you waiting for? Self-combustion? Death? If so, I'm close. To both."

I grinned, already pleased with the results. "I'm plotting."

"Less plotting, more action."

With the vampire venom only recently burned out of my system, the remnants of its influence still buzzed under my skin, stirring primal emotions that refused to fully subside.

I wanted to take my time. But that rational thought was giving way to the growing urge to fuck her until she shouted my name with her release.

She leaned in, her breath warm against my skin, and slowly ran her tongue along the seam of my lips. The touch was light, a mere whisper of sensation that invited and teased, a temptation that I couldn't resist.

I responded without hesitation.

I drew her lower lip between my teeth, applying just enough pressure to claim it gently, feeling the pulse of her desire a beat before she moaned.

That sound made the already overwhelming need to act on my baser instincts grow tenfold; it was a rawness that simmered beneath the surface of my calm outer facade.

My desire to claim her surged just as fiercely as when I'd first been bitten and was teetering on the edge of madness, perhaps even more intense now that my mind was no longer clouded.

I knew exactly what I wanted.

I wanted to mark her so no one would ever be foolish enough to try to harm her, knowing they'd face the chilling wrath of House Sloth.

A mark from a Prince of Sin was no small thing. It was like a small, magical tattoo, a bond that could never be broken, even in death.

I'd never considered giving one to any previous lover. Ever.

With her legs locked around me, her lips swollen from our kisses, and her eyes heavy-lidded with desire, it was becoming increasingly difficult to remember why worshipping her up against a tree was a bad idea.

Why I should at least scout for shelter or encourage her to transport us to a more comfortable location. But there was something carnal about losing ourselves in the woods, fucking like animals controlled by instinct.

I tried to focus beyond the immediate thought of dropping to my knees and tasting her. I craved her like she was my drug of choice, and I was already addicted.

Some small part of me wondered if there was magic at play before dismissing it. The Liber Noctem could choose far worse twists of fate.

I forced my senses outward, but the rustle of leaves and the cool evening air only heightened the charged atmosphere.

We were alone, and the glen was well hidden, but that didn't mean we were safe.

Every plot I'd come up with to drive her wild slipped away as she reached between us, slowly trailing her fingers over my trousers, teasing my hard cock.

I thrust into her grip, swearing, then resumed stroking her thighs, my thumb edging closer to her wet heat again.

Another tug at my thoughts pulled me away.

She'd mentioned something about a hunt and the horsemen, but I had to trust that I'd sense them before they became a true problem. The trees were densely packed here; no one would get near without making some noise.

I banished any more distractions.

Now my focus was locked only on her.

I finally shifted my hand where she wanted it, dragging my fingers through her slick folds before moving them away, stroking the area beside her entrance.

I hid my grin as she rolled her hips with impatience, her body moving sinuously against mine.

"You're being a rotten tease." Her eyes narrowed before a wicked smile curved her lips. "This means war, Blondie. Prepare to lose."

My beautiful, clever dreamweaver won.

She writhed along my hard length, igniting a fire that made rational thought a distant memory.

I shifted slightly, allowing her boots to drop softly to the forest floor, the leaves crunching beneath her.

Once she was steady, I leaned closer, pressing my palm firmly against the tree beside her, anchoring me in place.

Her victory was only temporary.

"How many times do you think I can make you come on my fingers before I use my tongue? Three, four dozen times?"

She blinked at me, seeming lost for words.

I reveled in the fact that I'd stunned her. Lore was usually unflappable.

"You're going to be the actual death of me. Aren't you?"

I nipped at her mouth playfully.

"Not anytime soon. Necrophilia doesn't sound appealing. I want your eyes on mine when I'm between your legs."

Over the top of her tunic, I rolled her nipple between my thumb and forefinger. Her breath rushed out as she sank her teeth into her lower lip.

"And when I fuck you from behind, I'll have mirrors installed so you can still keep those pretty eyes on me."

She huffed a surprised laugh. "You are seriously disturbed."

"You have no idea."

I slipped my free hand beneath the fabric of her torn tunic, the cool air brushing against her skin and pebbling her nipples.

My knuckles gently grazed over them and her eyes fluttered shut.

I bent down, teasing the hardened peak with a swirl of my tongue until her fingers plunged into my hair and she damn near growled.

I smiled against her flesh as I cupped her other breast, and repeated the motion until she squirmed beneath me.

"Good things come to those who wait, Peaches."

She muttered something about understanding why mortal cultures called orgasms little deaths.

By the time we were through, she'd know this was about celebrating life.

My hand continued its deliberate journey downward, pausing to skim over the weapons belt she still wore and then to trace an intricate design just above her pelvic bone.

She didn't realize it, but I was spelling out my true name—and I intended to confirm what she'd already guessed with her soon.

For now, though, I teased her entrance before finally slipping a finger inside her. I groaned as she clenched around it, envisioning how incredible that would feel when I slid my cock into her.

Her lips parted, and I captured the sound of her moan with a deep, lingering kiss.

I stroked her tongue with mine, feeling her grow slicker.

I gently gripped her chin and tilted her face up, deepening our kiss to let her know this would be a slow, drugging descent into pleasure.

That I would take my time and not be hurried.

This would be the only time I acted slothful the way mortals thought of it—I'd languidly stroke and tease.

She rocked against me, and I withdrew just enough to play with her clit before plunging it back into her.

A breathy moan escaped her, followed by a soft curse.

It took every ounce of willpower I could scrape together to not bury myself inside her now. But I wanted this to be about her pleasure, so I leashed myself.

I carefully added a second finger, pausing to let her adjust.

Once she rocked against me, I took over. I rhythmically pumped in and out, attuned to the subtle shifts of her body.

I slowed when she got close, then pumped faster again, drawing out to stroke her clit before driving my fingers back in and repeating the motions.

I varied the pace, watching her with singular focus as she climbed higher toward that peak.

"Oh, gods. Whatever you're doing, don't stop."

Her fingernails dug into my forearms, leaving small crescents in my skin as her teeth pressed into her lower lip, barely holding back a moan.

Her dark gaze was locked on my hand, where the heel of my palm pressed against her most sensitive spot. I couldn't stop the sudden possession I felt.

She was *mine*.

Her mind, her body, her pleasure.

I pumped harder and faster, mimicking the way I'd take her against the tree soon. Lore's gaze snapped up to mine, almost daring me to give her more.

To submit entirely to whatever *this* was.

Little did she know, I feared I already had.

Her hips met each of my thrusts and I grew impossibly more aroused.

I wanted her to come undone so many times that her pleasure blurred into an endless, incoherent wave with one hitting after the next.

I felt the slickness in my palm, warm and dripping, and I fought the urge to put my fingers in my mouth and lick it off.

I watched, completely rapt, as she took control. Her body moved with a confident rhythm as she started bouncing on my hand.

It was impossible not to imagine her riding me the same way, and I almost came at the erotic thought of her using me to chase her pleasure.

She was absolutely stunning.

Her cheeks flushed with a peachy hue, and her eyes sparkled with a sultry brightness as she drank me in, her attention roaming over the hard planes of my chest, my arms, the straining bulge in my leathers.

She wasn't dreaming of one of her characters, she was wholly engaged with me, and that, more than anything, turned me on to the point of pain.

Her breasts moved rhythmically as she rode my fingers, and my cock jerked at the sight of her grabbing one and squeezing it.

I leaned in, replacing her hand with mine as I cupped one breast and took the other into my mouth, sucking and teasing until she cried out for mercy.

"What did I tell you about mercy?"

I fucked her harder with my fingers as she drove herself onto them.

Her body slamming down onto my palm made a clapping sound that had my cock straining against my leathers with new urgency.

I withdrew them and flicked her swollen clit before thrusting them back in.

"Oh, gods..."

I flashed her a wolfish smile.

"The gods don't fuck the way we monsters do." I took the lobe of her ear between my teeth as she ground against the heel of my hand. "But if you wish to be on your knees, I'll give you something to pray to."

My sweet, sunny dreamweaver loved wicked words; she was drenched. I'd noticed it earlier in our journey and tucked it away in the vault of my mind.

I'd told myself it was strictly for intel purposes, to better understand her.

It might have been the first lie I successfully told myself.

Her breath hitched as she grabbed my forearm with both hands and used it for better leverage, guiding herself toward her own pleasure.

Each movement and moan elicited a deeper connection between us.

She dragged her attention from where my fingers were buried inside her and licked her lips as she took in my erection.

"I want to see you lose control too."

I would deny her nothing.

I tugged at the laces of my fighting leathers, feeling the cool air hit my skin as I freed my aching cock. Her eyes darkened at the sight of me, and her growing arousal added to what I was already drowning in.

This woman would be the death of me, and I suddenly welcomed my ending with open arms.

My hand wrapped around my length, pumping in sync with her as she rocked her hips harder, faster.

Within moments I was hurtling toward the edge of climax.

My grip tightened as I stroked over the crown, swirling the bead of liquid down my shaft, and thrust into my hand.

Her hooded gaze followed the movements, and I felt how much she enjoyed watching me lose control, fully aware it wasn't something I normally did, but I was willing to unleash myself for her.

She clenched around my fingers, dripping wet.

A primal satisfaction ripped through me, knowing I turned her on.

Mine.

I leaned into her, pumping my fist over my erection as her hips bucked against my other hand, each of our movements a desperate, jerky plea for our release.

Every stroke, every thrust, pounded the same word into my mind over and over until it was all I could think of.

Mine.

For a moment, it felt like she'd slipped into *my* head, chanting the same word too. It was a mental seduction that was the beginning of the end for me.

We were both teetering on the edge.

I sealed my mouth over hers, our kiss messy and frenzied as our tongues and teeth clashed.

Heat surged up my legs, coiling tightly in my balls, an intense sensation that signaled how close I was to coming.

I was on the verge of falling over that peak; one more moan from Lore and I fell completely, feeling her shatter right along with me.

My head fell forward as the force of my orgasm hit, a powerful wave that made my knees buckle. I spilled onto her hip and cursed.

In that moment of unending ecstasy, I sensed it—a magical tether that seemed to bind us. One that felt familiar. But impossibly so.

I was too lost to the moment to focus.

My chest rose and fell rapidly as I gasped for air, trying to ground myself in reality again, to pull my consciousness back into my body after such an all-consuming experience.

She'd spoken of the gods, and for a fleeting moment, I might have considered myself wholly devout instead of the sinner I was.

That was as close to an out-of-body experience as I'd ever come.

My mind, my body, my very soul, had all narrowed to her. Like she was the central point of my universe and I was caught up in her gravitational orbit.

"Fuck." My heart was still pounding, and I couldn't seem to catch my breath.

Lore's labored breathing matched my own, and her dark, beautiful eyes were still glazed with pleasure.

I had *never* experienced an orgasm that powerful before.

We hadn't even joined our bodies in that most intimate of connections—what had just happened was only a taste of what could be.

Instead of being spent, I was filled with a strange energy at the thought of forging a deeper connection. I was already getting hard again, my attention already narrowing on that insistent tug that demanded we complete our union.

My body was at complete war with my mind. Reason and desire clashed.

And I was so tempted to submit to that innate drive, to focus only on the woman before me, forsaking everything else.

One heated look from Lore and I'd cave.

I reached for her, tugging her close, needing to wrap her against me.

Her arms went around my waist, and she laid her head against my chest as if she needed a moment to process the intensity too. The physical contact helped quell the inferno of need still raging within me, but not enough to fully douse it.

My mind couldn't seem to wrap itself around what the hells had just happened.

My emotions never got so entangled with a physical relationship before. And now I couldn't seem to snip the threads fast enough.

I held her tighter, breathing in her sweet scent for one more moment.

This wasn't the time to analyze the future or any complications.

Nor was it the time to allow my desire to overtake logic and strategy.

Whatever this thirst was, this visceral craving, it could wait. It *had* to wait.

I finally let my arms drop from where I'd been cradling her close.

I retrieved the torn tunic and used it to wipe the proof of my desire and lack of control off her hip.

Once she was cleaned up, I tucked myself back into my leathers and retied the laces.

She watched silently, her expression unreadable.

A different sort of fear worked its way into my thoughts.

"Are you all right? If I did something you didn't—"

She shook her head, halting me from voicing any worries.

"I've never..." She inhaled deeply and exhaled, looking shy for the first time since we'd met. "That was—"

I leaned in and gave her a chaste kiss, then drew back.

"Intense? Incredible? I could recite a better list if I wasn't still intoxicated on that release." I tapped my temple lightly. "I think this is broken at the moment. Now I understand why Lust acts the way he does."

Lore's relief swept into the space between us.

"I thought that was just me."

"Not even close, Peaches." I tucked a loose strand behind her ear. "There's nothing I want to do more than bury myself between your thighs and experience that level of heaven again, but we need to move."

That strange tether was vibrating in my chest.

An insistent, frantic warning I couldn't ignore.

I had no idea if it indicated the Book of Nightmares was getting close, or if it had to do with not finishing what we started.

We'd already risked too much.

After Lore used the ripped tunic to clean herself up, I balled the offending fabric up and tossed it into the underbrush.

My feral urge to hunt down and murder the male who'd given it to her dulled *slightly* now that our combined scents were on it.

But I still wouldn't mind driving my dagger through his heart.

Seemed my savage behavior wasn't quite under control yet.

I carefully draped my tunic over her head and helped her into it, my fingers lingering as I laced up the ties and slipped her weapons belt over it again, wishing we could savor the moment.

Despite all the reasons why it wasn't a good idea, I wanted to lay her down on the soft carpet of leaves, making love to her slow and tender, exploring her every desire until she was sated and I could think of something past forging our connection in the deepest way possible.

But a thread of urgency had my senses prickling; there was a gnawing sense that *something* was wrong. It pulled me back to myself, banishing the remnants of whatever spell our releases had created.

We needed to keep moving.

I'd just stepped back when a glint of silver whizzed by, nicking my ear before embedding itself in the tree beside Lore's head.

One millimeter to the right and it would have hit her jugular.

An ancient, frozen rage gripped me in its fist.

She released a startled cry, and that storm of fury erupted in me as I whirled around, positioning myself between Lore and the threat.

Any tenderness, any distraction, vanished.

I embraced the monster bellowing at the cage I'd locked it in.

And I kicked that door open, releasing all my pent-up divine rage as I prepared my counterattack.

THIRTY-TWO
Prince Sloth

"ARE YOU HIT?"

My voice boomed across the woods, startling birds that had been roosting for the night. There was no need for us to be quiet; we'd been found.

I glanced over my shoulder, examining her swiftly.

She shook her head. "No. I don't think so."

I scented the air for any trace of her blood, but there wasn't any.

It was that small fact that kept some semblance of my sanity in check.

Once I was certain she hadn't been hit, I tore my attention from her. I wanted to scoop her up and bolt for cover. And that was not the best counterstrike.

If it was one of the horsemen who'd found us, they would pursue us easily.

This needed to end here, now. Even if I was seeing red and could barely think past the snarling beast that had emerged from within me.

My gaze swept over the dense undergrowth and shadows, searching for whoever had hurled the throwing star.

The wall of ice I was familiar with finally answered my call. It descended like an avalanche, calming the raging inferno instantly.

I rested my hand on the hilt of my dagger, my muscles tensed to strike.

When I found whoever was stupid enough to attack Lore in front of me, I would tear them apart piece by piece.

I closed my eyes and reached into the dwindling well of my powers, letting them flow through me like an unseen current.

My heightened senses stretched out, searching, until they brushed against the presence of our attacker.

A soft footfall sounded to my left, and instinct kicked in.

I pivoted, my arm whipping forward as I released my dagger.

It sliced through the air before embedding itself in flesh with a satisfying thwack.

Before he could even gasp in pain, I was on him, my fists pounding hard into his stomach, his ribs. Each hit was harder than the last.

I felt his bones break, but it wasn't enough.

He doubled over, and I didn't hesitate.

I jumped back and with a swift, brutal movement, I slammed my boot against the dagger still wedged in his gut, driving it in deeper.

"Fuck!" he shouted.

A dark, savage glee settled over me as he coughed up blood, stumbling backward with a look of fear and fury in his eyes.

He'd been close to hitting Lore.

Too close.

Rage reared up inside me again, far worse than when the dark book had been stoking my emotions in the temple.

I was close to becoming completely unhinged. I felt myself not just slipping but hurtling toward that seething pit of fury that lived inside me now.

Darkness beckoned, and I sank into its unforgiving embrace.

"What the fuck are you?" he rasped.

"Your darkest fucking nightmare."

I clasped my hands behind my back to keep from tearing his head off his shoulders. I was not in control of my emotions anymore.

I fought against an animalistic need to attack until the threat was not simply obliterated but scattered across the woods in several bloody chunks.

I glanced to Lore. "Is this the formidable War you spoke of?"

His scent wasn't the one from the tunic. Otherwise, he'd already be dead.

"Yes." Lore nodded, wincing a little. "That's him."

I turned back to the horseman.

"It was foolish to attack my woman after your friends took her." I stepped closer, my voice low. "You should have come for me first. And you shouldn't have come alone."

My hand shot out, grabbing the hilt of my dagger.

I twisted it as I wrenched it free.

For a second, I was reminded of when the Goddess of Night had done the same to me in my nightmare. It was the night Lore had almost died of hypothermia and the goddess had made me think it was her stabbing me.

I was becoming as monstrous as her dark book of power.

And when it came to Lore, I would become far worse to protect her.

In fact, I sensed that terrible power, but I could no longer tell if it heralded the arrival of the Liber Noctem or if it was my own darkness emerging.

"You're lucky you missed." I shoved a knuckle into the Fae's wound, gouging it open further. "Or else I would have ripped your intestines out and shoved them down your throat. And when the wolves finally found you, broken and weak, I would've made sure you were still conscious when they began feasting."

Blood spurted out, spilling down the front of his tunic, and splattered onto the mossy earth.

His teeth ground together, but he managed to not yell out as he staggered to the ground, falling to his knees.

His dark gaze burned with hatred.

I doubted it went as deep and dark as mine.

There was an abyss yawning wide, swallowing my sense of reason bit by bit. The Liber Noctem had grown more powerful, and it was urging me on, hungry for depravity. For once, the dark book and I were in perfect alignment.

"Wait. Don't kill him."

Lore's voice leashed me.

I forced myself to take a step back, to not break any more of his bones, to remember why punching a hole through his chest wasn't necessary.

The wound wouldn't kill the bastard, but it should slow him down long enough for us to escape. I couldn't seem to make myself move, though.

I'd incapacitated him, but the beast inside me demanded more. It would be so easy to shove my fist into his gut and eviscerate him.

My tattoo burned at the thought, seeming to crave his blood as much as I did. I drew my arm back, readying the strike that would see his heart wrenched out. I practically felt its dying beat in my palm now.

A gentle hand came down on my shoulder, stilling my movements.

"It's okay, Blondie. I'm okay. I'm starting to think this test might be about mercy—"

A sudden whoosh caught our attention and in the next instant a volley of arrows rained down from the dense canopy above us.

I didn't think, I acted.

I lunged toward Lore, wrapping my arms around her tightly, my body forming a protective shield as I knocked us to the ground.

The arrows struck with a sickening thud, piercing my skin as they embedded themselves deeply into my shoulders and the backs of both arms.

Iron points speared into me, and each shaft vibrated with the force of its impact, driving the arrowheads deeper.

A burning sensation spread rapidly from where the arrows struck, followed almost instantly by a cold, tingling numbness creeping through my veins.

Fucking poison.

I'd had enough of all the cursed venom, toxins, and now poison. Each one was slowly eroding my damned power, leaving me closer and closer to a mortal.

I gritted my teeth and waited a beat, listening for any sound of movement in the trees as I tried to banish the fire and ice lashing through me.

War laughed darkly from where he still bled out on the ground, and I regretted not cutting his head off.

"Death's here and he's in a pissy mood."

I ignored the Fae, concentrating on where his friend might launch a strike from next. There was no rustle in the canopy above, no sounds of arrows being notched. Death was toying with us.

I counted off another few seconds, and when no other attack was launched, I shoved myself to my feet and hauled Lore up, placing her behind me.

I had to get the damned arrows out before I lost consciousness, but first we needed a secure location. If I went down, I wanted to know that Lore would have a safe place to wait until I healed.

I didn't think I'd last long racing through the forest. I already felt the numbness spreading. Nor did I think I'd be able to cover our tracks well enough to avoid being hunted by the ruthless Fae.

Which left only one option.

"Will you try to shift stories?"

I glanced over my shoulder, my brows lifting in surprise.

Lore already had the phoenix tear in her palm, and she looked ready to enact vengeance of her own.

I turned to face her fully, sensing her churning emotions. "Lore? Stay with me. Will you get us out of here?"

"You're hurt."

"I'll be fine, Peaches."

"They're coated in *poison*."

I wasn't sure how she knew that. None of the arrows had missed their mark.

"I'll be fine," I repeated, my tone soothing. "Let's shift to a new book. Preferably one without pirates or Fae."

She didn't laugh.

Tension radiated from her, and her eyes burned with fury as her attention drifted from one arrow to the next.

I tried not to wince as the poison worked its way into my system.

Lore didn't miss the slight tightening around my eyes.

I sensed her anger growing more volatile by the second; it was already white-hot and it hadn't been fully stoked yet.

She inspected each wound, then flicked her attention to some point over my shoulder, and the fine hair on my body lifted. Not from the Fae who'd joined us—but from the forbidding, brutal expression on her face when her focus settled on him.

That look would put the wrath of the gods to shame.

I didn't have to turn around to know the second horseman had arrived.

"You did this to him."

Her anger was a blazing inferno, but her voice was cold, unfeeling.

I'd never heard that tone from her.

"If it makes you feel better, I *was* aiming for you."

His low drawl didn't hide the fear I sensed coming from him. He'd realized the same thing I had—the true threat wasn't him and it certainly wasn't me.

There was something far worse in these woods tonight.

And I was wholly captivated.

I kept my attention on Lore, sensing a chasm splitting inside her, growing wider the longer her anger simmered without an outlet.

She was a geyser ready to blow.

I released a small hiss as the next wave of ice moved through my veins.

Lore didn't miss the barely audible sound, as if she was now attuned to the slightest shift in me.

Her gaze darkened, like a shadow passing over the sun.

"You shouldn't have missed."

She took a step toward him, attempting to veer around me, but I held my ground. Given the crackling energy pouring off her right now, she was more than capable of leveling him by herself, but I was struggling with my own instincts.

There seemed to be an innate understanding that passed between us—an unspoken acknowledgment of what the other needed.

Lore didn't try to move past me again, but that didn't make her less dangerous to our enemies.

Her head cocked to one side, her gaze sharp and calculating as it narrowed on the male behind me. She reminded me of a hawk sizing up its prey.

There was nothing soft or forgiving in her face; there was hardly anything human in it. She wore a mask of vengeance that would make the fiercest archangels tremble if they dared to gaze upon it.

She was a perfect nightmare.

An inkling of recognition flickered in, but I couldn't sort out what was familiar.

My sweet ray of sunshine who burned hotter than the surface of the sun when provoked. It seemed like I was the only one who admired her ferocity.

I heard the Fae's boots catch on a rock as he stumbled back.

It was the wrong move.

Showing a predator any fear was the quickest way to ensure they attacked.

Right now Lore was no different.

I sensed the rising tide of power a moment before she detonated.

"You hurt what's *mine*."

Her shadow ribbons unfurled like a nest of vipers.

But I was momentarily fixated on her declaration.

She'd claimed me, out loud, and the second she uttered the words, it almost felt like a second heartbeat pounded in my chest. Something had awakened, something I hadn't even been aware of that slumbered deep inside me.

I had never felt something like that before.

I snapped out of the odd sensation, taking in the darkness that had suddenly descended, noticeable even under the cover of night.

Lore hadn't taken her attention from the horseman of death.

It looked like she was channeling the rage she felt while staring at him and turning it into something worthy of the Book of Nightmares.

"Now you'll pay."

Dozens of dark tendrils writhed through the air with a menacing hiss as they lunged at the horseman who had just leapt from the tree.

I twisted around to watch the magic she wielded with ease, staring at the sheer power and control she exercised over it.

She was focused, sharp. And utterly lethal.

She wasn't using the shadow ribbons to shift stories. She was wielding them like the true weapons I'd suspected they could be.

Lore had somehow unlocked the full might of her magic.

And it was a great and terrible sight to behold.

If this was her test for this Trial, I didn't doubt she'd win.

I'd had no idea she was capable of shadow magic, but it was clearly something a dreamweaver could command. It had to be a skill diluted from the goddess's bloodline.

Death's eyes widened in disbelief, a fleeting expression of shock frozen on his face, just before the dark magic engulfed him entirely.

I couldn't tear my attention away.

Shadows twisted and coiled around him like a living storm, and in only a few seconds a gut-wrenching scream came from inside its swirling darkness.

The keening howl was the embodiment of pure, unadulterated torment.

It was so harrowing and desolate, it actually sent shivers down my spine.

Another wail breached the shadow storm, louder and more tormented than the last. It sounded like his own nightmares had come to life.

I couldn't imagine Death's darkest fears, considering the starring role he played in so many others throughout the centuries.

My heart thudded solidly in my chest. The mass of shadows that kept pouring into the swirling storm was so thick, I couldn't see beyond them.

He screamed again.

It sounded like the shadows were feeding off his terror and reflecting every horror he created back at him until all he could do now was cry out, too lost to his nightmares to even beg for mercy.

I didn't think he was capable of speech anymore.

Lore was shattering his mind, and she hadn't lifted a finger. I thought of our lessons in mental shielding; she'd used that skill and speared into his head.

With her power to create reality from dreams, it made sense that she could also slip into someone's mind and bring forth the darker side of them.

Just like the goddess who held that same magic.

That same flicker of recognition hit me. Was Lore's magic coming from the Book of Nightmares itself, or was she using the goddess's magic some other way?

We were on a precipice, close to the truth but just out of reach.

I was wrenched away from my thoughts when his sounds of terror suddenly ceased. An eerie silence fell.

War didn't so much as breathe from where he still bled out on the ground.

A beat later, the shadows finally broke their hold on the Fae, and all I could do was stare at the pile of ash and bones that used to be the harbinger of death.

Lore had *annihilated* Death with her magic.

She'd plunged into the deepest well of her power and mastered it beyond what I had thought possible, even with decades of training.

All within seconds.

I had no idea what had set her—

Understanding slammed into me.

I swallowed hard, trying to come up with a more logical explanation for her sudden mastery, but even with all my years of study, I couldn't.

There was something far more powerful than dreams or nightmares, something so rare that not even the gods themselves could re-create it or destroy it.

A bond strong enough to overcome almost every obstacle. Something deeper than love, more passionate than lust, and far greater than hate.

I staggered back like I'd taken several blows, my thoughts racing as I tried to deny it, tried to find *some* other explanation.

There were none.

The primal instincts I'd been battling. My emotions that kept oscillating so wildly out of control... They were signs. It wasn't the influence of the Liber Noctem. It had never been about that.

Lore finally wrenched her attention away from the Fae she'd destroyed. A slight line of worry creased her brow. It was the first semi-human look she'd worn.

"Are you okay?"

"I—"

My pulse roared through my veins, driving the poison deeper.

But I couldn't calm myself.

I shook my head, not meaning to respond to her question.

I was trying to clear my thoughts. Not because I couldn't accept the truth but because I wanted to be *completely* certain before I said it out loud.

There would be no coming back from this revelation.

And I wanted there to be no doubt that it was true.

All the little pieces slowly came together, forming a larger picture in my mind. Now that I was searching for the threads, I found them easily.

When we'd been practicing her mental shields, I'd felt it then.

I'd been overcome with the *need* to claim her as mine, and she'd accepted. I felt the moment her mind welcomed the connection.

I'd dismissed it as impossible. As some strange anomaly of our intermingling powers. Had the strangeness ended there, I could still shrug it off.

But that hadn't been the last sign.

It happened again when I'd felt myself falling into that endless abyss the first time we kissed on the pirate ship; I'd thought I was going mad. That the Liber Noctem had been somehow stirring up hidden desires to distract me.

All the while it was the bond growing stronger.

When the sea monster took her, I'd never felt fear that potent before.

Then there was the tether I'd followed across the Isle of the Damned despite the logical route I would have taken to the lighthouse first.

This whole time I'd convinced myself it was the dark book, or the Trials. Neither had been the case.

I'd been jealous and possessive more times than I'd ever experienced in my immortal life. Fighting the dragon shifter, seething at the pirate king.

Nearly turning as feral as the vampires when I'd caught her scent mingling with another male's. It was irrational, and even being aware, I couldn't control it.

I'd come across ancient texts that claimed it was possible for my kind to experience such a connection, but I hadn't believed it was true.

To my knowledge, none of my brothers had felt it. Wrath and Emilia came close, but I wasn't sure if they were simply fated in a different way.

I also never read anything that indicated such a bond could form between a mortal and a Prince of Sin, which was the main reason I hadn't put much thought into it even after that odd claiming in our minds.

It was easy to dismiss my protective urges; I did want to keep Lore safe — she was the key to keeping Nyantha from being reunited with her power.

But it went deeper than that.

Even if she wasn't a dreamweaver, I would feel the same. I'd realized that long before tonight. I just didn't admit it to myself.

Fate was a fickle thing, I'd never placed any stock in it. It couldn't be weighed and measured; it couldn't be easily explained.

I lived in a world of logic and reason, and fate defied them both.

It made me uncomfortable to simply let go, to believe in something with my heart without facts or reason backing up them up.

Now I couldn't deny it.

I should have known the moment she plucked my true name from my head what it meant. She was the only one in *any* realm who'd be granted that level of intimacy without me uttering a word.

I dragged my attention back to her face.

My *mate's* face.

But her fury wasn't sated.

I was bleeding and struck with at least a dozen arrows, and she'd snapped, just as I had done when she'd *almost* been hit with *one* of the throwing stars.

Her need to protect me was as fierce as mine was to keep her safe. It had been fierce enough to unbind her magic in force.

I needed to temper the emotions roiling through me, the ones that wanted me to encourage her wrath, to watch the realm burn and destroy everyone in it.

The Book of Nightmares had played its hand well—it struck right after we'd begun to secure our bond.

My revelation had only taken seconds to piece together, and now that I had my proof, I delved deeper.

I mentally flipped through any information I could recall about the mating bond and how it worked. We'd need to guard ourselves from manipulation.

This was the most fragile time for a mated pair; it was when our emotions were the most unstable and heightened.

When we were the most likely to lose control at the slightest threat or provocation. It would remain this volatile until we'd secured it completely.

And that usually occurred after sex, the ultimate forging of two into one.

Which meant we were both standing dangerously close to the encroaching darkness, and it couldn't have come at a worse time.

The Trials *had* to be reaching an end.

And it would be even more challenging to keep our focus on the light, on remembering dreams were the way to overcome the dark book.

Though, looking at my mate, it seemed like she'd plunged into the abyss.

And I wasn't even sure if I could bring her back.

If this test was about mercy, I feared the outcome.

She turned to War and a new fire ignited in her gaze. Tiny embers of her magic sparked in the depths of her dark eyes, flickering with calculation.

There was little sunshine left in this version of the dreamweaver.

This was the opposite end of the spectrum of her magic—this was the weaver of nightmares. This was the worst of Nyantha's magic come to life.

There was no part of her I would fear, no place too dark I would not follow.

She was my mate. And I'd accompany her to the ends of the realms if I must. I'd vowed to not leave her side and nothing had changed. Nor would it.

She could strike me down and it wouldn't keep me from my promise.

If she fully accepted me, we'd secure the connection and then we'd take on the Book of Nightmares as a unit and end this.

Not even the gods themselves could stop us then.

But we needed to hurry before the book found a way to breech her defenses.

Lore's attention flicked back to my wounds, her jaw clenching at the sight of the dark veins of poison spreading out.

I felt the shift in her a moment before her expression hardened again — a lock snapping into place.

Whatever spark of humanity she'd clung to was now behind that door.

Her shadows rose like demons waiting to be unleashed.

I took a step toward her and halted.

Several shadows whipped out to block my path, throwing up a writhing wall that prevented me from taking her hand.

I cursed.

The shadows grew taller, thicker, more solid, like tentacles whipping around.

We weren't running out of time. We were already out of it.

Whatever happened next would either see the Goddess of Night reunited with her magic and the realms destroyed, or we'd survive and lock the book away for good.

Everything balanced on a knife's edge; Lore would either win or she'd lose.

And like the Goddess of Night herself, my mate didn't just submit to the darkness; she *became* it.

"Lore." She didn't give any indication she'd heard me. "Fight back, Peaches. You're stronger than the dark book and its magic."

Despite her being fueled by the Liber Noctem, our bond flickered. It was weak, barely noticeable, but I'd felt her respond.

I tried to take a step toward her, but the shadows buffered me again.

It took a moment to understand why she'd thrown the wall up.

Her magic wasn't keeping me away from her; it was protecting me from the nightmare that was about to be unleashed next.

I just hoped she didn't get lost to it.

Lore turned her attention back to the Fae.

The great harbinger of war promptly pissed himself from just one look at her face.

Her mouth curved into a slow, wicked grin.

"Leave nothing, not even ash this time."

THIRTY-THREE
Lore

I watched, strangely emotionless, as my shadows tore into the Fae.

They easily dismantled the vault surrounding his mind, and at my next command, they would wrench out his darkest fears and bring them to life for me.

I granted them a few uninterrupted moments to play that would feel much longer to War.

To him, it would seem as though weeks had slipped by in the span of a few heartbeats.

In the realm of nightmares, time held no meaning; each second could stretch into infinity if I chose to make it so.

Something sparked this...retribution, but the longer my magic toyed with his mind, holding it captive, the less control I seemed to have over my own thoughts. Intrinsically, I understood that I needed to let go or I'd lose myself entirely. But for some reason, I couldn't.

This was my final test, and I was prepared to fail.

I wanted him to suffer even if that meant I sacrificed a piece of my own soul.

There was a reason, one that eluded me, but I was certain I could hold on to my essence long enough to see him pay.

It was a dangerous game I was playing.

And for a fleeting moment, I had a sense that I wasn't really winning.

It felt like I was losing something vital, something I'd needed to guard against...

I was becoming and unraveling all at once.

My heartbeat remained even, unbothered by the notion of beginning and ending in an endless loop.

This story was one I'd lived before, in different manners, but in the scenes, the emotions or lack thereof, I'd been the orchestrator. Others had stood where I did now, bowed by my own will. And here I was, experiencing it all.

It was a strange thought, but somehow, I understood.

This was destiny in a way. Or perhaps it was hell.

To live out the punishment inflicted on others, to intimately understand how it felt for them in those final moments.

A flash of worry broke through the darkness enveloping me, and I swore it wasn't my own, but it vanished as quickly as it had come, snuffed out by the menacing power streaming from me.

I exhaled.

My focus needed to remain on the task at hand.

I gathered my shadows and flung them harder at the Fae before me.

I felt nothing except for a slight hunger to inflict more pain as my magic thrust itself upon War again, turning his fears into grotesque, humanoid forms that lurched out from the darkest recesses of his mind.

No one outside the swarming shadow storm would see the physical manifestation of his nightmares, but I saw them clearly. I knew this wasn't the real horseman, it was some character brought to life, but that didn't stop me from delving deeper into his psyche.

I cocked my head, a flicker of amusement breaking through my indifference. The great harbinger of war was afraid of faceless monsters with red-glowing eyes.

They haunted his dreams.

Which made them mine for the taking.

I slipped deeper into his mind, where his fears lay exposed like ripe fruit in an orchard. I reached out and plucked them one by one, savoring the power they offered as I worked my shadows up into a ravenous frenzy.

His hoarse shouts grew louder as those faceless souls surrounded him, his pupils blown wide with terror.

With half a thought, I directed my magic to drag out their torment.

They shifted their attack at once, now creeping with a torturous sort of slowness, their razor-sharp claws lightly grazing across the lush bounty of his mind instead of tearing into it.

I wanted each moment of his fear to linger like an eternal night.

The strange sense of retribution came over me again. He'd hurt someone important or had tried to. And now I would hurt him back tenfold.

Something tugged at me, at that reminder, some sensation I had no name for. I had an urge to turn to it, to shake off my shadow magic.

I shook my head to clear it instead.

Whatever that was, it *almost* broke through my mental shield before I slammed it back in place. Still, a slight fissure remained.

I ignored it.

I turned my attention back on War, my desire for vengeance returning.

I made sure every scratch of my shadow talons felt like a thousand daggers of ice against his mind. The mental assault wouldn't stop until his psyche lay in complete ruin at my feet.

But not yet. Now was the time to stoke his fear until he prayed for death.

Every scrape of my magical talons peeled back another layer of War's mind, a new fear or a new memory of the terror he'd inflicted on others.

I realized what those red-eyed faceless monsters were to him: They were the souls of his victims, haunting him, his own personal demons.

These were the specters, and now I understood why they'd also given Conquest a wide berth on the island.

Each of the horsemen was haunted by these creatures, the souls of those they'd doomed.

I delved even deeper into his memories, wanting to know who this male truly was at his core. The visions quickly unraveled for me like a dark, twisted scroll, with scenes from a life lived in utter brutality taking shape.

I flipped through the memories like pages in a book, searching for the worst of his deeds to reflect back at him.

Each memory was more corrupt than the last.

He'd been a nasty, violent thing. Seeking pleasure in mortals' pain for centuries. Stoking war and violence and bloodshed just for his amusement.

It was a familiar sentiment, one I did not like to acknowledge.

The long, immortal life he lived was not merely marked by cruelty; it was drenched in it.

He'd razed cities, turned villages against one another, created never-ending skirmishes and battles for land.

Tavern brawls, religious strife, he even stoked embers of discord in married couples.

War was a creature of pure aggression, relishing the agony he inflicted on mortals for hundreds of years.

His legendary "hunts" only scratched the surface of how deep his depravity went.

While in his mind, I *felt* how much he gloried in his identity as War, relishing that menacing title every time he overpowered someone weaker.

He delighted in the suffering he caused.

He thrived on the chaos of battle and got off on it.

But his battles weren't limited to physical assaults; he was well versed in mental wars. Toying with his victims until they went mad.

War wasn't simply a wicked bastard in this story realm; he was a monster—a true blight upon other Fae and mortals alike. I had known that hunger for power, for fear. Once, long ago, I'd been that monster. But I was no longer bound to those mistakes.

The scales of divine justice had righted themselves.

And I was merely the harbinger of *his* doom now.

His agonized screams only fueled my rage.

I didn't want his nightmare to end too soon.

I wanted him to suffer, to beg.

I wanted him on his knees, tears streaming down his face, blood splattered across the earth from where he bashed his head against it, hoping to silence the images. Only to realize he was no longer in control of this battle.

I wanted him to intimately know what it was like to gaze upon the monster bringing his death. The same way he'd stared down, cold and unfeeling, into the eyes of those who'd begged him for that same mercy he never granted.

Too soon, his cries stopped, replaced by a strange, insistent tug in my center. At first, I thought I imagined it. Then it grew stronger, more demanding.

I rubbed at my sternum, then flicked my attention up.

An angel of death suddenly emerged from the darkness I'd wrapped myself in, parting my shadow magic like it was a simple curtain being drawn aside.

No one had ever invaded my power while I was creating a nightmare before. They'd never been strong enough or foolish enough to try.

I couldn't decide if I was impressed or contemplating retribution.

I glared at his bare chest, finding myself inexplicably drawn to what was inked onto it despite the annoyance I felt at his bold interruption.

His whole upper body was almost entirely covered with a tattoo of a phoenix. Its feathers glistened like molten gold as they spread across his skin.

It called to me.

Each subtle movement of his muscles set the mythical bird into motion, as if it were poised to take flight at any moment.

The level of detail was astounding; every plume and talon had been rendered to perfection. I hated to admit it, but his body was the true masterpiece, a living canvas that came alive with each breath he took.

My gaze traveled higher, finally resting on his chiseled face.

Ice-blue eyes ensnared me.

They weren't the sort of tranquil blue pools that begged to be drowned in; they were the blue of an unforgiving sky.

Beautiful, terrifying. Powerful.

One moment passed, then two.

His pale gaze was spellbinding, all-consuming, and locked on mine as if in challenge. Some ancient, slumbering thing deep inside me woke, intrigued by the idea of meeting this male on a battlefield.

He would make an interesting opponent.

My thoughts suddenly flashed with different battle scenes—ones fought between silken sheets.

Vivid images of him lying back on a massive plush bed filled my mind, his toned arms casually tucked behind his head as he watched me drink him in.

I could easily picture his golden skin on full display in the soft, ambient bedchamber lighting. Every muscle and curve highlighted by the slight sheen of sweat.

The mere idea of him lying there, naked and fully aroused, cool eyes burning with desire, made my core tighten with need.

I banished my thoughts before they turned any more erotic.

It was a very peculiar reaction to a stranger I should be thinking of killing.

I forced my attention to remain locked on his, not giving any quarter.

He had a cold, ruthless sort of male beauty, but if he made one wrong move, I would just as easily slit his throat as I'd climb into his bed.

Though I couldn't deny the latter was slightly more appealing.

It wouldn't be the worst thing to take my pleasure from him and *then* tear out his throat.

With the power and confidence he exuded, he would no doubt know how to throw his weight around in the bedroom.

A spark ignited in his eyes, a glint that suggested he'd followed each of my dark musings and was eager to meet the challenge in any way I wanted.

There was *something* about him that stirred a distant memory, a familiarity I couldn't quite place. I knew him but I couldn't remember how.

It seemed an important distinction, but I couldn't grasp it.

His gaze remained unwavering and intense, like a hunter sizing up its prey. He hadn't spoken a single word, somehow sensing I needed time to adjust.

Or maybe he knew the silence was captivating.

The longer it stretched between us, the more the atmosphere hummed with tension.

If his plan had been to gain my full attention, he'd succeeded.

My entire focus narrowed onto him.

He extended an arm toward me, inch by inch, as if he knew any sudden movements might provoke a dangerous reaction.

His scent hit me as he closed in. Leather, parchment, and spice.

A bolt of awareness traveled down my spine, my senses sharpening with each careful step forward he took.

My body coiled tightly as he moved nearer, ready to respond to a threat at any moment.

He clocked the tension in my rigid posture, his mouth pressing into a firm line as if my response disappointed him somehow.

His attention finally relinquished mine only to fall to my lips instead. It lingered there, heating, laying claim to them without uttering a single word.

He must have a death wish; no one ever dared to stare at me so boldly.

My mouth curved despite my better judgment.

I remained perfectly still as he reached over and softly brushed his thumb across my lower lip.

The moment his skin touched mine, warmth spread through me, and my carefully constructed mental shield began to fracture.

My magic recognized him a beat before I did, my shadows dissipating back to the ether without my direction.

It took another minute for my thoughts to settle, for my mind to clear.

"There you are," he muttered softly, his thumb still gently caressing my lower lip before he finally let his hand drop back to his side.

His touch had grounded me, like an anchor mooring a ship during a storm.

I drew in a deep, steadying breath, letting it fill my lungs before slowly releasing it, and blinked up at Prince Sloth.

His expression was set in a careful, unreadable mask now, but I caught a flicker in his gaze—a flash of something I'd never expected to see.

I had the strangest impression that he was...afraid. Of me.

I glanced around the forest, feeling disoriented.

I must have fallen out of a tree or hit my head on a branch. I felt like I'd lost a few hours and had no recollection of what had happened.

Dawn was rising, birds were beginning to wake from their slumber, and I had a splitting headache that wouldn't quit.

"What happened?"

I rubbed at my temples.

The prince searched my eyes. "You don't remember anything?"

I shook my head and grimaced, silently cursing the invisible sledgehammer pounding against the inside of my skull. The pain was close to blinding now.

"I remember being angry. I think. But I can't remember why."

He was quiet for a beat. "Do you remember the attack?"

I cast my thoughts back as far as I could remember. There was a void I couldn't slip past. The harder I tried to think, the worse my head felt.

I pressed the heels of my hands against my eyes and squeezed them shut, focusing on breathing in and out slowly.

Gods. It felt like I'd downed all the Fae Fizz from...

I couldn't remember the title of the book, possibly because I was suddenly caught up in how odd the name "Fae Fizz" was for the strawberry-lime spritzer I'd made my brother re-create for my twenty-second name day.

Looking back, it was not the greatest choice to serve. Members of my book club had snorted and turned red every time they had to ask for more fizz.

Was it possible to die slowly of embarrassment years after the fact?

I guess I'd find out.

"Lore..."

I took a deep breath, allowing the cool air to fill my lungs, and let my hands fall to my sides.

"I—"

I started to speak but stopped short, blinking in surprise as I slowly turned around. The dense canopy of the forest had vanished, replaced by towering stone walls and an expansive arched ceiling.

Sloth moved closer, his arm brushing mine as a wave of apprehension washed over me. I had not shifted stories; I knew that with certainty.

The Liber Noctem must have brought us here.

Or maybe, another fear whispered inside me, maybe we'd been here all along. Maybe all the other stories were built in this arena.

I took in more details of the vast chamber around me.

At first glance, I thought it was an ancient temple.

But at the far end there was a raised dais with something that looked suspiciously like a throne. I couldn't see it clearly from this distance, but the dark, gleaming stone didn't look very inviting.

There was something menacing about it, something sentient. Like it was watching me with interest.

Clearly, I was in the midst of another mental break.

Thrones weren't ancient sentient beings of doom waiting for their masters' return. I exhaled. I didn't know any temples that had royalty, so that ruled this chamber out as being strictly used for worship.

It wasn't just a temple or a castle; it was a grand fusion of both.

Tall arched windows lined the walls, their stained glass reflecting prismatic colors across smooth stone floors that shimmered like a clear night sky.

I paused on the design; a giant golden phoenix blazed from the central panel, its wings outstretched in a burst of fire and feathers.

This phoenix was not a symbol of beauty; it was rendered for an angry god. It was *sharp*, angular. Every plume was bladelike, each feather catching the light like polished metal.

Its eyes were twin voids of obsidian glass, set so deeply into the design they seemed to follow me across the chamber. Flames curled up its wings, but the fire was the same golden hue as the rest of the bird. The phoenix rose from a pile of charred bones that looked like they belonged to a single figure.

Rebirth, but only after complete ruination.

Honestly, it was beautiful in that stark, Gothic horror sort of way.

The prince moved in my periphery, his attention skimming over every corner of the chamber, as if he expected someone to suddenly step out from the shadows. To be fair, I kept looking for that too.

I rubbed my hands over my arms. It definitely felt like we weren't alone, but I didn't see or hear anyone else.

I glanced up, my gaze tracing the towering columns that flanked us to form an aisle that led to the dais where the throne sat.

Each carved pillar featured grotesque figures writhing in agony with shadowy creatures rising behind them, then slowly morphed into landscapes engulfed in flames the higher the columns stretched.

Amid these cheerful images, there was the occasional dreamscape.

A babbling brook flowing under a luminous crescent moon, or winged figures dancing in a meadow of wildflowers.

Dreams and nightmares forever immortalized in stone.

My attention shifted to a tapestry on the nearest wall, and I wished I could erase it from my mind. It was worse than the columns.

Images of mortals being flayed alive, their blood running down in ruby rivulets and splattering over a snow-covered ground, made my stomach clench.

Then the scene *moved*.

Not with the illusion of motion, but with slow, deliberate pulses that gave the impression that the tapestry *breathed*.

Each scream captured in the thread seemed to cry out faintly, as if the fabric had absorbed every sound from the people who'd inspired the artist.

I wasn't sure what kind of magic was at play, but it wasn't pleasant.

Shimmering snowflakes fell, melting as they touched the blood. Behind them, shadowy figures stood watching.

Cloaked, faceless, unmoving. There was something about them that drew me, but I couldn't quite figure out why.

I glanced around, rubbing my arms again.

The prince had gone nearly as silent as I had. I understood why.

This place was horror in physical form.

I took a few careful steps down the aisle, stopping at the next set of columns. They twisted up like broken spines. They were carved with human faces, open-mouthed and eternally screaming, and realistic enough that I wondered if they were truly made of stone, or if the figures encased inside them had simply been turned to stone as one of their deepest fears.

It was terrifying to consider.

The floor beneath my feet resembled obsidian, but it pulsed faintly with a heartbeat that didn't belong to me or to the prince.

Fear was not just an emotion here; it was a *presence*.

Alive. Intelligent. Watching. And the longer I stood there, the more it felt like it knew my name.

A name I hadn't been called in eons. Which was an odd thought, considering I'd never set foot inside this place before.

I shivered in place.

Wonderful. I'd always dreamed about a nightmare castle confusing me for someone else.

My attention was drawn back to the columns themselves.

Ignoring the horrible images carved onto them, they weren't very wide, and it seemed like the slightest bump could send them tumbling to the ground like dominoes, crushing anyone unlucky enough to be standing nearby.

I subtly edged away, not wanting to be the one to send them crashing down.

Shadows danced across the room, swaying more frantically than before, and my pulse raced impossibly faster until I saw it wasn't my magic somehow leaking out against my will.

The shadows were the result of several large flames that burned in bronze bowls scattered across the chamber floor.

I stared at them for a beat.

It was strange that I hadn't noticed them right away. That odd sense of being watched prickled my spine. I glanced around again, searching for who was nearby.

No one but me and Sloth. Still, the unease grew.

The temple throne room was filling in with more details and I wasn't sure how that was possible.

But the proof was before me.

The fire seemed to burn eternally, reminiscent of sacred flames tended by the faithful servants to the gods, and if they'd been here when we first arrived, I would have seen them without question.

The flames filled the air with a warm, golden glow that was impossible not to notice.

But instead of a feeling of calm created by the soft light they cast, an ominous feeling permeated the chamber with their arrival.

It felt like the air around us pulsed with an ancient power that was waiting for...

Something terrible, obviously.

Nothing good ever came from a creepy temple throne room that heavily featured a Gothic dream and nightmare motif.

The bowls themselves were carved with scenes nearly as horrible as the tapestry and columns. Not scenes of torture but of worship gone wrong.

Figures knelt in blood-soaked robes before towering beasts with too many limbs, their eyes gouged out or turned skyward in twisted ecstasy.

In one bowl, a mortal's hands reached upward in desperate prayer, only to be met by a clawed hand descending from flame.

And yet... despite the gruesomeness, I couldn't look away.

Something about the robed figures sent a chill down my spine.

I stepped closer, needing to understand why they disturbed and captivated me so. And then I noticed the sigil etched into their robes.

Two crescent moons facing outward, a sun in the center, and a sword driven straight through it. My blood turned to ice.

I'd seen that crest before. On the old woman from the traveling caravan.

The woman who'd sent my life into chaos.

I slowly backed away from the fire and the sense of dread closing in on me. How was that symbol here? And how in the hells did it relate to the old woman? Logically, I knew she must be one of the faithful, but why she'd sent *me* on this quest was a question I didn't want the answer to just yet.

"Do you see them?" I asked.

Sloth stepped beside me. "They're Temple Knights. Religious warriors who serve Nyantha."

Wonderful. I hoped they were restricted to carvings and not about to attack.

Subtle traces of incense and herbs wafted through the space, a heady aroma that indicated someone had burned them recently.

Another new detail.

Or maybe we were just becoming more grounded in this scene.

I swallowed hard.

None of the other stories took this long to fully form. Which made me reconsider if this scene was *unraveling* instead of being woven into existence.

I glanced around again. I didn't read anything with this setting. It would have been immediately recognizable.

I knew with certainty where the Liber Noctem had led us, and it *wasn't* from any of my favorite books. This must be the Court of Fear.

This was where Nyantha had been banished.

And it felt as dark and forbidding as the goddess who was bound here.

I staggered backward, desperately reaching for Sloth's hand as if it were a lifeline. He'd been quietly observing it all.

"I think the Trials are about to end," I whispered, not wanting to attract any attention. I was sure we were being watched now.

In fact, the entire chamber might be teeming with the robed worshippers. The Temple Knights.

I wondered when the veil or glamour or whatever magic was keeping them hidden would drop, exposing them to us.

The prince's fingers threaded with mine.

He gently tugged me against him, his body tensed.

I waited for him to deny it, to tell me there was still time.

To coolly demand for me to use my magic and take control. That we would be victorious if I remembered to not sink into fear. Or something.

The silence was suffocating and an answer in itself.

When Lord Stoic had no advice, that meant the road truly was dark and it might be time to panic.

"Any idea how I can win this final test?"

I turned to look up at him, but whatever I was about to say died in my throat.

He peered down at me, his expression cold and hard, like a statue carved entirely from ice.

My attention moved from the harsh line of his mouth to his eyes.

They were no longer the familiar blue I loved; they were an endless sea of black, stripped of any recognition.

My heart thudded as this...nightmare stared down at me, void of all emotion. The prince had always been controlled when it came to expressing his feelings, but this was something else.

This was some ancient creature that had never known laughter or warmth.

Had never enjoyed a good book or a warm drink.

Had never known the meaning of family or friends.

Or even of duty and honor.

This was someone who felt *nothing*.

He didn't so much as blink as our gazes remained locked.

I wanted to run screaming in the other direction but remained by his side. Which wasn't an easy feat. The longer I kept looking at him, the more afraid I was.

The depth of the darkness in his eyes was unsettling; they seemed to absorb light itself.

Whoever this was, it wasn't the prince I knew.

Fear drummed in my chest as I tried to pull away.

His grip tightened, drawing me closer until his breath was a chilling whisper against my ear.

"You already lost."

THIRTY-FOUR
Lore

I HAD NO time to react or fully absorb what was happening.

One moment, I was trying to pull my hand away from the demon standing beside me wearing Sloth's face, its inky eyes locked on mine, and the next, he lunged at me with terrifying speed.

I just barely managed to sidestep him at the last second and felt the rush of air as he missed by mere inches.

We faced off again, only a few paces separating us, the shadows flickering wildly against the stone walls. I was breathing hard; he looked unfazed.

This was definitely not going to end well. For me.

I tried to remember the tricks Eddie the pirate had taught me. All the dirty fighting techniques that would now be very useful.

I could barely keep a thought in my head. But I remembered how much he'd emphasized the power of a well-placed kick to the groin, a subversive move that could turn the tide in my favor.

Still, I didn't think I could bring myself to hurt Sloth.

My heart pounded wildly as he shifted his feet, lowering himself into another fighting stance. His inky gaze locked onto mine with predatory focus, and I almost felt the tension crackle in the space between us.

Clearly, he had no qualms about attacking me. But it wasn't really the prince—the Liber Noctem must have done something to him.

There had to be some way I could wake him from this dark magic.

If our roles were reversed, the prince would never give up on me.

This was only the beginning of the ending of the Trials.

And I was not prepared to fight Blondie.

In all my musings, I never would have thought this would be the scenario I needed to train for.

"I don't want to fight you," I said, hoping to break through whatever spell he was under. "I think my subconscious fears somehow turned you into the sociopath I joked about."

His expression didn't shift from that cold, emotionless mask.

"Or maybe it's the Book of Nightmares."

That, apparently, was like some secret passcode that unlocked the demon.

Sloth lunged forward, then pivoted smoothly on his heel as I spun out of his grasp, stepping into the movement with a predator's skill.

I bolted away as fast as I could, but he was immortal, and his supernatural speed left me with little chance of escape.

His fingers clamped onto my tunic, and with a swift, forceful tug, he yanked me against him.

"Haven't you figured it out yet?" His voice resonated with such a deep, ancient power that it vibrated through me. "I *am* the Liber Noctem."

All the fine hair on my body stood on end.

"How—"

He shoved me away from him so hard I stumbled backward. I spun around, ready to kick him where Eddie the pirate had insisted but could only stare.

Sloth spread his arms wide, and I stood frozen, unsure of what I was seeing.

His skin began to shimmer, and beneath it, words started to glow.

They hovered there for a moment, then began moving at a dizzying speed, like some unseen hand was feverishly flipping through the pages of a mystical book.

A book that lived *inside* his body.

That was not possible.

I staggered closer, needing to confirm whether I was sane and this was real, or if this was the mother of all mental breaks.

Maybe I was still in the Faerie forest and sprawled on the ground with a concussion. Or maybe this was one never-ending nightmare.

Words and sentences raced across his skin, giving me fleeting descriptions that I slowly pieced together.

My blood turned to ice.

It was the story the Liber Noctem and I had been crafting with my dreamweaver magic—the dragon shifter, the pirates, the vampires and horsemen of the apocalypse…

Every plot, every character, was there, vividly inked beneath his skin, alive and pulsating. I read about the moment he'd snapped the pirate king's neck, the way he'd gone feral when he'd been bitten.

The tale was told in a voice that sounded so close to my own it was jarring.

Everything we'd been through…even our kiss was written there in his skin.

He hadn't lied.

Somehow, some way, Sloth *was* the Liber Noctem.

And he'd been with me the entire time I'd been trapped in this cursed realm. My mind raced as I tried to figure out what in the hells that meant.

How it was even possible. Was he ever really the Prince of Sloth or had this all been some elaborate nightmare? A delusion I was trapped in.

He'd told me he thought the book was using a host now. I thought back to each test, analyzing them with new eyes. My horror grew. Every time we shifted stories, Sloth had somehow stoked my emotions. When I thought he was about to kiss me in the cave, we'd ended up in the tavern. When I'd almost used my power to shift us to the pirate ship, things went haywire when he'd grabbed my hand.

In every instance, his connection had caused chaos. The book hadn't been with his master librarian or anyone else. It had *always* been Sloth, from the moment we'd entered this realm.

For all we knew, his master librarian had never even made it to this world. If the Liber Noctem had taken over Sloth back in the temple in Bellington, then everything that happened after was brought into question.

Not once had we ever considered the dark book was already with us, watching our every move, plotting our demise.

It felt like the floor beneath me fell apart and I went careening into the abyss. My knees hit the cool stone. I was still here. Still reeling.

Was it possible this was all just a vivid dream?

When he'd first told me about the Liber Noctem, he'd warned me it was far more cunning than anything we'd ever encountered before.

Maybe I was still lying on that mountain where we'd been attacked by the spiders. Maybe I'd been bitten and was trapped in my own dreams. Or maybe we'd never left Bellington.

Beware of waking the gods, beware of waking the gods...

I glanced around sharply. It sounded like a chorus of voices had whispered those warnings.

Maybe I really was losing my mind.

Beware of waking the gods, beware of waking the gods.

The chanting was getting louder now, the shadows along the walls seeming to pound to a beat I couldn't hear but almost sensed.

I thought of the robed figures carved into the bronze bowls. The Temple Knights.

Had they somehow cast a spell and trapped us here? Was Nyantha about to rise and strike us down?

Sloth watched impassively, his arms and chest still flickering with the pages of my story. The phoenix on his chest was now as bright as the rising sun.

I shielded my eyes with my hand.

The dark prince was still staring coldly at me, his fathomless eyes still black as night.

My hands curled into fists, my nails digging little crescent moons into my skin. I felt the urge to scream rising in my throat and choked it down.

Beware of waking the gods, beware of waking the gods.

The chanting echoed through the hallowed chamber, a dire warning continuously punctuated by the rhythmic stomping of feet.

Tears stung at the corners of my eyes, threatening to spill over.

The temple throne loomed before me, seemingly vacant, but it *felt* occupied by an unseen presence.

Someone was there.

Someone with the power to cloak themselves from view.

Beware of waking the gods, beware of waking the gods.

My attention darted around the chamber as the voices grew louder.

I was desperate to find the source of the haunting chant, but there was still only me and the dark prince and the last threads of my sanity snapping.

Goose bumps prickled across my skin.

Beware of waking the gods, beware of waking the gods.

My stomach churned violently, a visceral manifestation of the terror that gripped me in its fist.

All of a sudden, I understood why this was happening.

I was in the heart of the Court of Fear, and this was the power that fueled it. It wanted my terror; it needed it. And the chanting was absolutely haunting.

Beware of waking the gods, beware of waking the gods.

The chanting and stomping were both demanding now, a primal beat that was starting to do... something to me.

My chest felt strange. Like there were now two heartbeats in place of one.

I gasped, my throat constricting with each shallow breath I took.

My lungs felt like they were wrapped in bands, and no matter how hard I tried, I couldn't fill them completely.

Beware of waking the gods, beware of waking the gods.

Every stomp, every pounding, every word, was hammering away at some invisible wall I hadn't sensed before. Behind it, I was terrified of what I'd find.

There was something there, something I'd locked away. Or something that had *been* locked away, something that was banging to get free.

I didn't want to open that door. I silently begged for someone to help.

The chanting seemed to sense this shift; it grew louder, stronger, the stomping vibrating up through the soles of my boots, rattling my bones.

Beware of waking the gods, beware of waking the gods.
I wanted to fall back to my knees and cover my ears.
My legs gave out and I dropped to the stone floor, but even the coolness couldn't ground me from whatever was unraveling in me.
I cried out, my voice lost in the growing cacophony of voices that belonged to the ghosts of Temple Knights or my own imagination.
This *wasn't* real.
Please, I begged silently, *please, someone, help.* I was lost in darkness. I couldn't breathe. And that wall, that cursed wall inside me, was crumbling.
A shadow fell across me and I prayed that the prince had returned.
I glanced up and that little spark died as Sloth or the Liber Noctem moved into my field of vision. His mouth twisted into a cruel smirk as he stood over me.
"I like you on your knees."
His fathomless gaze glittered darkly as he seized my chin and tilted it up.
For a second, I couldn't tell if he wanted to kiss me or wipe my existence from this realm once and for all.
I should fight back but couldn't muster the will to do so. I was outmatched. If the Book of Nightmares wanted me dead, I had no hope of surviving.
Even if I'd passed my other tests and Trials, this...whatever this test was, I couldn't harm Sloth. No matter that he might not actually be the prince, but some dark glamour of him. If the Liber Noctem was Nyantha's power, then maybe this prince was created from my dream magic. I was losing all sense of what was real.
His thumb traced the seam of my lips until they parted involuntarily.
I swore a flicker of emotion crossed his face; it was like a shadow passing over the sun before it vanished along with his touch.
He gestured with a sharp nod behind me. "It's time to take the throne."
That sounded like a terrible idea.
I glanced over his shoulder and wished I hadn't.

The ominous throne was no longer empty.

A faceless figure rose with slow, eerie grace.

It truly was something out of a nightmare, and I was both captivated and unnerved by the sight. I wanted to look away but couldn't. It was as if my eyes were ensnared by the power radiating from her.

The figure had materialized from the very shadows themselves and was dressed in a gown fit for the gods. She was not corporeal, but looked like a ghost or shade of what she'd once been. The gown, though, that was real.

Even being terrified, I couldn't help but admire it—the fabric was unlike anything I'd ever seen.

Midnight blues and deep indigos cascaded like liquid shadows down her body, the fabric adorned with gemstones that glimmered like stars plucked from the night sky.

Her dress was not fit for just any deity; it was perfect for the Goddess of Night herself.

Which, as she hovered there, faceless and silent, I realized was exactly who she was. There stood Nyantha. Or the essence of the goddess. Her spirit.

The most wicked of the old gods. Even without physical form she was formidable.

And I was completely frozen in place. Not by fear or magic but by a strange reverberation that bounced between us. I should be falling to my knees, averting my gaze. Offering up a gift like so many in our village used to do.

And yet...the essence called to me. Softly, gently. Like it had been waiting for my return.

But somewhere deep inside me, I almost swore I heard another voice. A beloved one.

Sloth's voice haunted me even more than the chanting voices of our spectral audience. But it was probably just some twisted ploy by the Book of Nightmares.

My prince wasn't here. He hadn't been calling out for me.

He'd *never* been calling out for me.

Maybe he never existed outside of my imagination. Maybe the Book of Nightmares created a leading love interest from the depths of my dreams.

And that...crushed me. To think that I could have fallen in love only for it to have been one more figment of my imagination.

It was all some elaborate magic designed to tear me apart piece by piece. My dream had always been to be loved, truly loved, no matter my flaws.

The book knew that, preyed upon it. Turned my desire into something wretched. Nothing had been real between us. *He* was probably not even real.

I finally choked on a sob.

The truth of that cracked my chest open wide, my heart tearing in two. I was alone and terrified and had no idea how to escape this nightmare.

All the other tests, the other Trials, all my darkest fears, were now swirling together in one final attempt to break me. Or maybe they were seeing if I'd truly overcome them.

Beware of waking the gods, beware of waking the gods.

The faceless, incorporeal deity at the end of the aisle didn't move, but I sensed she was watching me, waiting. She wanted me to go to her, to accept my fate. Her spirit felt so...familiar.

All the while, her invisible Temple Knights' cries echoed around the chamber walls, bouncing back at me with a fervor reserved for zealots.

Beware of waking the gods, beware of waking the gods.

"Their dreams are often our nightmares."

Sloth's voice was still laced with the low timbre of the Liber Noctem as he spoke near my ear.

"I don't understand. That doesn't make any sense."

"It's time." He leaned in again. "Wake from your slumber. Unite."

Beware of waking the gods, beware of waking the gods.

The voices suddenly stopped, the echoes cutting off as if they'd been magically sealed away again.

I exhaled, relieved that was over.

Sloth's mouth curved.

"Your true essence must rise. Unite. *Carpe Noctem.*"

Magical chains whipped out and locked me in place.

I opened my mouth to scream and was swept away by a flood of thoughts and memories. They were unfamiliar and crashed through my mind one after another, with growing clarity.

Now I did hear screams bouncing off the walls.

I thought they might be mine.

More images crashed into me.

More memories that were mine and not.

Every scene I'd glimpsed during the Trials came back. Only this time I had clarity. *I'd* been the one watching the mortal drown. I'd been the architect of all the horror and fear I'd inflicted on others.

It wasn't Nyantha. Or it was...but we were not separate beings. She and I were the same.

I had no idea how. But I knew these Trials...they'd been testing *me*.

I wasn't Nyantha's champion, I was the goddess stripped of immortality, my soul split into two. One half of my essence had been birthed to humans while the other half remained locked in this realm. The gods had devised this ultimate test well.

I was given a chance to truly feel the way I'd made others feel, to live life as a mortal. To understand how fragile life was. How precious. Once I understood, once I passed, only then would both parts of myself reunite. And only then would I be restored.

There was too much pressure in my head, too much power for my mortal body to contain. It felt like I was being crushed from the weight of it.

The chanting started up again, quietly this time. Reverent.

Beware of waking the gods, beware of waking the gods.

This had been my punishment, my penance. The death of what I was, and an opportunity to rise anew, like the phoenix. To become what I'd been before things twisted. Before I'd created a nightmare monster out of boredom that had killed the phoenix's mate. I'd begun my existence as the goddess who ruled over the night and loved *dreams*. Power corrupted. I'd lost myself, the part of myself that was very close to the human I'd been born.

Either these Trials were meant to be my redemption or they'd become the last nail in my coffin. It all came down to choice. Would I learn the true power of love and dreams, or would I be forever lost to the empty hunger for power, chaos, and fear?

Somehow, I was halfway down the aisle now, striding toward the throne. I closed my eyes. When I blinked them open, I was even closer, that haunting faceless figure now mere feet away.

My body went taut. I didn't want to close the distance.

I wasn't sure if I embraced both sides of myself, if I would get swept away in all I'd run from.

Sloth's unhurried footsteps sounded behind me, the rhythm stirring my fears to new heights.

The male I'd started to fall for, the one I'd thought was my ally, was ushering me to my doom. I knew it wasn't really him, he was as trapped in this nightmare as I was, but it still *felt* like betrayal.

It was one more act of cruelty I could thank the dark book for.

I was now at the steps of the dais, the ghostly figure looming above me in her beautiful gown.

I dug my heels in, resisting whatever force kept drawing me to that throne.

I knew, without a doubt, I could not step near it or the goddess, or the world as I knew it would burn. I would cease to be. And I had no idea who I'd become—the nightmare or the dreamer.

Beware of waking the gods, beware of waking the gods.

The faceless goddess lifted an arm, holding it out to me as if she wanted to offer me a blessing that would only be a curse. I suddenly remembered the old gods sending a missive with their plan: I could choose to be born human, or I could remain in this realm with my monsters.

I'd chosen to give this up. I'd never wanted to be so cold, so unfeeling again.

"LORE!"

Torment. That's what hearing his voice inside my head was and knowing he wasn't truly there. I steeled myself as my boots landed on the first stair.

This was inevitable. This was my final test. The one Trial that would determine it all.

Magic pulsed around me, binding me to the will of the gods.

If I could not survive what came next, I would not be the phoenix. I would simply burn.

This time, when the faceless goddess reached for me, a chill rippled through me at her touch.

Then a crack rent the air.

Or maybe that was the invisible wall I'd sensed inside myself finally shattering. Whatever had kept us separate was gone. The time to reconnect my soul fragments was here.

Beware of waking the gods, beware of waking the gods.

I swore I felt the whoosh of fabric as a crowd knelt behind me.

My attention was locked on the faceless goddess. One moment she was standing before me and the next, she stepped *into* me.

And we were whole at last. My immortal essence taking its place in its new vessel.

My mind splintered. The power was too overwhelming. There was an endless darkness, followed by a blinding light. Everything I was vanished.

I dropped to the ground, heaving as power crackled under my skin.

My fingers splayed across layers of smooth silk.

All my senses were crystalline now. I felt stronger, faster, more of *everything.*

This was what it felt like to be a goddess reunited with her full power, to be immortal.

I scrambled back, staring down at my body. A body that felt so different yet still looked the same except for my clothing. I was no longer in the tunic I'd been wearing. I was dressed in the Goddess of Night's gown. *My* gown.

I tried to settle my thoughts, but they were too jumbled.

Memories that weren't mine but still cycled through my head.

I was getting dizzy from the amount of information filtering through me.

Sloth's black gaze found mine. But he wasn't really the prince.

He was the book. Or the essence of it given physical form.

And I...I wanted my power back.

He kept those dark eyes locked on me as he slowly took a knee.

"Welcome back, Nyantha." His mouth hitched into a mockery of a grin. "You've been trapped in dreams too long. Your court missed you."

THIRTY-FIVE
Lore

I WAS STILL grappling with the fragmented memories, of feeling detached from who I'd been and who I was and not understanding how to rejoin both parts of myself, when the prince ascended the dais, his body brushing against mine as he stepped behind me.

"But not nearly as much as I have." His mouth brushed against my neck. "Ascend, Your Majesty. Fully awaken."

I stared at the throne. The dark stone seemed to pulse with that strange heartbeat I'd felt before, slow and insistent, like the realm itself was holding its breath. As I lowered myself onto the seat, cold surged up my spine.

The moment my skin made contact with the obsidian stone, power roared through me. Not in a gentle swell, but in crashing waves.

I gasped as it filled me, rooted me to this body, this time.

For the first time in ages, I felt like I was finally... home. But not in the sense of the place, more in the unification. As if my soul had been fused together again.

The calm feeling didn't last. The hunger came next. It was a dark need that coiled around my ribs like a serpent, whispering for horrible things.

I wanted my court to be here, I wanted them to kneel. I wanted fear glazing their eyes as they finally stared up at me. I craved their blood on the floor, needing to hear the devotion in their screams as they begged for my blessing.

It hadn't always been that way. I hadn't ruled here by choice. And I'd taken my anger out on those weaker. This was not my true home. It was my prison. And I'd made everyone in this realm suffer along with me. It used to be a dreamworld, but I'd turned it into a nightmare.

I gripped the arms of the throne until my fingers ached. That wasn't me, that vicious, cruel being. I'd fought too hard to overcome those cravings.

But the throne remembered who I had been the last time I sat upon it.

And it wanted her back.

I breathed in and exhaled, refusing to submit to the lure of the darkness.

Something about this moment felt like part of a test, though I was starting to forget the specifics. The throne thrummed beneath me. It reminded me that I was the one who set the rules. Everyone else was beneath us.

And anyone who dared to chain me would suffer the wrath of a goddess.

The craving for that power grew stronger, sinking claws into the last remaining tender parts of me. The mortal vessel that had longed for love, and to be seen for who she was. Just to prove that her life was as adventurous as her books. The consummate dreamer.

The darkness seeping into me from the throne promised I'd never be weak again, never be fearful of the trappings of love. I would never be powerless.

All I had to do was let go, give in, allow the darkness to crown me its queen and use me as an instrument of its will.

I clenched my jaw, fighting against the pull. It was like a tidal wave dragging me under. And I had one fleeting thought before darkness swept in; I had to remember who I was, who I chose to be, before the throne and this realm decided for me.

I shot up from the throne and made to leave the dais, when the male who'd been standing by seized me by my waist, and in one inhumanly fast motion, he spun around and settled onto my throne, positioning me on his lap.

I felt the power of the throne reach for me even through his body. It was a siren's song. And I was getting lured deeper. Or maybe it was the Liber Noctem itself.

I struggled to hold on to the tether inside me, the spark of light.

The male chuckled, his voice deep and rumbling.

He'd made the sort of bold, possessive move that I enjoyed, but it felt... not quite wrong, but hollow. I was missing something.

A tug in my chest caught my attention. It felt like a thread someone else had pulled and at the other end I'd find all the answers and clarity I desired.

I considered following to see where it led.

The male, *Sloth,* I finally recalled, dragged me back against him, his hands firm and commanding. The move was meant to distract and it almost worked.

It would be easy to sit on his lap, enjoy his company, and feel the power of my throne surge through me, obliterating all doubt and worry.

I wondered what it would feel like, to no longer have fears.

The insistent tug grew weaker, releasing me from my curiosity.

I glanced up and drew in a sharp breath that had nothing to do with the male growing hard as granite beneath me. I didn't think it was my body, but my power that turned him on.

Members of the Court of Fear were no longer hidden in shadow.

They were bowed low in supplication, awaiting permission to rise.

My attention skimmed over the assortment of courtiers. Some were horned beasts with humanoid bodies; some were as beautiful as fallen angels.

All were dressed in fine fabrics and jewels. As if they feared my wrath for insulting me by not wearing their best.

Sloth suddenly started to trace his fingers along my sides in gentle, sweeping motions that were hard to ignore.

Perched on his lap, I felt the firm press of his arousal against me.

Part of me wanted to indulge in some fun, but a different part almost felt like it was screaming to wake up.

But I *was* awake now, wasn't I? After what felt like an eternity, I was here, in my court, with the dark book's host by my side. My magic was with me, no longer bound to a book.

And he was attractive, powerful. Everything I'd normally enjoy.

As if innately in tune with my thoughts, his hands slowly traveled upward.

There was nothing soft or gentle in his touch now; it was hot, possessive, demanding.

Was that what I'd just craved in my head? Had he plucked the thought from my mind? Something felt...off.

I closed my eyes for a moment, relishing the sensation.

If I'd been trapped in a nightmare, was this now a dream? It didn't quite feel like one. But perhaps the problem was me. I was unsettled. If I'd regained my full power from the Book of Nightmares, I wasn't sure why Sloth was still here.

It felt like an illusion or dreamscape; nothing was clear or solid.

Except for the male I sat upon. He was solid, warm. But that nagging feeling of him being another figment of my imagination wouldn't relent.

He seemed to be *too* in tune with my desires. Like he was plucking them directly from my head and making them real seconds after I felt them.

I peered out at my court again.

They remained in their submissive postures, heads respectfully bowed, as if they were statues lined up for viewing in a sculpture gallery. Were they real or—

Sloth ground against me a little, drawing my attention back to him.

He felt real enough.

Perhaps if I took him to my bed I'd feel more grounded.

Or maybe I was meant to be...his hips shifted beneath me again.

For some reason, I knew this seemed out of character for him. I couldn't picture him putting on such a public display.

But maybe I hadn't really known him that well.

Everything was so confusing.

The longer I sat on the throne, the more my thoughts grew muddled.

He began to trail open-mouthed kisses along the column of my throat, and my mind emptied.

The thought that we could indulge in each other right here on my throne, without my court daring to lift their gazes to watch us, filled me with a heady rush that had little to do with partaking in such debauchery.

This was the power of fear.

Heat pooled between my thighs, and I tried to force my thoughts elsewhere, but the male beneath me was determined to distract me. And my throne was sending a constant stream of magic out that felt too good to ignore.

He boldly cupped my breast, rolling its taut peak between his fingers.

I wasn't sure why I felt... nothing. Except that growing unease.

I slipped my hand into the slit on the side of my bodice, suddenly remembering the weapons belt I'd been wearing. My fingers closed around the familiar stiffness of the leather belt and pouch, and relief speared through me.

The phoenix tear was still in my possession.

It was the first memory I had that wasn't muddled.

And with it came a few others that grounded me back in my body.

I didn't let on that my mind was clearing, the fog dissipating. Somehow, someway, the stone was counteracting the dark power.

I needed to plot carefully.

Sloth continued to drag his lips and teeth over the sensitive skin of my neck, and the more he lost himself in my body, the surer I became that this wasn't real.

Lord Stoic was far too reserved to put on such a debauched show. This was the work of my dark romance-addled fantasies.

Ugh. The Liber Noctem was clever.

This nightmare was far too tempting, but having the prince lay claim to me in front of an entire court wasn't the scary thought the dark book believed.

It really had no idea, the sort of twisted fiction I enjoyed.

All my favorite romantic fantasy stories had some version of a sexy throne scene. And while it was very tempting to live out this fantasy, I would not be fooled into failing my test.

The Liber Noctem version of Sloth's hands were under my skirts now, his hand possessively clamped just above my knee.

His thumb moved in slow strokes along my inner thigh.

His hand moved higher, and—

I pulled the phoenix tear from the secret pouch hidden under my gown and let my magic carry me away.

Honestly, I deserved some kind of medal for being strong enough to leave Sloth when things were about to get good.

But there was no way I'd bring about the end of the realms because I'd gotten seduced by Dark Sloth on a throne and then went all Goddess of Night on everyone again. I was close to finishing the Trials; I felt it. And I *would* win.

My shadow magic unfurled, and I went crashing to the ground.

Sounds came at me all at once.

"Lore!" My brother crouched in front of me, his face a mask of worry. "Dear gods. Are you all right?"

I slowly blinked up at him, disoriented. "Fable? How are you here?"

My brother searched my eyes.

"We're at the caravan."

He spoke slowly, as if he didn't want to cause any alarm.

Too late. My heart was racing now.

"But I left the festival."

He was silent for a beat that set me further on edge.

"You haven't left." He shook his head. "A firework went off near you and you fell on a rock."

He pointed to where I was sprawled on the ground. I followed the direction his hand indicated. Sure enough, there was a rock.

I reached up, gently pressing the sore spot on my head.

My fingers came away wet with blood.

As if that realization sparked another, my head ached again. I'd forgotten about the splitting pain when Sloth and I had been in the forest.

Speaking of the prince...

I glanced around and was met with the worried faces of our neighbors.

The old woman I was convinced was a fairy godmother from hell and member of the Temple Knights peered at me from her wagon... The festival was exactly as I'd left it.

Sloth was nowhere in sight.

Fear pressed in on me. *Did I leave him in Somnia?* I had to get back there.

"How long was I gone for?"

Fable's mouth pressed into a firm line. "We should take you to a healer."

I gripped my brother's arms. "How much time has passed?"

My brother sighed. "You've been unconscious for a few minutes. Five tops."

I stared at him. That was impossible. I'd been gone for at least a week or two. Or more. Did time move differently in Somnia?

Fable helped ease me into a sitting position and the crowd that had gathered slowly started to disperse.

I watched them go, but my mind was still spinning with this revelation. Had I been dreaming this whole time?

I glanced at the old woman. "You gave me a stone."

There was a flicker of something in her gaze, there and gone in an instant. "A worry stone. You looked like you needed it, girl."

"You're lying. You told me I had a sacred duty. You told me I needed to go on a quest with my darkest fears to live out my dreams." I noticed the pin on her cloak. "And that pin. You said it meant you were a friend. I know it symbolizes the Temple Knights. Who *are* you?"

She gave me a pitying look.

"I don't know you or anything about a quest."

She was lying. A dark, seething annoyance rose inside me.

"Come on, Lore." Fable's voice was gentle. "Let's get you up and to old Hattie Jane's. She'll get something for your head."

"I'm not..."

I felt the power of someone's attention land on me and jerked my gaze up. The prince strode through the marketplace, parting the crowd around him like a river.

I exhaled. I wasn't crazy.

His hood was tugged low over his brow, his mouth turned into a deep frown as he loomed over me. I went to push myself up, but the splitting headache came back with a vengeance, and I stayed put.

I smiled up at him.

"I'm so happy you're okay," I said. "I thought I left you in Somnia."

His frown deepened.

He flipped the cowl of his cloak back and stared down at me, his expression set into harsh lines.

"You have me confused with someone else." His voice was low, dangerous. He jerked his chin at the stone I still held clutched in my hand. "I'll pay whatever you want for the portal stone."

He reached inside his cloak and tossed a coin purse at me. It hit the ground next to me with a strange finality. So impersonal, so...cold.

I stared at him.

"Don't you recognize me?" I asked, fully aware that my brother was looking on. I sensed his embarrassment for me. "I'm Lore. You're Blondie. We've—"

"I assure you my name is *not* Blondie, nor would I tolerate being called something so ridiculous."

His cool gaze slid to my temple, softening briefly.

"Brain injuries have been known to cause realistic delusions. I saw you right before you fell, and your mind probably created its own explanation for why I look familiar. We've never met before this moment, and I am afraid I don't have time to discuss this further." He nodded at the phoenix tear. "If the coin purse is not enough to cover the cost of your inconvenience, I'll pay you tenfold when I return. Do we have a bargain?"

My fingers closed around the stone possessively.

What he was saying made sense, logically, and with my brother crouched before me, his worry etched onto his features, I was starting to think maybe I *had* been dreaming.

The alternative was honestly the part that seemed too impossible to be true.

Was I really some reincarnated ancient goddess who'd been punished by the other gods, then forced to become a mere mortal vessel who held the power over dreams and nightmares and had traveled through all my favorite stories and played the leading lady to win a series of Trials designed to test if I had learned from my wicked ways and had overcome the darkness?

All so I could rise like the mythical phoenix and reclaim my birthright and be granted my freedom?

Or was I just a small-town librarian with an overactive imagination who'd sustained a head injury and had dreamed it all up?

My face suddenly burned with embarrassment.

I seriously just called a stranger Blondie to his face and had been convinced we'd been partners on an adventure quest across a nightmare realm.

This was why I would be single for the rest of my days.

I looked at my brother and he gave me a tight nod. He thought I should give the stone to the stranger and take the coins.

"Will you help me up?" I asked.

My brother straightened, but it was the stranger who offered his hand first.

I stared at it for a moment before slipping my hand in his. He gently tugged me to my feet and... his eyes flashed black.

When I blinked, they were pale blue.

My heart thudded. I must still be out of it.

"Thank you," I said, glancing down at the stone.

It was getting warmer in my palm, almost pulsing like a heartbeat.

An uncomfortable prickle started at the base of my spine and slowly worked its way up.

I let go of the stranger's hand and the sensation stopped at once.

He was watching me very closely, and something about it unsettled me.

"Do we have a deal?" he asked again, a little more of an edge slipping into his careful tone.

The phoenix tear pulsed again, the beat growing stronger and faster.

Maybe I hit my head, maybe it was all a dream or a delusion, or maybe this was one more test the Liber Noctem was throwing my way.

It was preying on my fear of inadequacy again. Making me doubt the power I held that had nothing to do with magic.

I'd already accepted the fact that logic wasn't my strong suit. And if I was wrong, at least I wouldn't be damning the realms by going Dark Lore.

But the more the stone pulsed in warning, the more I thought I understood why. If this was still an elaborate nightmare, if Sloth was possessed by the dark book, then handing him the phoenix tear was the absolute last thing I wanted to do.

Gods only knew what could happen if they were reunited.

And anyway, this couldn't be the ending to a story I dreamed up.

I scowled up at the prince. Honestly, who would believe this had all been some twisted dream because of a head injury?

The fiction lover in me revolted.

"You'll have to do better, evil book. I would *never* have such a contrived ending for my story."

Sloth's eyes flickered from black to blue before remaining inky.

"*Carpe Noctem.*"

He'd spoken in a creepy voice that wasn't his, and I hoped that meant I'd just passed another test.

One minute I was in Bellington with my brother and the next I was wrapped up in the prince's arms and we were careening across realms.

THIRTY-SIX
Love

I GLANCED AROUND at what appeared to be a bedchamber, struggling to recall how I ended up here. Dark sage curtains were drawn, a fire burned low in an oversized hearth, and the towering walls were filled with shelves of books.

I was currently sprawled on an enormous bed made up of an assortment of sage and gold sheets and quilts, and I wasn't alone.

Rough, calloused fingers brushed against my ankles as they curled around the hemline of my gown, slowly dragging it up.

My body tensed, wondering what fresh level of hell I'd ended up in now. I looked down my body and my blood instantly heated.

The prince knelt by my feet, and he was doing that thing again where his entire focus was set on me. His pale eyes were locked on mine, and I'd never been more relieved to see him looking less demon and more wicked prince.

"Hi."

Sloth's cool gaze flickered with something that almost looked like amusement but was replaced by raw, animal hunger.

"Something wrong, Peaches?"

I bit my lower lip. And his focus followed the movement.

"Where are we?"

"My home." This time concern marred his features instead of desire. "After you annihilated Death and War, you passed out. I brought us here as soon as I could. I needed to recharge my power or else I would have waited to move you. You've been sleeping ever since."

He hesitated as if to gauge my reaction.

I kept my expression neutral. I had no idea how he managed to get us here when we'd been trapped in Somnia, which made me automatically suspicious. He'd mentioned something about magical wards keeping us there. Unless I'd won the Trials, they should still be in place.

"You woke a few minutes ago and said you'd been having nightmares. That you wanted me to prove this was real. I think whatever you're feeling might be lingering effects from the Trials, but they're over, Peaches."

"How?"

"When you killed the Fae, you were lost in shadows, but you chose to come back to me. Instead of staying lost to that pull of dark magic, you chose the light, and the book lost. The wards broke and we were free to leave."

"Oh."

It sounded plausible. But it was rather anticlimactic.

And it didn't explain why I was pretty sure I was the Goddess of Night.

He sat back on his heels, letting his hands fall away. I missed their warmth almost immediately. "You still think you're in a nightmare."

It wasn't a question. He'd ascertained by my expression and whatever other methods of deduction he used that I was still wary.

Rightfully so. The Liber Noctem was a master manipulator.

"Where is the book?" I asked. "And how did your magic get restored?"

There were still so many threads I needed answers to.

"The book is bound in an enchanted section of my library." He gave me a boyish grin that melted my heart. "You and I are the only ones with access to it. I'll take you there now if you wish. I believe my magic was somehow fueling the book's power. Once it was rendered inert, I used the phoenix tear to transport us to my House. My magic is fueled by my court, so I'm fine now."

Huh. It *sounded* logical. But I wasn't fully sold yet.

"So the moment I decided to not go Dark Lore, the Trials ended?"

"Something like that." His mouth twitched up on one side. "From what I understand now, the Trials were always meant to test Nyantha.

To see if she still chose the dark over the light. It was a way to make her relive the way she'd tormented others—some mortals liken it to karma. The old gods have similar punishments they employ."

I thought of the nightmare with the faceless goddess ghost.

The one who'd stepped into me.

Questions with no answers flickered through my head, one after another. Had that all been an illusion? Another fear I'd had about not being in control of myself? Was he saying the Trials really were about redemption? That I was the Goddess of Night and I'd risen from the ashes of my cruel past?

And since I didn't go Dark Lore on the realms, I was now free? Poof, just like that? A terrifying, sadistic goddess was now...pardoned and could carry on?

It was very plausible, but I had some serious trust issues after the last few false endings.

This time, though, it seemed like the Big Bad had really been defeated.

It was honestly hard to wrap my head around the fact that I was the villain in my own damn story and didn't have a clue.

Though, to be fair, I'd always argued with Fable over this very thing. Most villains saw themselves as their own heroes. It was all very subjective.

Still, it felt...unfinished. Maybe I was just addicted to adventure now.

Or maybe the new, fully reunited parts of myself—Nyantha and Lore—were still a little bloodthirsty and I needed to keep myself on a tight leash.

Could I really be trusted to be out of my cage? Maybe the realms were safer with me locked away.

The prince had been watching me closely and tugged his tunic off, turning so I could look at his back. Several deep wounds were scabbing over.

I sat up in bed, heart racing as those final moments of reality came crashing back.

Arrows flying at us from above, Sloth shielding my body with his...

I'd completely forgotten that Death had tried to kill me and had pumped those poison-tipped arrows into Blondie instead.

I had gone feral when he'd been hit.

No wonder I'd gone over to the dark side for a while. I'd never felt more fear or rage in my life. I'd wanted to end the world and everything in it.

If Sloth was killed...I couldn't finish the thought.

A sob broke free as I scrambled to the edge of the bed and tightly hugged the prince.

He gathered me up in his arms and buried his face in the crook of my neck.

"It's okay, Lore. We're alive. We made it. The worst is over."

He held me while tears streamed down my face, muttering soft words of encouragement until my emotions slowly began to settle.

When the last of my tears dried up, he leaned back.

"There's something I've been meaning to tell you." He cradled my face in his hands. "I love you, Peaches."

He brought his mouth to mine, his kiss chaste and sweet.

My lips parted, and the moment his tongue touched mine, *I* ceased to exist.

He broke our kiss and whispered, "*Carpe Noctem.*"

So it was another damned nightmare.

"Lying bastard!"

And just like it had the last time he spoke those words, the world around me went dark.

I stood on the dais of my throne room, staring down coldly at the traitors who'd been found trying to break in and free the true prince.

I had him locked inside his own mind until I decided what to do with him. The Liber Noctem was only too happy to do my bidding and keep operating his body while he remained powerless.

Three mortals knelt at the base of the dais, their wrists bound in front of them. Bruises marred much of their swollen faces, and their tunics were splattered in blood and dirt.

They'd fought hard, but it hadn't been enough to escape.

When my shadow warriors were given orders, they followed through without question. My attention flicked to the army of Nocturnas lining the walls of the throne room. I'd called them in and told them to be ready.

The mortals shifted; the polished stone was not comfortable to kneel on. And I'd made them wait while I'd had my dark prince fetch my blade.

Something inside me seized at the sight of them; then as quickly as the emotion came, it was gone. Must be the last vestiges of human sentimentality.

My vessel was too softhearted.

"What's taking so long?" I asked, not taking my gaze off the humans.

I couldn't stop staring at their bloody clothing. I didn't like the way it made me feel even more off-balance.

"Where is Nightsblade?"

The Liber Noctem's host studied me with that fathomless gaze before presenting me with my favorite midnight blade. The weapon was a gift from a friend long ago, a friend whose name I couldn't quite recall. Nightsblade could kill any monster or man.

It was covered in silver runes and glowed faintly.

"Nightsblade. Your execution dagger."

My heart began pounding harder.

My memories were fracturing again; facts I thought I knew were getting hazy, less certain. I felt like I was losing my mind.

I stared down at the mortals, waiting for recognition to spark again.

I *knew* they were traitors, or at least that was what I'd been told, but I couldn't remember giving the command to capture them, nor could I recall deciding their fate.

In fact, I couldn't remember anything before taking the throne. It was as if a dark curtain had fallen, sealing me off from the rest of myself.

I glanced at the crowd of courtiers still bowing.

Was this why I'd called everyone to court?

My thoughts were scattered. I felt like me and I didn't. It was like two sides fighting for supremacy and neither was gaining the upper hand.

I saw myself take the dagger, felt the cold hilt as I wrapped my fingers around it. But I was wholly detached from the moment.

I felt compelled to look at the weapon. It looked like there was something missing from the end of the hilt, something that had been pried off it.

Something I was positive should never have been removed...

I faltered at that, searching for a memory that eluded me.

Whatever had been taken from the blade...I knew it was important but couldn't recall why.

What I did know with certainty was that I'd used this weapon countless times, on countless condemned. I'd stood by and watched mortals and supernaturals bleed out and hadn't hesitated. They'd ended up in the designs around my throne room, the tapestries, the columns.

These traitors should be no different.

The strange screaming was back in my head.

A howling, keening sound of pain. And fear.

It was feminine, familiar.

Was that the mortal vessel I'd once been?

I rolled my shoulders, easing the tension in them.

I stepped forward, facing the younger of the two males. His dark hair fell in a tousled mess across his forehead, partially hiding his features.

It bothered me. And it shouldn't.

"Look at me," I demanded, my voice sounding cold to my own ears.

He lifted his face slowly, his brown eyes meeting mine.

Not with defiance or fear, but with love. And a hint of sadness that tugged at some well of emotion I hadn't realized I possessed.

"I love you, Lore."

That name...it was the same one I'd heard someone bellowing in my head.

I wanted to obliterate it.

I felt my throne sending out that dark, seductive, pulsating energy. The temptation I could never resist.

My shadow magic descended in a fury, raging in time with my temper, then vanished a beat later. And so did my wrath.

The male was now sprawled on the floor, face down in a widening pool of crimson, his body still and lifeless.

Horror washed over me as the shock wore off.

I stared at my trembling hand; the dagger was slick with fresh blood.

There was something about the blade that almost felt like it was screaming at me. Some vital information I needed to piece together before it was too late.

I noticed one little shadow, slipping around my wrist and frantically twisting around the hilt. It was nearly frenetic as it wound itself around the hilt over and over in undulating waves. I called it forth and turned it into the nightmare creature it was meant to be.

"Heel."

The shadow writhed, swelling into a hulking hound made from smoke and nightmares. Claws scraped against stone, and its eyes burned like coals plucked from a fire. Its snarl echoed around the chamber.

My mouth curved.

"Good boy. Go outside and guard the castle. Kill anything that attempts to enter."

The shadow hound snarled once more, then tore through the throne room, sending my shadow warriors scattering.

The scent of blood drew my attention back to the matter at hand.

Each droplet fell with a soft patter onto the stone floor, merging with the pool spreading from the male's unmoving form.

That screaming inside me was back, and I almost tossed the blade away.

I squeezed my eyes shut. I...felt. I *felt*. That shouldn't be possible.

"Finish the other two."

Sloth's voice had a hard edge to it. But he forgot himself.

He did not command me. No one did.

I was the Goddess of Night. I was ruled by no man, woman, or emotion.

I stared from the slain mortal to the two left. The woman was strangely familiar. Tears streamed down her face, her silent sobs wracking her upper body.

The male's jaw was clenched tightly, but his eyes were locked on me.

"We love you, sunshine. No matter what," he said, his voice unwavering despite the hopelessness of his situation.

He had to know he was about to die.

And yet he chose *love* instead of fear. How pathetically mortal.

A sharp ache seared through me, an overwhelming urge to collapse beside them and let my own tears flow, to grieve together.

It was not fit for a god to feel such pain. And yet, I felt it strongly.

But a different resolve hardened within me.

I shifted my grip on the cold hilt of my blade, feeling its weight and purpose. That was the only feeling I needed.

With a quick, brutal motion to silence my own trepidation, I plunged it into his chest, piercing his heart.

When his body hit the floor, something inside me fractured.

It was as though a dam had finally broken, releasing a torrent of memories that surged back with brutal force. I was Lore, but I was the goddess and this was my final test. My last Trial. And I just...failed.

The Liber Noctem.

The Trials.

This was how it intended to break me.

And it was succeeding.

This was terror on a whole different level. This emotion would fuel this court, this realm, this whole universe, with its might.

My hands trembled as I stared at the lifeless forms of my father and my brother, their eyes vacant and unseeing.

I'd done that to them. Not some merciless goddess or dark book. But their daughter, their sister. No matter who I was, what reincarnated deity, I would *always* be Lore Brimstone at the heart of me.

And I had just committed the worst sin.

My hands were still slick with the evidence of my treachery.

A wave of nausea crashed over me and I wanted to hurl the dagger away from me and then empty the contents of my stomach.

But through the agony raging through me, I managed to steel my nerves, to *think*. The Trials and tests were fear based. If I was a character in the middle of the epic life-or-death battle, what would I need to focus on? What clue?

The weapon I held felt heavier, drawing my attention back to it.

And I suddenly recalled the odd feeling from before, the desire to really look at it, to piece together a vital clue. Of little Teddy the shadow's help.

The Liber Noctem wanted me to get rid of the dagger. It was doing its worst to make me toss the blade away.

I'd felt it was important, that I was missing something…

Tears streamed down my face, dripping into my family's blood.

I wanted to scream, to fall to my knees, I wanted to—

Oh, my gods. I stared at the hilt where little Teddy had been winding around, at the end where it looked like something had been pried off it. Something that was in a familiar shape.

I would know, I'd only been carrying the damned thing around since I first started this twisted journey. It was in the perfect shape of the phoenix tear.

Through the storm of emotions threatening to drown me, pieces of the puzzle finally slipped into place. I sorted through clues like the detectives in my favorite mystery novels. There had been little hints all along, breadcrumbs for me to notice or think nothing of. But now I knew I was on the right trail.

In order to win the Trials once and for all, I needed to take my power from the Book of Nightmares. In my last nightmare it had slipped and given me a bit of truth.

The book had been trying very hard to weave a perfect lie, and there was nothing more convincing than one that held a grain of truth at its core.

I thought about the prince, about his dwindling magic, his insistence it somehow tied in with the book.

And I knew. Without a doubt, he was partly correct.

Sloth's magic was fueling the book.

And I'd bet anything it had to do with his tattoo.

That was why his power was weakening. The Liber Noctem was draining him. It had to be the reason it had chosen him—the perfect host.

Immortal. Powerful. And someone who'd remain by my side throughout the Trials, so the Book of Nightmares would be with me every step of the way.

I glanced at Nyantha's blade. At the place where the phoenix tear had been pried away.

For some reason I knew, without a doubt, I needed to stab Prince Sloth to sever the connection. And I suspected the midnight blade I held, the one that was missing the phoenix tear, would help me accomplish that task.

Without his magic, the Liber Noctem would be rendered inert. And then we could really end these Trials. I just needed to not go dark once I had my full power.

And the book had almost won. By killing my family, it had broken something in me. But that wasn't real. None of this was.

I wiped my tears and subtly fitted the phoenix tear into the end of the hilt. It snapped into place, just as I thought it would.

I sent a silent thank-you to my little shadow pet.

Ignoring the bodies of my slain family members and the weeping dream version of my mother as they all slowly flickered out of existence, I channeled my best impression of a villainess and prayed I knew what I was doing.

Or I would end up really killing the male I loved.

THIRTY-SEVEN
Prince Sloth

My mate paced in front of a writhing mass of shadows, her lips moving too quickly for me to read. She was having one heated discussion with someone.

But I only saw her and her shadows. And the army of shadow wraiths waiting in the wings, ready to be dispatched.

The Nocturnas that had attacked in the temple in Bellington were only a small fraction of the legion of warriors that packed this chamber now.

When we'd shifted to the Court of Fear, the moment my boots hit the stone floor, a ward shot up inside my mind, trapping me in my own body. I could see, but I couldn't hear what I was saying or understand my actions.

I fought back, trying to use every last ounce of my power, but it only seemed to lock me further in my own head.

Lore hadn't noticed.

Whatever she was seeing, whatever nightmare, it had deceived her with its illusion. She'd been lost to it from the moment she attacked War.

I couldn't imagine the strength she possessed to have fought back this long. The Book of Nightmares must be furious that it hadn't outright won yet.

I wondered how much longer she could withstand the mental assault. I also couldn't help but wonder how long *I* could last, watching as my body moved and acted of its own volition while I remained powerless.

Her eyes were entirely black whenever I caught glimpses of them.

Another sign that the Liber Noctem was still in control.

I kept tugging at our bond, sending encouragement to her whenever I felt a strong wave of emotion barreling toward me. I was quickly realizing that the heart might be as ferocious as the mind. No matter how trapped I was, or how lost she seemed to be, there was still that bond shimmering in the dark.

Lore was ruled by her emotions, her love. And she was winning by that force alone.

I hadn't seen Nyantha make an appearance yet, but there was a dark suspicion that was growing stronger the longer I observed the dreamweaver.

And the shadow wraiths that were poised to strike at her command.

As far as I knew, those shadow warriors were loyal *only* to the Goddess of Night. They'd never acted on behalf of anyone else.

Which meant...

I knew what it meant but couldn't process the *how*.

Lore and Nyantha were one and the same. And I...loved her.

I bellowed her name again and simultaneously tugged on our bond.

I felt her, weakened, on the other end of that tether, but she was there. She wasn't lost to darkness and shutting me out. And I wasn't so lost to whatever magic was overwhelming me that I couldn't reach her, even in some small capacity.

And that gave me hope.

Lore was strong; she would survive.

No matter who she was or had been in the past, she was Lore now and that was all that counted. Everyone deserved a redemption arc. And it was fitting that this dreamweaver, obsessed with all things story, might get that wish.

Lore being Nyantha...It was a twist I hadn't seen coming, but it didn't matter who she was. She was mine. My *mate*.

The perfect balance of heart to my mind.

I poured every memory of her I had into that bond, all the sunshine and sass that filled her soul. How she'd looked to me in those cursed stockings with ribbons. The way her swagger on the pirate ship stole my breath.

The ridiculous way she'd ridden me into battle during the brawl.

She was so beautifully filled with light.

Nyantha had once been simply the goddess who ruled over slumber, who'd been more inclined to grant dreams.

From the texts I'd read on her, she loved to weave daydreams and joy; it was why she'd been so popular among the mortals who worshipped the night. When she'd been her highest self, she sounded very much like Lore.

Something twisted along the way. Something had made her forget who she was.

But Lore was the epitome of a dreamer, she simply needed to latch onto that with all she was. If she *was* Nyantha, that would be the way to win the Trials and set herself free. The realms would be safe. The Court of Fear would be restored to a court of daydreams. And we could have forever.

It also explained why her dreamweaver magic never manifested the way it should have. Nyantha was technically the queen of dreamweavers, but since her magic had been taken, that prevented her from fully accessing her magic. Just like Lore. And Lore's increasing power occurred after each test she passed. Which indicated her power was slowly being returned to her, just as I suspected it would be if she was the Goddess of Night.

Her wraiths grew agitated each time I tugged on that bond, like they sensed her darkness slipping further away.

She stopped pacing and squared her shoulders.

Whatever inner war she'd been battling, she won.

She faced me, and I couldn't help but admire her.

Dressed as she was in a gown that looked like the fabric had been stitched from the night sky itself, I couldn't help but think she really did look like a deity now.

It was the midnight blade in her fist that gave me pause. Even through the ward keeping me imprisoned I felt it's power thrumming.

I almost thought I saw the phoenix tear nestled in its hilt, but she moved it from my sight too quickly to be sure.

Lore stared up at me, and for the first time since we'd landed in the Court of Fear, when our gazes connected, I felt my mind unlock. I was no longer being fully controlled, but I sensed I wasn't yet free.

A bolt of awareness went through me, and I shuddered with the pleasure of it. If she felt that same ripple, she didn't let it show.

I drew in a deep breath, filling my lungs with her scent.

"Lore."

I took a step toward her, but she immediately retreated.

"Don't."

I halted in place, my muscles tense.

Her voice held no warmth or recognition. I searched her eyes. They were no longer black; they'd returned to her normal chocolate brown.

Still, unease settled between us.

My magic was almost depleted now; whatever had happened to trap me had used up a lot of power, and I couldn't get a good read on her emotions. If I didn't return to my court soon, I would be in serious trouble.

Her face was set in an expressionless mask that gave nothing away as she scanned me.

She studied my eyes intently, lingered for a moment on my lips, and then continued her appraisal, moving slowly from my shoulders to my feet.

The air between us grew charged, almost vibrating with tension.

She was my mate, yet somehow, she wasn't.

I couldn't tell whether she was pretending she didn't know me, or if her memories had truly been erased.

If my suspicions were correct, if Lore and Nyantha were one and the same, then maybe there was nothing left of the woman I loved.

When she brought her attention back to mine, a trickle of fear went through me. There was a hardness in her eyes, determination.

Behind her, her shadow wraiths began to pace. The Nocturnas thirsted for fear; they felt it stirring and it was making them ravenous.

"Lore. Whatever you're being shown, or told, it's the Book of Nightmares. It's meant to deceive, that's how it wins. You must trust in—"

Her arm shot out, the tip of her blade digging into the eye of the phoenix tattoo on my chest.

I didn't breathe.

A trickle of blood slipped down my body.

Her attention followed the line, a shadow darkening her gaze.

"Maybe you're the one who should *trust*, Blondie. I thought we'd bonded."

"I—"

I blinked slowly. Her expression was as unreadable as ever, but that name...

And she'd said that to me before, when I'd been impaled by the spiders. But now it felt like there was a deeper meaning woven into her words.

My mind raced. Lore *knew*. She knew we were bonded; she might not realize how, but there was awareness.

"Do you understand me, or do I need to teach you a lesson?" She pushed a little harder and I clenched my teeth. "I'm the main character; you're my sidekick."

If she was acting, I would make sure she had an awards ceremony.

But this *was* my mate. And I had to believe that our bond was strong enough to overcome any dark magic. She wanted my trust. I'd give it.

Lore was letting me know she was here and she was in control. Not the Liber Noctem or anyone else.

She leaned in, driving her blade deeper.

I gasped as something took hold of me; something was draining my power.

The tattoo flared brightly and began flowing into Lore's dagger.

My mate was going to kill me and I'd just—

Her gaze was steady on mine. I noticed the slight tightening around her eyes. She was not as calm as she appeared.

I breathed through the pain, then I started to analyze what I was *really* feeling, focusing on one aspect at a time.

Even though the blade was clearly draining magic from me, *I* wasn't getting weaker.

I *should* feel weak, but it was having the opposite effect. The more the light faded from the tattoo ink, the more I felt a thrum of power replacing it. The tattoo itself wasn't disappearing, but whatever magic fueled it was.

I considered that and understanding dawned. The tattoo and book were connected, and it had somehow been siphoning my power. That was what locked me away in my own mind—the Liber Noctem.

My gaze crashed to hers and a flicker of emotion passed through her. She knew I'd just pieced together what she was doing.

Lore was fucking brilliant.

My mate leaned in, so close I felt her lips brush against my ear.

That connection blazed between us, stronger and more powerful than before. This time I knew she'd felt it. Her breath hitched.

Our moment was shattered almost instantly.

A few feet away, a single stone split open in the floor, the tile shattering as golden fire licked up from the cracks. From the chaos, *something* began to take form; first a wisp of smoke, then the gleam of gilded edges forcing themselves into being, its cover hardening into blackened leather veined with living shadow.

The Book of Nightmares was now unbound.

Pages flared open, flapping like wings, words burning themselves onto parchment as if written by an unseen hand. With every line etched, the air grew heavier, darker, until the book hovered fully formed above the ruin, thrumming with a power that bent the very air around it.

My breath hitched; this was no artifact anymore—it was alive.

The shadow warriors closed in, their blades whispering against the stone.

"Halt." Lore's voice brooked no argument.

The Nocturnas stopped at once.

For one heartbeat, time seemed to hold too.

The book's whispering pages stilled, the shadows drew tight, and the silence pressed down like the weight of a world about to break. Only Lore didn't seem afraid. Her expression was one of pure determination.

"Rise, Aurora."

I stared at my mate, and suddenly I understood.

The pages snapped faster, a blur of gold and shadow, until the sound was no longer paper but the thunder of wings. Light burst from between the covers, molten and blinding, and the book tore itself apart in a storm of fire.

From the blaze, a shape unfolded. Vast wings stretching nearly as wide as the throne room itself, every feather a shard of flame edged in shadow. Its cry split the air, shaking the walls and damn near rattling the marrow in my bones.

I couldn't believe what I was seeing. The original phoenix hadn't disappeared from the world like legends and lore suggested; it had been imprisoned in the dark book this whole time.

The phoenix that had been trapped in the Liber Noctem rose higher, its body both fire and flesh, talons gouging through stone as though it were sand.

This was the very creature whose sorrow had broken a goddess.

Whose pain had turned Nyantha from the Goddess of Night into the Goddess of Nightmares.

Heat rolled across the chamber in waves, scalding the air, bending the blades of the shadow legion as if even steel bowed to its return.

For a moment, I could only stare, transfixed by the terrible beauty of it, the shimmer of gold in its inferno, the eternal hunger burning in its eyes.

It turned those fathomless eyes on my mate and recognition flickered there. Along with something much deeper and more tender.

Awe warred with dread in my chest as the bird lifted its head and cried out again, this time in victory.

This was no rebirth. This was a release. An ancient goddess of flame and ruin had been unbound, and we were all standing in its shadow.

Lore stepped forward, flames snapping at her skirts, but she didn't falter.

She steadily raised her hand, and the fire bent back, collapsing into sparks that floated around her like falling embers.

I held my breath as the phoenix dipped low, its massive head bowing until its beak brushed her palm. Magic pulsed against her skin, fierce but tender.

"We're free, my friend. Go. Live. I'll dream up a world where your mate survived. I vow on my life's blood."

The bird's chest swelled, wings snapping open with a sound like thunder.

A blast of wind tore through the chamber as it leapt skyward, crashing through the stained-glass mural of its own likeness.

Shards of crimson and gold rained down, glittering as light streamed through the broken window. For a heartbeat, the throne room glowed with its fire; then the brilliance was gone, carried with it into the night.

Almost instantly, the world around us began to fracture and shift. The grotesque art melted from nightmares into dreamscapes. The columns that had been carved with scenes of violence and brutality were replaced by devastating beauty. Winged creatures, flowers, joy, and love. This was what the Court of Fear had once been before Nyantha arrived: the Court of Daydreams. The walls turned opalescent and shimmered; the incense that burned now smelled sweet and inviting. It was one of the most serene, lovely spaces I'd ever seen.

All because the Liber Noctem, the book I'd chased across realms, across time, was no more. A strange sort of peace settled in me.

The feeling didn't last.

The Nocturnas turned their weapons on us, fury radiating out from them.

I swore.

"Maybe you should try calling them off," I said, slowly backing away from the encroaching horde.

Lore flashed me an incredulous look. "They're not like puppies. They are sentient, ancient beings and they are *very* upset right now."

I snorted.

That was the understatement of the century.

The shadow warriors had only known fierce loyalty for their deity. And they'd expected her to feed their thirst for fear in payment for their blades.

Lore wasn't providing them with sustenance. And they did not take the change lightly. They seethed with fury as betrayal burned in their eyes.

The Trials might be over, the Liber Noctem rendered inert, but we hadn't survived the story yet.

Nocturnas surged toward Lore, their amorphous figures solidifying with each forward step, swinging weapons that glinted in the firelight.

I hadn't known they could turn corporeal in this realm.

This was not good. But I was aching for a fight.

I gripped my dagger tightly, its cold hilt pressed against my palm, and launched myself into the advancing line of shadow soldiers.

I navigated the deadly dance of combat the way I always had. Each strike was precise, every controlled stab landing a lethal blow for maximum impact.

Every time one opponent went down, I spun to take on the next. My mind locked onto battle strategies, clear of all other distractions.

The clang and clash of steel meeting steel reverberated off the walls of the throne room in a symphony of violence.

I fought my way to Lore, felling soldiers and taking hits. I ignored the sting of a strike landing, knowing my healing magic would take care of the worst blows.

Now that the Liber Noctem had been excised from my body, I already felt stronger.

I had no idea how Lore pieced together the cause of my draining magic or that the key to removing it was the dagger and phoenix tear, but I wasn't surprised by her brilliance. She loved mystery novels and had solved this one in the nick of time.

Soon my mate and I stood side by side, our backs pressed together, creating a defensive circle as our enemies closed ranks around us.

I thrilled at the fight, throwing elbows and launching kicks.

My blade cut through the air, leaving trails of destruction every time I

brought it down. And as the shadow warriors fell, their bodies dissipated into nothingness, swept away on an invisible wind.

Lore released a battle cry and moved with lethal grace as she stabbed, retreated, and pivoted in her own brutal dance of death.

The warriors attacked with the unstable force of an enemy that knew they needed to give their all now or suffer defeat.

They charged me, roaring their fury, their swords crashing against my blade with all the power they had, pushing me backward with each frantic blow.

The lead Nocturna of this final bid for annihilation dove at me. I just managed to sidestep it and went to drive my blade into its chest but missed.

It doubled back, its sword slashing a line of fire down my chest.

Blood splattered across its face, its black lizard-like tongue swiping it away.

"Sick fuck."

I swung at it with all my might, delivering a powerful blow that severed its head cleanly.

The next group was on me before I'd recovered.

Their eyes burned with rage, and the desperation of having nothing left to lose made them even more perilous opponents.

I drove my fists into their jaws with the full force of a Prince of Sin's powers, feeling the jarring impact as they crumpled to the ground, unconscious.

While they were dazed, I sliced my blade cleanly across their throats, the sharp edge leaving a trail of crimson in its wake before they vanished to nothing.

Another Nocturna lunged at my shoulder with a snarl, its fetid breath hot against my skin.

I spun quickly, driving my elbow into what remained of its disfigured face.

The next wave of Nocturnas didn't fully form into physical beings. But with my magic at full force, that didn't stop me.

I unleashed my wings from where I'd magicked them and knocked several shadow wraiths back.

"You do have wings! We're going to have *so* much fun with them."

I spared a glance at Lore. She was still carving her own swath through her former army, her eyes bright and her face split into an infectious grin as she took in my true form.

Lust was going to lose his mind when he met her.

I thrust my blade into the shadowy chest of the nearest wraith, feeling its half-spectral body fully form before yanking the blade free with a spray of dark mist.

The next Nocturna lunged at me, its glowing eyes flickering with malice, but I was faster, slicing through its insubstantial form with a single stroke.

The battlefield was still a blur of motion as I continued fighting my way through the legion of warriors. Each fallen wraith dissolved into nothingness at my feet, and soon the chamber was nearly emptied.

I caught glimpses of Lore and had never been prouder to call her my mate.

I'd been distracted and didn't notice the last of the horde coming for me.

Lore didn't miss. She spun around, expression like that of an avenging angel, and unleashed a torrent of magic that burned a hole through the remaining warriors; they evaporated into nothing.

The sudden stillness that followed was almost oppressive.

Her chest heaved with exertion as she glanced around at the silent chamber. Sadness permeated the space around her.

"I'd been trying to avoid killing them all. It didn't feel right...all things considered."

She closed her eyes, and I watched, transfixed, as her shadows—now glittering, multitoned, and beautiful—swirled around us and shot through the broken windows and raced across the world.

I glanced outside and noticed the changes to this realm—the soft blue sky, the pillowy clouds, the winged unicorns soaring in the distance.

Lore was dreaming up the world she'd promised for her phoenix and freeing the nightmare creatures from their own hells.

I stood there in silent awe while she worked. Golden rays of sunlight replaced the dark skies, birds sang melodious songs, and bugs buzzed pleasantly from flowering trees.

Several moments later, my attention lifted to the glass ceiling she'd created. Above us, flying together, were the phoenix and her mate. Their joy could be felt all the way here.

Lore did it. In the span of a few minutes, she'd created a new world of dreams.

I tucked my wings away and strode over and tilted Lore's face up. "You are brilliant. And maybe I concede that you exhibited some main character energy."

She closed her eyes to avoid meeting my gaze, but I was infinitely patient.

She finally opened them, and whatever she saw in my face caught her by surprise.

"But I told you before, I am no damned sidekick."

"What—"

"I'm clearly the main love interest."

I tangled her hair in my fist and hauled her up against me, sealing her mouth with mine.

I kissed her hard.

Needing the reassurance that this was real, and we'd somehow fucking made it. Her mouth parted and my tongue claimed hers.

The sound she made had me rock hard. I pressed her closer, needing to erase the distance. My mate. My beautiful, fierce mate had won.

Lore broke our kiss much too soon and shook her head.

"I'm…"

"Finally admitting I'm the dark hero in your story?"

A smile ghosted across her lips. "Only if you finally admit you've read romance novels."

"For research purposes only."

"Mm." Her expression turned serious.

I waited, sensing that she needed a moment to process her emotions. I stroked her arm, soothing her.

She gently placed a hand on my chest and pushed me back a step.

"You know what I am." Her gaze held mine, unwavering. "You should go."

My brows shot up.

"I know *who* you are." I took a deliberate step closer, erasing the meager distance she'd put between us. "You are Lore Annabelle Brimstone."

She gave me the exasperated look that I'd seen before. The one that made me want to haul her up against the nearest hard surface and worship her.

"That's not what I mean, and you know it."

"Aren't you curious how I know your full name?"

"A lucky guess?"

I grinned.

"What I know is you may be the Goddess of Night. And perhaps you might be the scourge of the old gods, and the former blight upon mortal kind."

"Please, tell me more of my positive qualities," she deadpanned. "I think I might be swooning."

"But you fought against your inner darkness, and you won. The Trials tested you and you passed. You set the phoenix free and defeated the Liber Noctem. You just created a world of dreams. You are no longer bound to this realm as punishment. You are free, Lore."

"What if I go...dark again?"

"I'll be with you, Peaches. And you won't."

I watched her face carefully.

"But the only thing I want to concentrate on now is the fact that you're my mate and we're together and we survived."

Her gaze snapped to mine. "What?"

"You are my mate, Lore."

"That's impossible."

"Not really. Don't you sense the bond?"

She went perfectly still.

The sort of stillness only an immortal could manage. Whatever had made her human was gone, but I couldn't say I was disappointed.

She would live for eternity. With me.

"Are you telling me you're my fated mate?" Hope flickered across her face before she shook her head. "This has to be another daydream." She reconsidered that. "Or maybe it's your nightmare."

I leaned down, enjoying the shiver of pleasure that went through her.

"Keep delaying the inevitable, Peaches. I am a patient male. When you finally accept the bond, there won't be any doubt that you're mine. Goddess of Night or small-town librarian. The fact remains you are mine and mine alone."

She didn't say anything, but I sensed her desire flare at the bold claim.

Lore peered up at me. "Is it really over?"

"Not yet."

I fought to keep my expression neutral as her worry intensified.

"There's the mating bond to complete. We'll also have to make arrangements to move your things and your family to House Sloth. If you accept me..."

Lore looked at me like I might be crazy.

And maybe I was. But I was crazy for her and didn't care who knew it.

"Of course I accept!" She launched herself into my arms. "I've dreamed of this fate my whole life. Well, until I went evil there for a while."

I kissed her thoroughly until we were both in danger of completing our bond right there in the Court of Daydreams.

When we managed to break away from our kiss, I glanced around the throne room one last time, admiring its transformation. Where the nightmares had ruled, there were now dreamscapes. More brightness and light. More joy. More of *Lore*.

Her attention trailed around the room too before settling on the throne. What had once been a solid piece of obsidian was now a solid piece of rose quartz.

"I'll return here every so often, just to ensure the realm is functioning as the dreamworld it was always meant to be. Somnia was never mine technically. The other gods used it to bind my essence—sort of like a place for my soul to wait for reincarnation once the time was right. The throne is the true balance of power here; it's sentient and, until I came along, hadn't been subject to corruption. It's an impartial ruler."

It seemed to pulse sweetly at her, almost like it was bidding us goodbye. Lore smiled at it, then looked to me.

"Ready?"

I nodded.

She used the dagger that contained the phoenix tear, and her shadows whipped out and spun themselves around us as they transported us to my House of Sin.

We landed outside the steps of my castle, the snowdrifts rising to our waists. Several sets of fresh tracks led into the double doors.

I sighed.

Lore glanced at me sharply. "What's wrong?"

"We've got one more nightmare trial to deal with, I'm afraid."

"The book? I thought releasing Aurora destroyed it."

"Worse." I nodded to the boot prints. Six sets. "My brothers are here."

THIRTY-EIGHT
Prince Sloth

"YOU'RE FUCKING WITH us. You've got a *mate*, Cas?"

My brother Lust was as eloquent as ever. He leaned against one of the bookshelves in my private study that housed my most prized fiction, his arms crossed over his chest.

I gave him a withering look of disapproval, the least of which was due to the nickname I despised. He knew I preferred Lo to avoid any slips of my true name.

And he also knew I hated when anyone knocked those particular books out of their perfect alignment. He leaned back, pushing several books in, his grin growing more devious as I considered the merits of stabbing him.

I didn't feel like dealing with blood spatter.

"Considering the small fact that I can't lie, it would appear to the contrary."

Gluttony's grin was as wide and irksome as Envy's, and I regretted my response.

Unlike Lust, the rest of my brothers were seated in a semicircle in my reading area.

Gluttony sat forward, arms resting on his knees, and left the demonberry wine he'd pilfered from my side bar untouched.

Once I'd sent Lore off with a servant for a bath and change of clothes, I'd found my brothers in my private study. They'd helped themselves to my wine and bourbon.

No one mentioned how they'd known to arrive tonight, but one glance in Envy's direction indicated that he'd played a role in it.

His spies were as good as Pride's, if not an edge better.

On any given day, this room was my sanctuary.

It was adorned with floor-to-ceiling shelves brimming with books, several overstuffed reading chairs, and an eclectic collection of artifacts I'd gathered over the centuries. I could spend hours poring over texts without being bothered.

Normally, this room, adorned in my House colors of pale sage and rose gold, served as a serene escape from the world, an earthly backdrop to read and relax in. But now it felt like my personal hell as I faced an onslaught of questions from my brothers.

"You did hear me when I said the Liber Noctem is no longer a threat to our realm, correct?" I asked. Six pairs of eyes stared at me like that bit was the least interesting information I'd shared. For fearsome Princes of Sin, they were rather obsessed with romance.

"You're sure the mating bond is real?" Pride asked.

I gave a sharp nod of assent, and Gluttony barked a laugh. "It couldn't get any more perfect than that. Especially for you."

He was baiting me. I knew it; my cursed brothers and their shit-eating grins knew it.

"And why is that?"

"You, the biggest skeptic of romance, the one who's waxed poetic on the efficacy of logic over love, have been struck down by fate."

"Not to mention," Lust added, "you've spent years lecturing us on how foolish we are to waste time and energy on romance. Oh, how the mighty have fallen. You're just as foolish as we are. Maybe more so. At least we knew we were morons."

Gluttony looked like the cat that swallowed the canary. "The scandal sheets are going to lose their minds over this news."

"One might even dare to say you've been laid low by love." Envy's emerald gaze glittered with mirth.

The bastard was loving this as much as Gluttony and Lust were. Thankfully, Wrath, Greed, and Pride were keeping their opinions to themselves. For the time being.

" 'Laid Lo by Love' makes for a rather snappy headline," Lust said, his grin widening. "Especially since you're basically Lo Lo."

I clenched my jaw.

Gossip sheets were tedious to deal with at best. And that was typically when they were focused on Gluttony and his debauched antics.

I wasn't thrilled by the prospect of having my private life made into gossip fodder for the Seven Circles.

At least not until I spoke with Lore and prepared her for the spectacle.

Gluttony's betrothed, Miss Adriana Saint Lucent, would no doubt be given the exclusive information to break the story first. I supposed that was the best-case scenario. Adriana would be more respectful than others.

I sighed and pinched the bridge of my nose.

I was still filthy from the final battle and hadn't had time to bathe or eat a meal.

My brothers were lucky I hadn't stabbed them with my House dagger and sent them back to their circles for coming here without an invitation.

But they were here, and I'd figured there was no time like the present to get on with the news.

I knew it would be tedious to tell my brothers about the mating bond, but this was bordering on excruciating.

I'd rather be back in the realm of nightmares, battling monsters, than suffer through my brothers' jokes.

"I have to speak with Lore on timing," I said, turning my attention to Gluttony. "But I would appreciate your assistance with planning a ball to celebrate our union. Lore enjoys romance."

My brother lunged forward with such enthusiasm that I barely had time to brace myself before he flung an arm around my neck, pulling me into a crushing bear hug.

Lust joined in the hug, and the force of his embrace nearly knocked me out of my seat and sent the wine spilling.

Wrath cursed as his trousers were splattered and sprang up, his sin rattling the walls with his ire.

Pride swiped his glass from the table and shook his head, and Greed looked like he was considering leaving us all to deal with this embarrassing display on our own.

"Are you finally asking me to plan a party?"

"Yes, and I'm already regretting it."

"That's the spirit!" Gluttony punched me in the arm. "I'll make sure this is the most epic ball to celebrate a mating bond to date."

"It's the *only* post-mating-bond ball you've done to date," Wrath pointed out, clearly still annoyed that his pants had been sullied. His gold gaze narrowed on me. "Tell us about Somnia. While you were gone, the fabric of the Seven Circles became…unbalanced. And the old gods sent a missive."

That was news to me. But it made sense. With my power being drained, my circle would have taken a hit. Which would have impacted their courts.

"What did it say?"

"That the Trials were enacted and they'd do all they could to keep the wards in place. We tried to keep the rumors from spreading, but after the ice dragon situation, everyone was afraid."

I poured myself a knuckle of bourbon and leaned back in my chair.

Then I methodically shared the facts, from Xavier's betrayal to using a locating spell and finding Lore, to every story we survived. I skimmed over the parts that didn't concern them—kissing Lore, our moment in the Fae forest—they were ours and ours alone.

I finally shared how Lore overcame her dark side, how she ultimately chose to remember who she truly was. And how she freed the phoenix that had broken her to begin with. They were stunned when I told them she was Nyantha.

"You need to complete the mating bond and leash her magic," Wrath said. "She'll be a threat to this realm until it's done."

I flicked my attention to him. "Don't."

He crossed his arms over his chest, his mouth pressed into a firm line.

His wife was just as dangerous, but we never questioned her.

We were family, the good, bad, and ugly.

I would not permit anyone to make Lore feel like she couldn't be trusted, or that she hadn't already proven herself to the realms. None of us had a perfect past. And none should be judged for former mistakes.

"If this interrogation is over, I'd ask you all to kindly fuck off." I stood and jerked my chin to the door. "Get out."

Envy tossed back his bourbon and pushed to his feet, stalking toward me.

He clapped me on the back. "Don't get your panties twisted, Cas. No one meant any harm about your mate. House Envy supports you and your nightmare goddess."

Greed rolled his eyes. "As long as the dark book is destroyed, there's no issue from my House of Sin."

"The threat to the Seven Circles seems to be under control," Wrath admitted. "You have my House support as well."

"Even if Lore burned the realm down, I still wouldn't have an issue," Lust said, yanking me into another unbearably tight hug. "I'm just happy our little icy prick of a brother is mated."

I slowly pried his grip off me, trying and failing to hide my own smile. "No one hugged Gabriellis when he got betrothed."

"Nobody likes him," Pride deadpanned.

"Categorically false," Gluttony said. "Everyone adores me. You're the one who's all broody and secretive. I hope you reunite with your wayward wife soon."

"He's right," Lust added. "You're a miserable prick, Luc."

"Anyway," Gluttony said. "No one hugged me because *I* was never foolish enough to claim that the head was superior to the heart."

Gluttony swiped the unfinished bottle of demonberry wine and sauntered to the door. "I'll send over ideas for the ball tomorrow. Better get to completing that bond."

I silently cursed them all to find their happily-ever-afters. Soon.

After I'd taken a decent bath to scrub the blood and dirt from my body and changed into clean clothes, I found Lore wandering down the main corridor of my House of Sin.

Our House, should she decide to move here, actually.

I stood a few paces behind her, my chest warming with affection as I silently watched her admire the library. For the first time I could recall, I didn't fight the softness and cast it aside, dismissing it as distraction or weakness.

I felt anything but weak around my mate.

Candlelight gilded her dark hair as she reverently trailed gentle fingers over the nearest row of ancient books.

She paused at one of the towering shelves, tipping her head back as she took in the dizzying height of them.

Row upon row of old tomes I'd collected over the years were stacked toward a vaulted ceiling, the shelves winding through the corridor and chambers, all filled to the brim with books.

Her lips parted on a soft breath of wonder, and I watched as she stepped closer, like a moth drawn to a flickering flame.

There were plenty of half-formed calculations running through my head, but they slowed now at the sight of my mate's awe.

Lore loved stories with her whole heart. She read the way others prayed, devoutly, hopefully, always searching for her next favorite read to analyze.

And I, who'd guarded the knowledge in this House like a dragon that horded gold, found myself a little desperate to give it all to her.

Every locked archive.

Every forbidden scroll.

Every piece of me. Everything was hers if she wanted it.

"How does anyone without wings actually reach the books up there?" she murmured to herself.

"Enchanted ladders." I grinned as she spun around, one hand flying to her chest. I'd moved on silent feet, hunting my sweet prey. "Naturally."

"Blood and bones," she swore. "You scared me."

I tipped her face up to mine, my fingers brushing beneath her chin, slow and deliberate. Her skin was warm and soft as silk. And being this close, with our mating bond vibrating with need, made me act a little recklessly.

I let my thumb linger against the curve of her jaw.

"I was aiming for breathless," I said, lowering my voice. "I must be losing my touch."

Her breath hitched slightly, just enough to let me know she was as affected by my touch as I was by hers. I sensed her desire, and it nearly drove me to my knees with its force.

Her steady gaze held mine, simmering with heat as her lips curved into a small, devastating smile. She was my ending, my beginning.

My favorite story for the rest of eternity.

"I wouldn't say that." Her voice was rougher now, filled with need.

I let my touch wander, trailing lightly from her jaw down the side of her throat, slow enough to feel the flutter of her pulse beneath my fingertips.

She shivered a little from the pleasure of my caress but gave me a playful, challenging look instead of admitting that she very much wanted *more*.

I wanted to press against that defiance until it shattered and she admitted how badly she wanted me to close the distance and complete our bond.

"You're trembling, Peaches," I said softly, my thumb resting at the hollow of her throat. "Scared of something?"

"I'm not afraid of you," she said. "Obviously."

My mouth curved.

"I never said you were." I leaned in, close enough for my breath to ghost across her lips. "You're afraid of completing our bond. Right here. Where anyone can catch us."

Lore's gaze flicked down to my mouth, then back up again, a dark gleam in her eyes as she pieced together how close I was to shattering.

"You're playing a dangerous game with our bond," she said. "Teasing it so horribly. Or maybe you're playing with fire, teasing a goddess with a wicked streak and expecting I won't make you pay."

It wasn't a warning; it was a dare.

My fingers skimmed lower, lightly tracing her collarbone as though memorizing its shape and feel for further analysis.

I felt the tension of need coiling in her, and every nerve in me stretched taut, aching to close the distance.

"I could devour you." My voice was rough with need. "Right here. Right now."

"But you won't."

I smiled, slow and hungry. "Not yet. Because once I do, I won't stop."

A beat passed. Then two. Lore didn't move, didn't so much as blink.

Then she slowly exhaled.

"Good. Don't start unless you mean to finish."

I held myself still, fighting the urge to pull her in, press her against the shelves, and take what had always been mine. What was *ours*.

But this wasn't simply about want.

Much as I hated to admit it, this was fate. It was threaded through the very fiber of our souls, through magic older and more powerful than either of us.

I wanted her to feel it. Every inch of it, the magic, the romance. Everything she'd ever dreamed of.

I let my hand trail down the line of her sternum, pausing just before the first tie of her bodice. Her heart pounded a wild beat.

"It's not just the bond I desire," I said. "It's you."

Lore swallowed hard. "I want you too."

The space between us and our restraint was shrinking faster now, not with the growing need, but with the force of gravity.

I let my forehead rest against hers, our breaths colliding, syncing. We were already threading together, becoming one.

"You know what happens if we finish this," I said, my lips brushing against hers.

"There's no going back."

Her fingers slowly came up and slid into my hair. She pulled just slightly, enough to let me know she accepted. Me. *Us.* Our bond.

The last threads of my restraint snapped.

My mouth descended on hers and I kissed her like I'd been starving for decades, a lifetime, and just found a feast.

She gasped into my mouth, and I swallowed it, pressing her back into the nearest shelf as the books rattled with the force.

There was nothing gentle in this kiss, only desperation. My hands were everywhere, memorizing, exploring. Claiming.

I'd already felt her come undone, already knew intimately the way her body responded to my fingers when I'd buried them inside her against that tree.

But this was different.

This felt like the true first time I was touching my mate.

Her fingers curled against my chest, and when I deepened the kiss, she made a sound that made all thought fade and primal need take over.

The bond flared. It wasn't just a thread now; it was a raging inferno that razed all distance between our souls.

I pulled back just enough to read her expression. Her lips were swollen, her eyes dark with want.

"You're sure?"

She nodded, breathless, her gaze fixed to my mouth. "Claim me."

THIRTY-NINE
Prince Sloth

I WOULD HAVE. I would have hiked her skirt up and sunk into her right there against the shelves. But something in me pulled back. Not from her, but from the reality of our setting.

I would not have my mate shouting my name where anyone of my court could come upon us.

I would have her.

But not here.

Not like this.

I took her hand instead, pressing a lingering kiss to her knuckles, my breath still wildly uneven.

Lore's brows tugged together in confusion as I stepped back, putting some space between us, but I didn't release her hand.

"Come with me." I tugged her gently. "There's somewhere I want to show you first."

I held her hand possessively, anchoring her to me, and led her deeper into the library. The corridors blurred as we moved faster, book spines flying behind us.

We stopped only when the hall opened into a vast hidden chamber; the heart of the library, the heart of me.

The Library might be sentient, but it had gotten its spark of life from my own soul. No one knew just how connected I was to my library.

The tree of knowledge towered above us, its ancient roots curling into the floor, its trunk wide enough to cradle a small village. Leaves in a hundred colors flickered above, shifting like firelight to welcome us.

Lore stumbled to a halt beside me, her lips parted in wonder.

"Is this where we visited? With your magic?"

Instead of answering right away, I gripped the curve of her hip, pulling her back against my chest, letting her feel what she did to me, what she was to me.

"Yes." My lips brushed the sensitive skin of her neck. "This is the soul of my House. And the place I imagined taking you just to see your face."

She stilled in my arms, absorbing the words, almost like she savored them.

"You, Lord Stoic, imagined this? I think I might be swooning."

I grinned.

I might not be known for being a romantic, but I was a quick study.

And I was highly motivated.

"Every damn night since I met you."

I spun her around and kissed her, picking up on where we'd left off.

It was breathless and bruising, all teeth and tongue and heat.

She moaned into it, her hands already tangling in my shirt, tugging at it like she wanted skin, not fabric.

I broke the kiss only long enough to whisper to the room, "Library—veil the world. Then give me and my mate some privacy. I do not wish to be disturbed."

I felt the Library bristle.

You will not maul our goddess mate on the hard floor like some common miscreant. Please, allow the wizard of wisdom to do its work. You, Your Highness, are shaming us and our splendor with your...fervor.

"Duly noted."

The Library muttered several more admonishments, then got to work on the images I sent it.

I watched Lore's expression as the leaves rustled, and the air shimmered as magic poured into the chamber, creating our own private sanctuary.

The roots of the tree shifted, curling in a circle to form a nest that acted as a makeshift bed.

From the canopy above, translucent fabric drifted down, soft and glowing with the light of a thousand stars.

I wanted something fitting for a goddess who ruled over the night.

The shimmering fabric hung around us like a tent spun from constellations.

The floor beneath us softened into a bed of pillows, blankets, and silk.

Lore spun in a small circle, taking it all in.

"Your *library* made this for us?"

"No," I said, pulling her back against me. "I did."

She inhaled deeply, then glanced up. I watched as she dreamed up actual stars and placed them like flickering lights around the chamber. The night sky was so close we could reach out and pluck the heavens if we desired to.

I looked down at my mate, forever awed by her mind.

And then I kissed her again, rougher now, deeper.

Her hands tore at my shirt, and I let her rip it open, buttons scattering.

She ran her palms over my bare chest, nails dragging down my tattooed skin, and I hissed through my teeth as she lightly skimmed over my erection.

"Tell me you're ready."

Her eyes met mine, fire, hunger, and a hint of mischief all rolled into one.

"You're the one who's finally catching up. I've been three plot twists ahead of you this whole time, Blondie."

And then I was on her, lifting her, walking her backward into the nest of pillows as she wrapped her legs around my waist, our mouths never breaking from our kiss.

I laid her down on the silk as the canopy fell around us, keeping us hidden from the chamber and the world.

She reached for the laces at her bodice, breath hitching as her fingers slipped beneath the tight ribbon—

I caught her wrists before she could loosen a single knot, pinning them gently above her head, pressing them into the pillows.

"Don't." My voice was thick with desire and something dangerously close to awe. "Let me."

She looked up at me, chest rising with every ragged breath.

"I want to unwrap you." My lips trailed down her jaw, toward her throat. "Like the way I imagined in that cursed historical romance. All those fucking ribbons. I wanted to untie them with my teeth."

Her body shivered beneath me, soft and warm and already yielding.

Carefully, so slowly it made her whimper, I let go of her wrists and ran my hands down her arms, over the smooth lines of silk stretched tight across her bodice. The laces were intricate and tantalizing.

I tugged one lace loose, then another, watching the fabric give way with every movement. Each inch of exposed skin was a reward, a revelation, my complete undoing.

"You were made to be worshipped," I said. "And I intend to take my time."

I tugged another lace loose, the fabric parting beneath my fingers. Her skin glowed in the magical golden starlight around us thanks to my mate's magic.

I leaned in, my lips hovering over the swell of her breast, and she hummed a low, sultry sound, drawing my attention up.

"You know, if you keep undressing me at this pace, we might both die of old age before we actually get to the good part."

I let out a low laugh against her skin.

"Oh, is that what this is to you?" I traced my tongue lightly along the newly bared curve of her breast. "Just the *good* part?"

Her breath hitched, but she held my gaze, even as her cheeks flushed.

"Well," she said, licking her lips, "I *am* wearing an unnecessarily complicated dress because of our bond. I assumed there'd be a reward at the end. Sometime this century, though."

I dipped my head, teeth grazing the underside of her throat.

"Oh, there will be," I promised. "But first, I want to hear you beg for it."

She inhaled sharply, her hips lifting against mine in instinctive challenge. My cock was so hard it ached.

"You first," she whispered.

Gods help me, my mate would be the death of me.

A low growl escaped me, the sound very much *not* human, and her smirk vanished, swallowed by the heat rolling between us like a tidal wave of desire.

She lifted her hips again, trying to tempt me into action.

I continued to unwrap my gift, slower, more deliberate.

This was House Sloth after all. And I would take my time until she was begging for mercy I wouldn't grant her.

At least not in this arena.

She smiled again, still teasing, but it was starting to falter with every breath, every inch of silk I slid off her skin. She was trying hard to not appear as wrecked as I already was.

I pushed the loosened fabric from her shoulders, letting it fall slowly down her arms, baring the delicate slope of her collarbone, the elegant curve of her breasts.

I pulled the last lace and finally bared her fully. The globes of her breasts made my mouth water as I mentally plotted where I'd taste first.

She gasped as the cool air kissed her newly exposed skin, but it was nothing compared to the heat in my gaze.

Her hands clenched around the pillows beside her.

"Look at you." I cupped her breast, my thumb grazing the peak until it hardened. "Made of starlight and sin."

Her breath shuddered.

"You're really leaning into the poetry now, aren't you? Who would have guessed."

"Can you blame me?" My mouth trailed down the center of her chest, tasting every inch of her. "You're like a prayer I never thought I'd have answered."

I felt her heartbeat thundering beneath my lips.

I continued to slide her gown down her body, trailing open-mouthed kisses with each exposed inch of skin.

I kissed lower.

And lower.

And *lower* until she gasped and arched up into me, the silk pooling at her hips now, her thighs trembling.

"You're not teasing me anymore, Peaches," I murmured against the inside of her thigh, voice low and dark.

"I—" She swallowed hard, her wits finally abandoning her. "Please don't—"

I licked the inside of her thigh, then blew a cool, steady stream of air. Her breath hitched too sharply to finish.

"Oh, no," I purred. "Finish that sentence, my sweet, tempting mate."

She lifted her head to glance down her body at me, dazed and desperate, as if trying to remember who she was before I touched her.

"I don't remember what I was going to say."

"Good."

I kissed the place where her thigh met her core again, nibbling a little. She bucked up, trying to get me where she wanted me.

"I want you to forget everything *but* me."

Then I finally gave her what she needed.

The first stroke of my tongue made her cry out, head tipping back into the pillows, hips jerking against my hold.

I licked deeper, slower, circling and exploring her like a man dying of thirst finally at the spring. She was warm, wet, and tasted divine.

I dragged my tongue through her slick folds, feeling her legs shake around my shoulders as I slowly devoured her.

I wanted her wild.

I wanted her undone. I wanted her *mine* in every sense of the word.

Her hands fisted the sheets.

She gasped my name.

And I feasted like a zealot worshipping his goddess at the altar of her body.

She moaned, a sound so helpless and beautiful it made my cock throb against my trousers.

Lore cursed, her hips jerking against my mouth. "Gods, you—"

She didn't finish the thought.

I circled her clit with my tongue, then sucked it as I slid two fingers into her, slow at first, then deeper, curling them just right.

Her whole body arched off the makeshift mattress, crying out as I pinned her down again, driving my tongue through her slick folds.

"That's it," I growled. "Let me feel how close you are."

She bucked against my hand, and gods, the slick heat around my fingers was nearly enough to end me. Her inner walls fluttered, tightening, clenching.

I licked harder, fingers pumping, coaxing her higher and higher.

"I've got you," I whispered against her. "You're mine, Lore. Say it."

"Yours," she gasped, half mad with it. "I'm yours...please—"

I kept stroking her clit and thrusting my fingers, loving her taste and sounds. I could devour her all night and never be sated.

Her moans turned raw and desperate.

Her body arched, thighs trembling around my head, back bowing off the ground as she clenched around my fingers and sobbed my name.

Her climax hit like a storm.

I didn't stop.

I licked up every drop of her release, and I knew there would be no going back. Not for either of us. Not when the taste of her was still on my tongue.

Not when I'd barely begun to show her what it meant to be *mine*.

Only when she collapsed into the silk, boneless and glowing, did I rise—mouth glistening, chest heaving, cock so hard I could barely think.

I dragged my palm down her bare stomach, watching her tremble with raw need, her eyes glazed with pleasure.

"I want to own every part of you." I cupped her breast, squeezing a little. "Body. Mind. Soul."

The bond roared through my veins now, alive and electric, aching to complete itself. I hovered over her, every part of me coiled tight with need.

"Finish it." She tugged at my pants. "Take these off and fuck your mate."

I shucked my pants off, then rose over her, muscles taut, breath already ragged. My cock throbbed against her thigh, hard and aching, already leaking for her.

I needed to be inside her.

I caught her gaze as I settled between her thighs, dragging the head of my cock slowly through her slick heat.

She bit down on her lower lip, her expression filled with the same desire I was sure was written all over my face.

"Last chance to deny the bond. Once I'm inside you, there's no undoing it. You'll be mine. Forever."

She reached up, cupped my face in both hands, then kissed me sweetly. "Don't be obtuse. I already am yours. Like you're so clearly mine, Blondie."

That was it.

I drove myself forward, slow and deep, burying myself inside her inch by inch, her tight heat stretching around me, welcoming me like she'd been waiting for this moment for as long as I had.

She inhaled sharply, her nails scraping down my back as I filled her completely.

"Fuck," I groaned, jaw clenched, fighting the primal urge to thrust harder. "You feel...you feel like magic."

We stayed there, still for a heartbeat, joined, locked, the bond humming like a current between our chests.

And then she opened her eyes.

Our gazes collided. Everything in me stilled.

The final click of the bond locked into place, not a shackle but a vow.

A promise. It went deeper than blood or bone; it was infinite. Unbreakable. A claim carved across soul and skin.

I felt like lightning was lashing behind my ribs. Magic flooded through me, through her, a golden chain threading from my heart into hers and back again.

Her eyes widened.

"I feel you," she whispered, breathless. "My mate."

The bond hummed at that. *My mate.*

"I'm yours." I kissed her slowly, thoroughly, until she began shifting her hips against mine, seeking more friction. "In this life and any other."

I pulled out almost entirely and drove back into her with a groan that tore from deep inside my chest. I'd never experienced the kind of pleasure I was feeling now, being buried deep inside my mate.

Her answering moan reached the starlit canopy above us.

I set a rhythm then, deep, deliberate, designed to ruin her for anyone but me. My name left her lips like a prayer, over and over, her nails dragging down my back as I pounded into her, claiming her in every way I knew how.

Her body rose to meet mine, hips bucking, sweat-slick and desperate, as if the bond had set fire to her blood.

And then, with our bond blazing, I suddenly had a clear vision of what my mate craved. The dark romances she loved to devour.

If she wanted me to play that role, I would. I would become the darkest, filthiest bastard of her dreams.

My hands gripped her thighs, spreading her wider, lifting her hips to angle deeper, driving her onto my cock.

"Say it." I bit down on the lobe of her ear. "Say who you belong to."

She cried out, her voice raw, wrecked. And perfect.

"You. My mate."

I drove into her so deep she clawed at my back.

"Cassiel," I corrected.

Lore stared at me, her fingers digging into my arms.

"You were right. Back in the cave. Cassiel is my true name." I slid one hand up her throat, tilting her chin so I could watch her expression. "Now tell me who you belong to."

I slid out, then thrust back in to the hilt.

"You, Cassiel. I'm yours."

She was unraveling beneath me, her darkest fantasies coming to life.

"Good girl. No one else touches you. No one else fucks you like this. Like your mate."

"Oh, my gods." Lore's hips jerked up to meet each brutal snap of my thrusts. "Don't stop."

"Louder." I thrust harder, pounding into her slick heat. "I want the old gods to know whose name you scream. Who makes your pussy drip."

She shattered again beneath me, back arching, walls fluttering around me, her mouth falling open in a soundless cry.

The pressure built in me, unbearable and brutal, but I held on.

I wanted her to feel this.

Every thrust.

Every oath.

Every promise I'd ever failed to say out loud. I'd given her the dark romance, but only because she wished for it. She was precious to me.

I leaned down, pressed my forehead to hers as I thrust once, twice more—then came with a growl that was more beast than man, my body shaking with the force of it, shouting her name like a surrender of war.

I collapsed over her, still hard, our bodies slick and tangled, the air around us thick with the scent of sex and magic. And love.

Neither of us moved.

The bond thrummed through us like a second heartbeat, golden threads of power stitching us tighter together with every breath.

"That was...incredible." Her fingers drifted up my spine, slow and languid now, no longer desperate, just present. Claiming.

I buried my face in the curve of her neck, breathing her in.

She smelled like home.

"I feel like I've been struck by lightning," she said, her voice hoarse from shouting.

"So do I." My lips brushed her throat. "My mate fucks like a deviant. I am completely ruined for life."

A soft, disbelieving laugh escaped her, and I smiled against her skin.

When I finally lifted my head, her eyes were already on me.

Still burning with desire and tenderness.

She reached up and cupped my cheek.

"I never thought it could feel like this. So...right."

"Neither did I," I said honestly. "But if I knew love would feel like you, I would have searched for you a long time ago."

She flashed me an impish grin.

"My sweet sociopath. I had no idea you were such a secret romantic."

I nipped at her playfully. "Don't get used to it, Peaches."

She thrust her hips up, stealing my breath.

I was ready to go again.

"I wouldn't *dream* of it," she taunted.

And I was completely fucking lost to her, my mate, my goddess, my best friend. She could throw all her wildest romance dreams and tropes at me, and I'd gladly chase her through them, especially if it ended with us like this.

FORTY
Lore

My mate growled as I writhed beneath him again.

And I couldn't help but tease him more.

"Is that the sound of your inner romantic clawing its way to the surface again?"

"Lore."

His tone had no bite. He was still hard as granite inside me, and I loved the overwhelming sense of power coursing through me at the slightly desperate edge in his voice. Knowing he was falling apart just as quickly as I was.

That this male, this cold, unforgiving god among sinners, was so lost to us.

I could not believe this was truly life now.

It was far better than any story, and I wouldn't change one twisted thing.

I had a fated mate who put all my favorite dark romance characters to shame in the bedroom. I had a true partner who stood by my side throughout each of my nightmares, weathering the storm with me.

Encouraging me, propping me up, but never doubting my strength, even when it was different from his.

He didn't care that I had once been a villain. He loved *me*. The good, the bad, the slightly unhinged old god, all my imperfections were perfect for him.

Once our mating bond was sated, once I could think beyond how much I wanted to experience that level of euphoria again, I couldn't wait to see my family.

Those thoughts had to wait, though. Books got one thing correct: the mating bond was a horny deviant. I could not get enough of Cassiel.

Gods. His true name had me panting on its own.

I rolled my hips a little, loving the hiss of breath he released. He might be on top for now, but that didn't mean he was in charge.

He raised an imperious brow. Apparently, the mating bond gave him access to my thoughts. Well, he was in for quite a show.

"It's okay to admit I'm in control, Cassiel."

"Are you?" He pulled out slowly, then slid in, his strokes smooth and long. And utterly too good for my self-control.

"Mm-hmm."

I inhaled deeply and tried to think of anything but how close I already was.

"Come for me, Lore. I know you're close."

I bit down on a moan, refusing to give him the satisfaction.

"Suit yourself, my sweet, devious mate. I'll make you shatter."

His hands gripped my thighs, spreading me wider, dragging my hips flush against his in a rhythm that should've broken me, but I refused to go over the edge.

Not yet.

"Tell me again." His voice was rough with need, his normal ironclad control hanging by a thread. "Tell me who you belong to."

I laughed, breathless, a little wicked. Looked like Dark Lore would always be there a little. But only in the fun ways. I couldn't be more thrilled.

"Do you always get this needy when you think you're winning? You have to do more than that to make your mate come, Cassiel."

His hips slammed forward. I gasped, biting my lip hard enough to bruise.

He groaned with the next punishing thrusts.

"Careful." I dragged my nails down his back. "If you keep making those sounds, I might start thinking you're the one who belongs to *me*."

His pace stuttered, and I smiled. It was time he unraveled for me.

"You're playing a dangerous game, Peaches."

"Good." I slammed my hips up to meet him, thrust for thrust. "I came here to play, not talk."

His hand slid to my throat, not choking, just holding, just *claiming*.

Like he had before, and I'd nearly lost my mind. I'd always wondered if it was as much of a turn-on in real life as it was in my favorite novels.

It was even better.

His control, his power, it was all still there, tightly leashed. But so was mine.

And we both knew it.

I rose to meet him, slow and deliberate this time, taking the pace down, my breath grazing his skin. My lips brushed the stubble along his jaw.

"You want me to say it again?" I whispered. "Then make me. Make me forget every name but yours."

His eyes changed. Darkened. Turned feral.

And then he did exactly as I'd demanded.

His mouth crashed into mine, not a kiss, a *claim*. His tongue surged past my lips, demanding, devouring, like he meant to brand me from the inside out.

His hand fisted in my hair, pulling just enough to tilt my head back, exposing my throat as he dragged his lips and teeth along it.

The other hand slid down, rough and purposeful, slipping between us. His fingers found my clit and pressed hard. No warning. No mercy.

His cock was still working me and now with his fingers I could no longer hold off.

I gasped into his mouth, hips jolting against his palm, but he didn't let me retreat. He chased every sound, swallowed every short breath like they all belonged to him. And right now, they did.

As his fingers played with me and he drove himself harder and faster into me, I couldn't remember my own name, let alone anyone else's.

Only *his*. Only this.

And when I finally cried out his name, it wasn't in surrender.

It was victory.

My mate. My beautiful, ruthless mate grinned down at me. The challenge that sparked in the depths of his cool gaze made my toes curl with anticipation.

I might have won this round, but the battle to see who could make the other shatter faster was only just beginning.

Much like our love story.

THREE WEEKS LATER

I HURRIED DOWN the corridor toward the new romance wing of the library, trying hard not to lose focus and stop to admire the books. My mate's collection was the real dream. When we *finally* managed to stop strengthening our bond, Cassiel had taken me on a tour of my new home.

I still couldn't quite wrap my mind around this being real.

I glanced down at the pocket watch the prince had given me and swore.

I was supposed to arrive early, but when my cursed mate saw my gown, he promptly tore it to shreds and pounced.

Then we ended up making love against the bookshelves, over one of the research desks; I sank to my knees and worshipped him while he'd been sitting in his favorite chair in his study…

Needless to say, we were due some time apart.

I trailed my fingers along the smooth, well-oiled spines of the old books as I rounded the corner and grinned at the plaque hanging proudly above this wing:

Ruined by Romance

If my smile got any wider, I might start frightening the rest of our court. They'd probably worry that my dark side was back and I was about to lay waste to everyone. I didn't share those fears. I knew, without a doubt, I'd overcome my demons during the Trials.

I'd also forgiven myself. Which was harder than surviving the stories.

Life was about choices. And choosing the light, choosing love and hope instead of fear and power, that would never change for me.

And if that wasn't some serious character growth or epic main character energy, I wasn't sure what was.

I continued to rush down the corridor, grabbing my skirts in both fists as I came to the chamber, already hearing the sounds of activity humming inside.

I paused, jumping in place for a quick moment, then strode in.

House Sloth had never seen anything quite like it.

It was about time Blondie had a little fun.

A pale sage green banner hung over the arched library doorway, stitched in gold thread: "Ruined by Romance: First Official Meeting."

I stood beneath it, hands on my hips, wearing my favorite shade of morally gray, as was the dress code I'd sent out with the invitations.

The reading hall had been transformed into something between a lounging salon and a secret witch coven's wine night.

Star-orb lanterns floated lazily above the cushions and low tables I'd asked the Library to summon. The air was thick with candle wax, magic, and sugar. Lots and lots of sugar.

Pitchers of Fae Fizz sparkled with strawberry-lime glitter.

Platters of chocolate-covered raspberry jellies were already half emptied. And every single seat had its own soft tunic draped over the back, each one stamped with glowing silver script: *Fictionally Depraved & Morally Gray.*

I was so excited that my guests had already arrived for our first official meeting.

Prince Lust, Emilia, Camilla, and Adriana were already deeply engrossed in conversation, pausing when they saw me.

"Lore!" Emilia patted the seat next to her. "This was the best idea. I can't believe we never thought of a book club before."

I crossed the room and plopped down next to my soon-to-be sister-in-law.

"We're going to have the best time," I said. "So many questionable crushes, so little time."

Camilla flipped her long silver hair over her shoulder and smiled back deviously. "Envy has been prowling around, pissy over my new fictional husband. It's been delicious to see him so worked up."

I laughed. "I can only imagine how much it stokes his sin."

"It's been thoroughly entertaining. And inspiring."

Emilia handed me a raspberry jelly and glass of fizz. "Will your family be arriving soon?"

I nodded. "My parents both lost their jobs when I went missing and they've been struggling, so they were thrilled for a new start. Especially here in a giant library. Fable plans to finish out the year and then spend the summer here to see if he'd like to stay permanently. Hopefully by week's end they'll be here."

She squeezed my hand gently. "I'm so happy for you."

My friends Blake and Agatha would also be visiting soon, but they shared the news that they had a baby on the way, so I wouldn't be seeing them as much.

It had been bittersweet traveling back to Bellington. I'd given my notice at the library and then cried with my coworkers. Very un-nightmare-goddess-like. I was happy here, more than anywhere in the world, so closing that chapter wasn't as hard as I'd feared.

It was more saying goodbye to an old life, one that no longer fit the same way it had before I'd left. Bellington was very much the same; I was different.

I learned that not much in life was scarier in truth than the nightmares our minds often made from our worries over *what if*. Fear was a true monster, and I vowed to slay it whenever it reared its nasty little face.

Lust started teasing Camilla, and Emilia and Adriana just laughed at his quips.

I grinned. All my wildest dreams were coming true, and I didn't even have to use my magic to manifest them.

Camilla claimed one of the tunics and pulled it off her shoulder in that way that made it look like a fashion statement rather than comfort wear.

She caught my eye and smiled.

"I would kill for this shirt in every color. It's so comfortable."

"Please don't," I deadpanned. "It's a book club. Not a blood ritual."

"Speak for yourself." Adriana flipped through her annotated copy of this month's read, replying to something Lust had said. "I've got a list."

Emilia, who was terrifyingly elegant even when dressed like a morally gray menace, handed out discussion cards she'd somehow printed on orange blossom-scented parchment.

"Question one," she said primly. "On a scale from one to irredeemable, how sexy is the villain love interest?"

Chaos erupted. Drinks sloshed.

I may have heard someone shout "Ten and I'd die for him!"

That might have also been me.

That, of course, was the exact moment Cassiel decided to appear.

He strolled in with his usual maddening calm, hands in his pockets, like he hadn't just walked into a den of feral romantics high on sugar and our favorite tropes.

"Blondie." I beckoned him forward. "Please show them the tattoo."

His brow arched, but he didn't argue.

He shrugged out of the coat, then tugged the loose collar of his tunic to the side to reveal the new ink just below his collarbone.

Felled by Feelings.

Lust fell out of his chair.

"Oh, *fuck me,* that's real? You seriously got that tattoo? 'Felled by Feelings'? I'm—" He wiped the corners of his eyes. "Oh, gods. It's too much."

Sloth didn't so much as blink. He turned and gave Lust a slow, icy smile. The kind that made centuries-old demons feel like they'd misbehaved in church.

The sociopath was back.

Lust sobered up immediately.

I leaned into the prince's side with a smirk. "I didn't even have to bribe him. He got it on his own."

"Willingly," my mate said, unashamed. "I was feeling sentimental."

"And totally exuding some epic main love interest energy," I said, grinning. "Very hot."

"That's a permanent condition." He'd delivered it in such a perfectly deadpan way it made Camilla choke on her spritzer.

She recovered quickly. "I propose a new tradition. Every time someone cries over a morally gray romantic monologue, they get a tattoo."

I pointed at Lust. "You're next."

"Oh, come *on*," he said, flopping back dramatically. "If I were a romantic hero, I'd be dead by chapter five and replaced by a sexier version of myself."

I tilted my head, letting the grin curl, slow and wicked.

"Please. If you were the main character, you'd be a leather-clad, weapon-smuggling former god of sin with a tragic backstory and a poetry kink."

"That's slander," Lust said proudly, then paused. "Except for the poetry part."

"I *knew* it," Adriana muttered.

They were still arguing about whether Lust's true love would be a necromancer with a heart of gold or a morally upright assassin when I finally let myself sink into my cushion. I could see Lust with a woman who didn't believe in love at all. I wrapped both hands around my glass of Fae Fizz and took a long sip, letting the drink fizz pleasantly on my tongue.

This was perfection, a dream come true.

I had a book club, my family would be moving here soon, then we'd all live the rest of our lives lost between the pages of books. I had my mate. I had forever.

And when I looked up and met Sloth's eyes, the world quieted.

He was still watching me. Hadn't looked away once.

My heart did that soft, fluttering thing it only did for him. And I knew then, without question, that this wasn't the end of our story. Not even close.

This was only the beginning.

And, gods, I couldn't wait to turn the page.

ACKNOWLEDGMENTS

This book is my tenth published novel in as many years (?!?!?), and I still pinch myself daily that I get to share stories with you.

To celebrate such a huge milestone, I really wanted *Throne of Nightmares* to be my love letter to readers and stories.

Fittingly, my first thank you goes to YOU, dear reader.

Thank you for continuing to go on these adventures with me, but most of all, thank you for being a huge part of the inspiration behind this story.

To anyone who has ever tagged me online and asked the question "Which fantasy world would you choose to visit for a day and why?", for any reader who shared their love of romance novels, or favorite tropes, or book clubs, thank you.

I hope you find a little piece of yourself reflected in Lore; she is inspired by each of you.

To my editor Helen O'Hare, I am immeasurably grateful that you were equally excited when I said I wanted to write a book about multiple stories set within the story and trusted (and encouraged!) all my strange ideas. This book is the book of my dreams, and you helped to shape it into the action-packed, romantic fantasy adventure I'd hoped it could be. Thank you for your sharp editorial eye, your unwavering excitement, and wonderful notes.

To Molly Powell, my UK editor, who always, always cheers me on and has brilliant comments that make the scenes and chapters pop, thank you for always being such a big fan of this world.

ACKNOWLEDGMENTS

Huge thanks to my agent, Barbara Poelle, for checking in weekly and cheering on every chapter I sent her way and being just as excited as I was about this book. Porch Talk 2025 was one of my favorite things ever (Elli and Lucy very much agree) and I'm so lucky to have not only your expert career advice, but your wonderful friendship as well. Next time we're driving Miss Daisy, let's hope we avoid a torrential downpour ☺ Another giant thank you goes to Charlotte Poelle, my partner in crime who brainstormed House Sloth's official colors.

My family deserves all the love for being so supportive during my deadlines and listening to all my ideas and giving the first round of feedback on every draft.

Special shout out to my sister for reading every single draft and not strangling me by the sixth or seventh version, and to my mom for patiently listening to me pick apart the plot *repeatedly*. To say I agonize over every word is a massive understatement and I'm lucky you're all stuck with me ☺

To my whole team at Little, Brown — thank you for being my earliest cheerleaders, for loving these characters and this world, and for all the hard work that goes into publishing these books. To have such a massive support system in-house is beyond my wildest dreams. Thank you for always taking my ideas on board and finding ways to implement them. To Sally Kim, Michael Barrs, Liv Ryan, Kathleen Quinlan, Kayleigh George, and Gabby Leporati — aka my brilliant publicist who always makes me tear up when she finishes my books and sends me the best emails — I am so lucky to have this brilliant, creative team.

Huge thank you to Gregg Kulick, art director extraordinaire for never strangling me when I ask for ONE MORE TINY TWEAK. This cover is so gorgeous and I'm so thankful for the hard work that goes into it. Taylor Navis, the interior designs seriously blow me away every time and I cannot thank you enough for the attention to detail you bring these books. Linda Arends, I love getting to work with you while you take these manuscripts and usher them through production. Thank you to Emily Baker for coordinating! And thank you to my copy editor, Eileen

ACKNOWLEDGMENTS

Chetti, and to my proofreaders Jeffrey Gantz and Linda Feldman. To the entire sales teams at both Little, Brown and Hodderscape, thank you, thank you for every account you land and every chance you give my readers to find their favorite editions.

Virginia Allyn, you continue to blow me away with taking my map ideas and turning them into magnificent pieces of art. Thank you, thank you for this incredible library map! Sasha Vinogradova, thank you for the stunning illustration of the phoenix, I absolutely *love* it.

To my brilliant UK team at Hodderscape, Molly Powell, Vicky Palmer, Katy Archer, Francesca Russell, Helena Fouracre, Robyn Bowler, Alainna Hadjigeorgiou, Catherine Worsley, Sarah Clay, Kerri Logan, Jennifer Wilson, thank you for all the enthusiasm you bring to this series. I'm so excited for what's to come.

Heather Baror-Shapiro, thank you a million times over for getting these stories into the hands of readers around the world.

Sean Berard at Untitled Entertainment, thank you for always being excited to showcase these novels around Hollywood.

Gabrielle Greenstein, thank you for all your wonderful guidance for licensing and making my readers merch dreams come true.

Stephanie Garber and Anissa de Gomery, I live for our bookish talks and one day we seriously need to start our own book club. (And my sister, Kelli, too!) Thank you for being the Lore Brimstone's of my world. Bookish besties for life.

Booksellers, librarians, book clubs and every single reader both in the US and internationally who shouts from the rooftops about these sinful princes, I will never be able to thank you enough. You are the best readers in this realm and beyond. And I am forever grateful for you. Writing might be a solitary endeavor, but you've made this fandom into a wonderful, book-loving community.

Cheers to the next ten years and new bookish adventures, may we all be ruined by romance and enjoy every second of it!

ABOUT THE AUTHOR

Kerri Maniscalco is the #1 *New York Times* and *Sunday Times* bestselling author of the Stalking Jack the Ripper series, the Kingdom of the Wicked series and her adult fantasy romance Prince of Sin series, including *Throne of the Fallen*, *Throne of Secrets* and *Throne of Nightmares*.

Kerri grew up in a semi-haunted house outside New York City, where her fascination with dark, atmospheric settings began. To date, her books have been translated into more than twenty languages and have been viewed on TikTok a few hundred million times.